LITERARY LIFELINES

Edited by
Ian S. MacNiven and Harry T. Moore

LITERARY LIFELINES

The Richard Aldington–Lawrence Durrell Correspondence

THE VIKING PRESS

NEW YORK

Library of Congress Cataloging in Publication Data
Aldington, Richard, 1892–1962.
Literary lifelines.   Includes index.
1. Aldington, Richard, 1892–1962—Correspondence.
2. Durrell, Lawrence—Correspondence.
3. Authors–English—20th century—Correspondence.
I. Durrell, Lawrence, joint author.   II. MacNiven, Ian S.
III. Moore, Harry Thornton.   IV. Title.
RR6001.L4Z545   1981   821′.912 [B]   79-56268
ISBN 0-670-42817-5

Grateful acknowledgment is made to the following for permission to reprint copyrighted material:

E. P. Dutton, Publishers, Inc.: An excerpt from *Lawrence Durrell/Henry Miller: A Private Correspondence,* edited by George Wickes, 1963.
E. P. Dutton, Publishers, Inc., and Faber & Faber, Ltd.: Selections from *Spirit of Place: Letters and Essays on Travel* by Lawrence Durrell, edited by Alan G. Thomas. Copyright © 1969, 1966, 1965, 1963, 1962, 1961, 1960, 1959, 1958 by Lawrence Durrell.
Hutchinson and Co., Ltd., and A. P. Watt: An excerpt from *The Mist Procession* by Robert Vansittart.
New Directions Publishers: Selections from *End to Torment* by Hilda Doolittle, edited by Norman Holmes Pearson and Michael King. Copyright © 1979 by New Directions Publishing Corporation.

Page 236 constitutes an extension of the copyright page.

PREFACE

❦ Many of the great collections of authors' letters contain only one side of the correspondence; here we are indeed fortunate to have both sides of an exchange between two literary men, Richard Aldington and Lawrence Durrell. The letters published in this volume are housed in Special Collections, Morris Library, Southern Illinois University at Carbondale. The correspondence from Aldington was acquired as part of Durrell's personal archives, purchased intact by the University in 1969. Durrell's letters to Aldington were obtained from Catherine Aldington Guillaume, the author's daughter.

Our first editorial principle has been to give the full texts of as many letters as practical considerations permitted. Letters were left out which contained merely perfunctory acknowledgements, repeated information, or seemed of extremely narrow interest. Often these deletions were made with agony and regret since many otherwise pedestrian letters held sparks of vivid wit. Every effort has been made to include all letters required for interdependent passages to be clearly understood. Most of the letters are complete, but necessary deletions have been indicated by ellipses inside brackets: [. . .]. Ellipses without brackets so appeared in the original.

Silent corrections have been limited to restoring transposed letters and correcting evident typographical misspellings. Both writers occasionally coined original spellings, and where this was clearly the intention we have allowed the correspondent's version to stand, avoiding the pedantic [sic] in most cases. Thus Aldington's 'tripewriter' remains without comment. We have retained the highly individual punctuation and use of upper- and lower-case letters, except in a few instances where clarity suggested a change.

A very few brief annotations have been included in context within brackets. Longer annotations have been appended to the appropriate letters, where they appear without superscript footnote numbers in the interest of presenting the letters themselves with a minimum of distracting editorial apparatus. A few first names recur so frequently and in such easily recognizable contexts that the family names have usually not been supplied: Catherine (or Catha) Aldington, Roy Campbell, Claude Durrell, Gerald (or Gerry) Durrell, Aldous Huxley, Wyndham Lewis, Henry Miller. First names not given in context may be found in the index.

We would like to thank Lawrence Durrell for permission to print his letters to Richard Aldington. We are extremely grateful to Catherine Aldington Guillaume and Alister Kershaw, Aldington's literary executor, who have permitted publication of Aldington's letters. Both Durrell and Kershaw have read the manuscript and made helpful comments.

At Carbondale, gratitude must be expressed to many on the staff of Morris Library, including Ralph E. McCoy, Dean Emeritus of Library Affairs; his successor Kenneth G. Peterson; Kenneth W. Duckett, former Director of Special Collections; his successor David V. Koch; Alan M. Cohn, Humanities Librarian; and their associates. Susan Steier MacNiven has been indispensable at every stage of editing and preparing the manuscript and index. The previous scholarship of Miriam Benkovitz, G. S. Fraser, Norman T. Gates, Selwyn Kittredge, F.-J. Temple, Alan G. Thomas, and George Wickes has been especially helpful. To all these and the many others too numerous to list, our sincerest thanks.

I. S. M. and H. T. M.

INTRODUCTION

❦ In 1933 a young man of Anglo-Irish descent with a few unsung private publications to his name wrote what he later termed an 'enthusiastic effusion' to Richard Aldington, then an established writer well into the third of his literary careers. Aldington had been acclaimed successively as poet, critic, and novelist. Along with Ezra Pound, H. D., F. S. Flint, D. H. Lawrence, and Amy Lowell, he had appeared in the Imagist anthologies, had written on French literature for the *Times Literary Supplement,* and had seen his fiction, *Death of a Hero, The Colonel's Daughter,* and *All Men Are Enemies,* published successfully on both sides of the Atlantic. The twenty-one-year-old Lawrence Durrell's letter evoked a friendly and detailed response. After saluting his admirer as 'Mr Dumell', from a misreading of Durrell's rapid signature, Aldington discussed the Imagist movement, compared the merits of D. H. Lawrence and Ezra Pound, and ended with a general invitation for his correspondent to visit him in England. From so promising an opening contact between two men of congenial temperament, a close friendship might have developed quickly. But this was not to evolve for many years. With uncharacteristic diffidence, Durrell did not reply, and there was no further communication between the two men until he wrote to Aldington again in January 1957.

Nineteen fifty-seven was a year of crisis for both men, and each needed a lifeline from an understanding friend. Aldington had slipped from the eminence that once had been his, and Durrell, climbing to an eminence of his own, came to depend upon Aldington's critical judgement and even his proofreading skill. Two recent Aldington titles, *Pinorman* in 1954 and especially *Lawrence of Arabia* in the following year, had angered a number of British Establishment notables, offended many critics, and frightened most publishers. A virtually complete boycott by critics and publishers alike removed most of Aldington's books from the booksellers' displays and reduced his income drastically. English newspapers would not print his reviews or even, in most cases, his letters to their editors. An important author with a bibliography running to seventy titles had become either estranged from his public or at least unavailable to it. Durrell's financial prospects seemed little better. Since the publication of his third novel, *The Black Book* (1938), and of his first major book of poems, *A Private Country* (1943), he had received gratifying critical praise but very little in the way of remuneration. At the time of his resumption of correspondence with Aldington, he had recently resigned without pension from British government service. He had resolved to return to the exclusively literary life he had not enjoyed since his pre-war sojourn in Corfu and his creative and hilarious Villa Seurat association with Henry Miller in Paris.

Matters did not turn out to be so desperate as they had seemed for either of the authors featured in the present volume. The solid merits of Aldington's work; the re-issue of old translations, and the publication of some novels in new translations and even in English in the USSR; and the loyalty and assistance of a few friends, both old and new, combined to bring about a steady improvement in his fortunes. Significantly, Aldington's greatest triumph during the years after the Second World War occurred in Russia, culminating in his being the guest of honour at a lavish celebration in Moscow on his seventieth birthday, 8 July 1962.

The resolution of Durrell's monetary problems was to come in a still more dramatic fashion. Like a magnum of *grande champagne,* he had been maturing in the cellars of the Foreign Office for fifteen years and was ready to burst forth with the publication of *Justine* on 1 February 1957. The first volume of *The Alexandria Quartet* had been written from 1954 to 1956 on Cyprus, literally between calls for advice from the Nicosia Government House, press briefings with hundreds of journalists, and explosions of EOKA bombs. *Justine* was successful in England, the United States, and France, where, in the excellent translation of Roger Giroux, it was a *Club Français du Livre* selection. Other novels in the *Quartet* followed suit. *Mountolive* was named as a Book-of-the-Month Club choice in America, and *Balthazar* won the prestigious French *Prix du Meilleur Livre Etranger* for 1959. By 1960 the *Quartet* had been translated into French, and all or part of it was to come out in German, Italian, Danish, Japanese, and nearly a dozen other languages.

The wanderings which brought Aldington from his birthplace, Portsea in Hampshire, and Durrell from his in Jullundur (which he likes to describe as being within sight of the Tibetan Himalayas) to residence within a few miles of each other in southern France had been wildly varied. Aldington's boyhood was calculated to make him into an English gentleman for life; it did, but other factors were to turn him into an expatriate for half of that life, though he remained indelibly English. Durrell spent his first eleven years in Imperial India, fussed over by native servants and dazzled by the colours of the saris and flowers and by the rising white-peaked mountains. He in turn should have emerged a pukka sahib, but he did not.

Although Aldington disliked his public school, Dover College, his adolescence seems to have been reasonably happy and eventful. He spent vacations hiking over the chalk cliffs and the wind-contoured North Downs, and collecting butterflies under the guidance of the Reverend Francis Austin, the author and amateur naturalist responsible for turning Aldington's casual interest in lepidoptera into a lifelong passion. His father took him on a 'run over to Calais for lunch', and thereafter he made ever deeper explorations of Europe, first travelling to Brussels and later to Rome, meeting the German poet Stefan Georg on a train between that city and Paris. Aldington entered the University of London, already determined to become a writer in rebellion against his novelist-mother's wish that he enter a practical profession. His father's near-bankruptcy removed him from the university, but soon he met the graceful young American poet Hilda Doolittle, and the two began to write what Ezra Pound was to call Imagist poetry, giving the now famous name to what Aldington claimed he and H. D. had discovered and practised independently. During 1914 Aldington served as secretary to Ford Madox Ford and helped write *When Blood Is Their Argument,* one of Ford's attempts to answer George Bernard Shaw's anti-war propaganda. Either becoming tired of Ford's erratic ways, or because Ford wanted someone who knew the German language and culture well—depending upon who is telling the story—Aldington passed on the job to his friend Alec Randall.

Aldington and H. D. had been married since 2 October 1913, and although they were not divorced until 1937 and indeed continued to be affectionate friends until her death in 1961, the war upheaval and Aldington's military service left them both with shattered nerves, their marriage wrecked. Aldington's angry, sometimes cynically humorous streak was intensified and became fixed as that part of his character which caused Durrell's wife Claude to nickname him Top Grumpy, a designation he thoroughly enjoyed. That much of his supposed ill nature was either a pose or a downright slander is attested to by most of those who had any contact with him. From John Gawsworth, English poet and bibliographer, who never met Aldington though he had corresponded with him for nearly a quarter century, we hear that 'in kindness Richard was ever continuous'. Henry Miller met him only once, in company with Durrell and Frédéric-Jacques Temple, and pronounced him *'a good human being* .... Soon we will meet again—in that other world where time and space are meaningless. Then we will really get acquainted.' On Aldington's death, Samuel Beckett, who had known him well, wrote, *'J'ai moins de souvenirs que si j'avais six mois.* Among the ghostly few is that of the great kindness shown to me, in Paris, in the late twenties and early thirties, by Richard Aldington.'

Aldington's personal and literary friendships between the wars embraced many of the foremost writers of the age: D. H. Lawrence, Pound, Yeats, Aldous Huxley, Amy Lowell, Remy de Gourmont, Roy Campbell, to name only a few. Durrell stated in 1957, 'It is fun to let his memories run on . . . Middleton Murry, Katherine Mansfield, Eliot, Ouspensky, etc.'

After the Great War, in which he suffered severely from what was called shell shock, Aldington continued to write poetry (*Images of War, A Fool i' the Forest, The Eaten Heart,* and many other volumes) and gained a reputation as an astute critic of French literature. It was expected that he would eventually succeed Bruce Richmond as editor of the *Times Literary Supplement,* for which Aldington was, among other things, the principal reviewer of contemporary French literature. He once took over the *Criterion* during a prolonged absence of its founding editor, T. S. Eliot. Aldington's abrupt self-exile in 1928 was more an advance than a retreat. He preferred not only the wines and cuisine but, above all, the freer intellectual climate of France to the dour post-war disillusionment and banal struggle for profit of his beloved and always regretted England. He announced dramatically to a luncheon group which included Eliot, Flint, Herbert Read, and Richard Church: 'I am on my way to Paris.' Church reports that his voice trembled when he added with an obvious finality, 'I am leaving England.'

Durrell too is a stubborn expatriate. *The Black Book* is an explosion of revolt against that English middle-class phlegm which he termed 'the English Death', the 'grubby Bohemia' of arty London, and the English weather, which he blamed in his letters for reducing the population to 'sneezing voluptuously in each other's faces in a continuous cycle of reinfection'.

The first important product of Aldington's life in France was *Death of a Hero* (1929), which was especially well received in America, partly because Remarque's *All Quiet on the Western Front* had just appeared there. Aldington described his own war novel as 'a furious plea for peace'; the same is true of Remarque's book and of Hemingway's *A Farewell to Arms,* also published in 1929. Other novels by Aldington followed (among them *The Colonel's Daughter, All Men Are Enemies,* and *Women Must Work*), as well as translations (*Alcestis, The Decameron,* and Nerval's *Aurelia*). Aldington was married a second time, to Netta Patmore, and in 1938 his daughter Catha was born.

The romantic/classic tension which pervades Durrell's writings is complemented by the escape/check-rein sequence of his life. After eleven idyllic years in India, he was sent 'home' to school at St Edmund's, Canterbury, and hated it. What sensitive child of the colonies did not resent a similar violent rupture from all he had known? Kipling's 'Baa, Baa, Black Sheep' tells the story for all such sufferers.

After a few years Durrell's father died in India, and his mother returned to England, settling in Bournemouth to finish bringing up her four children. By age nineteen Durrell was in love with Nancy Myers, a young art student at the Slade, and with a friend he privately printed his first book of poems, *Quaint Fragment* (1931). Lawrence and Nancy were married, and at his insistence his mother moved the whole family in 1935 to the Greek island of Corfu, where he was to write:

> The roads lead southward, blue
> Along a circumference of snow.

This move was to confirm a pattern in Durrell's life: idyll followed by season of anguish and toil, which was in turn soothed by another peaceful interlude. The harsh and frenzied war years in Cairo and Alexandria were succeeded by the relative material and psychic peace of Rhodes; then came the fairly barren Foreign Office years in Argentina and Yugoslavia, which would have been relieved by a time of rest and creativity in Cyprus but for personal misfortunes and the tremendous upheaval of the ENOSIS conflict. In Provence, Durrell now seems to have found another haven.

To call his life in the years before the Second World War an idyll is perhaps misleading. The blue of the Mediterranean sea and sky, the hot sand of the beaches, and the genuine friendliness of the Greek farmers and fishermen did lend that part of his life an appearance of pastoral ease belied by the writing, travel, and editing work of those years. Durrell's *The Black Book* earned him the praise of Eliot, though Faber and Faber rejected it conditionally, citing obscenity. Durrell's exchanges with Henry Miller and Anaïs Nin led to a first meeting with them in Paris, in August 1937, and to a series of joint publishing ventures, ranging from the serious *Black Book* to the burlesques in the *Booster* magazine. Durrell was even able to tempt Miller, despite his declared preference for garbage cans and city streets over green nature and cows, to Greece for a few radiant months before the war arrived. It is typical of the contrast between Aldington and Durrell that while both loved Greece, Aldington translated classical Greek but curiously never visited the country, while Durrell spoke demotic, rendered into English the nineteenth-century Emmanuel Royidis's *The Curious History of Pope Joan,* and lived for long periods in Greece. Both Durrell and Aldington were intelligent observers of their surroundings, but the latter tended to live more and more in the past as found in his own library and in the ancient churches and monuments he loved. Most poignant is his mention of 'saying farewell' when, ageing and in poor health, he revisited Cluny and Vézelay.

Richard Aldington and his family spent the war years in America. He found life on the Connecticut shore pleasant enough, but chafed later in Hollywood at the frustrations of writing for the film industry. At first he felt the challenge of turning out scenarios and wrote with pretended modesty to Herbert Read: 'I'm not much good at present— my salary is only $1,000 a week—but I have a kind of obstinate hankering to master this infernal trade at which nearly all English writers fail.' Nevertheless, by 1946 he was back in France, where he soon separated from his wife and settled in Montpellier to rear his daughter. Before he left the United States, he had received the James Tait Black Memorial Prize for his biography of Wellington, had published in most of his favourite genres, and had written his autobiography, *Life for Life's Sake.*

Still, Aldington was relatively unproductive during the war, while Durrell wrote only some poetry and *Prospero's Cell* (1945) and edited *Personal Landscape,* a literary journal he published in Cairo in the early years of his British government service. The difference was that Aldington was near the end of his ability to produce fiction and poetry: in 1948 a book significantly entitled *The Complete Poems of Richard Aldington* appeared. Durrell, in contrast, was merely prevented from writing by what he referred to as his 'ten years solitary in the FO', and was saving up the impressions and ideas which would flesh out his 'foreign residence' books, *Reflections on a Marine Venus* (1946) and *Bitter Lemons* (1957), and his *Alexandria Quartet.*

When Aldington settled in Montpellier, he was cut off from most of his pre-war associations although he kept up a considerable correspondence. He turned to biography as his main artistic field and also wrote introductions for fourteen reissued D. H. Lawrence titles. He had once intended to be a naturalist, and this interest produced *The Strange Life of Charles Waterton* (1949). It was followed by a fair and balanced tribute to an old friend, *D. H. Lawrence: Portrait of a Genius, But . . .* (1950), and a more controversial view of two other friends, *Pinorman,* which some persons felt damaged the memory of Giuseppe (Pino) Orioli and Norman Douglas. The real fire and smoke, however, arose over *Lawrence of Arabia: A Biographical Inquiry.*

While the main point of this biography is that the 'Prince of Mecca's' daring exploits and military acumen were largely myths of his own making, Aldington's relentless documentation of his subject's mishandling by the homosexually inclined Bey of Deraa, and Lawrence's own tendencies in that direction, especially aroused the anger of highly placed Home Office officials, apparently including the Prime Minister. Pressure was exerted on publishers, and most of Aldington's books were allowed to go out of print in Britain.

The biography of T. E. Lawrence had been suggested to Aldington by Alister Kershaw, a young Australian writer who came to Europe in 1947 partly for the purpose of meeting him. Aldington's first impression was that the biography would be like his *Wellington,* a largely laudatory portrait of an English hero. But the more deeply he searched into the actual occurrences of Lawrence's desert campaign, the more he became convinced that the celebrated champion of Arabia had been falsely shaped into heroic stature by those in the British upper echelons who felt England desperately needed a popular idol in the dark years after the Great War, by the showmanship of the flattering lectures given by the touring American Lowell Thomas, and by the conscious efforts of Lawrence himself. Although Aldington realised that his view of Lawrence would be unpopular, his innate honesty compelled him to brand Lawrence an 'impudent mythomaniac'.

The negative impact of Aldington's T. E. Lawrence biography on his personal situation can scarcely be over-estimated. Journals which had attacked him because he had supposedly denigrated a national hero refused to print replies either by Aldington or by others on his side. The ethics of literary reviewing were violated by such friends of Lawrence's as B. H. Liddell Hart and Robert Graves: they had attempted to persuade the publisher (William Collins) to suppress the book, and after he courageously refused to do so, they wrote damaging reviews of it in various magazines. This is typical of the virulence against Aldington. In fact, no one has disproved what he wrote about Lawrence, and in 1978 the noted Oxford historian Hugh Trevor-Roper said in the *New York Times* that Aldington had been completely right about 'the Prince of Mecca'. In the years following the publication of his *Lawrence,* the British press stopped mentioning Aldington almost entirely; even when quoting a *Tass* article which named him along with W. Somerset Maugham and J. B. Priestley as three contemporary British writers who received royalties for works published in Russia, all but one English newspaper carrying the story retained the other two names but dropped Aldington's. His income fell sharply, and his sales were affected in the United States as well. When Durrell first met him in 1957, Aldington, who despised what he called the 'hugger-mugger' of bohemianism, was living in a single room in Montpellier, with books, writing desk, and bed in an incredible confusion.

Durrell was hardly in better financial circumstances. Having been driven by the ENOSIS conflict from the lovely old Turkish house in Cyprus which he described restoring in *Bitter Lemons,* Durrell and Claude Vincendon, who became his third wife, were reduced to living in the Villa Louis, practically on top of the railroad station in Sommières between Avignon and Montpellier. Space was limited, and plumbing consisted of an earth closet which appeared in the *Quartet* as the invention of Scobie's friend Toby Mannering.

The letters tell the progress of the friendship. Aldington was, as he admitted to his Cambridge friend Alan Bird, isolated and lonely, and he later mused that he seemed to be fated to write about three Lawrences, D. H., T. E., and Lawrence Durrell, although the biography of Durrell he had planned in 1959 never materialised. For Durrell, his new residence gave him a chance to visit a man he continued to admire, the scholar he credited with introducing him as a young man to French literature 'before I could limp along in French'. When they discovered they shared refined tastes for intelligent women, vintage wines, elegant cookery, wide-ranging conversation, and a thousand other necessary amenities, appreciation soon turned to trust and affection. In their correspondence, the 'Dear Mr Durrell' soon became 'Dear Durrell' and then 'My dear Larry', while Durrell followed suit. They had lived within thirty-five kilometres of each other for only five months when Aldington moved to the Kershaws' country home, six hundred kilometres north at Sury-en-Vaux in the Cher. Durrell relocated in September 1958 in the wild stone and scrub garrigue near Nîmes, where he duplicated his Cyprus feat by making a tiny farm cottage into a comfortable home. From January 1957 until Aldington's death on 27 July 1962, more than three hundred communiqués passed between the households, the flow of letters punctuated by occasional meetings.

Durrell tried to fend off the many visitors his new fame brought, yet he repeatedly chided Aldington for not dropping in: 'Richard, thrice wicked man . . . you passed without nobbling us for a drink!' Aldington's gift to the Durrells before leaving Montpellier was to introduce them to the French radio executive, poet, and D. H. Lawrence scholar F.-J. Temple, who became Durrell's close friend and literary ally.

From a low point in 1957 Aldington's reputation has been steadily rising, and the trend should probably continue as the extent of his contribution to literature becomes fully recognised. The passionate feeling and meticulous craftsmanship in his novels recommend them; some of his translations are still considered the standard editions, and in fact his *Candide* has long been accorded the mute compliment of repeated unacknowledged piracy by several American publishers; his poetry ranges from pure Imagist vignettes to graceful love lyrics to satiric verse; his biographies combine the excitement of adventure fiction with factual accuracy; and his criticism is still appreciated. His letters may be safely left to speak for themselves. The outstanding value of the present exchange of vitally written letters is their dramatically and intimately presented story of the changing fortunes of two writers, a rare and exciting literary event.

Lawrence Durrell has made serious contributions to the same areas as Aldington, except in the case of biography. Durrell has written three plays which have been produced in Germany, Great Britain, and elsewhere. His *Alexandria Quartet* was followed by *Tunc* (1968) and *Nunquam* (1970), a pair of romances published together in 1974 as *The Revolt of Aphrodite*. When Durrell published *Monsieur* in 1974, he stated it was not an end in itself, but a source of workpoints; Durrell has continued the thematic lines in *Livia* (1978) and promises more to come. Despite the acclaim his novels have received, a small but stubborn coterie still holds that his melodic, tight, and sometimes wryly humorous poems are his true masterworks.

Richard Aldington now lives in his books, letters, and the memories of those fortunate enough to have been his friends. Lawrence Durrell is still vigorously with us, seizing coloured ink pens from the scores which bristle from the bowl on his desk like the spines of a sea urchin and writing notes for his poems and his novels in progress, practising yoga, savouring the *vin neuf* of Provence, and seriously, humorously, eloquently talking. In the present book we find him exchanging ideas with a close friend who had his own expressional magnetism.

Ian S. MacNiven
Associate Professor
SUNY Maritime College

Harry T. Moore
Research Professor Emeritus
Southern Illinois University

2 August 1980

LITERARY LIFELINES

Dear Mr Dumell,

Many thanks for your letter and for all the nice things you say about my works—if they may be called 'works'. I'm very pleased that they interest you, and even more pleased that you find them an oasis of comparative sanity. I can only explain this on the grounds that I have always abhorred affectation and insincerity, while having a strong propensity to common sense.

Imagism as a *movement* undoubtedly ceased to function in 1917, when we voluntarily ceased to publish our anthology and agreed to go our separate ways. I think the association was justified, because it enabled a number of then quite unknown writers to put specimens of their work before a rather larger public than was otherwise obtainable. I agree with you that the early work of Pound has a lovely quality, which he afterwards lost through being self-consciously 'modern'. No writer should try to be more 'modern' than he really be; otherwise, he merely makes a fool of himself. Pound was technically far more accomplished than Lawrence, but Lawrence was incomparably the more gifted, and possessed a far richer and more vital nature. I find Lawrence improves with time and re-reading. You may be interested to know that sometime this autumn Secker is issuing a *Selected Poems* of D.H.L., chosen by myself. I think you will admit that Lawrence comes out admirably in this selection.

Yes, first editions of *Images* are hard to obtain, but Allen & Unwin keep an edition in print. In any case, during this month or next they are publishing my first four books of poems again, under the title *Collected Poems, 1915–23*. There was another *Collected Poems,* about four years ago, but that is now out of print.

Roughly speaking, my reviews in the *Sunday Referee* began about November 1929 and continued until about April 1932, when I dropped them to write *All Men.* I then started again in April this year, but only went on to the end of July, since I found they distracted me from other work, while no interesting books came my way.

To talk about the repetition of 'sort of' in the *Dream* is really very silly. The words occur five times in a book of between 8000 and 10,000 words, and three of these occur in the intentional repetition of the phrase 'a sort of a poet'. They'll have to invent something better than that by way of disparagement—to write something better would be a good way.

I write this from France on the eve of leaving for Spain, but I expect to be in England during the winter and should be very glad to see you.

Yours sincerely,
Richard Aldington

Lawrence Durrell wrote an appreciative letter (since lost) to Richard Aldington, and this is the reply. Durrell did not respond, and a silence of nearly twenty-four years ensued.

Aldington misread Durrell's signature and greeted him as 'Mr Dumell'; the goddess Error, balancing this outrage, caused Jean Fanchette (see note on p. 74) to address Aldington in 1959 as 'Mr Adlington'.

§ *Care of Faber and Faber, 24 Russell Square, London [January 1957]*

DEAR MR ALDINGTON: PLEASE FORGIVE MY TROUBLING YOU BUT I HAVE HEARD THAT YOU RESIDE IN

MONTPELLIER AND AS I AM HOPING TO STAY FOR A
FEW MONTHS SOMEWHERE ALONG THAT STRIP OF
COAST BETWEEN MARSEILLES AND BANYULS I WON-
DER WHETHER YOU WOULD PERHAPS OFFER ME A
WORD OF ADVICE AS TO PRICES AND POSSIBLE
PLACES. I HAVE TWICE HAD AN INTRODUCTION TO
YOU: THE SECOND TIME FROM JOHN ARLOTT. YOU
HAD LEFT YOUR PARIS RESIDENCE HALF AN HOUR BE-
FORE I PRESSED YOUR BELL HEADED SO THE CON-
CIERGE SAID FOR VAR.

I HAVE BEEN A STUBBORN ALDINGTON FAN FOR
MANY YEARS AND OWE YOU MANY A DEBT OF GRATI-
TUDE FOR INTRODUCTIONS TO FRENCH WRITERS
LIKE DE GOURMONT WHOM I WOULD OTHERWISE
NOT HAVE ENCOUNTERED. I AM LAZY AND SPEAK
BAD FRENCH.

I ADMIT THAT THIS SEEMS A POOR WAY TO SHOW
MY ADMIRATION—BY TRYING TO PICK YOUR BRAINS.
BUT YOU WERE ONCE KIND ENOUGH TO ANSWER AN
ENTHUSIASTIC EFFUSION OF MINE WHEN I WAS EIGH-
TEEN SO I FEEL THAT SUCH GENEROSITY CAN AL-
WAYS BE COUNTED UPON.

I AM LOOKING FOR SOMEWHERE CHEAPISH AND
PLEASANT!! ALL OF US ARE THESE DAYS.

YOURS VERY SINCERELY,
LAWRENCE DURRELL

[P.S.] I shall be in Paris about the 5 or 6 of Feb but as yet am unsure of
my address. You could reach me c/o E. VINCENDON 46 BLVD
DES INVALIDES.

John Arlott, the writer and broadcaster on cricket, was then a BBC staff
producer.

Durrell was actually twenty-one when he first wrote Aldington.

✿ *Les Rosiers, Ancien chemin de Castelnau, Montpellier, 1 February 1957*

Dear Mr Durrell,

Thank you for your letter.

I wish I could say: 'Go to so-and-so at such a place and he will put you up for "X" francs a day.' But I can't; and then I don't know your tastes.

If you want an imitation of the Côte d'Azur, the places near the Spanish frontier (so-called Côte Vermeille) are best; but avoid Port Vendres, which is a base for troops in Algeria. I hear Argelès well spoken of.

Martigues is pretty well spoiled now, cracking plants and so on close at hand, and many discontented Algerian 'workers'. As a fair-sized port town I suggest Sète, which is headquarters of a number of painters, and picturesque but noisy. Grau du Roi (near Aigues Mortes) and the Saintes Maries de la Mer are charming places, but small and half closed down at this season. There are also a number of small *plages* between Agde and the Côte Vermeille, but all were wrecked by the hero boys in 1944 (there being not one German in them) and they are ugly. Palavas, near here, is a little fishing village smothered in tourist shacks and villas.

For weather Montpellier is about best. As you move towards the Rhône you get into mistral, and towards Perpignan there is a worse wind.

Usually the further a place is from the sea the cheaper and more purely Méridional it is. And among the sea resorts, as a rule the smaller the cheaper. This is a very intelligent time to come, as the winter is ending, and the tourists don't really swarm in dangerous hordes until 14th July; but there are unpleasant short epidemics at Easter and Whitsun. This year they will be less pestilential owing to the admirable activities of the great and good Nasser which deprive them of petrol. On the other hand as a foreign visitor you can get plenty, so if you have an English driving licence I advise you to get an international (through A.A.) and run a 'scotter' as they used to call them. Otherwise, at least a push bike, for the interest of this country lies in the excursions.

There are some most ancient villages in the hinterland here where you could put up, but you might get bored with the isolation and antiquity.

There is a fair system of buses, but they are based on local needs. You can get information from the Syndicats d'Initiative where someone always speaks English.

It is a great help to get yourself officially designated 'Student'. Under these idiotic régimes a 'student' is to be favoured in every way because he is of no use nor ornament, while an 'author' is to be penalised and over-charged for he is obviously making fifty thousand a year.

If you come through here let me know, and my daughter (who is far more intelligent than I) and I will try to help.

Yours sincerely
Richard Aldington

❦ *46 Blvd des Invalides [Paris], c/o E. Vincendon [ca. 1–14 February 1957]*

Dear Mr Aldington. I can't thank you enough for the prompt and detailed response to my letter. I am really most grateful for the information and will slowly head south when I have wound up a few trifling affairs in Paris bearing your advice in mind. I'm looking for a really quiet and cut off place to finish a book—but I do so love the sea—Greece has rather spoiled me in this respect. I do hope it may be possible to call on you and thank you in person—I promise not to stay more than 5 minutes, as I know what a bore admirers are and you are doubtless a busy man—but as one of the giants of my youth I feel it would be wonderful to meet you if only for a moment. And how splendid to hear you have a daughter—your novels always suggested that you were not a family man and I think there is a passage in *Death of a Hero* where you say categorically you won't bring any children into the world! Odd how one takes statements by favourite authors at face value!

On behalf of your English admirers may I plead with you to give us a big novel soon? You haven't written one for some time—I think far too long.

Please accept my warmest thanks for your generosity. If there is any service I can perform for you in Paris I should be most honoured.

Sincerely

Lawrence Durrell

❦ *Les Rosiers, Ancien chemin de Castelnau, Montpellier, 14 February 1957*

Dear Mr Durrell,

By all means let us meet here, and no 5-mins limit about it.

The Hôtel du Centre, place Chabanon, in Montpellier is picturesque, not too uncomfortable and fairly cheap; but it may be filled with students. Place Chabanon is beside the Préfecture.

Since I wrote I have discovered that a number of refugees from Israel have been staying at Les Saintes Maries, but I believe almost all have now returned. This at least goes to show how empty the place is out of season. You are right in the Camargue there and close to the bird sanctuary and the last herds of bulls; but of course it is flat marsh country.

No, I think the alleged writer in *Death of a Hero* congratulated himself on not having a son. Nothing was said about a daughter.

Yours sincerely,

Richard Aldington

❦ *Villa Louis, Gare Sommières, Gard [ca. 14–27 February 1957]*

Dear Mr Aldington—There literally hasn't been a moment in our travels to sit down and write you a bread and butter letter to thank you for your kindness in having us to lunch and putting up with our chatter. We have been up and down the rather disappointing seaboard (so tame after the Balkans) and finally devoted a few days to the hinterland which is really marvellous. Finally we hit upon this v. primitive villa and took it for a few months, right over the railway station! I hope when we are settled in about three weeks you will visit us with your daughter? We are living like gypsies of course.

I've written to England to see if I can't review the Mistral book—
it seems absurd if, as you say, there is a boycott because of your TEL
book. Actually the only criticisms I myself heard of it were by people
who felt you had dealt unsportingly with a highly complicated and interesting character—sorrow rather than anger. I only had a few chapters of it in Cyprus when I was leaving so I don't know. But to hell
with the Establishment!

Very many thanks for your kindness. I wish it had been possible to
talk more shop but Claude chatters so—and yet had I not brought her
I should have been drawn and quartered.

Please visit us one day will you! All the trains have post horns and
make one feel like Louis Philippe on a progress. And it's quite near.

Sincerely
Lawrence Durrell

Aldington's *Introduction to Mistral*, 1956, is a critical biography of
Frédéric Mistral, Provençal poet and sharer of the Nobel Prize in 1904.

♫ *Les Rosiers, Ancien chemin de Castelnau, Montpellier, 27 February*
1957

Dear Durrell,

I am delighted to know that you have found a place at Sommières.
It is one of my favourite small towns in the area, picturesque in itself,
with charming surroundings and the walks along the Vidourle. If you
can find Ivan Gaussen's *Sommières* published by Demontoy, a printer
in the town, get it. I think the printer still has a few copies, if you en-
quire. It gives some of the history of the place.

Of course we shall love to come to see you, as soon as Allah allows
us some petrol. And you must come and see us when you are in
M'pellier. I don't know where the Gare de Sommières is. I'm afraid
the marché is not very good, but Claude should be able to find vegeta-
bles in abundance.

I should feel much indebted if you could say something about *Mistral*. It is absurd that such a book should be boycotted because the Establishment are sulking over the exposure of their favourite little sod!
The fellow [T.E. Lawrence] was phoney from start to finish, and only

got by because he was related to the Edens and Vansittarts—on the wrong side of the blanket. He was the mouthpiece of a powerful clique of Oxonians. Hogarth was one, and another was Lionel Curtis who for thirty years had a secret room at the Colonial Office. The whole mixed up with Cairo buggery—O good Lord! And that England has to make a hero of that! Pah. Burn the juniper.

With all good wishes to you both,

Richard Aldington

Les Rosiers, Montpellier, 12 March 1957

Dear Durrell,

I wish you'd drop the 'Mr'. You don't expect me to be a cher maître, do you?

I enclose obit of [Wyndham] Lewis. I knew him well, Horatio. And he really wasn't such a four-letter man as he seemed. But he did strange things. E.g. circa 1932 I got an SOS—he was in hospital, pissing blood, no money &c. I went at once, and though no Croesus, coughed up fifty quid. Do you know what the next was? The beginning of a satire on me as the phoney journalist who knew how to make money out of silly books—in this case *All Men Are Enemies*. It was witty and though (as I thought) unfair, a good satire. I urged him to publish, but that killed it.

Strange you don't like the *Apes*. The Rodker is unfair, but very funny; and the Osbert and Sachie [Sitwell] really immortal. I never knew who the saph was, but that surely is a splendid caricature? We shall have nothing but books about him for the next ten years. He always begins with superb energy and virtuosity and then peters out. Poverty and the need to get a book out. I'm sure he was a paranoiac. As I told you, what I couldn't take was that pro-Hitler book.

Such a nuisance this petrol rationing. We could otherwise have made a weekly pilgrimage to a 'cultural' or wine centre. Châteauneuf-du-Pape . . . I long to set you and Claude down to the hors d'oeuvre (such poutargue!) at the Mère Germaine, and then a little pilgrimage to the home of Anselme Mathieu, whose first name (I am persuaded) came from the best of the Châteauneuf vineyards.

Nostradamus is a very queer bird. I understand [Henry] Miller's feeling. Some of those prophecies and their fulfillment involve odds something like 30,000 to 1 in favour of N. having by some unknown means had insight into the future.

'Sire, l'avenir n'est à personne.'

There are going to be a lot of strikes here and in the homeland.

Ever yours,

Richard Aldington

In Provence, *poutargue* refers to a substitute for caviar made from mullet eggs and other substances.

✿ *Villa Louis, Sommières [ca. 12–18 March 1957]*

Dear Aldington: I'm so glad the little thing passed muster. I hope they'll carry it to tell a few people what a delightful book it is, and specially visitors to Provence. I have enjoyed it. We are getting on quite well—villa is nice but no bath and no lavatory—we have showers from a watering-can (weather somewhat cold for this); as for lavatory, I am of course a firm supporter of the Old English Humus group (Massingham) and believe in giving mother nature back as good as I get but . . . It remains to see how long the vines stand up to this Rupert Brooke treatment ('corner of a foreign field that is forever England'). We are now having a marvellous correspondence with an earth closet specialist in Arles. Sommières is terribly funny—strongly touched by the spirit of Raimu and Fernandel; I can see a pancake novel forming in Claude's mind on the pattern of *Clochemerle* with the Vidourlade as the high spot. The flood stories are really a scream; we have collected hundreds of first person singular accounts. I do wish we had a tape recorder.

I am now trying to get the Treasury to baptise me 'resident abroad' and the French to accept the idea; I know nothing about Income Tax etc here. We have seen a number of lovely peasant houses for three and four hundred pounds and perhaps next year we might buy one and make it over; but conflicting ideas beset us. We might go seriously broke in which case Claude, who is a tremendous speed-everything-executive girl, would get a job in the nearest big town; so we should have to be within commuter's distance of one. The seashore, I begin to fear, is out—and Perpignan way would be too far if C had to find a job in Toulouse. The best combination would be a house about five miles from Nîmes or Avignon on a swimmable river. (My daughter and Claude's two will want to come out this summer—perhaps both my daughters; the elder by the way is nearly as old as yours and is on the way to becoming a ballet dancer.) Well, all these little beasts will have to be lodged and fed for the summer holidays . . .

I musn't bore you with these problems. I never met Lewis alas; but of course he is great. Only with the *Apes* I felt the personal pleasure of the pejorative made the book good satire but somehow not on a 'universal' plane—don't know how to say it. It sinks under the weight of its own spleen. Will it outlive its subjects? And I felt this immoral because I always felt Lewis to have a greater equipment than Joyce, and he should have spent his time making some art instead of complaining about the lack of it! What a tremendous proser! I suppose the cultivated meanness that you write about is a sort of childish hangover—what children do if they feel unloved: be naughty to get slapped—that at least is some sort of attention. I knew someone awfully like that. I was told the humiliation of going bald worried him terribly. Just as the 'small man worry' was the central Lawrence problem (T.E.). His brother told me: 'He could never forgive himself for being tiny.'

Yours,

Lawrence Durrell

[P.S.] By the way, if you should ever want to take a day off and come up here the Autorail offers virtually door to door service! We live just over the station, the garden falls into the railway so to speak! But there's hardly any traffic.

The 'little thing' is Durrell's review of *Introduction to Mistral*, published as 'Poets' Kingdom', *New Statesman and Nation*, 4 May 1957.

The film and stage comedians Raimu and Fernandel were both from Provence, location of the fictitious town Clochemerle in the satiric novel of that name by Gabriel Chevallier. Sommières straddles the Vidourle, which periodically floods the town to the second storeys. These epic incursions are known locally as *Vidourlades*.

Durrell has two children, Penelope (born 1940) and Sappho (born 1951).

⚓ *Les Rosiers, Montpellier, 18 March 1957*

Dear Durrell,

[. . .] We have to turn out of here in a few months, as some building grafters are pulling down the pension to build a block of loafers' tenements; so if you come across a peasant cottage or small Mas with eau and électricity and don't want it, will you let us know?

You are perfectly right about Lewis. He should indeed have done more creative literary work and less grumbling. But he failed as a novelist, in my opinion. (Novels are to be read.) The early short stories were very good. I found the *Childermass* and *Snooty Baronet* etc boring. The meanness was just an uncontrolled resentment against anyone who helped him. The 'small man' complex in TEL was an alibi. What he resented was his bastardy. He wouldn't sleep in the same house as his parents, and changed his name to show his displeasure. He joined the RAF to get away from his mother. I can show a copy of the letter from him to Mrs GBS in the B.M. where he puts that in black and white. Also he was an impudent pederast, trading for security on his relationship to the Edens and Vansittarts. If that's one of England's heroes thank goodness I'm poor bloody infantry.

I want to come and see you, but I'm just put on a filthy régime and three weeks of drugs to avoid a physical and nervous breakdown. I've got stuff I must finish, and it takes me at least twice as long, curse it. But if I can get time free, I'll wire the day before. When are these fools going to give us petrol again?

These strikes in England look very serious, both the ship-builders and the A.E.U. are out or coming out, and there is already a terrific run on the pound. What a happy land is England.

Yours,

Richard Aldington

[P.S.] I am officially invited to USSR by the Union of Writers! What next? Bastards, they pinch my novels and never pay a kopek.

A.E.U.: Amalgamated Engineering Union.

⚓ *Villa Louis, Sommières [ca. 18–21 March 1957]*

My Dear Aldington: I am most concerned you are in a bad way; if there is anything I can do please let me know. I could always hop down to you. And I'll keep an eye open for a mas—but you'll have to be near Montpellier won't you? The estate agent in Nîmes spoke of a little place, propre etc with water inside the house for 500 at St Bonnet. But we have been too bedevilled with the Préfecture on one hand and the Whitehall boys on the other to really get about enough and see places for ourselves. Saw two absolutely mad, but rather fun peasant houses for 400 at Aucharges—but it would need almost the purchase price to make them livable. I am marking time until I transfer myself from the sterling area if I can; not that I have anything much to transfer—a few miserable hundred. But we are now going into the book market with a vengeance and either I keep afloat this and next year or I drop the whole business; for good. So it's shit or bust as the 8th Army used to say. Claude has just finished her second book which goes off and I'm wrestling with a brute, trying to throw it before end of June. I've just been taken in the States, only one book, but my goodness what handsome advances. One really could get by if one found a publisher to back one there.

Have the Russians been pirating you? It's the same with all Commie states—how I hate them. I did four years in Yugoslavia as Press Attaché and thoroughly studied the dialectic; I'm afraid I'm rabid on the subject. I suppose your books would represent a critique of the rotten social bourgeois conditions prevailing under democracy—hence they are good propaganda. You are in good company. When I was in Belgrade they were printing Dickens and saying that he illustrated the present day social set-up in UK. Now that Burgess and Maclean are running the IRD section of the Russian Foreign Office their propaganda will improve alas. I shouldn't go to Russia unless you want to see the place; but all 'Socialist' states smell alike—such moral and spiritual despair in the air you have no idea, and such poverty . . . Coolies. Orwell described the state of mind well. Besides, you will have to watch your reputation in USA—so if you do go be sure to make an anti-Russian statement the minute you cross the border into Europe, or you'll be frowned on this side, and might affect sales in USA. Do be careful won't you, if you go; they put press hounds on to one everywhere and do 'press pick ups' everywhere; and there's so little hard news that the text of a merely polite after dinner speech when transmitted will read like Paul Robeson!

If you have money try and get in on a currency swindle to get it out. The Panama Legation or the Peruvian Embassy always trade in Commie gold—and save their own more worthwhile currency. So does the press corps!

When I'm feeling low and ill I find it bucks me up no end to be accused of being my own worst enemy and to be inflicting pain on myself so I always read Groddeck's *Book of the It* and it usually shames me to my feet. But then I seldom get really ill; and when my nerves split I drink my way through it. No solutions to recommend after my present age I feel (Forty-Five) . . .

However: we shall see. I had an amusing note of fury from James Stern. 'By God: so you've found Sommières have you? I very particularly didn't tell you about it as it's always been sacred to me and I couldn't bear to think of it being spoiled . . . And now you've found it. Tell me, how is it etc.'

Miller wants me to drink the air and capture the intimations of Nostradamus' birthplace and tell him all I hear (this must be done in an American accent): the news has almost made him abandon the flying saucers he's been believing in so hard this year . . .

Yours,

Lawrence Durrell

Claude Durrell wrote three novels, *Mrs O'* (1957), *The Rum Go* (1958), and *A Chair for the Prophet* (1959), and translated into English Marcel Rouff's *The Passionate Épicure* (1961) and Marc Peyre's *Captive of Zour* (1966).

Justine, the first novel of what was to become *The Alexandria Quartet,* had appeared 1 February 1957. At this point Durrell was writing *Balthazar* (1958). *Mountolive* (1958) followed, and *Clea* (1960) completed the sequence.

Guy Burgess and Donald Maclean, senior British civil servants in the Foreign Office, defected to Russia in May 1951.

Les Rosiers, Montpellier, 21 March 1957

My dear Durrell,

I am very grateful to you for the expert advice about Russia. If I went I should end up in Siberia. [. . .]

The illness is simply a threatened collapse due to prolonged over-work and worry under the utopian auspices of Mr Roosevelt's four freedoms. Also as you saw I am too fat. ('A plague of sighing and grief.') And I can't knock off work, as I am under contract and tied to time. I must just hope the treatment will gradually improve me. But one can't hope much at 65.

Thank you too for the information about cottages. One or perhaps two friends are coming down from Paris circa Easter, and will hunt sedulously with the extra petrol ration we are promised. I just can't face it myself. The kilometre walk to the PTT just about does me in for the rest of the day but (toujours Anglais!) I feel I can't miss my bit of exercise.

You may tease James Stern by telling him I have been visiting Sommières regularly since 1950 and have taken a number of our coun-trymen there, including Australians. But of course no Americans. One Canadian, with misgivings.

Nostradamus was born at St Remy and lived and died at Salon. I have never read his *Centuries,* but a Wadham don of great learning but total absence of superstition, says that some of them are so minutely accurate for so far ahead that they can only be explained in our present state of knowledge by assuming he had some very rare insight into the future. Is this possible? I must say I can't believe it. I never believed in those women who got into the past at Versailles, and after all the past has been—the future is only potential being. Miller seems to have been captured by occultism, hasn't he? It is a not unnatural reaction against the gross and stupid materialism of the Americans. My theory is that commies are poverty-stricken yanks, and yanks super-wealthy com-mies. They have essentially the same outlook. It would never surprise me to see a sudden reunion at the expense of all the rest of us. After all they joined up with Hitler, and Ike [. . .] embraces such sturdy sons of democratic vistas as Ibn Saud and Nasser, not to mention Franco. [. . .]

Yours ever
Richard Aldington

[P.S.] If you and Claude are in Montpellier, do come and see me. If I can get a little better I'll try for Sommières.

'A plague of sighing and grief!': Falstaff in Shakespeare's *I Henry IV*, II, iv.

🔊 *Sommières [after? 21 March 1957]*

My dear Aldington,

Many thanks—and no, it wouldn't cause any strain Claude says to give you two lunch some sunny Thursday. The linden tree is a splendid venue when it shines! I'm so lucky never to have run across Leavis and Co with their ambiguities. Out of England one never sees their work—and I haven't ever met Vallette either; but he's always boosted my poems in the *Mercure* and been a good friend on paper. Seems to admire you v. much too. I should love to visit your grand old man of M[assane?], but won't a crowd put him off? After all, he may want to talk to *you* etc. But it's a lovely idea. I'm sorry you are not well again—what the devil can it be I wonder? Not age, at 65 and just facing up to your winter tales? H. Miller claims he can still dance a tarantella for his children without spraining anything. 'Like a doe' he says—always prone to self-admiration! I do hope he gets over this summer. I think you'd like him so much. He's a most endearing gentle and babyish character—not at all the cannibal he acts when he writes.

My brother Gerry? He is delightful, Irish gift of the gab on paper—but *loathes* writing and puts all his money back into expeditions. At the moment the little fool is down with bad malaria in the Cameroons and due home in June-July. I'm trying to persuade him to do a popular book on Fabre's life—to come down here and do it. Do you know these blasted books about animals sell thousands of copies. My agent says that it is the only sure-fire steady *eternal* market. I wish I liked animals enough—or even felt like Whitman about them.

Yours

Lawrence Durrell

[P.S.] What is the *Nation* (USA)? They invite contributions and I can't find them in the year-book we have.

Possibly Massane, home of the writer Joseph Delteil.

Jean-Henri Fabre, who taught at Avignon, was an entomologist and popularizer of science appreciated by Darwin.

✍ *Les Rosiers, Montpellier, 25 March 1957*

My Dear Durrell,

[. . .] *Entretiens* is run more or less by F.-J. Temple, who is secretary to the radio here. Delteil is quite well-known, but dead. His widow lives in M'pellier. It is perhaps mere misanthropy but except for Temple I avoid all the intelligentsia and artistry of M'pellier and Sète. One gets so involved in a small town—nearly as much as in a capital. [. . .]

This petrol-rationing (kept up artificially now) is maddening. I am so decrepit that I doubt if I could walk to the station here, and my only chance of getting about is to have Catha drive me in the Renault—at the moment lent to friends of hers who need it badly and can get petrol. We shall have it for Easter when friends of mine come from Paris.

After nearly 10 days of 'treatment' I feel worse than when it started, but perhaps that is intentional. I switch to another set of drugs to-day.

As to work methods—I think everyone works out his own. Lawrence was a marvel. Through having to work intellectually in his youth in the frequented miner's kitchen, he could switch off and write in a room with other people talking! He wrote always in a school penny exercise-book (sixpenny after he made a little money) and preferred to work out of doors. Huxley is wrong in saying L. never corrected but re-wrote. He did re-write, but that MS vol of *Last Poems* I edited was so corrected and crossed out and interpolated I had great difficulty finding the real text. Joyce as his blindness grew wrote laboriously in huge letters on separate pieces of paper and gradually put them together—an incredible labour. Pound in the throes of composition (prose on typewriter) hum-groans in such appalling cacophony that he can be heard down two flights of stairs, and big-game hunters look for their rifles. Still, his advice was sound: 'Know what you want to do, and do it.'

All good wishes to Claude,

Richard Aldington

Aldington's comment on Delteil can be explained only as a misconception based on the fact that the French author virtually ceased publishing new work in 1941, and Aldington must have assumed he had died. Joseph Delteil lived until 11 April 1978, and became a friend of both Durrell and Henry Miller.

✿ Villa Louis, Sommières, Gard, France [26 March 1957]

Dear Aldington—many thanks for the fascinating letter about writers' work methods, and the other tips; I hope to God things have changed. We have enough dough for about two more months here, by which time I hope the exchange control people will have done their stuff; otherwise I shall be driven back to England to try all over again. Expensive and silly. I'm racing to finish a book so I can get some dough next month. A damnable trade this: I am always being driven back into the foreign service to earn a living—which I hate.

Your 'drugs' sound suspicious to me: the standard prescription for nervous states these days is sodium amytal—which is frightfully depressive. Most purely sedative things are; unless you have something actually physiologically wrong I shouldn't let these devils load you up with barbitones and things. Have you had your blood pressure checked? As a sufferer from low blood pressure I know that most of these nervous and hysterical conditions one goes through are lack of oxygen—like a car with poor compression. Unless you are physically ill I should stick to aspirin and a heavy spirit in liberal doses—the coarser the better: Italian *grappa,* Bols Genever Gin—they shoot up the pressure at once. I tasted quite a good smoky fine of Langue D'oc in Montpellier but I forget its name. You'll probably laugh. I always use alcohol if I can, and a medium mild sedative like aspirin. But of course this would be no way to go on if I were in danger of being a real alcoholic. By the way, there is an awfully good *vegetable* sedative—what the devil is its name? Valerian. It's considered old-fashioned now but when I was lecturing in Buenos Ayres and going through a nervous spell I found it the most calming thing. It's still available—one of the old-fashioned remedies which the new pharmacopoeia scorns with its battery of new and powerful drug-series; but I don't think sal volatile, valerian, etc can be bettered. They have no physical effect—and are not depressive. But maybe it is just a change of scene and a month's holiday that's wanted—somewhere just above snowline!

I am passing on a card from Jacques Vallette, with whom I've corresponded for about ten years and always missed in Paris. He seems a delightful person. [. . .]

Henry Miller is also thinking of buying a house in France now. Silly man, he was briefly a millionaire in francs and hung about trying to get the money out; a devaluation came and about twelve thousand pounds melted to two! He should have bought up the first available château.

But no sillier than me I suppose who bought and made over a ravishing Turkish house in Cyprus which is now too dangerous to live in, and under present circs unsaleable! I should have moved into France and Italy while I had a little capital.

Yours
Lawrence Durrell

♫ Les Rosiers, Montpellier, 12 April 1957

My dear Durrell,

I have been trying to write to thank you and Claude for your kind letter and suggestions, but I seem to get worse instead of better and even a letter is an immense effort. I don't think there is anything to be done.

Please forgive this miserable scrap. I'll try to write again if I feel any better.

Yours,
R.A.

♫ Villa Louis, Sommières, Gard, France [before 18 April 1957]

My dear Aldington:

A brief note to thank you for a delightful lunchparty and to hope that your health is in better shape. Also I've been thinking hard about the problem of breaking the boycott. I had no idea of extent of your trouble over the calamitous Lawrence book. I mean it is one thing to annoy the press and so on, but quite another to damage your own circulation and alienate your readers—if this in fact [is] what has happened. I mean that one can't build up new confidence quickly—and even favourable comment in the press is comparatively useless if the chap in the street who has always bought you has suddenly stopped. It means re-grouping for an attack on the public rather than the critic.

Have you ever thought about films? Claude said the quickest way back to favour she thought would be a film; I've written off to a chap I know who writes for films to see what he thinks the chances are of an Aldington film script being bought. *All Men* was filmed wasn't it? I suppose there is no anc Greek or French classical love-story you could do—something gay and warm-hearted and as romantic as *Dream in the Lxmbg*? Why not the *Dream* itself? Will you think about it? I think the wretched girl may have hit on a good idea here—Why not also suggest it to your agent? Best of all would be an original love-story but as you aren't feeling well you could perhaps do a 'treatment' of some existing theme. What is *L'Arlésienne* about? *Tartarin*? I don't know. It's just an idea. See what you think.

Another thing I forgot to ask? Have you any MSS unplaced about which you are in difficulties in the U.K.? I would like to try and interest some houses if you have; but I imagine not.

If you decide to go to Russia, why not go with an object in view—perhaps a book about Tolstoy or someone? The idea would go down with your hosts; and in UK and USA it would be fully understood that you were going to study original documents at the request of the Russians. And you could do an account of the journey 'Quest for Tolstoy' in terms of your subject, which your agent might sell to a paper in serial form? This would obviate political dangers, and give us an interesting book? It would also provide a sort of serious raison d'être for the journey—to possible critics this side. No one can be blamed for going to see original letters and documentation for a book.

Very best wishes to you both.

Lawrence Durrell

§ *Les Rosiers, Ancien chemin de Castelnau, Montpellier, 18 April 1957*

My dear Durrell,

A bit better. Last week I almost passed out looking at Lurçat's tapestries, and was brought back by my friend Temple. The doc gave me a shot to steady my heart, and has been plugging me with B.12 and insists on complete rest. So I feel really better than I have for weeks, but of course I can't go on idling.

As to your suggestions . . . I have worked in Hollywood, and still have a most loyal agent who has tried my stuff everywhere. I always thought the *Luxembourg* could be translated into a screen play, but Jerry Wald (supposed to be a good producer) turned it down. I don't know about the British—never tried there. Korda once asked me for a script premising that he didn't believe in paying high prices to writers; and I told him I didn't believe in writing for producers at low prices. So that was that.

I can get my books taken in London (Eng) but they don't pay enough with their ridiculous income tax. And the yanks have gone back on me, at least pro tem. I suppose my recent stuff has been too highbrow. Everybody, agents and publishers, says 'Do a novel', but I can't write a novel unless I'm free from other work and also from worries.

The only unplaced MSS I have is an anthology of English poetry, intended as a follow-up to my *Poetry of the English-Speaking World* which has now sold in Yankosachsendom close on 150,000 copies. However, Heinemann turned it down because wages and costs &c now make the production of such a book prohibitively high. The last London reprint of the original anthol, though made from the same plates, is priced 30/- instead of 15/-! The other is a very recent translation of Mistral's memoirs, meant to supplement my book on him. But the English shy off Mistral.

This campaign against me is not just due to the bogus prince of Mecca. It has been going on since my earliest poems. I have *never* had a good press, and the same people who insulted me over that filthy little lying bugger—the Mortimers, Nicolsons and all the rest of them—have attacked every book since *Death of a Hero*, always saying how dull and obscene and inferior my books are.

I can't go to Russia now—travel out for a long time—I can scarcely walk a mile. If they reprint the novels and pay for them, that's all I want. I have sent the correspondence to Alec Randall, who is still on active F.O. duty as delegate to that fatuous U.N., so they can't say I didn't warn the F.O. He hasn't yet answered, so I suppose he is asking somebody at Whitehall for a hint. Evidently the invite was for this Youth's Festival to which Bertie Russell, that tender juvenal, has most appropriately been invited. Did you see that Washington says it will not refuse passports but disapproves? So it is just as well I can't go.

It is most awfully kind of you and Claude to bother about me, and I much appreciate your help. Of course part of the trouble is that I haven't touched the soil of the Isle Dolorous for 20 years. You don't know any periodical which might commission a few articles on non-controversial topics? I note by the way that N.S. is in no hurry to publish that excellent note of yours on *Mistral*! Hopeless to try there!

Ever yours,

Richard Aldington

[P.S.] A letter just in from Randall. He says much as you, urges caution, thinks I should wait to see if the promises about reprints and payments are sincere, and will consult the F.O. when he is next there. This is a great relief, as I don't want to go even if I could. But I want their dough. Filthy bourgeois that I am.

> The British film producer Alexander Korda once stated that he 'collects' writers since he believed that 'young, fresh writers are the life-blood of the screen'.
>
> At this time, Bertrand Russell was eighty-four years old.
>
> Aldington frequently refers to the *New Statesman and Nation* as either the N.S. or the New So-and-so.

§ *[Montpellier], 27 April 1957*

My dear Durrell,

Roy Campbell is dead, and the world is dark indeed for me who loved him and revered him—the only real poet we had. I hoped he might a little mourn me, not dreaming that I should grieve for him.

Tell dear Claude that letters shall be attended to.

I weep for Adonais he is dead.

Yours,

R.A.

> Campbell died in an automobile accident in Portugal. He was survived by his wife, Mary, and daughter, Anna.

◊ *[Sommières, 4 May 1957]*

It occurred to me that Mary Campbell may need some dough so I wrote to Faber suggesting they put *Taurine Provence* and the auto-biographies back into print. I don't know if they will respond. I also said that if they wanted anything written for a memorial volume not to forget that I'd gladly do anything. There seems so little one can do or think. Poor Roy, but how much poorer us. There's going to be trouble in heaven though when he gets together with Lewis, not an angel spared.

Yours

L. Durrell

◊ *Sommières [7 June 1957]*

MY DEAR ALDINGTON. OF COURSE NOT. IF IT'S AS FINE AS IT ISN'T TODAY THE LINDEN TREE WILL BE NICE TO EAT UNDER. Claude can manage okay and would like to. Can I take you at your word and ask you to bring a few of your fattest books? Biography or novels or anything—Korcybsky's *Cybernetics* if you wish. I read everything avidly; living on Greek islands one gets used to doing without what one can't buy. But I do regret the loss of my Cyprus library, a good reference one; I adore encyclopaedias! And further to impose on your good nature may I ask the binder to send you a small packet for me—bound MSS of my latest novel which Claude is typing? He will deliver to Les Rosiers. Very many thanks. Today is black friday. Just been offered four hundred pounds by the *New Yorker* for serial rights which were sold for twenty last month! Cupidity dies hard. Never been offered anything like that before: I could have bought a yacht and sailed round to Montpellier to visit you! No matter, we'll soak them yet.

The Stevenson sounds fun.

Glad health is improving.

Yours

Lawrence Durrell

Norbert Wiener published his *Cybernetics* in 1948; while Alfred Kor-
zybski pursued investigations in the same field, he apparently did not
write a book of that title.

Aldington was writing *Portrait of a Rebel: The Life and Works of Robert
Louis Stevenson*, published later in the year.

§ *Les Rosiers, Montpellier, 9 June 1957*

My dear Durrell,

How heart-breaking for you both to miss the *New Yorker* and its
money. Is it not possible to buy back the serial rights from the other
people? I really think the *New Yorker* can do more for an author than
any other periodical in USA—so many influential people read it.

By all means have bound MS sent here.

With much reluctance we must call off the Thursday meeting.
Catha points out that it is only week before the Bac exams, and that she
must cram. I would run over alone but while I was lying on the flat of
my back (like old Bill Barley) my international driving licence expired,
and it takes time to get another one from London (Eng.).

Here is a minor piece of sales information. I hear from my agent
that Poland will issue an edition of 10,000 'cheaps' of *Death of a Hero*
in 1958, and will definitely pay. The money works out at only about
115 pounds for the whole edition, and they are allowed to transfer only
35 pounds at a time! As I have similar deals pending with East Germany, Czechoslovakia and USSR, all promising payment, this becomes
a little more interesting.

Also, my agent reports sale of an article on Provençal Bull Games
to the *Queen* (!) for a miserable 12 guineas. This represents the first
break through on that front since the bogus prince of Mecca affair.

Apropos my Roy letter in the New So-and-so, I got a query from
Scotland asking if by 'cockneys and half-men' I meant Keats and Hunt!
(They're about 120 years behind the times.) I replied that on the contrary I revere Keats and respect Hunt, as Campbell did. What I referred to was MacSpaunday, the contemporary more or less bi-sexual
purveyors of crypto-commie-rot who had their heads cuffed for insulting a great poet.

Do you remember a striking phrase of our old friend Wyndham to the effect that England under the coming socialism would consist of 'a lot of peons locked up in a large rainy island'? Prescient. Apropos, in Stevenson's rather voluminous work I discovered an essay on Socialism which Fanny suppressed until long after his death for royalty reasons. But for one or two slips it is a quite amazing preview of the Hellfare State. Oscar's *Soul of Man* in comparison is damned silly.

Ever yours,
Richard Aldington

'MacSpaunday' is the collective name for MacNeice, Spender, Auden, and C. Day Lewis coined by Roy Campbell.

♫ Les Rosiers, Montpellier, 24 June 1957

Dear Larry,

Last week I received two pleasant gifts. One was your *Selected Poems,* which have comforted my vigils. A great pleasure to have a poet who knows what he wants to say and says it agreeably. I'm surprised you haven't been assassinated by MacSpaunday.

The other gift has a more complicated story. In Montreal (Que.) there dwells a widow-lady I have never seen who is probably a bit cracked, since she collects my firsts and scripts and similar bric-à-brac. Out of the blue she sends me a review of my *Complete Poems* by the old Roy himself and in his hand, which seemingly appeared in *Poetry,* Chicago (Ill) circa 1948. It is amazingly generous and amusing in its gunning after the cockney parasites, but the strange thing is I never saw it and never knew it existed! It was written before we ever met, but he must have thought me what Claude's compatriots call a 'skung' not to have thanked him. This silence of friends would have pleased Rochefoucauld, for (as you doubtless have experienced) anything insulting or malicious is instantly sent along by half a dozen people—'I thought you might be interested in this.'

I look forward to *Bitter Lemons,* which sounds exactly the kind of book I like. Wish they'd let me review it.

Great minds thinking alike. I laughed at your 'Lawrence of Arabia dressed in a sheet'. When the Battle of the Bastard was on, Roy wrote to the press an incredible number of extremely violent and abusive letters which of course were all rejected. One of them had a word-vignette of the bogus Prince of Mecca 'mooching about London dressed in a gippo's nightie and a gold dagger'! You both had the same vision independently.

The unfortunate Bac children had to translate a text of Willie Maugham in the English section. The old Maugham has always been very civil to me, but entre confrères would you have left this:

'He had led for years a useless, selfish, worthless life, the sort of life which maybe *it* will be impossible for anyone to live in the future, but he had lived *it* without regret and had enjoyed *it.*'

It is one of the difficulties of English that it often entraps the stylist into the ambiguous use of 'it'. I have found and exposed a honey of RLS.

We are struggling with the problems of packing my damned books and getting them transported to the Cher. My friend Alister has the house, which actually has running water, a lavatory and a shower, and we can transport ourselves as soon as the bureaucrats have been thrown in their pound of flesh, and condescend to transfer the property. There we can live rent free, and emulate the lamented Tolstoy on bread and onion soup and gros rouge.

Hope all is well with you, and the Muse punctually turning up.

Ever yours, and many thanks for the inscription in your poems,

Richard Aldington

Alister Kershaw came to France from Australia in 1947, in part to meet Aldington, whose secretary and close friend he soon became. Kershaw and his wife, Sheila, provided him with both friendship and material aid during his last years.

❧ *Sommières, Gard [22 August 1957]*

DEAR R.A. I HOPE THAT YOU ARE COMFORTABLY SETTLED IN NORTH OF THE LINE AND THAT ALL GOES WELL WITH YOU. ALMOST THE DAY YOU LEFT OUR INVASION STARTED, MASSES OF CHILDREN, AND MY SISTER AND *HER* SON, AND OUR LIVING CONDITIONS

SOON BEGAN TO RESEMBLE CENTRAL MACEDONIA.
BUT THE SWIMMING QUITE GOOD AND THE COURSES
LIBRES A GREAT SUCCESS. HUSH. NOT A WORD TO
SEND TOURISTS DOWN HERE! THE SUMMER ESTI-
VANTS WERE MEAGRE AND INOFFENSIVE AND HAVE
ALREADY BEGUN TO FILER. HAVE YOU READ DE
ROUGEMONT'S REALLY GENIAL *LOVE IN THE WEST-
ERN WORLD?* A LOT ABOUT LANGUE D'OC AND A NEW
THEORY OF PROVENÇAL LOVE POETRY, CATHARS' BE-
LIEFS AND HERESIES ETC. DO YOU KNOW ANY GOOD
BOOK ALONG THOSE LINES? THAT THE LOVE-
CONVENTIONS OF THE POETRY DISGUISED A KIND OF
METAPHYSIC OF MYSTICAL ILLUMINATION SHARED
BETWEEN LOVERS? AND THAT CONTINENCE NOT
LICENCE WAS THE TIP? IT SOUNDS VERY ODD BUT HE
CITES HINDU EXAMPLES OF SAME TYPE OF LOVE-
BELIEFS. DAMN THE STOVE IS SMOKING. I HAVE JUST
MADE A LITTLE BIT OF MONEY TO SEE ME AWAY
UNTIL THE SPRING BY WHICH TIME TWO GHASTLY
FAT NOVELS MUST BE DONE. BUT HOW, WITH THESE
BLOODY CHILDREN—YOU SHOULD HEAR THE NOISE.
THEY LEAVE IN SEPTEMBER THANK GOD.

YOURS
LARRY DURRELL

The *course libre* is the Provençal form of bull-fighting.

Maison Sallé, Sury-en-Vaux, Cher, 24 August 1957

Dear Larry,

Very nice to have news of you. Temple wrote he was going to see you and would be taking 3 children to add to the reposeful silence.

This is rather a weird kip. The house is new and has only been camped in. The walls are still being painted—by an Australian poet, a protégé of my friend Kershaw. Apart from beds and the kitchen equipment hardly any furniture is in yet. This morning circa 7 a.m. my books arrived from M'pellier and now block the garage. We are eagerly using the smaller bookcases as shelves. Trouble is, all or nearly all furniture shops in this area contain hideosities which I should hardly have expected in Portugal. Anything in plain wood must be made by a village carpenter, whose notions of speed are pre-machine age. The house is wholly tiled, which is clean but will be bloody cold in winter. Some of the anomalies are more amusing to think of than to live with. An entrance hall, wasting much space, is paved like a Roman villa but the lavatory flush goes off with a roar which suggests a Shakespearian stage direction 'peal of ordnance shot off within'. The bath-room has a plug-in for an electric razor (which I scorn) but seemingly the water can't be heated without starting up the whole system of central heating &c. As so often the 'conveniences' have been installed by persons who have never used them and don't believe they ever could be used, and so are more in the nature of eye-wash than practicalities. But doubtless in time I'll get fixed up. Catha is still in the Midi, camping somewhere near Agde.

Very glad to hear you are in funds until the spring. Pity you can't have a spit and a dror, and get to work later. I've got quite a schedule of prints and reprints ahead. On 9th Sept the RLS book comes out with Evans. For the same month Elek are re-issuing my translation of the *Decameron* as the first of a new series of 'world masterpices' or some such burp. Have you heard of the other new series of reprints, 'Four Square', backed by Philips Tobacco (!) and edited by Landsborough? They are kicking off with 4 reprints, of which one and I think the first is my book on the veracious Oxonian [T.E. Lawrence]. To my joy, L. agreed at once to include 3 postscripts of documents received since the book first appeared. I trust this will cause gnashing of molars. Four Square also want to reprint *Death of a Nero* [sic] and *All Men* &c, are negotiating with Heinemann [. . .]. Viking of N.Y. will reprint my anthology with a few modern additions. This is a mild triumph of common sense over impudence, for Auden and a Yale prof named Pearson persuaded Viking that my anthol is 'out of date' and produced a very highbruff one in 5 vols, which has naturally been a flop. Finally I hear Officially from Moscow (Russia) that *Hero* is to be issued there in English in 1958 for the tormenting of commies taking English courses in higher education. What next? The muscovite point-edly ignored the boujois topic of dough, which in my boujois way I made quite a point of in answering.

Have you been sent a copy of the privately printed *The Sweeniad* by Myra Buttle? Obvious pseudonym. It is very amusing and makes some excellent points. The main idea of the thing, the process of beatification, is taken without acknowledgement from my *Stepping Heavenward,* and no acknowledgement is made either of my lecture on Pound-Eliot [. . .].

I don't know the De Rougemont book, but should say the thesis is questionable. If you read the poems of the troubadours, and not merely theories about them, it is obvious that in the pre-Albigensian Crusade period they are pour le bon motif, i.e. the poets think it would be a good idea to have their mistresses naked in bed. But after the atrocious crime of the Albigensian Crusade and under the influence of R.C. shits the metaphysical-mystical was developed, as you have doubtless read in Dante's *Vita Nuova.* The original Provençal amour courtois was certainly taken from the Arabs of Spain, who were far indeed from mysticism, though I believe they started that too. You will find Robert Briffaut's *Les Troubadours* very well documented, and he brings out the Arabic origins and the sensual love very well indeed.

There are towerists in Sancerre and Route 7 is a pandemonium, but not one here and the silence is really most restful. Also it is nice to get real milk, butter, eggs from the paysans, while the village butcher has meat such as I haven't experienced for years.

Warmest greetings to you both, and enjoy life and one another while you're young. At 65 one might as well be Tom Eliot at 30—appalling thought to dwell on.

Ever,
Richard

P.S. I hope your Cyprus book had a really good sale. I read and re-read it and enjoyed it more each time. You have some of the mysterious DHL gift of making one feel one has lived personally your experience.

'A spit and a dror', British army slang for a smoke, was used in World War I to mean any rest break.

Myra Buttle is a pseudonym for Victor Purcell.

ℑ *Sommières [early September 1957]*

Dear R. A. Have had no chance to answer your delightful letter owing
to the bloody children; however we ship them off on Sunday by flying
boat from Marseilles with relief. Sommières has now gone out of season! The weather is excellent and the bathing superb; and hunt as I
may I can find no reference to the town in any of the posh guide books
to this area—things like *La France à Table*. It isn't even on the map;
whereas dustheaps like Frontignan are heavily cross-indexed. It is quite
inexplicable but delightful. I don't think the summer rush has consisted
of more than a hundred people, mostly visiting relatives; meanwhile
the heavy traffic roars on down the Lunel road, and the sealine to judge
from pics in *Midi Libre* is like Blackpool. And the Madame at our café
has stopped ordering ice cream because she says sighing 'All is over
now.' It is the most mysterious summer season I've ever witnessed
anywhere; we are delighted. It may be due to the lack of lavatories. I
must say our two camp jobs have been a wonderful godsend; if you
ever have to go really rural invest three quid in a Racasan, and a bidon
of the most delightful blue rinse to go with it—colour of Stephen's
Blue Black. The burial service comes about once a fortnight when the
children and myself stalk out by night like Burke and Hare, or Sir John
Moore, and consign all to the earth. Many thanks for the pointers on
the Troubadours; I'm doing some desultory reading around the place.
De Rougemont arrived from HM and that set me off. But it's pure
pleasure and instruction and I shall never write a piece about Sommières and risk spoiling the summer season! I'm glad you are going
into action again on the reprint front. I knew the tide would turn. I'm
still at the cross roads but have had the odd stroke of luck here and
there. *Justine* has got away to a good start in the USA; and they are
setting the 2nd vol. As soon as I have them both I'll inflict them on you
to see what you think, if anything; it's annoying to do books spreadea-
glewise, as the criticisms of a single volume aren't valid for all four.
However, patience and industry! Claude's first novel should be out this
month and I'll send you a secret copy for Cath to read; Claude is determined not to send copies to the eminent for fear they might review
her and shame her—she's right in this: the book is a lightweight; but
something of her warmth and candour comes through in the writing—and the factual account of the Irish pub she ran for a couple of

years in Cork is interesting. A Continental's reaction to the Irish. But
she's spoiled it with an invented love-story. I think she was scared of
the book being formless, just a tissue of anecdotes; which it should
have been, for the material weaves up better in *Tristram Shandy* form
than otherhow. But there, it's a first book; far more skilled than mine
was I must admit, damn her eyes. Next week we fall to work again
with a will to boil the pot for the spring. My beastly brother has started
a Zoo in Bournemouth and travels everywhere with a giant ape called
Chumley. Dreadful scenes in the dining car of the Bournemouth Belle;
but I must admit it is a good way to call on one's publishers when asking for money. Our techniques are widely different. I find that Fabers
get awfully scared when I put imaginary titles to books. For a long
time I convinced them that *Justine* was to be called Sex and The Secret
Service or Not Now Your Husband's Looking. This worried them into
a defensive position; they were so relieved when they got the MS they
offered quite a decent contract. Gerry, who is cruder (with Hart-Davis
one must be tougher I suppose), always threatens to write a life of
Jesus.

I expect they'll come down here and make my life a cicada ridden
mystery before long; my sister enjoyed ten days of courses libres. I'm
expecting my ballet dancer daughter to appear too for a short while.
Money! I must press on.

Every good wish to you both
Larry Durrell

William Burke and William Hare raided cemeteries for bodies, which
they sold to medical schools, in the 1820's. The English general Sir John
Moore made a night march during the Peninsular Campaign to escape a
Napoleonic army under Soult.

§ Sommières [after 11 October 1957]

Dear RA: Forgive laziness in not writing you sooner; actually not
really laziness. But around page 100 I began to suffer from the dreadful nausea which accompanies all creation—ahem: morning *and* evening sickness. A Dead stop. So we packed a suitcase and went off down
to Arles to stay with an old friend David Gascoyne: I wonder if you
know his slender, bitter but rather fiercely true mystical poetry? Any-

way he belongs to my 1938 Paris period and we spent long nights punishing the bottle and jeering at one another. I'm so delighted you are back on the field and in good fighting heart; and the reprints should fan you out again to the public as a living and thinking producer. But do meditate another novel, will you? As a writer of nice little island books, glutted with critical praise, I now realise that really it is only novels which are read. My poor old Alexandrian whore of a *Justine* has gone into three impressions in UK and USA—small beer by your standards; but it means I can stay here at least till next autumn, pay all my alimony (holy state of alimony) and keep on making love to Claude a bit—who has just sold her third novel. She was touched that *Mrs O'* amused you. She knows how thin and slender it is; the circumstances under which it was written . . . well. A woman driven half insane and on the point of going bats. In a bomb happy situation. She was running my French section of Radio Cyprus. Always wanted to write, always wrote, but couldn't. So I used to make her come round to the villa at bomb time and set up a typewriter on the dining table. We drank red wine and worked like maniacs—I was finishing *Justine*. Every twenty-five minutes there was a boom and something in the town went up; the telephone rang. We disregarded everything. I answered the duty room, staff room, Government House, Police Press . . . and back to *Justine*. I doubt if anyone has written a book under such conditions. So that when *Mrs O'* was accepted, we of course got drunk. It wore Cyprus out of her hide. And now in two or three books . . . who knows? She may write a book. *Mrs O'* was a Rubicon. *Justine* is still a mess—a relativity novel in four books. What insanity! Never mind. I have now got French German Italian and US contracts lined up for it. We can live on a minimum of 800 pounds a year here. Forward! Claude is dropping C a card just to let her know there are friends to hand if needed. How is RLS going; and is Temple's story of the Balzac true? Do tell me if you are doing a Balzac; and tell me (and Miller) what you think of *Seraphita* and *Louis Lambert*?

Affectionately,
Larry D.

[P.S.] Anything we can do for you at this range—speak! But why not come back?

Durrell was writing *Mountolive* at this time.

32

Dear RA—Many thanks for the *Lawrence*, an unexpected bolt from the blue, which I had planned to order anyway. I am in the middle of it. Don't think you can be factually contested at any point, and of course much of the truth was known and whispered about. I'm only sorry *politically* that the legend has to take such a hard knock; will give Arab nationals and Russians another small axe to wield. But of course the truth must out. Curiously though for me the trickster and morbid story-teller is in a way even more interesting in your book than the story-book hero of legend. I only read a few pages of *The Mint* (expurgated version) and thought I saw VERY strong repressed homosexual drive, as there is in Byron. And of course the IRISH thing (which I recognise in myself) of blowing things up for the story's sake! And then the *Adlerian* power mania of the *small* man. His brother whom I met in Argentina agreed that he had a marked Napoleon complex and added 'He could never stand a joke about his height.' I think public school overcompensation brought in asceticism and pistol stuff. The same drive turned me into a quite good boxer—timorous mortal tho I am! That fucking English system! No repose about it. Takes you ages to unlimber in Europe. The anti-French thing is quite inexplicable! Puritanism? At any rate we have reaped the fruits now in the ME. What fools we can be! I saw the little man once in a pub circa '31 talking about books; he looked rather nice. Had the face of a very tired Puck. I wonder why the great cover-up of the Bureau? Surely it makes him more not less interesting the way you explode him—for Freud anyway. A thousand thanks. Enjoying the book.

Larry

Dear RA. Delightful present—very many thanks for the offprint of the *Dream*, an old friend. We are going to have it bound up! Still working like maniacs but beginning to make a small headway at last on old serial rights. Weather lousy but not cold. Sommières is perfect—so beautiful in autumn. Occasionally we go to Nîmes for a movie and a blow-out at La Louvre. I'm just proofing vol II Justine for February publication. I'll send you both vols together as soon as the 2nd comes in to see what you think. My brother is giving tea to his fans at Harrods—imagine sitting with an anaconda round one's neck in Harrods! Claude [. . .] has finished her 3rd novel now, much less flimsy [than *Mrs O'*], *and* got a publisher in the States. We are prospecting for a canoe to use on the river when the children come. If you run across any catalogues etc pl. remember us. Nice card from Catherine who sounds okay. We'll look her up when next we go into Montpellier. Hope you are at least enjoying a good *café* life in the north. Saw a v. good review of the TEL reprint in *Books and Bookmen* by one Atkins. I think you've turned the corner now. Try and see a movie called *Les Espions* and also *Celui qui doit mourir*—about Greece the latter, wonderful.

Every good wish
Larry

🍷 *Maison Sallé, Sury-en-Vaux, Cher, 21 November 1957*

Dear Larry,

Don't waste good money binding that Songe (or Singe) but hang it in the loo. A poor thing, but mine own, save for few quotes acknowledged in Gustave's notes—whereas the modern poetic masterpieces are like those of Ausonius, centos of quotes.

Have you read the *Sweeniad* yet? Coming from a Cantab don, and a historian at that, 'tis something of smack in the kisser for TSE. But it won't do him any harm—to sales, I mean. The press and the timeservers have labelled him 'God' and God he will remain.

Do you really think anything of the bogus prince of Mecca legend remains (or ever existed?) in Arab countries? Desmond Stewart was a prof of some sort in Baghdad until they fired him recently for being insufficiently subservient. He wrote me that he once asked his most advanced English class: 'What do you know of Colonel T.E. Lawrence?' After a long silence one lad asked hesitatingly: 'Was he any relation of the author of *Lady Chatterley's Lover?*' It is in *England* the lie (not the legend) is so strong and so unscrupulously bolstered; in England that it has done and still does harm; and in England—and USA—that it must be rooted out. [. . .]

I wish I could work, but after the long break I find difficulty in getting started again. I simply *must,* for I have a chance for articles again in USA. And a book contracted for which I haven't even started. Pray for me.

Do you know I haven't seen the Atkins article on TEL which you speak of, and oddly enough this morning he sent me a copy of his book on Orwell and a long letter—but no article and no mention of it. And my agent is offended and has stopped sending me cuttings because I said I wasn't interested in British praise—it's their money I want.

Rob Lyle sent me a magnificent poem (or part of a poem) on Roy and a photo of the old Roy togged up in a singlet emblasoned as a jouteur of Martigues—the only Oxonian who ever had the right to wear one. These have gone to Temple for his plaquette. I have sent him some feeble prose. Keep Temple up to the mark. He starts things and gets discouraged.

Movies. Cafés. My dear boy, this cottage is a mile from the nearest weinstube and at least 5 miles from a pitcherpalass, and anyway I haven't energy, time or money for such things. I go to bed at seven p.m., rise at about ten a.m., have one meal a day, and spend the time in futile attempts to write and lying down to rest. *Celui qui doit mourir* indeed.

My books are in fearful confusion still—too decrepit to get them straight. But I picked up an odd volume of Pepys and read it or rather re-read it with much profit. [. . .] A real inspiration to British youth, Pepys.

> Love to you both,
> Richard

Aldington's *A Dream in the Luxembourg* was translated by Gustave Cohen, medievalist at the Sorbonne, as 'Un Songe dans le Jardin du Luxembourg', published in *Table Ronde,* October 1957.

Aldington's early friendship with T. S. Eliot turned to active dislike, fueled in part by Aldington's conception of Eliot as a literary dictator; this, rather than personal animosity, is behind most of Aldington's unkind witticisms. In his contribution to *Richard Aldington: An Intimate Portrait,* Eliot wrote: 'But that quarrel had since subsided and I exchanged letters with him a few years before his death. . . . I . . . have nothing left but feelings of friendliness and regard. . . . I was the first to give offense, although unintentionally, which made a breach between us.'

Desmond Stewart taught English in Iraq at two colleges, which later became the University of Baghdad, from 1948 to 1956. In 1977 he published a biography of T. E. Lawrence.

The writer Rob Lyle was a good friend of Roy Campbell.

Aldington, Durrell, Lyle, and Edith Sitwell were among the contributors to *Hommage à Roy Campbell*, edited by Temple, which appeared in 1959.

⑨ *Maison Sallé, 1 December 1957*

Dear Larry,

I re-read your *Esprit* (which it indeed is) during the sleepless night hours, and write to confirm my first impression. This is Wodehouse born again and born greater. I wanted to send out scores of copies, but the res angusta, you know, old boy. However I have ordered one for Alec Randall KCMG, who will find it when he gets back from UN next week. And another has gone to a member of The Aussie Embassy, as I foretold. I have also sent one to Breen, who had your job in Berlin (Germany) and gave me some ammo to use against le Prince de Mecque.

Apropos, have you seen Philby's book? I am told he has 'answered' me, though what can be said to the unanswerable? I gather from the Daily Drip that the 'answer' or part of it is that his friends knew the 'Secret'. Well, I knew that and said so. The point is the effect on a clever and extremely vain *adolescent* of finding out the 'secret'—why Daddy and Mother never went out together, why he and brothers never went to parties, why no girls ever came to the house, etc etc. He minded though when the other boys did not, and that was why he was allowed that bungalow in the garden. I really think he may have run away to join the R.A. [Royal Artillery] and that when bought out he made a condition that he should not sleep in the same house with them. I have a letter from a High School head-mistress who says that she lodged next door to 2 Polstead Rd as a student, and heard from the owner that before the bungalow was built (not by Mr TEL as the veracious Graves assures us) he rigged up some way of sleeping in a *tree*.

Of course it is hearsay, so can't be used, but I don't see why they should invent it—except that people of the landlady type do invent. And how.

I am wholly on your side in any literary troubles. Make a note of it.

Love to Claude,

Ever

R.

P.S. I have ordered a copy for the King of Poland, and hope he may comment on your attitude to Slavs. Shalt have the dope if it arrives. Do not neglect the K. of P. He is part of the (alas, pianissimo) gaiety of nations.

A memory—I was sitting in the boat-train for the *Normandie* at Waterloo circa 1937, with four ghastly N.Y. Jews 'kaddy-kornered' from me and making offensive remarks about England. Tea was served, and towards the end a small cockney in fancy dress as a page came round with a large stale cake cut in slices, and offered it to the yids with the beaming remark: 'Kike, sir?' [. . .]

Harry St John Bridger Philby, the father of Kim Philby who defected to Russia, was a British civil servant, explorer, and writer. He was the most famous Arabist of his generation, and the book referred to here is *Forty Years in the Wilderness* (1957).

Potocki de Montalk, New Zealand-born poet and translator also known as Count Geoffrey Wladislas Vaile, who used to dash around Bloomsbury in kilts, claimed that he was rightfully the King of Poland.

✿ *Sommières, Monday [9? December 1957]*

Dear R.A.

A few fluish days in bed, hence no word to you to thank you for your last letter. Nasty weather down here, and we have been plunged into annoyance by absurd attempts to evict us by a hysterical landlord. I think we have the drop on him but am not sure. We are consulting a high powered character in M'pellier. Wants to get us out by May which would wreck summer plans. No other news much; emboldened by your amusement at *Esprit* I am getting together another slim vol. of my foreign office memoirs called *Stiff Upper Lip*. Serial sales seem quite good on them and I'll be sending you the odd tear-sheet to amuse you. I hope your health isn't still giving you a lot of trouble. I'm expecting a copy of *Balthazar* in a while (publication date is April 15) and I'll send you the two novels for fun. You'll probably find them surchargé (secretly I rather agree with my adverse critics but what can one do? Except be oneself I mean). I am rather a hysterical and surchargé literary gent anyhow. We are seriously thinking of making a down payment on a 'mas' somewhere around here. Think you should have done the same really. It's possible if I sell my Cyprus house that I'll have about £500 to do it with. However, this remains to be seen. Temple came out for the day last week—enjoyable time and span us around the landscape in his car. We have bought a very handsome racing canoe for the river (and the children). A fluke buy of marvellous value—they cost nearly £90 new—we got it for £15, plus sail, tiller, mast, centreboard etc and a carriage for towing it. The children will be delighted.

I am 'resting' up until April when I attack the last volume of the quartet. Doing some features for the *Sunday Times*. The Americans are getting interested in me at last. Who knows? Come this time year after next I may be squarely afloat and not terrified of being forced to return to the F.O.!

Every good wish
Larry Durrell

Maison Sallé, Sury-en-Vaux, Cher, 13 December 1957

My dear Larry,

You are a fine poet, a fine novelist, and a fine lyer-abroad for your bitter country, but in *Esprit de Corps* you have written a witty book which ought to sell MILLIONS. I am anxiously brooding over my exiguous bank balance and recalling my Duty to my Daughter, but some copies SHALL go out as un-Xmas presents, Xmas now being beyond a joke. I have 'ear-marked' a KCMG (diplomatic), a female member of Er Mejesty's Orstrilian Hembassey in Peris, and a Cambridge don.

Lately, craving for a little relief from high tragedy, I was sent a recent Wodehouse, read it with involuntary groans and official grins for old times' sake. If you could have heard me laughing my boyish laughter over *Esprit de Corps* you would have noted the difference. What is the matter with the silly bastards who run things that you are not receiving at least ten thousand a year? I gather these admirable pieces had no periodical run? Your agent should at once be crucified between A.S. Frere and T.S. Eliot.

I rejoice in you. I think the happiest are 'Frying the Flag' with its superb malaprops (how many will dine out on them!) and the inimitable portrait of the pansy in 'Noblesse Oblige'. Eton and Caius is good. Might I put in a word for Harrow and Queans?

You are a great man, and nothing is good enough for you.

An aged but enthusiastic Serb,
Ritching Aldington

[P.S.] Bacchus bless you both!

A. S. Frere was editorial director of William Heinemann, Ltd.

Ø Sommières [ca. 18–25 December 1957]

Dear RA,

A swift shot in your direction on icy typewriter keys; we just got back and are trying to undampen the house. Rain and sleet here in our absence! The London trip was terribly exhausting, but the cowbell episode most amusing. The Queen mum was really a charmer and was rather more terrified than I was, which is odd. I said: 'But don't you get a lot of practice Mam?' 'Yes, but I'm always scared stiff.' However, we carried the whole thing off manfully; the place was stiff with earls and dukes, and I longed to hear Antrobus' account of it all. The old familiar faces! The odd thing was that the very architects of our silly Cyprus policy professed to be deeply moved and repentant—after reading the book: and of course after the damage was done. Salisbury came up and made me a tender little speech. I took my radiant 17-year-old-ballet-dancer daughter—blonde as yours—and she propped me up when I seemed to totter; Earls of Saius and Antrum said 'Hear

Hear' gruffly in chorus throughout my little mock modest speech of thanks . . . I felt uneasily like TEL and wondered whether there wouldn't be a withering exposure of me in the spring lists!

Glad you liked *Esprit*. And yes, I did awfully well from the serial rights . . . More than I shall make on any serious book. I talked Faber into the plan of a short Xmas book on these lines every year to make me a bit of dough, and earn time for better (?) things. I had noticed that a cheap Xmas funny was a money spinner usually . . . Osbert Lancaster told me. I hope next year to follow up with *Sauve Qui Peut!* It's a coarse-grained humour but the best I can do; and I'm delighted to have coaxed a laugh out of you in your snowy fastnesses. My Foreign Service colleagues are buying the book—and two on the Council of Europe seem highly delighted; but there will be pursed lips (stiff upper) in Various Circles I don't doubt.

I'm just on the last lap of *Mountolive*, the third of this bloody quartet; and shall have two fat novels lined up for next year, April and Autumn. Phew! But as I have wasted ten years of writing time poking about the world I have to do three years steady in order to start the money rolling in! Did I say rolling? Trickling in. But we are so happy here in spite of the characteristic discomforts of Langue D'oc that I'd settle for five hundred a year from writing rather than the five thousand and perks I earned in Yugoslavia. We have now got a tiny record player—music at last! What bliss it is in this silence. We lock ourselves up at night and play Mozart by candlelight. Claude has just sold her third novel to Faber and a US publisher is after the first two. A bookseller told me your Stevenson was 'moving along briskly'—a trade expression I gather; I think you are over the hump with TEL; but in talking about you with your fans I gather that what everyone hopes to see from you is a big warm-hearted novel of sorts. I think you would make up all the lost ground with a novel or two in your own spanking style! Here's hoping. Will you be coming down this way for Xmas to see C?

Lovefromusboth,
Larry Durrell

Durrell journeyed to London to accept the Duff Cooper Memorial Award for *Bitter Lemons.*

Lord Salisbury (Robert Arthur James Gascoyne-Cecil, Fifth Marquess of Salisbury) as elder statesman of the Conservative Party in 1957 was effectively adviser to the Queen between the resignation of Anthony Eden and the appointment of Harold Macmillan as Prime Minister.

Sir Osbert Lancaster, knighted in 1975, is a theatre designer and author of many humorous books; he also contributes cartoons regularly to the London *Daily Express.*

Sommières [January? 1958]

The Higher Criticism

Like veteran critics of the arts
Dogs smell each other's private parts,
But less confused and slow,
They never simply smell for show
But follow instinct quite at random
With no Quod Erat Demonstrandum.
Between the better and the best
They can distinguish by a letter;
A dog's critique of the proboscis
Is like a sort of Higher Gnosis;
Quite unlike Empson or like Murry,
Their findings are both warm and furry.
In dogs the Opposites *do* marry,
The thrust is equal to the parry.
Nor do they simulate the hearty
Like critics at a cocktail party.
A single sniff and then a wag
And love is simply in the bag.

Nevertheless I *did* have an impression that the patient's tone had altered for the better vis-à-vis your work. May have been an illusion . . . I hope not. *Bitter Lemons* continues slowly, but has sicked up two fan letters, one from Harding and one from Foot, the man who is reversing the policy . . . in which direction I can't say! Jolly glad to be out. The Dutton edition of *Esprit* will have a few extra makeweight stories in the same vein. Heigho I'll send it to you when it shows up. I've just finished and am articulating the 3rd of my Babylonian quartet,

120,000 words of refined prose no less. We have nearly been swamped out by a burst reservoir; reduced only to the habitable kitchen where the crash of typewriters is deafening. Claude has just sold *Mrs O'* in the States for a handsome advance. Can afford some Tavel for meals this next quarter. I have forsaken poetry for prose but from time to time manage to put words (which infuriate Claude) to an olde songe

> Come to these arms, my dear old Dutch
> But firmly bar the door.
> I could not love thee half so much
> Loved I not doing it more!

> On which ribald note I duck under,
> L.

[P.S.] The *Observer* want me to go to Algeria! Such is fame. But I won't.

Durrell was Press Adviser to Sir John Harding, Governor and Commander-in-Chief of Cyprus from 3 October 1955 to 1 December 1957, a period of EOKA terrorism. Durrell left the island for England late in 1956; Sir Hugh Foot succeeded to Harding's position.

Sommières [18 January 1958]

My dear RA

Just a swift line to tell you how touched I was by your kindness in error-spotting *Esprit*. Really I was most awfully grateful—and you know the book was proofed about 4 times—quite extraordinary how errors bury themselves. You obviously have a special eye—electro-magnetic?

I've nearly finished the new novel 140,000 words Phew! And it must be in London next week so Claude is typing night and day poor girl. *Esprit* has fulfilled your prognostication to my surprise—6000 copies and several papers clamouring for new Antrobi. What luck. Many thanks.

Larry D.

❦ *Maison Sallé, Sury-en-Vaux, Cher, 14 February 1958*

Dear Larry,

[. . .] I am very glad to hear about the *Stiff Upper Lip*. You've got something there which fits the mood of the times. I have only failed with one Proselyte and that was a silly blunder on my part. I said the *Esprit* is better than Wodehouse to a bigoted fan who thinks that Wodehouse practically invented literature.

You are quite right to rest. One of the great mistakes in our trade—which I have made myself—is to work too hard. The writer's capital is his talent and nervous energy, and if they are drawn on too heavily the result is bad. [. . .]

Has the *Sweeniad* come your way yet? It has already sold about 5000 in US, and is due out with Secker in April. Of course I said most of it twenty years ago, but it doesn't pay to be ahead of the times.

The paperback of *Hero* is due out today—which takes me back to the Île de Port-Cros in the autumn of 1928 when I was beginning it, and DHL and Frieda were living with me. Three disasters happened—Aldous's *Point Counter Point* was a Book-of-the-Month success; DHL got those appalling notices of *Lady C.*; and Frieda to whom I had read the first part of *Hero* went babbling to DHL about how good it was. Result: I was told that within a year or so Aldous would be dead or in a bug-house; 'and you too, Richard, you're worse than he is.' There's a letter of his, which Aldous very rightly published, in which all this is duly set down. Alas for the prophecies of a dying man with shattered nerves! Within 16 months poor DHL was gone and we are still more or less extant. It is so curious to me that both during DHL's life and after people can't see that these wild accusations were nothing but the nervous exacerbation of a man whose lungs were gone and who had a damnably rotten deal all round. If DHL had been a boot-licking time-server like Dick Church with his 'insincere and unnecessary opinions', they'd have given him the O.M. and perhaps even a little of their money.

I hope Claude's novels go well in USA. It is a fat-headed but large public with money but little sense, and quite unpredictable. But one real success on the Daph du Maurier scale would set up for life. As Daph made her reputation and dough by re-writing *Jane Eyre* for a generation which can't read, I wonder other people don't re-write Victorian successes. Perhaps they do and I don't know it.

All good things to you both,
Richard

P.S. Catha's latest best friend is a communist. Il ne manquait que cela.

Richard Thomas Church was a well-known poet, novelist, and literary critic.

🕊 *Sommières [ca. 14 February–1 March 1958]*

Dear R.A. Many thanks for the splendid letters and the really good sales news. I knew you were round the bend again—if you know what I mean. I think the Lawrence shock has worn off and of course the *Hero* goes on forever as it deserves to and will. It really is splendid. Things aren't going too badly with us either and we've beaten down our landlord so that we can clear the summer here before moving. I have a mind to put down three or four hundred upon a small mas or villa or something and see if I can't make this a permanent way of living. And now the Yanks have bought all my old dusty back titles and propose to print two books a year until they have me all in print . . . Unbelievable luck! *Esprit de Corps* is 12,000 up and reprinting. What a good judge you are but: master, master, I am afraid I sympathised a little with your recalcitrant friend. I know these have good contrivance, but they really aren't creations in the manner of my beloved P.G. And writing them you wouldn't believe how hard it is to avoid Wodehouseisms. The brute has invented an entire language of frivolity around *dished diddled foozled* and so forth; I have to cut out at least three plagiarisms in every story . . . Try one and see. [. . .] Incidentally what a legacy you left me in Temple; pure gold and a magnificent friend to have. He brought a lawyer out and routed the landlord over five rounds!

I have just delivered the third of my blasted quartet and Fabers seem quite excited, while the French press on *Justine* was quite unexpectedly blush making. I shall pass your note about the Roy MSS over to Temple so that if C forgets he can remind her. My friend Alan

Thomas writes 'Even the London *Times* seems to be taking after the *Balkan Herald* these days. A headline on the leader page today says MASS INVASION BY FOREIGN TITS. I wonder if Wolfenden knows?'

Henry Miller is in cracking form and has sent me a set of recorded interviews on discs which bring him back to me larger than life. What a delightful person he is and how crazy. You would have loved him. Everyone has a picture of him as a sort of ghoul from his work; but a gentler, more honourable, considerate and devoted man it would be impossible to find. And what a clown! A real Grock.

Claude is now writing a book about France and England; it should be interesting because it is from ground-level so to speak, steering clear of abstractions. And O yes, I did get the *Sweeniad* and enjoyed it. It was well done. But I think you are right in hinting that it had been done before and somewhat better. Roy's *Dunciad* did the job better I think; and you have had several knock down blows at the subject yourself. I also wonder whether the angle of attack today hasn't shifted away towards the provincialism and triteness and deliberate self-glorifying common-ness of the Dead End Kids? Eliot doesn't any longer present a danger with his anodyne conservatism; the boys which frighten me are the undeclared Burgesses and Macleans in the Labour party ... However not living there I feel rather out of it all. How lucky to have food in the larder for a year ahead! We arrived with £200 and not a hope of righting the ship.

every good wish.
Larry d.

The *Balkan Herald* is the fictional newspaper famed for its typographical errors as featured in Durrell's 'Frying the Flag', published in *Esprit de Corps*.

Among the many public offices held by Sir John Wolfenden was service on the Departmental Committee on Homosexual Offences and Prostitution, 1951–57. Thomas's reference to him in connection with the 'Invasion by Foreign Tits' was apparently intended in this context.

'Grock' was the performing name of Charles Adrien Weltach (1880–1959), the legendary circus and later stage clown, tumbler, and musician.

Claude's manuscript, 'French Habit', was never published.

🌶 *chez M. Alister Kershaw, Maison Sallé, Sury-en-Vaux, Cher, 1 March 1958*

My dear Larry,

That mass invasion of foreign tits is very gratifying, but I must tell you that the influence of the *Balkan Herald* on the *Times* certainly began in the 1930s. I distinctly remember A.S. Frere ringing me up one morning and making me look at the centre page of the *Times* which had a letter from some ornithological peer headlined:

TWO GREAT BEARDED TITS SEEN IN ESSEX

I do most heartily congratulate you and Claude on these marvellous successes, and hope you will both 'profit'. I think the idea of a mas is excellent if you can also put up the dough to make it habitable according to our W.C.-bath-and-heat notions. Have you seen the place Temple and his donna have outside M'pellier? Charming. And of course the children are as pleased as a waggonload of monkeys.

I have got the bulge on you pro tem in one 'field'. Seghers says I am a 'très gran poète', and is going to publish the Songe in his 'Autour du Monde' series, with the English if the shylock-grip of Heinemann can be released. Seghers says this series is not 'commerciale' but 'd'estime', from which I gather that he will claim the kudos as well as collecting the dough, as usual nowadays. Ah! when we can hang the last publisher's 'editor' in the entrails of the last Sunday reviewer!

Claude's book on France-England should be an event. I wish she'd tell us why 99% of French abuse their government as a set of pickpockets etc and yet are thrilled to the marrow when the pickpockets give them the Légion d'Honneur. Some mystery here.

I hear from Landsborough that he is making enquiries and calculations to determine how many copies of *Lawrence of A.* he shall order for the new impression, and that 10,000 is the minimum.

I never thought Eliot had any political significance whatever. [. . .] By the way, Purcell, as you know, is one of the best sinologists we have, and he tells me Pound's alleged Chinese culture is all balls. I always suspected it.

Catha in trouble at school and with me in consequence. No rest for the wicked.

Much love and congratulations to you both,
Richard

P.S. I don't think Wodehouse is better than you are.

🏵 *Sommières [ca. 1–10 March 1958]*

Dear Richard:

I'm just knocking together the successor to *Esprit* which is coming from Faber in November and is called *Stiff Upper Lip.* The illustrations will be by Nicholas Bentley. Would it gêne you to find on the title page the dédicace 'To Richard Aldington, who encouraged these follies'??? I know it's hardly the sort of thing to offer to one of one's Reverend Seniors in the Magic but . . . Let me know, will you? Sometimes one does these things out of friendship and rocks the boat in the wrong direction. And I have no bones to break. So speak thy mind! Meanwhile the *Times* proposes to carry the book in parts monthly until August by which time it will be in the press. I would of course ship you an extra proof with the option to cry off. Meanwhile here are carbons of the title story and one other ['Something à la Carte?'] which as a francophile you should get a laugh out of . . . Antrobus seems to be settling down nicely in the *Times*. Why the hell shouldn't we have some fun too?

Yours
Larry

[P.S.] Don't return carbons—they are spares—destroy!!

🏵 *Maison Sallé, Sury-en-Vaux, Cher, 10 March 1958*

Dear Larry,

[. . .] And now let me accept (with indecent alacrity) your most welcome and flattering idea of dédicace of *Stiff Upper Lip*. Wonderfully kind of you, and I am really touched. I wouldn't accept if I thought it would harm you, but I am sure the Establishment has been defeated by the good Landsborough. And I am so rejoiced by your success, which is most heart-warming. The new pieces contain many a chuckle, and the eating a bit of horse by a Colonel in the Blues was a trouvaille of genius. Yet I am not sure that I am not even more delighted by the wine-tasting spree and the heroic diplomat who refused to take his posterior off the breathing. Floreant, old boy, floreant.

Did Temple tell you that Mary has cut about three quarters of that awful letter of Roy's? Hope he didn't write many like that or the Position will Become Awkward. One might defend that one as a series of galéjades. Funny, he never bullshitted to me in that way. The old Roy as a Fellow of the Royal Society was a genial burp.

Love to you both,
Richard

P.S. I'm not going to destroy those carbons. I'm going to forge your moniker on them and sell them at Sotheby's for wodges of paper money.

Galéjades: Provençal word for banter, jeers, hoaxes.

✪ *Maison Sallé, Sury-en-Vaux, Cher, 5 May 1958*

Dear Larry,

Excuse silence. Health is a jigzag up and down, with downs unfortunately exceeding ups. The fine weather did help, and I got to walks of nearly 2 miles—then went down with a crash again, and feel—oh awful. Never mind.

Justine is a wonderful book and that Claude is right to be very proud of you. The book has such an effect on me I can read only a few pages a day—it is so vivid and 'emotioning' to coin a word. Don't misunderstand—it reminds me of my feelings when I first read Loti at about 18. I mean the introduction to a quite unknown (to me) exotic area and set of characters, and a (to me) new style of writing as well as a new mind—so that I feel 'here at last is something that will live and be read 50 years hence'. It is a great achievement. I want greatly to see what you do in *Balthazar*.

48

Catherine *says* she is working hard and perhaps she is. They certainly seem to be cramming her, for in a short period she had to write a philosophical discourse on Courage (what is that? something civilians talk about, I believe) and a historical essay on the State of Germany in 1914, and demonstrate the whole process of digestion in vertebrates. [. . .]

Love to both,
Richard

♫ *Sommières [ca. 10–14 June 1958]*

Dear RA:

Many thanks for your suggestion; I'd like to do the book. But a proof if you have one is best, rather than waste a copy. Shall I write direct to Dutton . . . how to go about it? Are you better these days? I meant to write before but the motor trip down from Paris with my two daughters was tiring, and on arrival we all went down with fatigue colds; everyone obliged with a characteristic performance—Claude with a grand bronchitis and my smallest with chicken pox! Disinfect this letter if you've never had it. Only just staggering to our feet with the help of Tavel.

Paris was fun; and we did a little country housing with friends, leaving terrible marks in their baths. What bliss the hot water was after nearly a year of bathless art! I even enjoyed the cocktail party to my surprise; ten years of cocktails and insipid pleasantries had, I thought, blunted me; but vanity surmounts every obstacle! After all, this party was for ME!

Justine is going slowly but steadily; it beats me why, but it has opened me up to markets in German Italian French—but best of all USA. I have now contracted for two novels a year in three languages until I can boost readership to around seven thousand which will I calculate free me from working! Already *Balthazar* has tipped that in two months. Another big novel *Mountolive* (part III) comes in November, together with *Stiff Upper Lip*. I gather Bentley has done a smashing cover for the latter squib; I've asked them to send you the first off the press.

It's been a hard year, but I've dented the enemy's line; I just want to keep the pressure up for a year or two, and then we'll see. We must start househunting again soon—we leave in October from here, damn it.

I'm sorry I didn't have a moment to contact Kershaw; by a stroke of luck all sorts of friends seemed to intersect with me in Paris, and took up all my time. We are also threatened with a stream of visitors this summer. And the children . . . Ouf! And I want to finish the quartet by Xmas.

I hope you are fully well again by now and working. I must fall to when my ballerinas have gone back next week. The wine has quite demoralised them.

Every good wish, and thanks for the hot tip and the shove up from behind!

yours
Larry

Durrell reviewed Alister Kershaw's *A History of the Guillotine* for *Australian Letters,* published by Geoffrey Dutton.

Corréa, Durrell's publisher in France, gave a party in his honour.

𝕁 *Sommières [after 19 June 1958]*

Dear Richard

The review is airborne! A pauvre 1200 I'm afraid. [Kershaw's] book is good but rather slender—more a monograph really; anyway we'll see—and many thanks again for the hot tip. *Claude* has now caught S's chicken pox with a temperature—I'm now cook and *bonne*—hence such scrappy letters. Sorry!

You mention the boycott again—what new sickening developments have taken place? O God!

I have a novel to finish by Xmas but don't see a hope in hell at the moment.

I've found an old mazet with 3 sq. kilometres of garrigue to rent for October—more roughing it! O to have been born rich!

Every good wish
Larry D.

§ *Sommières [ca. 4–14 August 1958]*

Dear RA. I didn't write to spare you the feeling of being obliged out of kindness to reply, in case you were feeling rotten, as Temple said you were. We have more or less lurched to our feet after chicken pox, false appendicitis, all the fun of the fair . . . house full of huge children, expensive to feed and maddening to live with, and no hope of release before Sept 8 when they return to school. I am supposed to produce the 4th volume of the blasted quartet by February; so far not a line written! We have found a tiny mazet on the Uzès road, on the edge of the garrigue, windy forlorn and rather Brontë where I hope we'll be moving in September; but it is completely unfurnished and it's tricky work planning for basic furniture etc. But I'm going to take a plunge, rent for a ten-year lease with an option to buy if I can, and . . . well: once more into the breach . . . It maddens me to think of my beautiful bathroomed furnished house in Cyprus unsaleable and unlettable. Everything down to a huge fridge! Fruit of ten years solitary in the FO . . . Now I have to start again. But things are, if not rosy, better than they were. The quartet is sold in four languages which is something and the Yanks are going to put all my books into print at the rate of two a year. I calculate that with ten chickens and the excellent potager out there I shall just squeeze by! But of course I shall still have to press on hard to secure the back door for next year. I should have copies of *Mountolive* and *Stiff Upper* to send you quite soon I think, though they are scheduled for November.

I'm now doing a Henry Miller reader for the USA; such a lot of fine work, but a tightrope in near-bawdry to be delicately trod with the author quite prepared to slip in an odd four-letter word and stick to it . . . and torpedo the project! I'll see you get a copy when it's out. At his best Henry is a V. great American I think.

Now that I have formally put poesy aside until I can earn a living with prose people are pestering me for it, the BBC intoning it and other smile-making things . . . what is one to make of the British. In *Mountolive* the only cut they insisted on was the word 'fellatio' which I shouldn't have thought anyone knew, save the late Havelock E. and Norman Haire . . . It baffles me to be unable to get a sense of rapport with the way they think; they shy like a nervous horse at a piece of paper in the road . . . Anyway, what the hell; if I have to do six more thrillers to stay here I shall do them with a good grace. I have now cased up this joint, as Henry would say . . . To live within bike-shot of Nîmes, and with the Stes Maries as my summer resort (I have two excellent tents) seems heaven to me, mistral and all. Ouf! I suppose I'm getting old, but I'm sick of travel. As always, everyone is trying to make me start travelling again; *Balthazar* has had quite an extraordinary advance-press, for it isn't out in USA till next month, and next year in France, while the Germans have lagged behind with translation-troubles over the blood clots in *Justine*. But the book has been reviewed in three languages on the english ed and the result is two invitations to tour america, one holland and one sweden! But I'm going to stay with my chickens; they need me (and I need them until I see how the money shapes)!

Sorry about C's 'bac'; but it may indicate real intelligence. Neither I nor my brother could ever manage an exam from common entrance upwards. [. . .] Glad about the health! That is *important*. Ever thought of trying to write a thriller when all else fails? But you have not needed to, have you?

every good wish
Larry

P.S. No, I'm not anxious to take up with Potocki again; I didn't approve of his affiliation with Mosley and adoration of Adolf, and would be unable to support the dementia praecox nowadays. It is all so *english* this studied eccentricity. His funny little eldricto brother, however, joined up in the RAF despite his views and was quite a good officer they say.

I'm afraid my anti-jewishness doesn't extend as far as Belsen, and never will. What is one to say to someone who publicly approves? Silence were better . . .

The Henry Miller Reader was published by New Directions in 1959.

Havelock Ellis and Norman Haire were pioneering writers on sex.

At the time considered a politician of outstanding ability and promise, Sir Oswald Mosley resigned from the Labour Government in 1931 to form the New Party, which initially attracted many leading intellectuals, some of whom contributed to the party's journal, *Action*. The New Party soon became the British Union of Fascists with Mosley as leader, and he was interned in England throughout the Second World War.

52

🙊 *Sury-en-Vaux, Cher, 14 September 1958*

Dear Larry,

I have owed you a letter for too long, and yet you and Claude have been much in my thoughts, for I've been wondering how you are getting along, and if the housing problem is solved. Ridiculous situation where scores of milliards are wasted on futile and dangerous atomic toys, and decent people have nowhere to live.

Is the book going on? You have been so very kind in suggesting outlets for me, but—well, exactly 50 years have passed since my first lit'ry work, a bad sonnet, was published. People eventually get sick of a name and the inevitable limitations of one mind, though I have suffered by being too versatile. The law of diminishing returns comes into action, and the more one writes, the less one gets. The clue for me now is to shut up as far as new books are concerned, and to trot along on what comes in from the old ones, and on little jobs such as reviews, introductions, anonymous translations, and so on. Perhaps in a year or two. When my agent returned from USA recently, she wrote that she had 'several proposals' for new books. This is new, because a year ago they wouldn't hear of me. I told her, no, I'm not inclined to write another book at present.

I am sorry you are against the king of Poland. He has his little affectations to be sure, but I find him a really warm-hearted friend, and in some ways a good writer. I discovered the other day that his translations of Miscewitz (spelling!) [Adam Mickiewicz] are standard in the American universities. As to Mosley—frankly, his editorials in the *European* are the only intelligent comments on international politics which I read. His old time apeing of the Fuehrer was a ghastly blunder, but he was never dangerous. He wanted to avert the 1939–1945 war, which the 'Left Wing' were hell-bent on having, after dodging the column in the first war. It rises my dander that he was jugged by the draft-dodgers of 1914, just as I resent the insults to dear old Roy from that pack of pansy-cowards who now rule the roost in 'poetry'. Surely you can feel the difference here, in France, when there is a man at the head of things, and all those yammering do-gooders are in the discard.

A cholera epidemic confined to communists and *New Statesman* socialists would be a Very Good Thing.

Catha is in London (Eng.) with her mother, and, I believe, visiting various 'family'. Strange to say, she doesn't seem to enjoy my native land—for you are Arish, are you not? Anyway, Catha sends gloomy letters deploring the rain and dirt, longing to get 'home' to France. Her only consolation seems to be that she found one or two of Roy's books in the Chelsea Public Library. This astonishes me—I should have thought they would have been burned to the greater glory of the TUC by the 'Left Wing'. I wish to god you'd write something really satirical about the 'Left Wing'.

People from London (Eng.) drop in to see me during their absurd 'holidays' (they don't know the elements of travelling) and I note with interest that the 35–55 group are nearly all 'Left Wing' (may Allah blacken their faces), and the under 30s are nearly all pretty Right of Centre.

I hear a strong latrine rumour that Steinbeck is to get the Nobel—a world scandal, when Aldous is denied it, and it has gone to his inferiors such as Hemingway and Faulkner. The scorns which patient merit of the unworthy takes.

If you and Claude come driving up Route 7, do make this a night's stopping place. Given two days' notice, I can get Alister–Sheila's bedroom made fit for you, and get in a little prog and boose—'peck and boose' was the phrase in 18th century Ireland. And glad indeed to see yer honour and the beautiful lady. Make a note of it.

I wanted to get the king of Poland a press, so that he could print for me my answer to the Lawrence Bureau, which of course can't be issued in England, since the motto will be 'spilling all beans'.

All the titles of good fellowship come to you,
Richard

TUC: Trades Union Congress.

𝕊 Le Mazet Michel, Engances près Nîmes, Gard [ca. 14–24 September 1958]

DEAR RICHARD. GOOD TO HAVE A LINE FROM YOU AGAIN. YOU SOUND IN BETTER HEART. I'm so glad. We are in the throes of a move into Wuthering Depths, which is a stone mazet pitched on the wild garrigue between Nîmes and Uzès. Very very Brontë; but this time I'm on a long let and can't be pitched out within five years, and also have an option to buy if I like (and can). Pray for Antrobus!

I have nothing against Potocki. Please don't think so, and don't let him think so; I always found him engaging and interesting despite the Freudian hair-do, and I still have among my books in England several issues of his review, and *Whited Sepulchres.* Yes, he's a good writer. But I wish he'd write more; but I think I can't go along with Mosley, who is a dangerous little pathologue. You know, Richard, I believe if you could see what happens in a Fascist state—could see the behaviour of the Cyprus Police, Malaya, Palestine police, you would be scared at the strong vein of brutish fascism the British have in their unconscious. The minute Habeas Corpus goes out, and the hundred juridical safeguards which we have built up, it is astonishing how jackbooted and truculent we become. Ultimately both systems are the same. One-party Government supported by a secret police and army. I had two years of Fascism in Greece under Metaxas; it really didn't differ much from Tito except that it left the economics of the country alone and didn't smash the middle classes. But the same barren boring demagogy, the same mental route marching . . . No. I can't go along with people who could wear Per Ardua Ad Buchenwald on their shoulder flashes. And if I loved Roy it was precisely because he turned down Joyce's overtures; he was invited, did you know, to become the official poet of Fascism? And if I am a Royalist it is in the biological sense— the only political creed possible to a poet I think, who is ultimately *only* interested in values and not politics at all . . . Enough. Don't let this rubbish bore you. And nowadays I have become a positive miser over my time and energy; and the thought of dear old Potocki or dear old Prince Monolulu strolling up the drive would make my heart sink purely by association. That grubby little English world; the Fitzroy Tavern; Nina Hamnett; Aleister Crowley . . . O dear, I don't feel the slightest contact with it any more, and prefer to frowst; but I mean harm to no man. And I should certainly perform any service I could for P, out of respect for him as a person and despite some of his ideas . . .

We have one month of furious settlement before us and then I must secure the larder for next year and get down to the fourth volume of this blasted quartet. Still, there is some rough shooting to be had on the garrigue, a potager to mind and twenty chickens to look after; we plan if all else fails to live thus. It's been a hard two years but the wind is now shifting rapidly in my favour; a bit more slogging. Do you know people are beginning to take me really seriously? Germans and Americans and French, believe it or not. And the old bitch *Justine* was short-listed with Musil for the Best Foreign Book Prize in Paris. She didn't win, and justly; but what a compliment! Like being short-listed with Proust! I don't know what poor Antrobus will say to all this. I'm tempted to let him do the Preface to the next volume just for a lark! He should be along soon, a copy for you coming direct.

Satire on the left? I think the best way is to pinprick; how about a letter to the *Times* opening subscriptions for a bronze statue of Burgess and Maclean to be set up in Turnstile Square? Our modern Heroes! But then they wouldn't print it I suppose.

every good wish.

Larry

William Joyce, known as 'Lord Haw Haw', made wartime broadcasts on behalf of Nazi Germany.

Peter Charles MacKay, a London character and racing tipster who styled himself Ras Prince Monolulu, told his life story (*I Gotta Horse,* 1950) to Sidney H. White. MacKay's colourful pseudo-oriental garb of flowing robes and ostrich feather head-dress was a familiar spectacle on British race-courses.

Nina Hamnett was an English painter and a highly visible figure in the London and Paris bohemias from the years just before the First World War on. She held court at such landmarks as the Fitzroy Tavern and Bricktop's, where she was known for her spirited renderings of bawdy ballads.

Aleister Crowley was a prolific author and diabolist who called himself the Great Beast.

Robert Musil (1880–1942) was an Austrian writer whose *Der Mann ohne Eigenschaften,* a massive unfinished novel, appeared in English as *A Man Without Qualities* in 1953 and was translated into French as *L'Homme sans qualités* in 1958.

56

My dear Larry,

I reply at once to your most welcome letter, to send you and Claude terrific gratters on your mazet. You are entirely right. You will be infinitely happier and freer there than in most places. All that disturbs me is your reference to rough shooting, which sounds as if you intended to take out a licence. Claude is ceasing to be French, or she would insist on your being a braconnier. In the Gard there are still sangliers. [. . .]

But, dear Larry, I *have* lived under Fascist guvverments, namely, Musso in Idd'ly and Salazar in Portugal, and I can affirm they were a damn sight better than the proletarian anarchy they supplanted. Moreover, I was in Spain under the 'Republican' régime our dear old Roy pretended he fought (did he?) and that was a mess, if you like. But in fact I agree entirely with all you say, except that I find Mosley's articles in the *European* extremely well-informed and intelligent, rather a contrast to [. . .] the New Shithouse, and all that gang of cryptos.

By God, on Monday I received a wire of about 60 words practically ordering me to attend some damned Conference in USSR to protest about Asia and Africa. What next? Of course I said I couldn't on account of health. Which is true enough. Temple came down, and was delightful, but—for heaven's sake don't tell him—I was so exhausted that when he left at 3 p.m. on Sunday I came straight home to bed and stayed there until 9 a.m. next day. One just can't fight on all fronts at once, and the losing battle is with A.D.

Nina Hamnett—poor Nina—a curious mixture of slut and whore, but a very decent chap. Why did she commit suicide? [. . .]

You must get hold somehow of Robert d'Harcourt's *Goethe et l'art de vivre* (Payot, 1935). Long out of print of course, but a positive bible on how to save oneself from the philistine world. The old Goethe of course had cards we haven't got. He always arranged for bores to call between certain afternoon hours, dressed himself as the Geheimrat, put up his gongs, assumed an air of glacial stupidity, and whatever was said, coughed importantly and uttered only 'Ja, ja'. In the evening when his real friends came, he was in a dressing gown, every man had a bottle to himself, and a good time was had by all.

I don't wonder you are having success—or rather, I do, because you write so damned well. Temple's visit interrupted my reading of *Mountolive,* but I am getting on with it, and wish the book hadn't to end. I'll write again about this. Is 'diamonos' classical Greek? I am perplexed. [. . .]

All the titles of good fellowship come to you!
Richard

[P.S.] Most surprisingly, Alister's Guillotine book has had quite favourable reviews in *Times, Times Lit, Express* etc and even the *Oxford Mail.* The Huns have bought it. What next?

PPS I shall never forget poor old Nina coming to see me in London (Eng.) circa 1933, and announcing with joy that she has found a nice clean old man with lots of money. Hélas, it didn't endure—tout lasse, tout casse, tout passe.

PPPS In 1914 Nina discovered that her boy friend of the epoch was a Boche. She denounced him to the coppers, and he was interned. It takes a woman to do that sort of thing. True, he had no money, and she had ceased to love him.

Mazet Michel, Engances près Nîmes, Gard [3 October 1958]

Dear Richard:

Just a swift line to thank you for your splendidly encouraging letter which set me up no end, about old *Mountolive.* I have been made suspicious about myself recently because all three of my *publishers* seem mad about the quartet and shower me with compliments! Corks, I thought, *publishers;* but they have hearts of stone and only think of saleability. Perhaps I've gone and done a pretentious middlebrow job without meaning to! Praise from a critic of your standing made me reach for the brandy bottle . . .

We are in an utter mess, trying to build a minuscule lavatory (dreams, idle dreams). The masons have feet like mastodons and carry mud sweat and tears all round the house on them; and tomorrow the plumber comes to bore holes all round us and fix pipes. I sold a couple of pieces of stuff to *Holiday* mag, and decided to splash out with a real lavatory . . . Arrangements permit me to do alterations under common agreement with proprietor. If in three years I have the permission and can cough up the rest I can keep the place. It's rather a fine property really with about a thousand trees (all dead!) and a square mile of garrigue around it. Mountains of flat rocks which I hope to build into terraces walls etc.

To my surprise the garrigue in climate, colour tone—everything—is pure Attica; even the sky. Quite different from Languedoc. I like it very much; and this year if fate is propitious I shall be able to count on living here. Think of it!

But it is going to be a month before we can do any work. And the dirt!

every good wish
larry

𝓈 *Sury-en-Vaux, Cher, 6 October 1958*

Dear Larry,

Your letter, postmarked 3rd, says nothing of pluies diluviennes, floods and suchlike inconveniences, yet from the map you and Claude seem to have been right in the danger area. And as you were undergoing structural changes you may have had rain through the roof, damage to books and clothes, que sçais-je? I hope all is well, and that you escaped. Clearly, Iaveh is a communist, and thus vents his spite at the result of the referendum. I have my doubts about the wisdom of the Général's policy. The English and the Irish were far closer than the French and Arab-Berbers, and yet the attempt at 'integration' failed miserably. Even if the Général succeeds in keeping Algérie Française he runs the risk of making la France Algérienne. Patriotism is not enough. [. . .]

There is no doubt that you are a great writer, and the wonder is that the bastards accept you. In these matters I am another Robespierre (a pea-green incorruptible) and would not praise even my own daughter if I thought she did not deserve praise. I will confess that the scene of Mountolive and the child prostitutes hurt me—but then I am a sentimentalist about all children, and have an exaggerated respect for ambassadors. The F.O. will never speak to you again.

Don't trouble to send a letter, but let me have a postcard to say you are both all right.

Love to Claude,
Richard

♨ *Mazet Michel, Engances près Nîmes, Gard [9 October 1958]*

No! happily we are not sinistrated by the floods on our hill top, but bedevilled by carpenters. Thrilled you cared for *Mountolive,* and I quite understand, yes, about the children. I wanted something almost unbearably fierce at that point to counterpin the Leila business and the chute totale! But it is of course true of the Egypt I knew and bears upon Justine's child in vol IV. Ach! I'm sick of this damn quartet. Antrobus comes on November 10, right on top of *Mountolive*!!

Every good wish
Larry

♨ *Mazet Michel, Engances, Chemin d'Uzès, Nîmes, Gard, France [ca. 15–20 October 1958]*

DEAR RICHARD:

MANY THANKS FOR THE GOOD LETTER, AND THE BETTER NEWS THAT THE OLD QUARTET IS BRAIN TEASING YOU A BIT: I WONDER HOW ALL THESE PEOPLE WILL LOOK IN CONTINUUM, SO TO SPEAK, AFTER VOL FOUR, WHICH BLAST IT I MUST SOON START. I STILL REGARD IT AS A SINGLE NOVEL IN FOUR MOVEMENTS! BUT THINGS ARE BEGINNING TO LOOK UP A BIT AND THERE'S A GOOD CHANCE OF MY OWNING THIS BLASTED MAZET: MEANWHILE AN AMERICAN PAPER HAS COUGHED UP 1000 DOLLARS FOR A PIECE OF DRIVEL AND WE HAVE DECIDED TO START BUILDING A REAL LAVATORY! YOU'D THINK IT WAS A

BLASTED CATHEDRAL THE WAY THEY GO ABOUT IT,
THE MASONS! NOT TO BE FINISHED TILL THE THIRD
GENERATION.

An amusing and wildly excited U.S. press on *Balthazar;* some
screamingly funny anti's. One chap says that I am a pompous prig and
adds 'all his cornices are hung with rhetoric'! Another very grave chap
(J.G. Junior) ends a frightfully tentative review with the words: 'Interesting as it all is I do not think the inhabitants of this part of South
Carolina will find it much to their taste'! But some very good pro's,
too, in the middlebrow section (*Times*). *Sales* perhaps? Who knows.
The *Boccaccio* is a splendid gift; I've just torn it from Claude who loved
it; I think it must be in your translation that I first read it in Rhodes,
years ago. Familiar feel. What does a slip or two matter when the
sweep and tang of the original are there? Glad to hear you are writing,
or at least have twinges of conscience about *not;* Temple and family
came out yesterday for the day, and he gave a good account of you:
back on form, and comfortably housed. But he was much concerned
about you saying you weren't going to do any more books, and invited
me to invite you to jolly well think again! I hereby do! [. . .]

That's all I think.

every good wish
Larry

*✈ Mazet Michel, Engances, Chemin d'Uzès, Près Nîmes, Gard, France
[before 6 November 1958]*

Dear Richard

A swift line to thank you for the donnish appraisal. I thought it
rather just and indeed flattering; yes, blast it, I am a romantic! I know
the weakness too which lies in the supercharging! Always remember a
blistering attack on Conrad by Lewis in which he said he was the Gau-
guin of prose 'romance laid on like chocklate cream'! Ugh! And yet
somehow I think Lewis has failed more seriously than Conrad on a
smaller scale—who did the work. I must admit I admire Gautier rather
also! Well, I can't help it; but the books are making quite a dent in England and America, at least from a press point of view. And *Mountolive*
has sold 10,000 in U.K. which [is] the best trade picture I've had so far

and has excited Fabers into bursts of the wildest generosity; in fact my advances are being bumped up to 500 on both sides of the Atlantic now. Is this where I begin to make a real living? Fingers crossed. But anyway I shall clear the bar for next year and can allay my mortal terror of being driven back to Chipping Sodbury! And once I own this mazet I won't know myself. I believe you would enjoy this life but of course you'd have to have someone as capable etc as Claude to help with the solitude. But the garrigue is wonderful; really wild with blue Attic skies. Temple writes that you are planning a visit; now do try and come out to us will you? I'd love to see you and have a good gossip about eng lit; I have also learned to dry-stone wall and can show you a beauty I built. It's wonderful work to do, nicer than writing, harder than walking!

Perhaps the most encouraging sign of all is the number of undergraduates writing to me about the books. I think that does mean that they are hitting the target area. I always believe the young have a nose for what is new, if not extra good!

We have just made a lamp out of an olive tree which is absolutely lovely. Cost 400 francs. It would sell for 12,000 in a shop. Bricoler, that's the game; I could ask for nothing nicer than bricoleing here; thousands of tons of stone all pre-cut in the form of soup-plates. You must come; and we'll give you a decent lunch with a non 7-degree wine. It's a promise.

I don't know what to think or advise about Catha; is she trying to get a job or study or what? If a job, you should let her attack Paris for a month. Anyway when you come we can talk!

every good thing
Larry

Bricoler literally means to dodge or shuffle, but in the Midi it refers to the construction of mortarless stone walls.

🜨 *Sury, 6 November 1958*

Dear Larry,

After the critical don, the enthusiastic poet:

'I am reading *Mountolive* and now want to re-read the others. I

was transported by the first, got tangled in or with or by the second—
now am swept clear into the vibrant and inspiring third. I don't think
he has any rival of his time, can only think of him as out-standing,
alone, unlike in philosophy, but comparable in mundanity and wit to
Norman Douglas. His fire or flame of consummation gets me where
dear old Lorenzo at times seemed smouldering—while Durrell crack-
les and champs and his Phaëton takes us with him—but won't topple
us, himself, or the fiery steeds over!'

I don't altogether go for the N.D. comparison. True he was in the
F.O.—placed en disponibilité at an exceptionally early age—and had
the cosmopolitan outlook. But there wasn't an ounce of poetry in him,
and his affectations, of cynicism, etcetera, become irritating. Moreover, he wasn't a novelist, and you are. *South Wind* is perennially
amusing, but really it is a kind of opéra bouffe agreeably truffled with
all the scandal of Capri of the belle époque. His other novels are fail-
ures, whatever the toadies may claim. His travel books are A-1, about
the best we have of that kind, but you are far more than a travel-book
writer. So, as Norman would have said, sucks to him!

The don was interesting to me, as showing the resistance to genius
of the well dug-in academic mind. They all ride to literary hounds, but
we can't give a rouser when they see a first-class run. As to poor old
Wyndham—he was greatly gifted, but was never able to concentrate
his powers, and he has rather silly ideas picked up from the avant-garde
in Paris. You are perfectly right about Conrad. Lewis never wrote anything so sustained as *Typhoon* or so moving as 'Youth' or so disturbing
as those tropical pieces. What trips me up a little is that Conrad writes
English as the Italian humanists wrote Ciceronian Latin—perfectly but
artificially. [. . .]

If you get an offer from Hollywood or London for film rights ponder well before accepting. There are many snags.

I couldn't get worked up to righteous indignation over Pasternak.
It seems to me nearly as much a misuse of political power and attempt
to stifle free speech that Winston Churchill, as P.M., signed two snivelling and quibbling letters on official Downing St paper, and sent his
emissary, a journalist hack called Liddell Hart, (a) to try to bully Collins out of publishing my TEL, and when that failed (b) to bully editors
and journalists into writing and publishing the stuff I showed you. The

only difference is that the Russians have no Pecksniff stuff about it. I may add that Collins only published the book to get back their advance. As soon as that was done, they closed down, and said there was 'no demand'. Landsborough has since sold nearly another 40,000, but one gets nothing on those reprints.

All good wishes to you both,
Richard

Sury-en-Vaux, Cher, 15 November 1958

Dear Larry,

[...] I am now going to see what can be done in Dublin (Ireland). Have you any particular foes there? I'm rather surprised the new novels haven't been put on the Index and banned in Australia, but doubtless that will come. [...]

Of course it would be far better for me to live in the Midi, not too far from you, for the climate here is simply one mot de Cambronne after another. Worse than England. But then Alister partly bought this house, at a fearful expense to himself, as a refuge for me—surely a most noble gesture of friendship? I certainly don't deserve it.

And, my dear boy, before I forget it again. Just turn to page 235 of *Mountolive,* and observe your boner. You make Balthazar check the other man's *Queen!* No wonder things go wrong in the world when the F.O. plays that sort of chess.

I am re-reading *Stiff Upper* for the third time, and still laughing out loud with delight at the top scores. Uncommon stupid of me to think that these new Antrobusses when I first read them were not as good as the earlier vintage. They are just as good, though I can never recapture the first fine careless rapture of meeting De Mandeville, travelling on the express with the Brothers Karamazov as firemen, and revelling in the *Balkan Herald.* I suggested to some fans of yours who called here that probably you originally had Wedding Balls Ring Out, and that Tom Eliot thought the dear archbishop would be shocked and made you put Bulls. But they wouldn't hear of it. Durrell can do no wrong.

I am a frightful cad. Yesterday I received from H.D. a script about

Ezra and herself—she knew him as a schoolgirl in Phila, Penna. Coming to the time when she and I were married and living in Kensington, she says: 'Wyndham Lewis called and used R.A.'s razor. This greatly annoyed Richard.' I should have refrained, but rather 'annoyed' by this sneer, I replied:

'I did not tell you, but the reason I was annoyed with Lewis was that I found out that at the time he was using my shaving things he had gonorrhoea. I thought that a dirty trick to play on a man with a young wife. I may add that in the 1930s he sent me an SOS and I found him in a shabby nursing home (I gave him 50 quid to pay his bill there) suffering in consequence from a bladder infection which made him pass blood instead of water. And you will remember that in his last years he was completely blind, a not infrequent consequence of that malady.'

I oughtn't to have sent that, but it riz my dander to be treated once more in the 'poor Richard' style, when I was damned right to be 'annoyed'. I am told dogs never bite bitches, which puts them one up on us.

Love to you both,
Richard

❦ *Mazet Michel, Engances, Chemin d'Uzès, Près Nîmes, Gard [ca. 20–22 November 1958]*

DEAR RICHARD.

A MOMENT MASON-FREE IN WHICH TO DOT YOU OFF A NOTE. I do hope the Xmas venture brings you our way, it would be such fun to talk. I don't know whether it is your championship or what but the current has started to run quite hard now and I shall end in sanctimonious affluence as yet. I am getting all sorts of commissions from U.S. papers offering sums the size of book advances; the *Sunday Times* is retaining me for next year and so on . . . Anyway I still have this blasted fourth book to tackle (and several walls to build): have you ever tried 'dry-stone walling'? It is without exception the most wonderful game, second to none. [. . .] I do loathe artists so with a few exceptions: much rather talk to boxers or fly fishermen really, wouldn't you? These dry-stone wallers of the garrigue now, they really broaden the mind I find! O, before I forget, about the chess howler you signalled; this was picked up in proof by Alan Pringle and I was asked to amend; before I could I got another letter saying that they had looked it up in the biggest Oxford and it was okay, queens were checkmateable. I know nothing about chess; it is like double entry book-keeping, I've never been able to understand it at all. There is good chance that our lavatory will be finished this week and I'm meditating an ode 'On a Lav in Lovely Languedoc'; then comes whitewashing—a huge chore. Twenty years of fly blown dust and filth; then the garage has to be turned out and made usable. And we are hovering on the edge of winter. Mighty cold days and gray; and I've been cutting olive wood like a maniac so that we have a stock in hand against rainy weather. But my wall is really beautiful—fifteen feet long and a metre high; I wonder if it will fall down before you get a chance to admire it?

Yours

larry

Alan Pringle of Faber and Faber, who died in 1977, was Durrell's editor until his retirement.

Sury-en-Vaux, Cher, 22 November 1958

My dear Larry,

If I can possibly manage it I shall run down to the Midi next month. I'd like to take Catha into Italy again if she can spare the time, for Mondadori tells me they are allowed to advance 100,000 lire to any of their foreign authors visiting Italy. Remember this, in case you and Claude want to kiss the Pope's nose, for we come under the insane regulations of the French—limit of 20,000 per person per year. [. . .]

My dear boy, I wish I could claim any credit for your success. But I have no more to do with it than one fan yelling 'Go it, England!' wins a rugger match at Twickenham. No, you've done it yourself, partly because you are a damned good writer, partly because you have hit the lit'ry public's taste, and partly because there simply is no one else in your class at the moment.

Alan Pringle has mistaken his reference. It is possible that the term 'checkmate' may have been applied metaphorically to a living Queen, but it cannot possibly be used for the Queen in the game of chess. Though the most powerful piece, the Queen can be taken, and if a chess-player was in a position to take the Queen the last thing in the world he would do would be to let the other player know. Checkmate is the anglicised form of shah mat—the King is dead. At chess when you have your opponent's King in a position so that at the next move you could take it, you say 'check' because *the King is the only piece on the board which can't be taken.* When no escape of the King is possible it is checkmate, and the game is over. The whole point of chess is that it is a silent battle, and a player would be crazy to give away a threat to any piece of his opponent, except in the case of the King when he is obliged to do so. You tell Mr Pringle from me to look again. I have been playing chess since I was ten, and I know that a checkable Queen is nonsense. You *can't* check the Queen.

Apart from the Balbus of my Latin gradus (and I don't know that he was a poet) the only other poet I know who built a wall is Robert Frost. When it fell down he wrote a poem which seems to attribute this misfortune to supernatural influences. It is really fantastic, that you should have been upset all this time by the building of a mere lavatory. The unions must have got things into a beautiful mess. I think the cold you have been having is just a snap, but there are snaps all through the winter, and if you are up on a hill you may be exposed. It is well to have a cache of tinned things in case of snow, but if your 15 minutes to the village is 15 minutes afoot, you scarcely need that. How about the wine problem? Have you got a place to store safe from heat or cold? They tell you to keep wine at 51 ° Fahrenheit, which is a damn sight easier said than done.

Love to you both,
Richard

ᛐ *Sury-en-Vaux, Cher, 23 November 1958*

My dear Larry,

Not two hours after I had posted my last letter to you there arrived here, to take a modest evening snack with me, a young friend of mine and his wife. He has a pretty good job with NATO, and sees the great world much as you used to do. On my advice he has bought your last three novels, and said they had arrived from London just before he left Paris. After a modest bit of Durrell-boosting on my part, I mentioned our bitter and discourteous wrangle about checking the Queen. My friend is much more of a chess-player than I am, and it seems that we are both right, but you are righter. 'Checking the Queen' is absolutely unknown to the rules of chess, and of course it was on that fact that I was going. But, some time back—he doesn't know how long—it became the custom in chess tourneys for a 'courtesy warning' to be given to an opponent whose Queen is in danger, and this has crystallised in English in the (really meaningless) phrase 'check to your Queen'. But you were writing a novel, not a treatise on chess! Your observation was clearly excellent as usual, and Balthazar's remark is fully justified. There is nothing for me to do but to apologise lavishly to all concerned, and to evaporate ceremonially. [. . .]

Love to you both,
Richard

Le Mazet Michel, Engances, Chemin d'Uzès, Nîmes, Gard, France [ca. 23–26 November 1958]

Dear Richard:

Nevertheless I think you have given a signal, or something: at any rate the good news is now steadily accumulating—the latest and best is a Book-of-the-Month choice in the States for *Mountolive* sometime this autumn . . . There is a buzzing in my ears, as it means I shall be able next spring to buy this place, pay off the last seven instalments of the car . . . secure Saph's school fees: and stop feeling hag-ridden for a while. Now if I am a wise little man I shall not drink this windfall away in the inimitable manner of dear Dylan but consolidate firmly and by pushing out a few more books try and exploit this valuable penetration into the middlebrow public! Congratulate me, please: and let me thank you at the same time for the generous shove up behind! It remains only . . . the hardest job; to put the bloody tail of the quartet firmly in its mouth. *Justine* has just got away to a serious rave press in German. *Die Zeit* gives the book a whole page headed 'A sure contestant for the Nobel'! It is all a little overwhelming; and my dear old Henry, whom I warned that he would loathe *Mountolive* (his bête noire is the 'naturalistic treatment' of anything) has weighed in with a four-page rave letter which no bobby soxer could have bettered. Altogether having achieved such distinguished suffrage among the writers I admire it feels almost super . . . how is it spelt? . . . erogatory? to have a bundle of greenbacks added to it all . . . Yes, do come south, and don't cross us off your visiting list. I shall cut down a whole olive tree for us to burn and lay in some Tavel. Such a barbarian as yet about wine; but at the end of our road is a newly arrived Marseilles cook of epic style . . . fish expert. He is so pleased by my unfeigned reverence for his art that I know we can count on him for something suitable to the meeting. I suppose I am a bit mad about visitors . . . The psychology of an escaped press officer! The truth is I am getting odious fan mail of a rave sort from females in the Waldorf-Astoria; I answer all letters as from Paris or London now. Provence is too near, you know; all those fat port-swilling bores drivel down here every year. Why should we be a comfy port of call? You see, for years now, I have not only met journalists at the airport but in the case of ones who might prove hostile to our policy line have actually housed them so that I could poison their minds more easily. In Cyprus I had six hundred pressmen in six months; the house was a river of gin; no time to myself. But I inspired several million miles of prose in praise of a highly questionable policy . . . Every day that passes without an alarm at the front gate is balm! But we have been lucky really, simply by refusing to reveal our address. Another year as good and I shall get *Clea* off my chest. What a relief. I'm so sick of them all . . . tempted to drown the lot!

Now I am tied up firm in the four chief European languages for the quartet; it's been a hard bit of sledging but well worth it. You won't I suppose know how it feels having always been your man, living by your own mind's work.

Anyway, here goes, I'm opening a small bottle of Côtes du Rhône (Gigondas) 1958. A health to you.

Yours
Larry d.

Sury, 26 November 1958

My dear Larry,

On receipt of your last letter I stood to attention and recited 'Om-kroop-der-soup' five hundred times, and then made the rafters ring with hearty British cheers.

Book-of-the-Month! Attaboy! That's the stuff to give the troops. Well played, sir. To carry your bat for a century not out for England is no mean achievement.

Yes, now don't be a bloody fool, and muck it up by boozing or any other nonsense. You have a damned fine girl in Claude, and all you have to do now is to lie low (as you plan) and get rid of *Clea*. But do be careful, and take expert advice before consenting to filming. I pulled an awful boner by allowing *All Men Are Enemies* to be done. I got 15,000 dollars, but the bastards made such a mess of it, I never got another sale. With income tax what it is, a big film sale doesn't benefit the author—it goes to the bloody income tax. Try to arrange that your Bk-of-the-Mnth money is straddled over two years. The US Inland Revenue will fight you over that, but it can be done.

Word has again gone forth to Mrs B. that your address is sacred. I regret my indiscretion—une fuite, quoi? But I don't think it will harm you. Of course those Waldorf-Astoria females hope you'll treat them as Narouz treated the bats. Don't you bother. Claude will get rid of them. Pah. What a pack of shits.

Have you heard that the town of Meran gave Ezra Pound the 'freedom' of the city? The Mayor, who had never heard of him, had to introduce him to a pack of citizens who had never heard of him, and did so in these immortal words:

'This great poet believes that all men and all races are equal, and has for fifty years expounded his simple creed in simple words that all can understand.'

You must admit god or chance sometimes does things handsomely.

By chance Alec Randall was in Rome for the Conclave and Coronation, which brings me an almost perfect Polk-Mowbray letter. What next? [. . .]

Try Châteauneuf-du-Pape, Père Anselme, 1947.

Love to you both,
Richard

In 'La Valise', one of the Antrobus stories, the Netherlands ambassadress recites 'Oom kroop der poop', Durrell's parody of Dutch poetry.

In *Mountolive* Narouz attacks flying bats with a rhinoceros-hide whip.

Polk-Mowbray is the fictitious British ambassador who appears in the Antrobus stories.

Le Mazet Michel, Engances, Chemin d'Uzès, Près Nîmes, Gard [15 December 1958]

Dear Richard: A swift line to thank you for the unexpected and welcome gift; I thought at first it must be an EOKA bomb and so made Claude open it! I am sorry that we won't see you yet awhile, but the stocks of dead olive will hold out until you come. Meanwhile, too, we are working wonders with this little mas and I shouldn't be surprised if you found it an ideal hideout for a couple of boozy writers. But of course the prospect of actually being able to buy it next year has made us look at it with entirely new eyes; I've got quite a little building project in my head. There is a mountain of dry freestone to play with and I can do the work myself; I have an awfully good mason friend who comes and brickles whenever I need something really professional done for the pleasure of borrowing Chauvet's books which he wraps up and carries away reverently. They are extraordinary people—*all* of them anxious to paint and write, the artisans. The plumber's wife is a lauréat of the Beaux Arts and the painter who is rather languid does appalling but very professional water colours. But one senses quite clearly here that one is in the Panurge country . . . they talk endlessly of belly wearying meals with emphasis on quantity always—a thousand oysters, a million pigs of garlic, a fifteenth helping; and they are always down with ferocious liver crises! But delightful honest chaps (deeply suspicious of each other's honesty!) Yes, this was a good ploy indeed. I gather Antrobus is going well in London. I am hovering about like a wet hen before beginning *Clea*. Ouf! I'm tired by the thought. I'd so much rather be a plumber or paint in oils! Another ten days and we'll be quite straight and then the merry rattle of typewriters! No, I haven't had any bites from the movies; I nearly sold *Labyrinth* once but after two attempts at 'treatment' they gave up.

every good thing
larry

p.s. I've never heard a word about the review of kershaw I did for australia, neither acknowledgmts nor cheque nor nowt; perhaps it's a
quarterly? I've also lost the chap's address. larry

Maurice Chauvet, long a resident of Montpellier, was a barrister, critic,
novelist, and folklorist.

ℐ *Mazet Michel, Engances, Nîmes, Gard [10 January 1959]*

DEAR RICHARD: Just a swiftie to hope you got safe home; it froze
the night you left and I had black visions of you slithering all over the
frosty roads. It was so wonderful to see you, if only briefly; and coura-
gio giving to hear you so enthusiastic about the bloody old quartet; it
rather got me over my panic about *Clea* perhaps not being up to
scratch, or showing tired developing marks round the edges. This sudden load of spontaneous cheering has rather unhinged me, no less than
the promise of money and four walls. We calculate that the whole of
this property will cost us about £1200; not bad really for a square mile
of land, two springs and the little mazet which is a bit crushed for the
children but okay for us two. Is it? I am planning to pay my baby
daughter's school five years in advance which will lift one great preoc-
cupation off my mind. Meanwhile this barber's shop mag *Holiday*
offers me a three-piece-a-year engagement at 1000 dollars a piece—an
income pardy, and the *Sunday Times* is contracting for more Antrobus.
Altogether it is a bit shy-making—to happen so soon I mean when two
years ago we were practically desperate for dough! I must soon get
down to it; but I must make sure I don't fall off the ladder. The Temples stayed till midnight nearly. We ate scraps and talked shop. They
really are good people and his devotion to you, touched in the French
manner with deep respect for cher maître is a real pleasure to see. He
was only sad about you not working but I was able to console him by
reminding him of your preface to the *Collected Poems*, mentioning
Oscar who talked of an artist 'revolving in a cycle of master pieces';
saying it was a boutade and that everyone has periods of sterility which
are hard to endure with patience. This much consoled him; perhaps it

will console you if you look it up. It much consoled me at a time when I hadn't even a respectable imagist imitation to my credit!

best to you as ever

larry

Pardy: French interjection, *pardi.*

⚓ *Mazet Michel, Engances, Chemin d'Uzès, Nîmes, Gard [19 January 1959]*

Dear Richard: Thanks for the dope. I didn't explain child-circumstances clearly, but all is okay on this front. My ex and I work in unison; child adores school. Spends four months a year in France with me; will later, having got english, come to a french lycée for a couple of years. My ex is next the school and was once in charge of the junior section, which is full of friends' children. Child regards it as a holiday so far! It is Bedales, by the way, co-ed without being crank. I'm working like hell, but ouch it goes stickily; I wish I hadn't scored an outer on vol 3. Wiser perhaps to drop project and not risk an lbw on 4th? Craven fellow! The Xmas papers have just come in, Books Of The Year, and we have been having some malicious fun doing spoof titles of our friends.

Poxus, or the Last Stage, by Henry Miller.

Bunyan's Sex Life by T. S. Eliot.

The Coachman Always Knocks Twice by Lady Diana Duff Cooper.

Cathedrals I Have Personally Dusted by John Betjeman.

Justine at Roedean by L. D. (this is Claude)

Asterisks and Figleaves, a selection from Catullus with a short yet long-seeming preface by H. Nicolson.

We thought for hours about how to nail you and at last after numerous tries . . .

Shakespear's Sonnets Elucidated (rather grimly) by R. A.

The only one who eluded us completely was Gerry; we still can't nail the little bastard down; but Claude says given time she'll do it. She still hasn't quite forgiven me for 'The Schoolgirl's Wonder Book of Booze and Sex'.

> every good wish
> larry

'Lbw' stands for the cricket term 'leg before wicket'. The batsman is retired when a ball hits his leg which, in the umpire's opinion, would otherwise have hit the wicket.

♫ *Mazet Michel, Etc [23 January 1959]*

DEAR RICHARD

JUST HAD AN AWED LETTER FROM JEAN FANCHETTE SAYING THAT ALDINGTON ('HIMSELF') HAD AGREED TO DO A SMALL TRIBUTE TO THE OLD QUARTET. It was very moving for me and I remembered all those solitary pipe smoking tramps across the moors when I was 18 with *Death of a Hero* in me pocket and a grim determination to write a printable sonnet graven all over my mug. If then I had been stopped and told 'One day this chap Aldington will ("Himself") write a small tribute to something you haven't even finished . . . ' I must say I should have disbelieved it. I don't know who your literary influences were and how you thought of them but when I was young just names like Roy Campbell, Aldington, [D.H.] Lawrence were like clouds in the sky. Like I suppose the Olympians, Zeus Hera and Co. I never somehow *visualised* an actual meeting with these great nobs of eng. lit. much less a day when tributes would flow from their pens . . . This is just to thank you; but apart from this I am seriously hoping that *Two Cities* comes off and that Jean succeeds in making it what he wants. I also privately think that you, as a sort of doyen of Anglo-French literary relations, may find in it a vehicle for much that as yet is unwritten; and a point of contact with these sharp younglings on whom I suppose the next wave depends as it goes over the top . . . I wish to God you weren't cooped up in Cher, however beautiful, but somewhere within striking distance of Paris. Incidentally when you go next, will you look Jean up? He's only a kid but a v. good one; when I send my 18-year-old daughter to Paris Jean and Martine look after her, tuck her into ballet schools and pensions. I believe that Jean could find Cath something to do pronto there as he knows everyone. The odd thing is that he's a brilliant doctor as well. How I wish I were! Damn prose.

best wishes
Larry

Fanchette, a young poet, doctor, and psychiatrist from Mauritius, launched his magazine, *Two Cities: La Revue Bilingue de Paris*, with an 'Hommage à Lawrence Durrell' consisting of five essays and an interview with Durrell.

✿ *Sury-en-Vaux, Cher, 26 January 1959*

Dear Larry,

Herewith carbon of my hasty burp for Fanchette. I have told him that you are authorised to make any cuts or changes you think fit, but you'll have to write him *at once* as time is short. If I had had more time I might have been less inadequate.

Kershaw and spouse will be coming down on Weds for a week, which will be very pleasant. I must try not to fall asleep like Scobie. Bugger those sailors. They should have let the old cow off.

My solicitor brother has sent me an extraordinary report of the Law Society on buggery and so forth. I find it very funny. Obviously, old man, they all have Tendencies. I'll send along later for you and Claude to laugh over.

Did you get a copy of the *European* with my Roy piece in English—a bit better than old Temple's French. I can't understand why the *European* people printed that fantastic lie about my writing it in French and then translating etc. I wonder if Claude agrees with a doting dad that Catha's French reads better than old Temple's? Did *you* know that curry-combing a horse in French is bouchonner un cheval? Damned if I did.

Forgive such a feeble piece on you—try to do better next time. I was awake for HOURS last night groaning to think what a balls I've made of it.

Love to both,
Richard

Aldington's article on Campbell first appeared in *Hommage à Roy Campbell* in Temple's translation.

🪧 *Mazet Michel, Engances près Nîmes, Gard, France [26 January–1 February 1959]*

Dear Richard: I am more delighted and moved by your little essay than I can rightly express. I never expected anything *half* as favourable or as long. I was struck dumb. And it's particularly heart-warming for it to have come from a writer of your standing. Many many thanks! Christ! I must really live up to this . . . And not fall down on *Clea*. The criticisms were so right, too; I was amazed not to be had up for melodrama by the theatre guild. But I've been deliberately trying to Elizabethanize, keep near *Maria Martin*, restore freedom of action to the novel which has been lacking a bit I think! We must see if the bloody thing comes off; I know the palette is over charged and the paint runs off on the floor here and there . . . About the continuum idea yes, perhaps you're right; but I wanted to chivvy english writing out of the time-bog and restore a little blood circulation to it. Ambitious fellow. Also, I wonder if you realise that with Freud having *dépouillé* what Lawrence calls 'the old stable ego' and with Einstein having evaporated 'matter' eastern and western metaphysics have come to a confluence? Lawrence says: 'Don't look in my novels for the old stable ego' and talks about hunting 'allotropic states'. His divine intuition told him that the old formal psyche with which we had to deal was getting dispersed. But I don't think (hating science so) he quite knew who was doing it! But now the space-time scientist is as much of a mystic as Duns Scotus! What I hoped to achieve by this piece of cookery was to dig us out of the time-bog and also to indicate the prodigious variety of facets which make up one human identity who wears a costume—name, race, job, sexual make-up. Seen in continuum you do (Christ, do you?) see people in sort of allotropic states, all divine, all perverse, all good-bad. Anyway when next we meet I'd like to talk more about all this; first I must see whether the bloody thing comes off as a continuum or not. Mathematicians have the right to laugh of course, for it's only a relativity-poem. It is to space-time what in algebra would be a naming of objects. I mean just an *a* plus *b* satisfies the mathematicians. They don't ask if *a* is Mountolive or Justine or just sacks of potatoes. The principle satisfies them. I am simply 'personalising' as *Holiday* mag calls it, journalising! But, as Henry says: 'How wonderful when you expect a high enema from a critic and he turns around and says you're a lulu.'

The poem! How the devil did you unearth it? It's marvellous and I've been reading it to the garrigue in what I imagine must be Scobie's voice (Scobie by the way is Tiresias!) He embodies in his humble way the spiel in the Oxyrhincus bits which the Bible doesn't print about the male-female 'when the two shall be one' (Apollonius of Tyana also says it!). And really he has absolutely no connection with sodomy as such, but symbolises (what high talk all this is!) the unio mystica. Only 'a novel is written to be read' as Aldington said somewhere, and one's symbols have to be somewhat crudely objectivised to keep the pot boiling.

Ouf! I've given you a headache, I can feel it. Anyway, one gets nowhere by being too conscious; finally the books decide for themselves whether they get written this way or that. One can only put in self-discipline and a bit of work (ouch! I've only pushed *Clea* to page 40) like Bertie Wooster pushing that pea up Piccadilly for a bet. But (excuse) it is I think not more or less anachronistic to choose Ulysses (Homer) for your form-model if you are Joyce or Kazantzakis than to choose Heinz 57 varieties with a book on each as Balzac did; I agree it ain't important unless there is such thing as a continuum which is more than an equation—a reality of sorts. (Lewis was bald headed after it in *Time and Western Man*. Stated it. But couldn't write it.) Perhaps he painted it? [. . .]

I don't think that you realise Richard that your general prestige and reputation completely outweigh any brouhaha about one or other book; I wish one could get you to Paris installed somewhere within bowshot of your café where your admirers could prove it to you every Monday. Claude is always saying you are too cut off, and it ain't fair, and I think she's right. That is why I'm hoping that some group of younglings like Fanchette's crowd get a chance to pester you a bit and convince you that the place you occupy is an important one and can't just be vacated like that!

By the way, we have been talking and thinking a deal about Catha and your general problems; I must be rather stupid, I didn't realise she hadn't got dual nationality. I've asked Claude (who has five nationalities and is a wizard office and business type) to write you direct about our lucubrations on the subject. I have an idea that she is right. Anyway SHE does all my income tax forms, she must have *something!*

A thousand thanks, Richard; I'm all swollen up with pride like a gumboil. It will take quite a lot of stone-walling to wear the exultation down!

I didn't see the piece on Roy, but had an indignant card from Temple about the Third Programme spiel because it included old MacNeice whom every[one] said was an arch-enemy; but Spencer told me that MacNeice (whom I've never met) as an Irishman was delighted by every new onslaught and liked Roy!

(the concrete paving is cracking a bit in parts but others are coming up a treat. my *mixtures* are a bit erratic—as in art so in life alas!)

every good thing!

Larry

Maria Martin, or The Murder in the Red Barn is a classic Victorian melodrama based on a notorious murder case of the time. In a letter to the editors Durrell has described the play as 'a barnstormer full of 'orrid and gruesome 'appenings. . . . The dialogue suggested the theatre of Dickens's time, pure Victorian melo.'

§ *Sury-en-Vaux, Cher, 1 February [1959]*

Dear Larry,

You vastly over-estimate my modest tribute, which I fear will do you little good, though I wish it could do a great deal. My prejudices have mostly been against Marx, Freud and Einstein—all rhinos, man—though I have nothing solid to back them. I know nothing about political economy, but make it a rule only to take seriously those economists who make their own fortunes. A man who pretends he can make nations rich and himself lives in a little back room in Bloomsbury must be a fraud or he would make himself comfortable first. Keynes at any rate cornered the paper market in 1919 and cleared 100,000 pounds.

I know nothing about psychiatry, but I am told by medics that Freud's percentage of 'cures' of neurasthenics etc is just about the same as those of persons left to chance. Modern medicine more and more recognises mental disorders as symptoms of physical disorders, and treats them accordingly, with the result that for the first time in centuries the bug-houses are beginning to empty.

Einstein no doubt is a far more serious proposition, though again I am told that he—because he was a rhino—was given the exclusive merit (which he decently didn't claim) for work which was done by many people in many lands. I know nothing about his bloody relativity. In the 1930s when I visited Cambridge pretty often I once or twice asked mathematical physicist dons if they would tell me about it. They always began briskly: 'Well, starting with the Calculus, you know . . .' I don't know the calculus! So that was that. Trying to get the dope on the 4 dimensions, I asked humbly: What is time? Ans: The finger-post pointing to entropy. So I gave up, and went empty away.

Anyway, don't you worry, man, those rhinos make no difference at all to the achievement of your books. Talking of which—Have I missed or mis-read a relevant passage, or have you not yet explained why Nessim married Justine? Of course, it is very good psychology on your part to make her a successful society lady and hostess and so forth, coming almost off the streets. A woman of that kind would have that skill. Surely Nessim didn't care enough about those Palestine Jews and their plot to marry her for that? Obtuseness on my part somewhere.

I was very pleased to drop on the full version of Scobie's poem—a very spirited ballad. I am suspicious about the alleged authorship of William Drennan, son of William Drennan, since another collection of Irish poetry gives different initials to W. Drennan's poet son. Of course, he may have had two. The original W. Drennan has much to answer for. I am unhappy to say that he invented the phrase 'The Emerald Isle'.

I incline to think we tributeers are doing you a disservice by intruding our unnecessary opinions on you just when you need nothing but luxe, calme et volupté, to trot on with *Clea* in your own time and in your own way. You must long ago have noticed that he who can write books does, and he who cannot writes articles about other people who can.

Apropos which—have you had the money from *Australian Letters*? Geoff Dutton vows it was sent off to you at Sommières early in Jan. If you have NOT had it, please tell me, and I will sound a blast on Roland's horn, if not on Gabriel's trumpet.

Seem to be differences of opinion about MacNeice. (I met him once, long ago, in New York, and didn't at all like him.) By the same post as your letter came one from a Roy devotee in London saying: 'MacNeice, I think, is the worst poet of the gang, and you should hear Neame (a genuine scholar) on the subject of MacNeice's "scholarship".'

By the way, a friend of mine who has great possessions writes confidentially of being 'very uneasy about the financial situation', hints of possible re-imposition of 'restrictions' in France, and advises me to go straight to Catha in case of 'any upheaval'. This may be merely rich-man-itis, but I thought I'd pass on the warning, which of course treat as coming from M.I. 5.

My dear boy, why wish me the purgatory of Paris, cafés and tout ce qui s'ensuit? I am miserable in the noise and stink of big towns, particularly in Paris which only 40 years ago was really lovely. I never go to cafés if I can help it. And should not know what to say to French or cosmopolite intellectuals. This sounds beastly ungrateful, but as soon as Catha gets herself settled, I don't care if all my books are obliterated. But I shall hearken most gratefully and closely to anything Claude and you can tell me about getting Catha launched. So please go ahead.

Yesterday received following telegram:

'Let us know address to remit royalties for our publication of your novel—I Metelkin Director Foreign Language Publishing House Moscow.'

Bastards. Cost me nearly 2000 to reply. I suppose this is the edition of the *Hero* in English, with which they propose to torture deviationist students of English who are too bad to send to Siberia. Seriously, the colloquialisms and soldier talk in that book are unfair to any students. Typical that I have no contract, wasn't asked if I wanted the book done, simply told it was being done, and haven't the faintest idea what they will pay. I'll let you know what happens. Almost by same post Los Yanquis offer *25 dollars* for an article on *T.E.* Lawrence in the new edition of *Collier's Encyclopedia.* Bloody insult, and if I do it they won't publish it. The Japs, by the way, are translating the chapter on 'TEL as Bugger', which pleases me, though of course the yanks won't let them transfer a cent to a British author. Perfect yentlemen, of course.

If you've done 40 pages of *Clea,* the rest follows almost inevitably. There is only one rule: Know what you want to say, and say it. I must say I look forward to that book.

All the titles of good fellowship come to you both!
Richard

M.I. 5: Military Intelligence.

ℒ *Mazet Michel, Engances, Nîmes, Etc [after 1 February 1959]*

Dear Richard: many thanks for the good letter; you are wrong about the 'trib', it's wonderful and I glow all over like the man in the Sloan's ads! Yes, I do agree with you, really do about the horsehair couch brigade, and my own favourite doctor is no Jew but Father Groddeck, who invented the psychosomatic approach, is full of laughter, and says in the first para that medicine is bunk! I expect you've come across *The Book of the It* at some time; I adore it. The only point which interested me in Father Freud was the fact of the psyche being dethroned in the old Nietzsche sense, and Plato coming back; in the Einstein thing the quirk is the discovery (only too apparent in the atom bomb!) that matter is a form of unconverted energy. I think these two ideas were seminal ones for our age; but you know, I regard ideas as fun and not *facts.* Everything we believe today will be disproved sooner or later. But they do turn up the ground and give the roots oxygen. And it is very funny after such a long murky detour through the Christian Javeh thing (which has soaked the place in blood and puritan repression) to find science coming out almost into the Eleusinian mysteries! Einstein's view of matter is only separated from Buddha's by a hair; only as a rationalised intuition it also carries the destructive QED in an actual bomb which converts matter into energy and blows up the whole bloody issue. I suppose because it has no metaphysic and ethic really! But I can hear the laughter of Sri Ramakrishna from where I'm sitting. As for the old Zen dogs in Kyoto they must be splitting their sides at our dilemma! And all this ant labour to prove something they said in 2500 b.c.

anyway, as I say, it is damn right to question chaps knowledgeably taking things like space-time to try and manufacture a smaller variety of bomb! I'm afraid my very scanty knowledge of psychics I get from JNW Sullivan whose little *Limitations of Science* was a great help. Barzun on 'Number' is fun too. But I hate maths really. Blast them. And probably I shall end up with something like *The Purple Island* by the lamented Phineas Fletcher. Wonder if you've ever seen it—you must have. Such a feat of literary torsion.

but there again, the choice of a form seems a big hurdle these days; *why* should the majors like Joyce choose to rewrite something so remote in space and time (and fun) as Homer? It's a literary problem. They want to restore the epic sense I suppose; but is that the way to do it? It doesn't even work in the coarser range of production like a Cecil B De Mille. So I wanted to choose something unliterary and see what happened . . .

anyway, get on with it, and shut up talking about what you *want* to do! I had planned to deliver *Clea* on Feb 1st but she [is] only at page sixty dammit; but Scobie is coming up quite nice I think as a patron saint. More of this anon.

Jean, by the way, is in touch with Embassy and Council over *Two Cities,* and could doubtless be useful when you do go up to paris to whisk Cath around a bit and push into offices with her. I don't think you need to worry about her; the first break she gets and she'll be away.

every good thing (sorry—headache)
Larry

⦿ *Sury-en-Vaux, Cher, 7 February [1959]*

Dear Larry,

[. . .] With this I enclose a page out of a forgotten poem of mine [*Life Quest*] published in 1935, which I fear is a little disrespectful to the atomic physicists and their new religion. It was in 1933 that Eddington predicted the A bomb, and I issued a challenge (in some scientific periodical) to all scientists to take the oath of Hippocrates. There was a good deal of ha-ing and hum-ing and infinite humbug, and nothing done. So that a doctor can be prosecuted for murder if he puts a cancer patient out of his agony, and physicists are rewarded, adulated and honoured for contriving methods of mass murder, maiming and permanent damage to human chromosomes, and handing them over to the political thugs and charlatans and the militarist morons. Pah. Some civet, good apothecary.

I never tackled Joyce on that Odysseus issue, and anyway he was cagey as a waggonload of monkeys and would have evaded. The Homer idea was at best a scaffolding, and a good advertising point. The analogies are pretty arbitrary. I think myself he deliberately put it out as a red herring, to conceal his immense debt to the minor French naturalistes (such as Mirbeau and the early Huysmans) and the R.C. Church. The spirit of the book is unHomeric and unpoetic. Of course it contains an encyclopaedic knowledge of Dublin pubs and pub types. He was the typical mauvais prêtre—didn't marry the mother of his children until Giorgio was married and protested. 'Dear Mr Shame's Choice', as someone began a letter parodying *Winnegans Fake*. I believe one of the objects of *Ulysses* was to produce a work which would kill the novel for keeps. Well, you've proved that didn't succeed.

Nearly every morning I re-read a bit of Durrell—but not on a lectern as Storrs boasted that he read his morning Dante! I went over again that section of Leila in her retirement, veiled and cobra'd. It is quite terrific, all the more for being done so quietly, and I see why it scared H.D. into fits!

Strange to bask in sunlight up here and to read of the Midi under snow and rains.

Hope *Clea* is racing along.

Love to you both,
Richard

Aldington is apparently referring to a letter signed by Vladimir Dixon which begins 'Dear Mister Germ's Choice' and contains the phrase 'dear mysterre Shame's Voice'. This letter was published in *Our Exagmination Round His Factification for Incamination of Work in Progress* (1929), a collection of writings about *Finnegans Wake*.

♫ *Le Mazet Michel, Engances, Nîmes, Gard [9 February 1959]*

Dear Richard: Just a swiftie; I didn't do anything about the Australian thing in order to give Sommières time; sometimes there are quite long holdups—once a letter took three weeks from Cyprus. But they *are* readdressing them, and last week I had two which had sauntered round by way of Sommières. So I'm not unduly anxious; but if by chance you are writing to your friend ask him approximate date despatch, and if it was a cheque or an international mandat and I can tool over and hunt in the postmaster's beard. They did, some time last month, post two letters in the now deserted Villa Louis, which were found by the electric light man and given to my landlord who kept them on his mantlepiece 'until we met again'. He is distinctly daft; completely by chance I went to Sommières and nearly ran down the man who jumped into the road waving his arms with a glad cry 'I have some letters for you in my bedroom'; one was an invitation to lunch from Kenneth Rexroth, about a month old! So don't blame your friends unduly; the trouble is most likely to lie this end and will sort out at the Midi tempo!

I [am] still buried in this blasted book; I can never feel the 'form' much before 40,000 and have the illusion that it will be too long; then from fifty up it shrinks like a pinafore and feels too short.

Justine is turning the corner to a 4th edition in Germany; it's thrilling to get press one can't read. I'm like a monkey with my German cuttings, turning them this way and that, sniffing them . . . It's no go; neither readable nor eatable. Miller and family are coming to You-Rope for a several month trip, landfalling Paris around the twentieth April! First meeting for twenty years.

> every good thing.
> Larry

❦ *Sury-en-Vaux, Cher, 25 February 1959*

Dear Larry,

[. . .] After much meditation I've decided that your four-dimensional novel is the cleverest literary racket I've struck for years. You make people so interested in your characters (ah poor Melissa!) in the first vol, that they simply have to go on and get the others, so you seduce the public into buying four vols instead of one. Were you ever in Armenia?

Good news indeed about the fourth impression of *Justine* in Germany. She's too good for them. I can never rally round this pro-German movement.

Apropos which our old friend the king of Poland wants to start printing again. I suppose it is rather reckless on my part, but I sent round the hat for tenners, and got enough for him to take delivery of a small hand-press at once. I shall have to collect the balance—it isn't much—later on . . . you were a wicked lad to say he keeps a crown in a cigar-box. Why I myself keep five silver dollars in a drawer here, just to show how democratic I am. All I hope is that H.M. won't discover (and print) that De Gaulle is a JEW or some such undiplomatic move. I prize eccentrics more than you do, even if a trifle self-conscious. Think of the Welfare State, double it, take all the silly bastards out of it, and what remains? There is a nice eccentric in Australia—P.R. Stephensen, who printed that book of DHL's pictures, the only remaining record of many.

I have for some time been in correspondence with a Nottingham postman who has a great admiration for DHL and has collected a library of nearly 1000 books, so he says. He besought me to find him some 'relic' of DHL, and from Temple I got him a photostat of an unpublished DHL letter which Alister gave him. The postman is very pleased, adding negligently that he has offered to lend it to the exhibition of DHL relics to be shown in Nottingham in 1960, 30th anniversary of death. What next? But get this one. I told my unknown friend about the immense 3-vol *Composite Biography* of DHL just completed by the University of Wisconsin. The complete thing costs $22.50, at least eight guineas. Assuming that he couldn't afford such a sum, I suggested he might induce the Nottingham Public Library to buy it. To which he replies airily that he prefers to buy a copy as he never really enjoys a borrowed book. Can you afford eight guineas for a book? I can't. Why are we not postmen, leaving Claude and Catha to write the books?

The sunniest Feb I ever remember up here.

Love to both,
Richard

Aldington wrote the introduction to volume 3 of *D. H. Lawrence: A Composite Biography,* edited by Edward Nehls.

✦ *Mazet Michel, Engances, Nîmes, Gard, France [9 March 1959]*

Dear Richard: Sorry I've been such a lousy correspondent; overwhelmed by a flux of work and a lot of correspondence about dough with States, and also with Nîmes tax people. I haven't done too badly this year considering the tattered condition in which we arrived three years ago; now with a little care and caution I can look a year or two ahead. Why don't you buy a mazet instead of propping up eccentrics? I've booked the Millers a room or two in Sommières for the summer months; I hope they'll like it. But with two kids, American kids (Henry says they are 'full of piss and vinegar') one can't be sure. Your english text on Roy was indeed very much better than the translation, I found; indeed it was a real piece of Aldington whereas the French didn't quite catch your accent, your touch. I hope the Muse is gradually reviving and that in a year or so you'll suddenly feel that interior click (which always seems to desert as if it never meant to return) and reach for the typewriter. I've only pushed *Clea* to 130 so far, and am racing along to clear a draft at least before we get invaded by Goths and Vandals (our own three kids) or Picts and Scots (the Millers); once I have a draft I can easily chip it about; it's the sheer damn roughage that is such a bore to put together. I've always hated work, and pined for a rich widow to buy me tiepins. I hope you are going to like old Scobie's reincarnation in this volume; I think he's back in good form again the old roysterer. But such a lot of ends to tie up; and I'm low in second-hand metaphors! There was a chunk about the books in *London Mag*, patronising rather, but I suppose not too out of whack; 'Romantic' is a term of abuse these days—but who wouldn't rather read *Wuthering Heights* than Trollope? The *Mercure* for March had a smashing eulogy of *Mountolive* in it. Clear hard analysis and very high praise. Jean says there's a conspiracy to kill me off from swelled head by praising hell out of me; April brings a triple event, French and German *Balthazar* and yank *Mountolive*. Esperons.

every good thing.
Larry

✥ Engances, Nîmes, Gard, France [14 March 1959]

Dear Richard: Extraordinary that you say, almost word for word (ref [Osbert] Sitwell) what I once indiscreetly printed in an essay. I complained as a middle class boy who had to compete for his publisher's attention against 'country-house art'; unhappily the word Sitwelliana crept in somewhere and showed what I had in mind. Damn! The next thing was a long letter in trembling outraged handwriting (I had written him on behalf of Miller: his water colours were to be shown, and S was arranging matters). Well, a rather splendid letter, beginning: 'Sir, it is clear that you are no gentleman.' I made a spirited response naturally, but gay too, and indeed affectionate because for a chap of my generation all the first war group regardless of differences in size, seemed to me a great band of heroes and poets who had delighted and nourished me when I was a youth—Graves Aldington Sitwell Sassoon (Benn's Sixpenny poets it was at the time. I was broke!). But as Connolly said: 'You have made a dangerous enemy. The elephant never forgets!' Somewhere in the memoirs there is an attempt to score off me by quoting a very funny letter I received from Amanda McKittrick Ros and which I had to sell when broke. Sitwell must have bought it. Like a fool, for surely there could be no fear of libel, he calls me, I think, an Anglo-Italian poet! It's a very funny and cutting letter indeed, and of course he should have said it was me, in order to get back properly. I would have been delighted. Why should all the laughter be in the next room? But this squib was lost. Yes, it isn't bad in a podgy way, his rigamarole; but God it is depressing the airs and manners. Compare it to 18th century memoirs. No tang. No punch. Just feeble mannered anecdotes. The Beau Nash of Rickshaw Hall! Ouf, pressing on with this thing; Gosh I'd be proud to be compared to the [*Arabian*] *Nights* in any way at all. But I think for anglo-saxons I feel sort of Pierre Loti or filtered down Poe. We shall see! Vallette in the *Mercure* for March has a marvellous boost for the first three (more swelled head). No, I told you I think that far from being in any way against P[otocki de Montalk] I respected him. But in my disobliging way I don't want to be typed by an association with him; how shall I make it clear what I mean? If, for example, as a Royalist I were offered a title I should feel bound to refuse because it would hamper my opinions on the subject. People would discount my views, believing that I held them in order to creep up on a gong. So with him. One is hampered always by associations like that. I want to keep my sword arm free!

every good thing

Larry

Cyril Connolly became a regular reviewer for the *Sunday Times*. In 1940, together with Stephen Spender, he founded the magazine *Horizon*.

Amanda McKittrick Ros (1861–1939), the novelist, was ridiculed, often affectionately, for her euphuistic prose. She sometimes responded to criticism with angry broadsides.

Mazet Michel, Engances, Nîmes, Gard, France [9 April 1959]

Dear Richard; *Clea* is mocked up at around 110,000 and I've sent her back for a quick clean retype before tackling the revision. Anyway I'll have the little brute done by next month. I've an odd feeling she's good; but you know how these things betray! Claude says it's the best of the four. I certainly hope so; let's see. But the *work* is done. Ouf! *Two Cities* comes next week; I gather that several important tribs failed to get copyright-cleared in time notably Gerald Sykes of the *New York Times* who did a swinger! & So I shall be half homaged. But your noble piece and a caper by Henry lead the van I hear. What luck I have had with my elders and betters; and all so different. I mean I know you loathe TSE's work, and probably Henry's too. It's quite miraculous to find myself winning such diverse approvals. I swell from day to day with gluttonous pride. Yesterday the Smarts came to lunch and I found that Amy, who is a Copt, painter, had met you long ago and admired you. Smarty (Sir Walter!) told me, in talking of your book, that George Antonius told *him* that once when reading the *Seven Pillars* he had a sudden sense of familiarity, turned up the *Times* files and found an article unsigned called 'Desert Epic' which matched *Seven Pillars* episodes word for word almost, years before the thing was written. Apparently . . . As a matter of fact I've often thought of engaging my dispraisers in the press under a pseudonym and thus defending myself! I had intended to go to paris this month but must await this final revision. Only when the MS is in the post will I be able to breathe. Meanwhile I've done a stunning freestone wall on the lower patio side which I'm still enlarging. It's something you should take up. Also I've had a fan letter from a film star, David Niven, who longs to play Mountolive; well, why doesn't he sell the film rights I'd like to know? I would immediately buy a lot more stone and cement! Nothing else seems to matter much these days.

every good thing; Temple says you are déprimé these days; hope not.

Larry

As Oriental Counsellor of the Cairo Embassy, Sir Walter Smart had hired Durrell in 1941; they remained close friends until Sir Walter's death in 1963.

ℱ *Sury-en-Vaux, Cher, 11 April 1959*

Dear Larry,

This is most excellent news, and I am persuaded Claude is right and that *Clea* is the best of the four, and therefore must be pretty damned good. You can now knock off for a spit and a dror.

I should have thought Niven would have 'typed' Scobie rather than Mountolive. I suspect (perhaps wrongly) that he (Niven) would like you to make a stage version of *Mountolive* ('starring Mr David Niven'—he was a bogus colonel, wasn't he?) for the legit. I think you will have Hollywood after you for one or other of those novels—and may the Lord help you, for they will vulgarise them to tatters. Can't be helped. You could keep some control if you insisted on writing the screen play in collaboration with some H'wood hack—he would do the work and you take the salary, but you could avoid The Worst.

The 'Desert Epic' mentioned by Antonius might have been written for the *Times* by TEL himself—depends on the date. He did an article on his gloire as a guerrilla leader for the *Army Quarterly,* and this with a few frills was reprinted by Liddell Hart as the *Encyclopaedia Britannica* article on 'Guerrilla'. I need not remind you that all contributions to encyclos are supposed to be original—otherwise the thing would be a mere anthology. Shows the impudence of that crowd—but then TEL was related to Edens, Vansittarts, Wingates and even Churchill. Apropos, I have just done the article 'T.E. Lawrence' for the new edition of *Collier's Encyclopedia.* A neat execution.

I am cross with you for not subscribing to the aid of our old friend the king in his legitimate desire for a printing press. You could have subscribed through me, like the others, and neither the king nor anyone else would have known. When you say you don't want to encumber your sword arm, you mean you don't want to put your bloody hand in your pocket! I shall persuade him to call it The Mélissa Press.

I have been feeling absolutely lousy since the Easter visitors departed—perhaps exhaustion through too much talk and laughter, perhaps 'reaction', perhaps a normal recurrence of whatever it is that gets me down. We had wonderful weather through Feb–March, but now April is laughing her girlish laughter and shedding her shrewish tears.

Did Temple show you the little note on our Roy pamphlet in *Le Parisien?* This was certainly put in by Ancelot, a friend of Kershaw. Everything to piston—nothing to merit. Temple tells me the book has been completely ignored in England. What a pack of so-and-so's.

I heard from Fanchette, who spoke of 'legal hurdles', but regret very much to learn from you that some of the 'tribs' haven't been cleared. That is a pity, because in a show like that the more tributers there are the better. However, nobody much reads amateur periodicals, so it won't really affect your fame one way or the other.

I hope Claude continues to be happy in your mazet and that she is writing. Already you and she have made the place so pleasant and non-bourgeois, and I often think of it and of you both in it with great satisfaction.

Excuse dull letter, and don't get old, it isn't worth while.

> Affectionate greetings to both,
> Richard

David Niven has suggested to the editors that Aldington might have been referring to the movie *Separate Tables* (1958) in which Niven played the part of a 'bogus major'. He received an Oscar for this performance. Niven's real military record in World War II was a distinguished one. A Sandhurst graduate, he served in the Phantom Reconnaissance Regiment, a commando group; after Normandy he was promoted to lieutenant colonel and made chief of the Allied Forces Network.

✍ *Sury-en-Vaux, Cher, 14 May 1959*

My glorious Copperfield,

I didn't write sooner to congratulate on the Prix because I wasn't sure how long you and Claude were staying in Paris (France). A letter from Catha leads me to infer she has heard you have returned, so herewith at once all my gratters on the event, which is satisfactory from every point of view but especially as a smack in the kisser for those ill-affected persons who tried to oppose you.

Did you run across Baron Hisse la Juppe in Paris? I should like to hear more of this excellent and respectable character. [. . .]

Morning and evening I ask myself why I was so silly as to survive into an epoch so idiotic and barbarous. I suppose I must shelter behind Catha—a poor excuse.

> In health lousy, in temper testy,
> But ever your affectionate bedesman
> Richard

Balthazar in Roger Giroux's translation received the *Prix du Meilleur Livre Etranger* for 1959.

Baron Hisse la Juppe is a wine connoisseur in Durrell's story 'Stiff Upper Lip'.

✍ *Mazet Michel, Engances, Nîmes, Gard, France [19 May 1959]*

Dear Richard: With three féries to delay this it will seem a tardy answer to your note of congratulations for which many thanks indeed; I know you have been through all this laurel gathering yourself so you will grin at my naïveté in enjoying it all so much; but the best thing was meeting H.M. again after twenty years and finding him so damn spry and in every way unchanged. We did a couple of prodigious walks across Paris at the old breakneck speed and he had me puffing; he must be a couple of years older than you. At my publishers' he played seven consecutive games of ping-pong wiping the floor the whole way with us all. If this is the fruit of Boodhism, as he says, it's something we need. We also enjoyed being turned into a two-man act for radio and press purposes and talked the most prodigious nonsense to everyone, I espousing his opinions and he mine. Claude, who loathes his self-portraits in his books and expected to hate him, immediately fell in love with him as everyone does, he is such a delightful innocent. And now all the dirt of the books which shivered her timbers so much seems as natural as soiled napkins on a three-month-old. It was a relief too to find splendid, beautiful and well behaved children and his latest wife a magnificent very unamerican girl—a true european by instinct I should say. So with all these misgivings aside we hope to have a grand summer with all our blasted children. Last night a surprise visit from Cath and Temple delighted us and we hung on to them until nearly midnight. Cath in excellent form and planning a raid on Paris this year. All sorts of plans to get you down for the summer, but knowing you are not in prime fettle I wonder if they'll manage to persuade you. I do hope so. But ouf it was a relief to get back to my half completed downstairs wall. In another fortnight I should have the bottom patio done. It's ravishing with all the freestone. Fanchette says that *Two Cities* is selling steadily, twenty-five copies a day, and he has cleared the hurdle. I think he too rather felt it was editorially a bit of cock-up. But your essay in the middle firmed up the jelly no end. He had just won a poetry prize and was all ballooned up with joy and indeed barely coherent. As soon as I finalise *Clea* for the printer I'll tidy the carbon for you to see; hope you'll like it and not feel it's a muckheap. I wish I could do something about your health; why not visit england for a consultation?

love from us both
Larry D.

𝕭 *Sury-en-Vaux, Cher, 25 May 1959*

Dear Larry,

Yes I sent the piece on Roy to Temple, though he has not acknowledged. I thought the piece a little 'lit'ry London' but that can scarcely be avoided when the inhabitants of the Isle Dolorous have been forced by the Hellfare State into the condition of 'peons locked up in a large rainy island' as Wyndham Lewis so prophetically foresaw. Needless to say, the author is a pansy, but as Roy used to say 'you can't walk along Upper Regent St without treading on them, man'.[. . .]

The present position is that three books about me are in progress or planned, and the point of debate is to which to entrust the [T.E.] Lawrence papers. One of the books is an Italian PhD thesis—I've had them before, and nobody reads them; so that's out. Another is planned by a yankee prof, who has written about DHL, but he is so occupied with teaching and bread-and-butter books that I hesitate. The third is planned by Michael Harald, and the article in *Action* is a trial run. He is doing a much longer one for a quarterly in the autumn, and will then try to get a publisher—very doubtful, I should say. But I think I shall let him have the bogus Prince stuff, though of course there is the English 'law' of libel to consider. At the worst, I can send the papers to the King of Poland, and just issue them as documents via the Mélissa Press.

Harald has just got back from Italy, where he saw Ezra, who is evidently on the last lap. (I believe the vile Nazis released political prisoners at 65.) Anyway, while he was at Rapallo a letter arrived from Hemingway containing a cheque for 'a few thousand dollars'. This is one up to the old Hem, who did owe a lot to Ezra, like a good many others, but he seems to be the only one who has thought of re-paying. It is all the more meritorious since we know how writers are cheated by publishers and agents, and robbed by the fisc.

Did you and Claude go to the Saintes Maries? I believe some friends were to take Catherine.

Always,
Richard

[P.S.] Last month Field-Marshal Auchinleck sent me a message about the TEL: 'Tell him the book is a contribution to history which the officers of the Army have been hoping to see for many years.'

Pound was released from St Elizabeths Hospital for the insane in Washington, D.C., in 1958 at age seventy-two after the U.S. Government dropped treason charges against him.

✈ Nîmes [ca. 25–30 May 1959]

Dear Richard:
   Glad to have your line. I shall of course mention nothing to Girodias. I must have expressed myself badly; he's redoing my *Black Book*

in Paris. He has just done the highly controversial *Casement Diaries* among other things. He prints in english a certain amount of porn; but some good stuff too, like Henry and Beckett and Genet etc. His only merit is that he could do something which couldn't be done in UK and pays normal publisher's advances and royalties. I don't think a private press could print a requisite number of copies of a hypothetical R.A. vol to pay the author properly . . . However. The Germans are now going to play my play [*Sappho*] in the autumn! After fifteen years I am surprised. We plan after this holiday to take the children back to england and collect my elizabethan books. I've always wanted to do one on the elizabethan writer and it may be possible next year; I might steal a few months from money-grubbing to do a non-saleable. It occurred to me vaguely that you might like to spend three weeks in this house; but will Cath still be in the Midi in Sept? I gathered she had plans to attack the Paris end of things. I myself liked both the *Action* articles and think the chap [Michael Harald] could sell a book-form job; it's not profound but quite spirited and well shaped. I gather le mouvement (which I view with vieux jeu distrust) is going to lodge some MP's this year! Don't you honestly think the *Pisan Cantos* are punk? One should be irreverent about one's elders in the game but . . .

> every good thing
> Larry

Maurice Girodias, founder of the Olympia Press, is the son of Jack Kahane, whose Obelisk Press in the 1930's published works by Durrell, Miller, and Anaïs Nin.

ℐ Sury-en-Vaux, Cher, 28 May 1959

My dear Larry,

I am pleased by the Claude Roy article (two names which should not be hostile to you) not because of any La Rochefoucauld reason ('there is something in the misfortunes of our best friends which is not altogether disagreeable to us') but because it means you are really there, at the top.

This miserable petit commerçant trade of writing is infested with myriads of parasites (Parisites?), scabs etc. On the one hand the prosituted [sic] journalists, on the other the highbrows with incomes or bureaucratic jobs. Both parties long for SUCCESS. As Aldous pointed out, they will pardon it in another writer if he writes crap; and they will pardon a succès d'estime if they know the author is not being paid. But the unpardonable sin is what you have done—to make a little money by writing well. They'll never forgive you. [. . .]

I exhort you to cancel your press-cuttings sub, and to read nothing that is written about you for at least 3 years. Loaf and invite your soul. Even if you never write another book, you have done enough. Be warned by me, and don't go on writing after you have ceased to please. Your wall-building is a great strength to you, and comfort to me. The heart of Ireland is sound. Why do these bloody frogs call you English? You are as Irish as Scotch whisky. Now I am English. In Italy the guides and touts always mistake me for a boche.

This morning I was standing at the cottage door, 'snuffin' the morning air' when a red-headed woodpecker alighted on the fence not 20 feet from me. I never saw one so close for so long. Fascinating. What most struck me was what DHL called 'the horror of the wild', i.e. the intense and unremitting watch, left, right, front, back, for DANGER. I kept as still as an archangel waiting to blow the last trumpet. Very beautiful plumage.

[. . .] I don't want to write any more books, not because I couldn't but because I won't. What I hope to find is a publisher who will gradually take over the old ones—I have all pre-1939 copyrights, and am recovering post-1946. But this is probably a dream. And as one's books must die perhaps as well early as late.

Love to both,
Richard

✥ *Sury-en-Vaux, Cher, 30 May 1959*

My dear Larry,

Of course the *Pisan Cantos* are punk, and so are the other *Cantos*, and so is much of his poetry. Under separate cover I send you the last copy of a reprint of my Pound-Eliot lecture, given at Columbia Univ Extension Course in 1939. A small edition of the lecture (about 100 copies) was issued on a private press, and this little undergrad periodical reprinted it. But none of the pundits has ever mentioned it, not one periodical ever reviewed or quoted it. I say it is unanswered because it is unanswerable, and that it is not reprinted because the Pound-Eliot faction or coterie practically control ALL literary means of expression except the Communist and Fascist. Which is why I have to take up with Mosley's lot, not that I like them or approve, but nothing else will have me. Remember that except for the notices written by you and Roy, the *Mistral* was either boycotted or dissed on from a pizzy altitude.

Don't lose that copy of the P-E, but return it in July. Catha wants me to come down for her birthday, and the excellent Temple has most kindly offered his flat. Too rich for the likes of me, but I suppose we can camp in it.

You are most kind to suggest your mas for September, but that is the very time when Catha MUST start job-hunting, and I shall have to try to go along with her, much as I loathe Paris (France). But I must try to save her from the Hellfare state, and yet keep her British passport.

I don't think Mosley will get in after all. Instead of keeping his *Action* paper keyed to election level and election problems, he has carelessly allowed some of the old gangers to trot out their obsolete pro-Hitler anti-Roosevelt twaddle, which nobody but morons like Ezra now believes. Apropos, the yanks have just issued a Casebook of E.P. with quotes from those broadcasts, which the US govt could not publish pendente lite. Well, I don't give a stuff for these bloody international squabbles, but after reading those extracts I can only say that he was damned lucky not to be shot at sight. No govt can accept such war-time stuff from a national. But it shows he must have been crackers. I said in 1928 that he had paranoia. So had our old pal Wyndham Lewis. Apropos, I am told that Sir Mosley (who is apparently very witty) gives a wonderful imitation of himself meeting Lewis (the latter in disguise) in some secret spot, and Lewis saying reproachfully that he was running terrible risks of assassination by 'them' for meeting O.M. But as the Bart cogently remarks: 'What about *my* risk?'

Don't publish that Elizabethan book until you are super-firm as novelist and lots of dough. Highbrow stuff knocks down novel sales. It was one of my many blunders to think one could keep up novel sales and also work for literature.

Love to both
Richard

Pendente lite: i.e., while litigation was pending.

⑰ Sury-en-Vaux, Cher, 29 July 1959

My dear Larry,

I sent card as directed. Infinitely grateful to you. The damn thing isn't worth a tenth that sum. I was hurried by that ridiculous Mauritian, and anyway I can't write any more. But hold! My miserable ex-nonconformist conscience whispers me that you are probably paying this out of your own pocket, and inventing an Irish story to cover it up. I mustn't sponge on you—so recently have you escaped the indigence of artists. I can't cash the cheque until I have your assurance as English (not Irish) gent that the bloody publisher is paying. But in any case endless thanks for the thought and deed.

Feel worse for my four weeks MD's treatment than when I left here, BUT he *has* stopped the constant cramps which afflicted me. I must persevere and hope the pregnancy and beri-beri will run their usual course.

I was much impressed by that show of local characters in action which Claude gave us; and so, I discovered, was Temple. We think she might be able to work it up into a profession. But it might be unwise to suggest. She might become as famous and rich as Mistinguette, and never again speak to outsiders like us.

I liked Miller very much, and having read his *Big Sur* profess myself a humble disciple. He is right about most things. What a frightful shit was Moricand.

Must stop—feel *ghastly.*

Love to you both
Richard

The card Aldington sent confirmed the sale of first French serial rights to his 'A Note on Lawrence Durrell', originally published in *Two Cities,* by Curtis Brown for £40.

'Mistinguette' was the stage name of comedienne Jeanne-Marie Bour-geois, who often appeared with Maurice Chevalier and was known for her stage personality and beautiful legs.

Conrad Moricand was a French astrologer who visited Henry Miller at Big Sur; the disastrous consequences are detailed in Miller's *A Devil in Paradise* (1956).

ʄ *[Engances, after 29 July 1959]*

Dear Richard

A swiftie to assure you that my golden ploy was a ploy. Have no fear about it. I have so savagely belaboured my english publisher about American promotion methods that they are really outpulling fingers and are going to spread themselves in unheard of ways over *Clea*, for example a whole page in the *Times Lit* and other unheard of practices! It is lucky I've spent some time in the fleet street aura and can help on ideas of the shoddier sort. I did so enjoy our evening; and Henry was delighted with you. Had the same impression as me, of someone with plenty more books stacked inside! And what a good picture Temple took—has he sent you one? He says that *Midi Libre* will print it. Dear Richard, fight it out; it is only round twelve—often the most gruelling of the match. I saw Cath briefly at the Saintes astride her new bike, very lovingly revving her motor (a little too much). We were attacked by lightning which blew the pump wiring to blazes. And the lack of water has blocked the lavatory, so I've been all day trying to clear it with wires and sticks. Somehow I always seem to find myself in an Augean position. I think you'd find Henry's *Black Spring* a great book if it happens across you; but don't try *Sexus*. It keeps one swallowing! But he is a natural. His approach to obscenity is perfectly presbyterean (?) Total catharsis! Girodias comes on Tuesday. I'll try and get him to make you a black offer for something . . . what? I don't know. A Catullus complete (it never has been)? We shall see. Rowohlt is here and I've been talking about his pocket book series in German hoping to unload a couple of your novels. But doubtless they have been done ages ago and are still rolling. I'm reading a vol (yours) of the three-decker Lawrence which Temple lent me for a few days. Good job, no? And everything Lawrence touches, even a postcard, curls up at the edges with fire and liveliness. What a pity the methodist thing drove him to prophecy; and his thinking box is often in a bloody muddle. But he's the darling of eng lit despite every reservation. Currents run through him. And of course it is precisely being faithful to the current that makes him a genius not a journeyman. He follows the ignis fatuus just as Henry does—often into a bog. *How* he would have profited from understanding Freud! Incidentally if you go on being ill I'll send you Groddeck's *Book of the It* and see if it doesn't help.

Ah, here comes the plumber. More soon.

every good thing
Larry

Ernst and Heinz Ledig Rowohlt worked as a father-and-son team running the Rowohlt Verlag at Reinbek bei Hamburg. Until Ernst's death on 3 December 1960 it is often impossible to discern whether 'Rowohlt' refers to father, son, or press.

Durrell incorrectly attributes a Methodist background to D. H. Lawrence who, in his essay 'Hymns in a Man's Life', says he is glad that he was brought up not as a Methodist but as a Congregationalist.

✍ Sury-en-Vaux, Cher, 26 August 1959

Dear Larry,

Might it not be a good idea for you and Claude to go to Hunland for the production of your play? You can have the gurnalists write you up before the production, and leave hurriedly for the Riviera if it flops.

You are most generous in trying to help me. Apropos, have you seen Vansittart's memoirs? I needn't tell you who he was. Speaking of TEL's claim, made in letters and in print that he had been 'offered Egypt by Churchill' and Hankey's job at the Privy Council, V. says:

'There is no truth in Lawrence's intimation that the job' (i.e. H. Commissioner of Egypt) 'was offered to him. Even less substance is in his claim to have had the chance in 1922. The appointment lay with Curzon. If Winston had ever foolishly proposed Lawrence I should have heard, for Curzon would have laughed him out of court, and the

laughter would not have been kind. Still more untruthful is the suggestion that anyone ever thought seriously of pushing out Maurice Hankey to let in Lawrence as Secretary of the Cabinet. Lawrence would
have been fantastic in any high officialdom . . .'

Now that is what I said and proved, though expressed by V. more
contemptuously. Yet Liddell Hart went to Collins behind my back and
swore to them that Lloyd George had told him Lawrence had been offered Egypt. When they asked him to prove it, he went to Churchill.
Now in answer to the direct question from my intermediary, Churchill
said *'quite unfounded'*. Yet at L.H.'s behest he signed two letters, dic-
tated by L.H. (I've got copies) on Downing Street paper, evading his
first denial by a quibble, and saying that 'knowing L' he (W.C.) felt
sure he 'must have' offered Egypt. He couldn't; as I showed long before Vansittart it was not in Churchill's power as Colonial Sec. But
those Churchill letters were shown to every editor in Fleet St, and the
whole filthy Lawrence gang from Graves up to the Gutter-press, were
mobilised to vilify and insult me, and call *me* the liar. And like a perfect
English gentleman the former Permanent Secretary of the F.O. kept
discreetly silent, though he reviewed the book evasively. Such is the
Establishment, such the English gent. Shits. And on my part guerra al
cuchillo. Let me get back health . . .

It was kind indeed of you and Claude to go to see Catha—she
must have been very proud. I do hope though that she won't think of
writing for a living. It was possible up to 1939 for ordinarily gifted
people, but since only for the lucky and gifted exception. She must try
for a job and be an écrivain de dimanche. Even if a writer makes decent
money now it is all stolen by the tax-thieves, as you know.

Thank you for the recommendation to Rowohlt. We must see
what happens. I believe I told you the Muscovites are to do *All Men*
(circa Dec) but no whisper of payment. Boulgres are to do *V Heaven*,
'59 royalty, payment in Dec 1961. I got 250 dollars last month by
writing an intro to a (bad) translation of *Eugénie Grandet* to be published in an edition de luxe by Mrs Macy, relict of the late shopkeeper
in N.Y. (N.Y.). [. . .]

Very pleased to learn from Henry's telegram that *Justine* and
Balthazar are going strong in Germany. Mrs Kershaw told me when
last here that even the Unescows are 'raving' about you now.

Hope so much you are resting and having fun after your enormous and successful efforts of the last few years. Where are my proofs of *Clea?*

Love and all good wishes to both
Richard

The Mrs Macy referred to here was the widow of George Macy of the Heritage Press and was not connected with the New York department store.

𝕊 *[Engances, 26 August 1959]*

Dear Richard—

Very many thanks for your cogent advice which I have passed on 'Express' to Girodias. Most useful and wise. Three more days and we must pack in order to face London! How I dread it, and yet like *visiting,* it is so full of the frightful nostalgias of a 12-year-old mad about Shakespear and who had to wait 12 months to *see* Tower Bridge!

every good wish
Larry

𝕊 *Mazet Michel, Engances, Nîmes, Gard, France [August? 1959]*

Dear Richard:

Yes, it is a thorny problem because, as Henry admitted, our protest would cover quite a lot of garbage, mostly put out by our friend Girodias. The beastly Daimler stuff for example. But I don't see how the principle of freedom is divisible; for example *Sexus* is in my view just as indefensible as De Sade. I could attest in a court of law that Henry was pure-minded and that his intentions in this book were genuinely artistic, that his curious form of sexual mysticism had carried him far away off course . . . but I would have to admit by all ordinary standards it was a shocking book! How the devil to demarcate the line between the permissible and the other I don't know at all. Girodias has redrafted my thing, cutting out Harris I think; but then what about Genet? I find him steep too. The problem really is whether it isn't worth a hundred pornographies in order to hold the gate open for one *Lady Chatterley* or *Ulysses*. I rather feel it is. By the way, I don't really hold with my own *Black Book*'s excesses, but I know that I tackled the subject matter with no thought of doing anyone dirt! I feel that in the longest run the dirt will kill itself and the good stuff float; but it is really a matter for your own mature views, and your own reputation. There is no doubt that apart from Durrell, Nabokov, Beckett, Miller, you would also, by signing, implicitly support work which as a man and a writer you find abhorrent; and I don't really know whether it was proper of me to wonder on paper whether the subject was one of interest, or would start a conflict between the lion-hearted supporter of good art that you are and a man of substance and reputation who should not, even implicitly, lend your name to a lot of dirt as well . . . It is most confusing. The only clear thing to me is that if the British Government are going to try and close Girodias down (*Chatterley* and all) they might as well arrogate to themselves the right to close the Folies Bergères on the grounds that it harms the health of tourists and excites them sexually. No. It is stupid and bigoted I think. I think dirt will founder under freedom; and in the long run a good overdose of it can only end in what . . . onanism? Well, we have enough of that at home as it is! Anyway the finalised version will come to you in due course; scrap it soundlessly if you feel you can't ride along, and no hard feelings whatsoever. Nice letter from Catha; our picture and article she will have sent; but I wonder whether she sent you the hair raising garble from *Méridionale* in which you were described as the leader of the 'nuageiste' movement, and I was supposed to be writing a 'théologie' in four vols? It was a scream; as I told Temple this always happens to Press Attachés when they phone out copy to press analphabetics. (Mr Maurois entourée par les amis de lèvres) damn this machine and my french.

I'll keep chasing Girodias, and do you also.

> Every good thing
> Larry

❧ *[London, before 22 September 1959]*

Dear Richard—a swift line from Antrobus Lodge. I'll get the Rome piece typed and send it to Hammond at Curtis Brown: ask him to approach *Holiday*. Claude has had to go into hospital for a minor operation and our plans are all awry as she can't travel till mid next month, which means I'll have to go to Hamburg to kick the play off and to Paris etc alone. I have done 20 interviews and 3 television jobs. By the way have spoken about you and for you to many many people; the whole problem, as I see it, is that there is an empty chair marked R.A. You may have enemies among the middle-aged, but it is a more serious thing that many of the young do not know your name at all. I believe from a study of the form here that you could rectify your whole rapport with your public by three television appearances. It is amazing how ubiquitous this beastly gadget is. At a blow you could alter the Aldington image (people seem to think you are both grumpy and cantankerous and 'superior')—the young I mean. And with your film-star physique you'd have them bowled. Seriously, *please* plan a trip to England to recover the fortress; a carefully planned campaign, well thought out, would put you right back: I really mean it. This would be the best and quickest way to help Catha. Don't groan! You'll have to face them to win them back; and God has sent you the idiot's lantern! You can talk to the whole bloody country at one blow at the fireside. This is not only *my* opinion but also that of many admirers and pro-A types, notably, for example, John Davenport whose last words were: 'Tell Aldington to come back for a bit.'

Every good thing
Larry

The 'Rome piece' refers to Aldington's introduction to *Rome: A Book of Photographs* (1960). His text was printed separately by Potocki de Montalk as a Christmas greeting.

John Davenport was a British critic and reviewer.

❧ *Sury-en-Vaux, Cher, 2 November 1959*

My dear Larry,

You have vanished, perhaps inevitably, into the Ewigkeit; and I know not whether you are in England, Germany or civilisation.

What is the news of Claude? Is all well?

Our great news, which you may have heard from Temple, is that Catha (armed with her 'useless' Bac) was interviewed by two Psychologues of high degree. The upshot is that she is taking Sciences Politiques at the Un de Paris, and has a 3-year subsidy of 200 dollars a month—private enterprise. If the S.P. turns out too hard, she can transfer to another course. At the moment she is waiting to move into a small apartment, most luckily available, and contemplating her first university essay which is on the palpitating topic: 'Discuss the Rôle played by the Bourgeoisie in France between 1780 and 1830.' Perhaps this is all wrong, and she should have gone to work as a waitress.

Owing to your kindness, I think I shall get the German job for the book on DHL—heaven send me strength to do it. Then, again owing to you I'm sure, the Beer Beer Cows propose to TV Septem contra Reeves, paying 100. The Mosscows write that the Russian *All Men* should be out before the end of the year; a new translation of *Hero* into Russ is being made; the Russ version of selected short stories [*Farewell to Memories*] is nearly finished; and the local literary Mr K. is considering a short story selection in English. Also the Bulgars will do *Very Heaven*. I'd better hurry up and become a commo, nicht?

Your suggestion of personal appearance on TV was made in all kindness, but I am sure it would be even more disastrous than Aldous's attempt was for him. The sin is not exile (you too are an exile) but Huxley and I have published satirical novels, wherein we laugh consumedly at Brit pretentions, and I have debunked 2 local heroes, old Doug and Colonel Mecca, both sods of high degree. For this there is no pardon. The only way to treat them (Brits) is to kick them again, which I propose to do, if ONLY I can get back health and strength.

Meanwhile, I toil away at this super-blasted anthol for the *En Brit*. I *must* keep my word and get the script off before Xmas. E.B. now say that it will run to 2 vols, making at least 900 pages in all—BUT that they are having some permissions trouble. I knew it would be—[. . .]

publishers always try to kill other anthologies either by asking prohibitive fees or by actually refusing. In my *Poetry of Eng-Speaking World* (which in spite of opposition and 'critics' has now had Anglo-yank sales of over 150,000) I had to contend with limitations of Hardy, Yeats, Masefield, and many others. Dame Edith refused to come in (telling people cheerfully that would 'kill the book') because I would not use a poem published after my date-line of Sept 1939. It would have meant revising the whole modern section.

Apropos doing myself harm by publishing one article in Mosley's *European*. The harm was in praising Roy and denouncing the little squirts who dared to vilify him—just as nearly 30 years ago I stood up for DHL against the vilifyings of Jimmie Douglas, Jack Squire, Lynd, *John Bull* etc. I sent that Roy article first to the *Times*, to Haley personally, and he bunged it back. I knew it was utterly useless to send it elsewhere, so I gave it to Mosley deliberately. I believe in a 'free press', not a press which kisses the backside of the Establishment and boycotts any author who tries to tell the truth. Roy was a great poet— Auden, Spender, Lewis, etc are a set of more or less cunning phoneys, who study intrigue more than art. 'Mediocrity weighing mediocrity in the balance' and 'usurping the judgment seat when it should be apologising in the dock'.

How did the play go? What is your news? Above all, how is Claude?

Ever

Richard

[P.S.] Did I tell you that after hesitation the University of Southern Illinois (there's glory for you) will definitely set up and publish a yank edition of *Mistral*. That breaks the boycott there—the E.B. anthol was an old affair, held up because of a change of 'editorial staff'. [. . .]

Commissioned by Rowohlt, Aldington wrote the text for *D. H. Lawrence in Selbstzeugnissen und Bilddokumenten* (1961).

The poetry anthology Aldington compiled for the *Encyclopaedia Britannica* was never published.

James Douglas, Sir John C. Squire, and Robert Lynd were literary critics who frequently attacked the writings of D. H. Lawrence. Under the editorship of Horatio Bottomley, the British newspaper *John Bull* was strenuously anti-Lawrence. These four contributed to the suppression of *The Rainbow* in 1915.

Sir William Haley, an admirer of Aldington, was at various times Director General of the BBC, editor of the *Times* (London), and president of the *Encyclopaedia Britannica*.

Sury-en-Vaux, Cher, 7 November 1959

My dear Larry,

This garden is full of tits. Now, none of your of Leila and Melissa insinuations—they are tom-tits. 'Great Bearded Tits seen in Essex', as the *Times* once headlined a communication from 'yours faithfully, Birdshit'. Strange that the Natural Forces which produce such lovely little creatures should also produce Auden and Spender.

In 1870 Rossetti published those poems he had buried in his wife's coffin, and his publisher Ellis advertised in the *Athenaeum* that next week he was publishing a book of poems by DGR. Only that, and nothing more. Rossetti was white with rage and shame, protesting against this odious puffery, this violation of a lifetime of integrity.

Well, as you say, TV has changed the literary infrastructure, and the ultimate product is Mr Charles Van Doren. Interesting that the cheat who is fired [. . .] is instantly hired as literary critic.

My dear boy, it would be useless for me to appear before 9 million Brits (appalling thought to dwell on) for I should instantly offend 18 million.

I am much relieved that Claude is out of the garage and back with you. Temple put the wind up me by mysterious hints about a serious operation etc. I don't believe he knew any more about it than I do, but wrote under the influence of TV.

The amazonian Catha was down here for Toussaint, went out with some of the peasants, and came back with a couple of guineafowl, saying she had shot them. *'What!'* I said, with creditable public school horror, 'But they're poultry.' 'Oh yes, but otherwise you have to chase them and cut their heads off, and the peasant let me shoot them with a .22.' No wonder she still pines for her beloved Roy.

My *Encyclopaedia Brit* anthology is finished all but the Intro, which I hope to finish this coming week. I have had to cut out all living authors—an immense relief. The reviewers of course will squawk—the main reason being that recent verse and the Oxford book form the whole of their reading in poetry. The British section winds up with Roy and Dylan Thomas. I asked Mary to choose Roy's, and she chose two magnificent poems, 'The Skull' and 'The Clock'. Then I asked one of D.T.'s (appropriate initials) ladies to choose, and she chose a villanelle (not so labelled) imitated from Dowson, and some whimsy-childhood stanzas unpleasantly reminiscent of De la Mare. I leave them side by side—the popular kitten mewing after the outlaw lion's roar. What's the matter with the Brits? Are they all feeble-minded since Hitler scared them to death?

No, I have not seen *Clea* proofs.

I like very much the story of building rooms for the children. Can you manage to keep it as a surprise? They will certainly be happy.

Catha says the Sorbonne profs give very nice lectures. The Economics bloke began: 'Je vous préviens que je ne suis pas Marxiste—question de biologie.' There are several Juifs in her sub-section of Sciences Politiques. I see that the man who failed to shoot Mitterrand is a diplomé en Sciences Politiques, so it evidently leads to positions of great dignity and emolument. [. . .]

Let me know how the play goes.

Ever
Richard

P.S. Rather dismal news of Ezra Pound. I hear he has left Rapallo and gone back to his daughter's 'Slosh' near Meran, saying he has 'come home to die', that there is 'something wrong in his head which no doctor can cure'—a very accurate definition of Paranoia. Still raving about 'the Jews'—surely anti-semitism is the hall-mark of the raté?

R.

Charles Van Doren won $129,000 on the television quiz game 'Twenty-one' during 1956 and 1957. In 1959 he testified under oath to the honesty of the programme, but later admitted to having been coached. He resigned from Columbia and was suspended by NBC.

Toussaint: All Saints' Day.

✻ *Engances [1 December 1959]*

Dear Richard;

Hope the medical trip was of some use and fixed you up. I wrote from Hamburg saying how thrilled I would be at the idea of a book by you, but I do hope that it is financially worth it, and not just another characteristic kindness. I can't understand about Faber, but I know they sent you their own last copy; the text is not quite fully corrected and each day a new corps of misprints comes in. I think that is why they asked for it back when you had finished. Unluckily I haven't even an MS here or a proof to send you. The foreign rights people filched the three I ordered in order to stagger their production—Germany France and Italy are trying to harness production to make maximum use of each other's press; and my agent has skimmed off everything including my MS and carbons. I will try and get a copy back from Dutton—but they have been circulating a proof to critics. There are now five critics doing long pieces about the form of the quartet; two Yank, two French and one Brit . . . they are all having to return the bloody proofs. At any rate for you there is no urgency, except that I'd like you to see it before undertaking the book, as you may find it a flop. I have also asked for *Sappho* and *The Black Book* to be sent you; you'll probably wince at the latter, as I do now, despite its qualities. It's pretty rough; but you'll remember that a young man who can't find his voice, like the octopus in captivity, gnaws off his own tentacles! Apart from that the only other general book is my book on poetry, with which you'll probably disagree heartily. But if your resolve still holds after these essays I shall consider myself a lucky man indeed. *Sappho* was, to my surprise, a great success and got a huge press; but I'm dead beat. More soon.

Larry

[P.S.] Raining like hell!

Harry T. Moore suggested to Aldington that he write a critical biography of Durrell. The book was never finished.

✒ *Sury-en-Vaux, 4 December 1959*

Dear Larry,

[. . .] Hope you twain were not troubled by the downpour in your region. A great misfortune if rain leaks through.

Apropos, we are pestered with sparrows under the eaves of this cottage. From frequenting your brother (and similar animals) have you any views on getting rid of them? The only thing I can think of is to get some of the village kids to raid the nests, which they would do joyfully—but then my sentimental heart yearns over the nestlings.

The trip to Zürich was rather pleasant, in fact very much so; and I enjoyed wandering about the old part of the town by the Limmat. The one-way streets there are a proper bugger, especially with limited parking. I was an hour getting into the hotel. The medicos were amiable and struck me as very up to snuff, particularly the physical (not psycho) bloke who resembled one's infant ideal of Sherlock Holmes and was impressively named Schlegel. He was greatly disappointed that I hadn't an enlarged prostate. He announced it to me confidently, but after his exagmination round my factification he exclaimed in tones of bitter chagrin: 'He is not great—normal at your years.' So I shan't yet (I hope) be took up for criminally assaulting little girls.

I have to await the combined report of their medical wisdoms. Meanwhile Schlegel gave me some tablets which acted magically on my hyper-acidity. He explained that bicarbonate of soda is a blunder. It over-corrects, with the result that the stomach immediately starts manufacturing more acid; et ainsi de suite. It is called Alucol, and obtainable in France.

What you tell me about the rush for *Clea* proofs puts a different complexion (as the stylists say) on Faber's rather curt note. When you next have to write them will you point out my reason for wanting the proofs, and ask what they want me to do? If I have to wait until Feb that holds up the book. Let me know what is decided. I think it will do you no harm to have a quiet book about you circulating among los yanquis for the next decade.

Thank you for *Sappho* and for *Black Book*—just in. What a silly remark of Miller's that is.

I am dumped with a chore by that ancient English character Melvin Lasky. Katherine Anne Porter, peeved at the immense vogue of DHL and the publicity about *Lady C.*, has written a would-be catty article, in which she calls Connie 'stupid', says Lorenzo didn't know what he was doing (!) and is 'all wrong about sex'. Who, one wonders, is all right? KAP? I loathe these idiotic wrangles, which get nowhere. But if I refuse to bother, the still vocal anti-Ls in London will say 'Ha, ha, Aldington couldn't answer her'. As a matter of fact I think *Lady C.* one of his least valuable novels as a novel, and deplore the critical and public stupidity which sees only the 'lurid sexual specialist' and never the 'genius' and the remarkably complex character. Voltaire says fools were sent us pour nos menus plaisirs—I must say I don't find it so. You owe a lot to DHL's valiant fight—if your things had come out between 1912 and 1928, as his did, you'd have been in all sorts of woes.

Rowohlt sent me good news of *Sappho,* and also very kindly a dozen free copies of the war poems—for which I must thank him. Claude says in her letter that Rowohlt is looking for hun translations of my novels. He can look till the cows come home. The only one existing is the *Hero*—done by the List Verlag of Dresden, Eastern zone in 1930, who reprinted and got rid of about 10,000 some years back. *Hero* was ill-received by the late Schicklgruber and his pals then rapidly coming to the fore in Germany, and as soon as he got in I was auf strengste verboten. I don't know for certain if *Hero* was burned, though I was told so. Howsomdever, one J. Schwalbe perpetrated a work: 'R.A. Der literarische und weltanschauliche Weg eines modernen Englanders'. Berlin diss. Wuerzburg [1941]. According to some weird Nazi psychology I was classified as a Typus C., which meant that owing to my Celtic origins I am rebellious and suffer from hallucinations. Fearful bunk. So if Rowohlt is going to issue any, he has an open field in which to expatiate. Mondadori told me that the Duce personally read *Hero* and forbade it (it appeared first in Italian about 3 years ago) but allowed the others. The régime of the Maréchal was not friendly, and in patriotic ecstasy Heinemann allowed all my books to go out of print and destroyed the plates during the last war—ditto Doubledays. After Pearl Harbor, Archie MacLeish wrote an article for the *N.Y. Times* in which he blamed the war on the sapping of America's morale by such books as *Death of a Hero.* Writers like me don't make for the sale of armaments.

You won't have had time to look at those war poems Rowohlt has issued. I think it feeble of Middleton to exclude Fred Manning and Roy—both real soldiers—and to include such chair-borne warriors of the knife-and-fork brigade as Auden and Spender. Damn it—the essence of the modern poem is that it is the sudden flowering of personal experience, not 'picked out of the air', as Goethe said. That poem of Auden's is journalism—reflections about something he had read in a newspaper.

Rest a bit after all this hamburging and Sapphism. Tell Claude that I send many thanks for her letter and the address of her step-sister, which I've forwarded to Catha.

Can you do anything to get periodical publication for a few of H.D.'s unpublished poems and perhaps an article on her? She is 73, crawling about still on crutches three years after breaking her femur, lonely in that Klinik. Temple is doing 3 poems in his *Licorne,* and I'm alerting an Australian friend. It would cheer her greatly if we could get her a little attention—Ezra and Eliot pushed her aside ruthlessly.

Love to both
Richard

During the Second World War metal was urgently needed, and the British and U.S. governments pressured publishers to let slow-moving books go out of print and melt the plates so that the old metal could be used for printing new books. Aldington should have known this was common practice, although in fact Ken McCormick of Doubleday reports that according to his records the plates of only three Aldington titles, *The Colonel's Daughter, Seven Against Reeves,* and *Very Heaven,* were destroyed during the war (in 1942). Doubleday scrapped the plates of an additional seven Aldington books in 1947.

§ *Nîmes [ca. 4–7 December 1959]*

Dear Richard:

A cracking good letter, and the very strong suspicion that it won't be long before you are in midstream again throwing punches. I've written Alan telling him not to be a fool and to try and get those *Clea* proofs back to you unless it means a complete production muck-up; in which case to borrow a set from the three or so he has farmed out to would be crits. Meanwhile to my fury I have to rush back to england and collect my young daughter for the Xmas hols; her ma is down with a minor operation of no great consequence except that it cuts across the Yuletide season. So I'll have to bring her here; which is a great joy, of course, except that I have to go and fetch her. I'll be back by the 17th, and will ring up Alan from Bournemouth about *Clea* and see what can be done. Are you still really minded to do this marvellous book: and what the devil can you put in it? My metaphysical ideas (ahem) are all borrowed from your generation. My 'space' business is from Lewis. I owe to you most of my knowledge of French Lit (until I was twenty-two I read very stumblingly; afterwards I got launched). I was damn lazy, too, and still am. Lawrence gave me such a thorough going over as far as style was concerned that it unlimbered me but I still don't go for L's ideas. Style is the man! I don't see the sort of work you have in mind. Perhaps a real genre essay knocking me to hell on various counts? I only ask this because—what books should I send you? I really believe *The Black Book* was my first essay: and I was defeated and thrown back on myself. Couldn't advance from there. The islands books are okay but don't lead anywhere (except the islands). I think the *Key to Modern Poetry* not bad; the poems are a very true and slender voice, rather Gautier-ish; not major alas. But then everyone can't be major; one must get used to the idea sooner or later. Anyway let me know in the fullness of time. But also reassure me that you want to write it. That it isn't a kindness, and that it will be properly based financially to make it worth while for you. Rowohlt by the way is interested in the option for his handsome little series (your Lawrence will be one); but it contains a lot of pics. If you haven't seen it I'll send you a couple. The Proust and the Rilke, they are charming. I've already told you about his DHL plan for Germany with you, as always, spearheading the attack. I was *touched* by Germany; so lost and yet so warm and kind; in spite of the industrialization it was the sort of world psychically of the Paston letters! This sounds absurd. But Rowohlt is a good man, a tremendous gambler, and with a real nose; his old firm was in east germany. The recent new firm has now six Nobel prize authors including people like Musil; real judgement. Tell him direct will you about German translations? I would not have believed him about the dearth of translators had I not seen it with my own eyes. He has a

team of five pidgins and does the work himself; but obviously he can't
do all the books himself with such a huge house. It's God's mercy that
he has done mine. He paid off and scrapped three lots of translators
because he liked my books; took a month off; locked himself up with
three poets and got down to them. The result is they are apparently
good German! he's terrified of englishmen and of his own english; so
bear with him. He's just sent me a telegram to say that *Sappho* is still
playing to 'absolutely cramped houses' and will I please send another
play! He's a crazy old duck, but one couldn't ask for a better man; as
he is polishing his specs he says: 'Aber Larry I must be honest; I love
your work. But I am a publisher too and I don't want to go busted for
them. You must play with me a little, no?' After advances of five hundred quid (by telephone from Hamburg, after he had read *Justine*) I
quite understand: however I haven't lost him a penny so far. 'Aber if
you are worried I put you on a salary, Larry. But you stop at once to
write the tripe please. No more Antrobus please until you are famous
and free to play. Give me five years of your seriousity please dear. I
must think of your reputation if you don't. No wasting the time; write
THE BEST you wish!'

I will have a think about H.D.; you know that despite the middlebrow acclaim my stock is low in England, due I expect to my pert crits
of ourselves. Smarty [Walter Smart] tells me that he is engaged by annoyed people every time he mentions me. However here and there
there are oases. I [will] see what I can do about a very well merited
H.D. number: didn't I see a *Poetry* (Chicago) once entirely devoted to
her very clean and racy and nervous (in the French sense) poems?

Ach. I am so sick of travelling about and sitting up in trains.

But I'm delighted at these hints of your recovery; really 'a writer *is*
only when he writes'.

Henry has just fallen in love with a 24-year-old girl, to the immense amusement of Eve; he says he feels he is giving off magic rays!
But he's heading for Japan and a Zen master at the end of this month.
Always new horizons. I rather love his childish rubberneck attitude to
the world. 'Gee! Think of the Orient, Larry. That great . . .' And one
thinks of the smells and the swarms of beings like winged ants.

Love
Larry

In a letter to Ian MacNiven, Durrell stated that he had derived his ' "space" business' from Wyndham Lewis's *Time and Western Man*.

Eve McClure had been married to Miller since 1953.

✣ *Engances [before 7 December 1959]*

Dear Richard;   Just back from Montpellier where I cut a long tape for Dominique Arban, hooking up with Paris via Temple's station. I hope you are back and have tracked down the virus and slain it. Are you still thinking of that offer for a book about me or has wiser judgement prevailed? I was in Rowohlt's office when I got your letter and I showed it to him together with the enclosures about your other titles; this must be the reason that *Der Spiegel* in a long article about me says 'Richard Aldington, famous for his books on D.H. Lawrence and for his debunking of T.E. Lawrence, is now turning his hand to a third Lawrence: Durrell!'

If the thing is worth doing, and who would not love to be written about by Aldington?, you must tell me what you need from me; are there any books you haven't seen? I don't suppose you need to see everything—so much is potboiler or just downright bad. I sent you a *Black Book* however which is just being reviewed in France. To my surprise the Yanks say they will produce it next year with a preface by Gerald Sykes. I am just reading your admirable Laclos translation [*Dangerous Acquaintances*] with a most interesting preface; a lot of books here I must read. Huge gaps in my information. I regretted very much that you had to send the *Clea* proof back without a quick look-see, but bound copies should be off the machines in about a month and your copy will be the first. So far no really discouraging reactions from anywhere, and some ecstatic ones!

By the way ref D.H. Lawrence, I don't know if Rowohlt has told you—he's a poor correspondent and diffident about his english; but your monograph is to form the spearhead of an attack. He has bought Lawrence out, and plans to issue three of his novels all at once together with your monograph—to give him a big push. I think Claude already explained his intentions for your own work, and his troubles about translation. It seems the chief post-war shortage in Germany—translators of calibre.

The play was a great success, and I learnt so much from watching them that I'm now going to try my hand at something a little better constructed—*Acte*. My trouble I suspect is a secret hankering for good old melodrama in a green light with lots of gore. I am so downright sad not to have been an Elizabethan; I really do feel close to Tourneur and Ford and Dekker and co; and far away from anglo-saxon attitudes and so on.

I must not forget either to send you Groddeck's *Book of the It*; you'll see where I get my psychosexual ideas!

We are both pretty tired and snappy and colded up after Hamburg; but dying to get down to work again.

Much love to you from us both
Larry

Dominique Arban: See p. 159.

♫ *Sury-en-Vaux, Cher, 7 December 1959*

My dear Larry,

Who is Dominique Arban?

Who is Gerald Sykes?

Without waiting for the report of the Zürich medicos I have told Professor Moore that I'll do the book on the third Lawrence—evidently a fatality in my life. BUT, goddam it, Katherine Anne Porter has written a silly-malicious attack on *Lady C.*—all the old tripe, and an appeal to the example of the great Henrietta James—for *Encounter*. They grinning derisively suggest I 'might like to reply' to what in their ignorance they think unanswerable. I MUST do it, Larry, or the bastards will leave it unanswered, and say I couldn't reply.

Then suddenly Temple drops a tile on my head. I promised to introduce *his* book on DHL, and Seghers without sending me proofs, demands script by end of the month, because he wants to publish in March, i.e. 30th anniversary of Lorenzo's death. Bastard.

A DHL Miscellany in today from N.Y. contains an appalling letter from Katherine [Mansfield] to Kot, describing from Zennor in 1916 a ghastly scene in which DHL beat Frieda up, pulling out her hair, beating her on the face and breasts, and patata. Fifteen minutes later he was discussing French literature with Murry (who like the little hero he was didn't go to F's rescue though she screamed for him) and then L. and F. cheerfully discussed maccheroni with rich sauce!!! Next day he was taking her breakfast in bed, and trimming her a hat! What a shit Kot was to keep that letter. Later I'll let you have the letter—copy—if you want.

Do you see that Alec Guinness is to be hero in the yank film on the Prince of Mecca, done by the *Bridge* [*on the River Kwai*] people? Clearly, it is dulcet and decorous that the chief part should be played by a clown, and of course the theme song will be 'Colonel Bogus'.

I didn't send the *Clea* proofs back—waited to hear from you. Shall I keep them? Longing to read *Clea,* and cursing these fools for taking up my time with dead stuff about DHL.

The *Sappho* success is really important, I think. Very few novelists, especially good ones, can write a play which goes over on the boards. Evidently you can. Instead of writing about the Lillibetians (a mistake at present for one with your big public) you should do plays, I think. If you can hit the right whatshername, you and Claude will be as rich as Robinson Croesus. The Hollywood advice they gave me is good I think: 'Never over-estimate the knowledge of the people, and never under-estimate their intelligence.' Shakers in *Troilus* makes one of the Heroes of Troy quote Aristotle. So What? How good Thersites is— preview of the abuse of Falstaff and Timon. I like Timon—what he says about Athens is just what I feel about London (Eng).

Evidently you were not washed out by the deluge. Good.

Love to both,
Richard

A D. H. Lawrence Miscellany was edited by Harry T. Moore.

Samuel S. Koteliansky, known as Kot, was Lawrence's close friend from 1914 on.

Peter O'Toole, not Guinness, eventually starred in *Lawrence of Arabia* (1963). Guinness, who took the title role in *Ross,* Terence Rattigan's stage play on the same theme, appeared in the film version as one of the Arab leaders.

◊ *[Engances?, ca. 14–24 December 1959]*

DEAR RICHARD
    THE MONOGRAPHS LEDIG REFERS TO ARE SUCH AS
THESE: IF EVER THE BOOK ABOUT ME CAME OFF AND
HE BOUGHT IT TO TREAT IN THIS MANNER I COULD
SUPPLY YOU WITH QUITE ENOUGH DATA AND PICS TO
MAKE IT FUNNY: I HAVE ALL SORTS OF STUFF, IN-
CLUDING A PICTURE OF ME HOGGING EDEN'S AP-
PLAUSE IN BELGRADE, SOOTHING THE GOVERNOR OF
CYPRUS AND BATHING NUDE WITH HENRY! I ALSO
HAVE A WONDERFUL INSULTING LETTER FROM BER-
NARD SHAW WRITTEN IN A TREMBLING HAND WHICH
WARNS ME AGAINST PEDDLING PORNOGRAPHY. SOME
LETTERS FROM DYLAN. AND SO ON. THERE IS PLENTY
OF THE STUFF!

                                    LOVE
                                    LARRY

> Covering note for one of Rowohlt's brief illustrated paperback mono-
> graphs. Rowohlt wanted to consider adapting Aldington's proposed book
> on Durrell (see note on p. 107) for his Taschenbuch series.

◊ *Nîmes [before 17 December 1959]*

Dear Richard;
    I am delighted with myself; I only half expected this gambit to
come off. Since Mahomet won't go to the mountain . . . Corresponding
with David Jones and his [BBC] team about their trip here I casually
mentioned that you might be visiting! Here is their response. Now
don't be difficult this time and foul up this most important departure
will you? Fabers are so thrilled at the idea of your book that I can bang
you straight on to publicity expenses and make them stand you a couple of nights in Nîmes plus train fares or petrol. What do you say?
    Please believe me about the importance of this idiot's magic lan-
tern; it doesn't matter if one mucks it up, the interview, gives offence,
any damn thing; *the mere fact* of being on television puts one right into

the ordinary news picture. In the old days the equivalent would be having the *Daily Express* quote a poem of yours in a leader! Even if you do not gain one new fan, you will find publishers sitting up. You are now half way round the bad turning; this should put you steadily back into the fairway.

Now this programme, too, is the most highbrow and serious of them all; they do camera studies of various poets and painters at work. Sometimes this sort of thing is wonderful, like the little Clouzot film of Picasso; and the marvellous one on Maillol at work. David Jones is a sensitive and serious person, who will probably surprise you by quoting poems of your own which you forgot you wrote; as he did with me.

Anyway will you drop him a line direct agreeing en principe to be available here on the 8th; for all I know they might come up to Sury. But it would be more fun to see you down here for us. And we could all be passed through the wringer in the same week. Alors to *DAVID JONES MONITOR PROGRAMME.*

I believe they pay too; but I don't know what. Really we should pay them. Just off to England for 24 hours to collect my infant.

love
Larry

Sury, 24 December 1959

Catha pushed off yesterday with two other students and her skis in a 2 CV, bound first for Nîmes, in hopes of riding in the mounted torch-light procession for midnight mass at the Stes Maries; and on the 26th to Mégève for a week's scrambling in the snow. Her Lambretta is here, so I doubt she'll get out to Engances this time.

Of course—it is Durrell, the Man and his Message. But seriously, we must have a bit of biog, and prove you're no goddam Saxon, but in the tradition des libres esprits (R. de Gourmont). I don't know if I'll be able to get down on the 5/1/60. The Renault is older than the rocks among which it sits, and we have just done a deal whereby we turn it in, and get a Simca on the système achat-louage—delivery unhappily not before end of Jan or beginning of Feb. Anyway, I must grit the old (false) teeth, and polish off the 30,000 on DHL for Rowohlt—who obviously knows nothing whatever about him apart from what he has read in the papers and heard from you. I want him to push off with *Sons and Lovers,* and *Sea & Sardinia*—two of the most attractive to non-fanatics. *Lady C.* is almost the worst of DHL's novels—you've no idea how utterly worn out and dying he was; the marvel is that any man in his state could have done anything nearly as good. He had nearly croaked in Mexico in '25, and again at the Mirenda a year or so later. When I saw him in Oct '26, just before he started *Lady C.,* he did, as Pino [Orioli] said, 'look like J.C. just taken down from the cross', and so ill he could hardly eat. Sickening the way the swine sentimentalise about RLS and his TB, and never once give a much greater man the slightest mercy. I do more and more loathe the British—what fearful shits.

Anyway, we should get the Simca-6 by Feb, and as soon as I have got the DHL off my neck, I'll tootle down and we can have some sessions of loud talk about you.

I don't think Snow could do you much harm. He didn't do me much good with the little book he wrote in my favour. If he does seem menacing I'll get in touch with him.

Damn Xmas, eh? But I hope you're having fun with the little daughter. They really enjoy life at that age, if the grown-ups aren't too fatuous and grumpy.

Got such a hearty message (on a card with a spoutnik) from the Soviet Union of Writers that Catha says must keep it to show the Russians when the invasion comes. Doubt it would protect against nuclear radiation.

I wonder if *Encounter* will use my counter-attack on K.A. Porter—there are swipes at Eliot and Pound and MacSpaunday, so they may retire.

Love to both,
Richard

[P.S.] You know, man, the chair-borne warriors of the knife-and-fork brigade. Did you ever see Roy's parody of Hopkins? The skite-hawks on the cookhouse roof?

𝄢 *Sury, 25 December 1959*

My dear Larry,

This is to say that I will never desert Mr Antrobus.

Miller and Rowohlt are poops, imbeciles, very likely, catchpoles. They know nothing. Antrobus is a very nice man, and his inventor is a very good writer. So SHIT to them. Vive Antrobus.

Ever

Richard

[P.S.] Catha has gone to Camargue. This is the second Xmas I have spent alone, and it is a good idea. The other one was on the boat train from London to Paris, in 1929, and I was the only passenger. The unfortunates who had to run the mail train and boat thought I was a King's Messenger—such a good lunch at Calais. And it was all for a woman. What next?

𝄢 *Engances [after 25 December 1959]*

Dear Richard; I do hope you manage it, and don't foul up this valuable bit of publicity; we have had a pleasant quiet Xmas with just the usual troubles of countryfolk—the well overflowing into the pump housing so that the motor has to be rebobbined: and me meanwhile having to draw it up from the depths by hand. But it is good for the silhouette they say. I agree with you about DHL, your choice. But I think I know why Rowohlt wants to lead with *Lady C.* Anyway it's good to know you are pounding the old machine again.

Juliet [O'Hea], my agent, has given me rather a start; she's been trying to locate a book of mine long dead and out of print, consisting of some lectures on poetry [*A Key to Modern Poetry*]. At last she has found a couple of copies. 'I note with delighted malice a somewhat belittling remark about Mr Aldington's poetry. Wretched youth! You had better burn these copies. Otherwise you will be just nicely placed for one of those famous right hooks, what with your own versicles in process of being printed . . .' What the devil can it be? The awful thing is that I want you to see the book, not for the poetry criticism (some of which was fudged up from a book to suit a planned study course), but because of the general essay on linguistic disturbance. Anyway it can't have been too awful because Roy read the book: he didn't think the essay much good, far too cerebral. But I should certainly have been knocked for six had there been something unpardonable. Anyway I'll send you the damn book when it arrives, and gladly take a hundred lines if there is some bitchiness in it! Or any other suitable penance. I never reread my own books alas, as Henry does (with joy and delight!) so I can't tell what I was thinking (if at all) ten years back! I've also ordered you a Groddeck and a copy of my brother's wicked pen portrait of the genius at the age of twenty-one. Wow! I'll assemble all these for when you come down.

God knows what sort of weather the filmers will find; it has been pouring and pouring: but Xmas day by some odd fluke got inserted into the calendar from late June, windless and very hot.

No, I don't think there's anything to worry about; I don't think Alan meant Snow himself, who I'm sure couldn't care less about my experiments; I think he meant the Snow circle of admirers, but I'm so out of touch I wouldn't know who these are. It is all rubbish of course, and publishers are fools to want a book to get a uniformly good press; it isn't in nature. Any expression of temperament cuts across somebody's own nature. Just like people. Some one can't stand; so with books. We are all prima donnas and all unjust in this way; and tactically a very bad press is quite as intriguing as a very good one no? Poor TSE, don't throw rocks at him; he's married! I have written him some fierce letters when he was directly my poetry publisher; but he was quite unruffled, and often came back with a left to the nose, very gently, but quite on the target. I understand your dyspathy; but even old Roy at the end got to love him. The old sobersides. He's dealt very handsomely with me I must admit; and I must admit to liking the *Quartets*. On the other hand I made him quite angry by describing Pound as really no poet at all! What the hell! We all have areas of tone-deafness; Charles Williams, for example, makes me writhe. Why? I cannot understand it. I must go to town and buy bread.

Don't dare to wish you happy Xmas; remember a diatribe against it in some book (*Hero?*) saying you liked spending it in a train!

every good wish
Larry

Sury-en-Vaux, Cher, 30 December 1959

Dear Larry,

[. . .] When Moore wrote of '200 pages' I visualised a pocket-book of about 35,000 words. Now he speaks of *Mistral*—and that is 70,000. A book that long on a contemporary would drag—have to be padded with such bunk as 'The Art and Craft of Fiction in Durrell's Books' and 'Durrell's Place in Modern Thought', which must be avoided.

I have to go to Sancerre this afternoon about the car. The driver's seat has gone wonky. Catha thought that the other seat could be moved over, and that one properly repaired. I should have gone earlier but for these blasted fêtes. If they can mend the seat and if the weather keeps open without too many floods I'll try to make it. Can't risk it if there is snow, and train is out of the question for me. The use of disinfectant daily has not yet attracted the attention of the SNCF (more interested in loafing and striking, as Roy says somewhere) and after these fetid holiday crowds I should certainly arrive with double pneumonia.

The posts are fantastic. Yesterday I got a letter postmarked 'Dover 23/12/59' and one postmarked 'Tokyo 25/12/59'. Even the Xmas rush scarcely excuses that, for both letters had to come through Paris.

I am rationing myself on *Clea*, but to my grief have already got through all of Part I, and who will go on with the tale when Scheherazade is executed on the last page? There are one or two signs of haste, Larry—you have one sentence of mixed metaphors worthy of Hart Crane at his worst; but otherwise the whole thing is superb and perhaps an advance even on *Mountolive*. All the part about Melissa's child is wonderful. You are the only person since DHL I've read who can write about a child with perfect tenderness and pathos and yet not a hint of sentimentality. (Do you remember the child in *The Rainbow*, crying her heart out for her mother in child-bed, and the farmer gradually quieting her by taking her to feed the cows?) Then the dawn air-raid is spectacular, superb. Pity you weren't in the war, instead of skrimshankin' it in the F.O. And then the joy of having a bit more of dear old Scobie—you're the only person in the world who could have made that ghastly old sod so lovable—and the cackling Bliss of finding him made a saint by those idiot Moslems. I wandered around Tunisie and Algérie-hinterland, Kairouan, etc—and know what fools they are about their saints. The rattling of the keys to scare away the efrits—exact.

One thing I wondered about the child—you make them all so real I believe in them! Darley had been father and mother to that little girl for a long time, and children care more about the person who tends them than the real parents if they are absent. They are loyal to the hands that feed and tend them, in expectation of more to come. Would she have left Darley so easily for Nessim whom she'd never seen? True, Darley had most charmingly prepared her with fairy tales, so that she thought that rambling country place 'a palace'. Anyway, all this may be answered later in the book.

Publishers are wrong in attributing so much to reviews—look what DHL survived. You never saw that spate of hate against him 1915–1930. I think my answer to K.A. Porter on *Lady C.* (for *Encounter*) will, if published, make a lot more enemies. I am pleased with a sentence when I say the reviewers of *Lady C.* (I give specimens of their foulness) evidently 'came from the great schools of Eating and Shallow, and the universities of Oxter and Cambronne'. I also have a swipe at Eliot and the other yankees established in London for the purpose of high-hatting the natives and creating 'opinion' in matters of art and literature—illustrating this by the fact that in the week Henry James got the O.M. three of his books were remaindered.

Why do you say Hypatia was fanatical? The fanatics were those bloody monks who murdered the girl so atrociously, cutting her up alive with oyster shells. And there is no such word as 'temeritous'—it is 'temerarious'. Haven't you an OED?

I've done the first chap of the DHL for Rowohlt, and-but work with difficulty. A wealthy person (truly) offers me 500 quid to shut up for a year—and I'm sorely tempted. I have in fact tentatively accepted, on condition I first do DHL, you, and the *Enc. Brit* anthol proofs. No word from them, but an official Xmas card from the chief of staff in Chicago, Ill. The bastards still owe me 750 dollars—I had to sell it outright to get cash for Catha, so the book will be a success, and bring me nothing.

Love to both,
Richard

SNCF: *Société Nationale des Chemins de Fer Français.*

'Temeritous' is in the *Oxford English Dictionary* and the meaning fits Durrell's usage, so the judgement goes to him!

§ *Sury-en-Vaux, Cher, 2 January 1960*

Dear Larry,

It's no good. I've arranged for the old car to be patched up by this evening, had even got out my suitcase, ready to start at dawn on Tuesday. And my Balaam's ass won't let me. During a feverish night I have realised that I have nothing to say to the British—apart from things they don't want to hear and the BBC wouldn't send out anyway—and that to acknowledge them even to this extent is hauling down the colours. I have been against them for 40 years and I still am. Make any excuse to Davy Jones—but don't let him come here.

I have finished *Clea*—alas. So there is nothing more to read. I'll write more about it. At present, I am suffering for you, suddenly sensing that women must have made *you* suffer intensely. But, as Scobie might have said, that is 'prying', so I say no more. Of course you are a bloody genius, but the apotheosis of Scobie—culminating for me in the shower of rockets from H.M.'s Navy—is sublimity. I laughed until I had to stop reading because I couldn't see the page for tears of mirth.

What I want to do—all things conducing—is this: To get the DHL booklet off to Rowohlt. He will presumably cough up 1000 DMs, and I shall then have the new car, and it will be spring. Then, you and Claude permitting, I'll come south for a few days, staying at Uzès or some village (not bloody Nîmes) and we can start cocking up Sketch of a Bloody Genius without a But. The only But is how to deal with these guys in S. Illinois, but you will advise on that.

I feel like Xtian when he dropped that rucksack of his in the river, now that I know I'm not BBC-ing.

Love to both,
Richard

[P.S.]   Did Roy ever tell you of how he went to his BBC job the first day? Well, you see, man, after I was demobbed and spent all me blood money, I was working in a Soho restaurant washing up the dirty plates

to keep Mary and the girls going. Then I got a letter from Desmond
MacCarthy, telling me he'd got me a job at the BBC. Being a senior
NCO I thought he meant I was to be a Commissionaire. So I put all
me gongs up, and went down there, and said to the bloke on duty: 'I
believe I'm to relieve you, mate.' 'First I've 'eard of it,' he said. 'What
makes you think that?' So I showed him Desmond's letter, and he said:
'You've made a mistake, mate. You got to work with them bastards
upstairs.'

Aldington still planned to write a biography of Durrell, and he is point-
edly referring to his D. H. Lawrence book, *Portrait of a Genius, But . . .*
(1950).

✿   Nîmes [ca. 8 January 1960]

Dear Richard; I felt somehow you'd foil me; a great pity as David
Jones was anxious to do a programme on you without reference to
TEL and also to enlist your help in a special DHL programme for
some centenary or other is to be celebrated soon . . . you'd have been
able to announce the forthcoming books of his and yours etc sitting in
front of the fire! However it can't be helped; but it was a chance in a
million. Wicked man. I'm delighted about the other news, about the
money; you do really want to down tools, do you? I think you'll die of
boredom if you do. However a year or two of vegetation might turn
the inner tide. I'll be sending you Groddeck soon; probably infuriate
you. I'm rather worried that you may be more infuriated by what
David Jones tells me [is] a 'nasty slight' on your poems in my bloody
poetry book; so hold your horses until I send it you. (I can never reread
my own books.) The book is dead; and if such a slur occurs I trust you
will forgive me; and it certainly shall be atoned for in any reissue.
Sackcloth and ashes. It chimes however with your story of Lewis's base
ingratitude; I mean that it must be due to the fact that for so many
years I basely imitated you! Boundless the egotism of writers, and bot-
tomless their ingratitude.

About the Yanks; can't you do your shorty for Europe and then
add a lot of muck? For example Alan Thomas has just finished a defin-
itive bibliography which he might let you include (at least 50 pages!).

Or print some specimens of the baddest work I done. Or something which needn't involve you textually; exhibit a and b (see appendix). I can't think of anything else except direct refusal. And obviously it isn't humanly possible to 'treat' me in a grand old man fashion; it is far too premature I agree for the wide angle lens.

The mazet is turned upside down; three huge vans full of cameras and mikes; and seven people in all. We've all been turned into film actors. Blazing lights. They've just come from doing Robert Graves, so I appear to be moving into the grand class at last in UK. But what a *pity* Aldington foiled us. Jones's programme has been very well written up as adult work; and certainly both he and the interviewer Wheldon are intelligent chaps.

Saph has been thrilled of course at all this 'acting' and will see the programme on the 14th of February in London. We won't ourselves however. I'm glad *Clea* didn't seem a 'chute'; just had a grumpy letter from a German physicist saying you can make word-continuum nohow. All right. All right. But he's only reached *Balthazar* as yet. The quartet is now sold in 14 languages, can you beat it? What would a Jap make of *Justine* I wonder?

Must run down and post this; they are back for more filming of the garrigue with me maundering poetically about it.

every good thing
Larry

🌲 *Sury-en-Vaux, Cher, 9 January 1960*

Dear Larry,

I don't know anything in literature which moves me more than the scene of artificial respiration of Clea. (What a bloody fool Balthazar was—needs his arse kicked.) I think you express there an ultimate tenderness for Woman which nobody else has ever reached. Lorenzo used to talk about it, but mainly ended up in punching Frieda's face, pulling her hair and calling her a shit-bag. In my lower middle class way I could never quite rally round that.

Conceited bastards like us naturally can't read their own books.

Now if we had Miller's public school modesty we could re-read with bliss.

I think you'd better ring up Antrobus again over the yank imbroglio. I have written an interim letter to Moore, and will eventually write Sternberg. I want to get free of all obligations as soon as possible. I can't go on working—an article even gives me sleepless nights. The annuity arose out of an offer, first, of a sabbatical year, and then the suggestion came to make it for life. You will find that 50 years of earning a living for self and others are quite enough. There comes a time when one can no more. It happened to Arnold Bennett. Ralph Pinker told me that in the delirium of his last illness Bennett went over and over and over the almost impossible misery of writing even one more *Evening Standard* article. However, I haven't yet got the full official notice, and don't even know what the amount is. If it's a 100 dollars a month I can manage.

> 'Only one more kit inspection,
>   Only one more church parade.
> When this bloody war is over,
>   Oh, how happy I shall be.
> I shall tell the Orderly Sergeant
>   to stick his etc etc.'

Love to all both
Richard

Vernon Sternberg was Director of the Southern Illinois University Press. Ralph Pinker was at one time Aldington's agent.

Sury-en-Vaux, Cher, 15 January 1960

My dear Larry,

Always a delight and a privilege to hear from you. Shit to the *Figaro*. They are not good enough to clean out your stopped-up lavatory pipes. JEL—because you have smashed all their bloody little writers. Another injustice to Oireland. Let Erin remember.

I have my pension—100 dollars a month. If the great and good Kroutchef keeps up his 250 pounds a year—O is K.

'And silence is most noble to the end' . . . Signed: Algernon Charles Swinburne.

You are the bloody lit'ry genius of your time, and nuts to you. Keep out of Westminster Abbey as long as you can.

All love to both and the children,
Richard

ℐ *Sury-en-Vaux, Cher, 27 January 1960*

Dear Larry,

Hope you are both back from your excursh, 'safe and sound in wind and limb'. You had better lie doggo in the mazet until this epidemic of 'flu and Algérie Française is over.

Herewith a letter from USA. Sternberg doesn't realise that you are a European author and becoming a world author. And of course we have never considered Faber—at least I haven't—but rather Rowohlt and your other Continental publishers. I don't think there is a possibility of combining the light-hearted illustrated book you have in mind with the academic yank university study. But as they have priority, the only course is for me to bow out. There will certainly be some swell guy in Illinois who can do the kind of serious study they require, and more and more I feel that one of your younger friends should do the pocketbook. I am getting rather more than less unpopular, and it would be much more useful for you to be boosted by some youngster who is dong le mouvemong—as Ezra used to say. However, I won't definitely break off until I have your permish.

I also want to return Rowohlt his 1000 DM's and get out of doing the DHL book. I spent my Xmas writing a letter and a longer memorandum to Rowohlt on DHL, and he didn't even bother to acknowledge. Moreover, I find from Temple that Pollinger and the Lawrence Estate (i.e. bloody Angie [Ravagli]) are demanding a fee for every quote from DHL or Frieda in a critical-biographical work. I consulted Frere and Moore—and they both side-stepped. So I wrote Rowohlt that I won't go on with the DHL unless he is prepared to indemnify me against any Pollinger claims. He hasn't answered that either.

I was furious with that *Figaro* creature for that article—and in fact started to write him a letter stating that he is a goujat and a tas de merde. However, Catha happened to come down for the week-end, and said that it really is meant to be good-humoured and to advertise you. She amiably pointed out that 'Larry's French isn't all *that* bad', to which I replied: 'You and Claude know that, but do the readers of [. . .] *Le Figaro Littéraire* know it?' I shall write the guy politely but firmly that in my opinion he is grinning and girning like a blue-bottomed Barbary ape on a precarious perch of his own finding and fouling.

Temple says the old Roy's poems (collected) are at last coming out. Too good for the bastards.

Do you remember I sent you a typed copy of an article by Roy, supposedly a review of my *Complete Poems,* but actually a splendid diatribe against MacSpaunday? I sent this at the same time to Mary—and she has not since written a line! Most fortunately, Rob Lyle very generously provided for Mary and the grand-children—otherwise the wife and descendants of the greatest English-language poet since DHL would have starved.

Don't have any worries about *Clea.* There are 'faults' one could pick on—but goddamit the only perfect work of art is a dead work of art, an ersatz, a Henry James novel or a TSEliot 'essay'. [. . .]

Love to both,
Richard

P.S. I don't think it is just to criticise the untersee mishap of *Clea* as 'improbable'. It might happen, and a novelist has a right to all probabilities and possibilities. What puzzles me is the homunculi—marvellously done—you are a bloody genius—but warum? Do you merely want to tell us the old Capo is nuts? Or is there a 'message'—as your friend the Churchwarden of Modern Literature would say?

'Churchwarden' may refer to T. S. Eliot, but more likely to Pursewarden, the writer portrayed in *The Alexandria Quartet* who is given to making mock-portentous pronouncements about literature.

✍ *Engances [ca. 27 January–1 February 1960]*

Dear Richard; Just got back exhausted from London, with raging colds. The snow has melted so it is possible to start tidying up a bit here. I think you are right about the Yank book, and I would be glad to see you shrug it off your shoulders and withdraw, so please do so. There are masses of time anyway for that sort of thing to be done. And now that you are financially free, start with a good long rest of a year or so, and then look around and see if you can't give us a new novel! Rowohlt has been in Switzerland recently where his girl friend broke her leg on an alp, which may account for him being off the air; is there any hurry with the Lawrence text after all? I'm sure he'd pay for quotes ... Anyway I do so heartily rejoice in your miraculous new-found freedom. What a joy. It is of course the dream of every artist, not to be pushed to write, but to wait for it! Only I don't believe as yet in your farewell to eng. lit. See how you feel in a year or two.

Clea comes out the seventh; I expect the white ants will nibble away all the green shoots, but really now I don't care. If only I can go on quietly journalising for *Holiday* I can make a decent living without troubling critics with my foibles. And maybe a new play which is half done. But I must go to Avignon next week for a few days to 'set up' a 'piece' for *Holiday*. The homunculi! I tried to suggest that the new science (the new middle ages) was going to have to revalue the old obsolete ones. Hartmann contends that the modern scientist is a near-mystic, has thrown Aristotle overboard for Heraclitus. Also I bet you have seen Jung's work on alchemy and psychoanalysis in which the search for the Philosopher's stone is studied ... and so on. I'm trying to use these things like crude symbolisms. I may later do a book on Da Capo in Smyrna; we shall see. But I would awfully like to try a big comic book if I could; something like the *Satyricon*!

But I first must write some articles to secure my back door for this year; we have a few months ahead of us now, as the children problem won't arise before July. As for *Figaro* I don't mind being shat on, but I was peeved that [. . .] first of all passed himself off as head of the literary section when he's only a freelance, and next that having devoted a whole day of care and food and driving to him he shouldn't at least have let me see his text in case I might be hurt. I need hardly add that he hasn't sent me a word of thanks for the whole day, lunch to dinner he spent with us; and that he broke his word not to mention Claude in the article. These are trifles, but they annoy one much more than a slap in the belly. The moral of the story however is don't encourage morons.

Henry is heading for Japan where a lovely geisha and a Zen master are waiting for him on the pier (so he believes). In Paris I saw the boys of *Two Cities* and lunched the Fanchettes, who were pale with rage about *Figaro*. Dear Martine cried all night with pure rage! Lucky I'm not Keats. But I shall get harder beatings yet I feel sure, probably in England.

Invitations keep pouring in to lecture and travel. Thank God, at last I am free from *that* sort of thing. After Feb 27, my 48th birthday, I am not reading any more criticisms in any language. I used not to before, but with promoting the *Quartet* from a business point of view I felt I had to. Now it's done, and I shall [take] whatever beating I deserve with blithe heart.

Why do you say you are getting more unpopular? I know one fan who is reading all your contributions to the *Criterion* because you won't supply him with new stuff.

Love

Larry

℘ Nîmes [ca. 10 February 1960]

Dear Richard; Sorry for the delay in answering you but I've been somewhat in Avignon these last days on a blasted reportage. I was very touched by your solicitude in the matter of the silly [. . .], but despite what you said about my duty, I couldn't bring myself to act! Besides your excellent programme would have made him celebrated overnight; and as he's a freelance, not on *Fig*, I wouldn't get him off it. But what does it all matter? *Clea* came out a few days ago and got the most incoherent full page of praise in the *Times Lit*—the middle page, a real rave all through. They've always been good to me but this accolade was quite out of the usual vein; I was startled and delighted of course. Haven't seen the rest of the press yet; believe I've been manhandled in the *Observer* by Toynbee—leader of the jeunesse croulante . . . But fiddle de dee what care I? I expected a thrashing after all the things that indiscreet bastard Pursewarden said. It's an unanswerable indictment of those who perform the functions of literature but are too lazy to try creating! It must have got into Toynbee I suppose; he's one of Britain's Open Wounds, old man. Why, I saw an article in which he gave Goethe a good shaking and warned him that he must be careful not to write things like *Werther* or he'd never get on in Lit. The staggering impertinence slew me; avert the face. The *Observer* gang are using 'Charles Morgan' as a smear agin me. ('I cried all the way to the Bank.') Nothing else much. I really am delighted about your dough, and sorry you won't have the punch to do at least old DHL; anniversaries and things coming up in England, and Penguins announce the unexpurgated *Chatterley;* do you think my lambasting has helped to produce this? I wonder. The books are rolling along merrily; my friends like *Clea* very much, or at least they say they do (The new *Sparkenbroke?*). Well there's lots of justice in the world and I've had a very fine slice of cake taken all round, so no complaints if I get my tail twisted now and again. To be free, pay my way, live here! I really don't ask for much more; and didn't believe it would come true three years ago in Sommières. Now the orders are coming in so fast from USA that I shall have to engage a couple of ghosts to fill them. Lousy lousy weather though, and the work held up on the kinderwing. I have bought four marvellous pure wool tartan shirts to rockbuild on chilly days; marvellous colours, like horse blankets. Must be careful in case Scots visitors trap me dressed in Mactavish.

Claude sends her love and hopes the health is mending; we had an evening in Montpellier with Temples and spoke of you. He has a marvellous coloured movie of us all in Sommières; you are very film actor, and watching it I doubly regretted the television fault. You'd have been a wow. All our literary giants look like moulting owls or diseased fish.

every good thing
Larry

Sparkenbroke was a best-selling novel (1936) by Charles Morgan.

❀ *Sury, 16 February 1960*

My dear Larry,

I often wonder why the F.O. call so many of their little blunders 'TOP secret'. Is it because their bottoms ceased to be a secret long before they got to Eton? [. . .]

Did you have much difficulty getting a French driving licence? I have had a British and International for 30 years, renewing annually. Now the land of the free refuses to renew the International—so I have to take a driving test, if you please.

I sent you a card yesterday about the BBC. They wanted me to authorise casting of a poem called 'After Two Years', which I wrote at 20 to show extempore how easy it is to fake ye olde Englysshe lyric. Like a fool I carried the joke too far by putting the poem in a book—since when it has been my Innisfree. The abandoned ruffian in London wanted it for a 'series of religious features' entitled 'Man meets God'. I wrote 'REFUSED'on the contracts and sent them back to my agent.

Love,
Richard

P.S. Grove Press (which fought the *Lady C.* case) are publishing as their big noise in April a novel by H.D. called *Bid Me to Live*. It has a lot of amusing stuff about DHL and Frieda in 1917 when they took refuge in H.D.'s apartment in Bloomsbury. I ignorantly upset the arrangement by inconsiderately coming home on leave—blasted nuisance those damn tommies. It is of course not a conventional novel—but written in her beautiful English. I hawked that script round the clever London publishers, who rejected it with various insults. They'll now have to pay the yanks five times as much.

Did you happen to see that article of Philippe Barrès about the French maternity clinics? They induce or delay births, not for the sake of agonising women, but to suit the convenience of the staff, which doesn't want to work at night or over the week-end. What an epoch of shits we've lived in to.

I wish you and Claude would let me take you both to see H.D. some time. She is 73, but still a noble-looking woman and bright as sunlight. She has to go around on two supports like ski supporters— the angel on two sticks.

♫ *[Engances, 18 February 1960]*

Dear Richard

Of course you must come and have lunch with your friends—I won't hear of you paddling round the region and not coming in for a pipe of mead. And I'm glad about DHL for his own sake and R's and mine. Glad you have shed the other chore too; there really isn't any hurry.

> every good thing
> Larry

⟡ *Sury, 1 March 1960*

Dear Larry,

I enclose with this part of a letter from Michael Harald (which return at leisure) describing an ITV about Roy. [. . .]

By the same mail I got a letter from the prof in question—one Gardner—who wants to get what he can out of me for his book.

Temple has done a very creditable book on DHL [*D. H. Lawrence: L'Oeuvre et la vie*]—the first book on him in French which shows any real knowledge of DHL's books and of the more important books about him. I have managed to churn out a preface for him, and posted it to Seghers yesterday. Now, my only rock of Sisyphus is the little book for Rowohlt, which is en route. Then, I hope, no more.

Under separate cover I send you proof of the reply to K.A. Porter's attack on DHL in *Encounter*. A poor thing, but mine own.

I have been doing some sums about these Russian editions. From the colophons I find that they issued 20,000 copies at 10.50 roubles of *Hero* in English, for which they sent me 362,000 ancient and fish-like francs. That works out at about frcs 1.80 per gross rouble. *All Men* has just been done in an edition of 225,000 at 14.40 roubles; so by the same reasoning the Russ public shell out 3,240,000 roubles; which at frcs 1.80 to the rouble should give me ancient and fish-like frcs 5,830,000. What hopes. Mr. K. is recklessly throwing away milliards of roubles on worthless wogs in the Orient, leaving himself not enough to pay his small but interesting debt to me. A letter from one Hanna Tshekoldina announces for sure a Collected Short Stories [*Farewell to Memories*], whereof she is the translator.

That hateful article of [. . .] still rankles with me. Is it not a sign of European depravity that the vilest insults are levelled at the greatest writers—DHL, Roy, yourself? [. . .]

I suppose I'm wrong and your other friends and publishers right, but I wish we might hope for another glimpse or two of the great Antrobus.

By the way, did Claude know, that until the Mollet govt. the lads at the Institut de Sciences Politiques had to wear bowlers? Even now Catha says that the débraillé of St Germain is not tolerated in either boys or girls. The profs seem to be pedants and doctrinaires of the purest ray serene. All Cath's essays come back marked: 'Style déplorablement littéraire, et je dirais mieux, affectif.'

Love to both, and praise old Temple for his DHL booklet for me.

Richard

P.S. Moore has gone to Texas to lecture on DHL. But if you haven't heard from the Uni of S. Illinois, tell me, and I'll prod.

Did you see that le G. has now forbidden the use of goads? How the hell does he think anyone gets oxen to plough and pack-donkeys to run? Essential to stick pins in their arses.

§ *Sury-en-Vaux, Cher, 7 March 1960*

My dear Larry,

[. . .] H.D. was so much upset by the under-water scene in *Clea* that she had to put the book aside. I was afraid something of the kind might happen, but she was always desperately over-sensitive. Did I tell you she has now got the American Association of Arts quinquennial award of a gold gong and 1000 smackers? This morning I got from the Grove Press a pull of the wrapper for her novel *Bid Me to Live*, which they whoop up strenuously in a long and not too loathsome blurb. It will be a success, as she is being groomed as the G.O.M. of yankee letters. What a bloody racket.

Temple's effort on DHL is really very good—takes away some of the reproach of French dumbness about him. What you say is perfectly just—the translations take all the rainbow out of his style, and they are serenely incapable of registering his life-struggle, which they would interpret as a 'strug-for-lif'. I remember laughing aloud when I was first reading Proust and M. de Charlus calls someone 'un strug-for-lifer'.

By all means send the *Encounter* article to Miller. I should be happy for him to have it. Bloody Henrietta James. I'd much rather have Artemus Ward with his 'snaix' and looking down on 'a C of Fiz-zogs'. Crude, yes, but not phoney, like that old sissy. Do you remember in that rotten book of his about the Midi, James says he viewed Carcassonne from a cab (which you can't do) and he has nothing to say about Arles except that the cobbles in the street hurt his pore old feet? Why go anywhere but Boston Common, Mayfair, and the Faubourg St Germain? Of course he went to Venice for his buggers. Just the sort of guy the Establishment would make into a literary saint.

Haley sent me a note to say that Frank Flint died, and was incinerated at Oxford on the 2nd. The ten little nigger boys of the first Imagist anthol are now reduced to three—H.D., Ez and me. A letter from Ez, who is in Rome (It'ly). He writes about Flint, but some bastard has evidently showed him my lecture on Ezra Pound & T.S. Eliot, and he is Patriarchially reproachful. Don't like that—would rather he had cussed some.

Damn Geneva. Why don't you say it's a shit-house—in parliamentary language of course. The only part to like is the lake and the distant mountains and that sluice with such a blue Rhône running out of the lake—too good for them. [. . .]

. Love to both,
Richard

[P.S.] How are the children?

At this time Durrell was writing on Geneva for *Holiday* magazine.

✍ *Sury-en-Vaux, Cher, 3 April 1960*

Dear Larry,

Too late I perceived we had gate-crashed. I hope Claude will eventually forgive.

The Duttons were charmed.

Back here I found a letter from Rowohlt, already fretting for the DHL pamphlet. I have sent him a final revised version of the first 3 chapters, and have done another in the last 36 hrs, since the Dutts left. I'll get the rest done as soon as I return from Suisse—and then, I devoutly hope, not another word for publication until apt incineration's artful aid removes me from the possibility.

It was wonderful to see you again, and to hear the Scobie's songbook stuff. You are a bloody genius.

Raining up here, and I start tomorrow to bring Catha back from Zürich (Switzerland) after her dreary interview with the 'orientation specialist'.

Love to both
Richard

[P.S.] No need really for me to repeat that you are the ONLY writer of your time, true successor of DHL and Roy.

Ninette and Geoffrey Dutton were visiting from Australia.

Ᵹ *[Engances, 2 May 1960]*

richard; excuse fatuous p.c. we are heading north to catapult the kids back to u.k. you didn't need to talk intrusions about such a splendid evening; Claude had more professional designs on your stomach—something simmered for nine days over a slow fire. That [was] all she regretted! Nice letter from Dutton with a vol of good poetry. And then Cath suddenly appeared smoking a pipe like the infant Rimbaud, full of wise oaths and curious instances. A nice anecdote about a Yank juvenile delinquent who was as a last resort turned over to the Catholic fathers. After his first day of school he came back very chastened and thoughtful. Asked how he got on he replied: 'They ain't kiddin' those guys; first room they put me in there was a dead guy nailed to the wall.'

much love from us both
Larry

[P.S.] have you seen the new *Encounter*—a blistering attack on my critics by Hilary Corke! V. amusing. Also a mew for you for your Lawrence piece.

Larry

The 'Lawrence piece' is Aldington's 'A Wreath for Lawrence?' It had appeared in the April 1960 *Encounter* as a reply to Katherine Anne Porter's 'A Wreath for the Gamekeeper' in the February 1960 issue of the same journal commemorating the thirtieth anniversary of D. H. Lawrence's death.

Sury-en-Vaux, Cher, 8 May 1960

Dear Larry,

Just getting to the end of the book on DHL, and killing Lorenzo over again, quoted 'Bavarian Gentians', which is so beautiful and still so moving, I can't go on with my pedestrian tripe. But I'll be able to finish and post it to Hamburg this week.

Rowohlt sent a longish letter before Easter, to which I replied, enclosing the first chapters of the DHL. Long silence, and then a firm's letter in hun, acknowledging receipt, and stating that a contract would be sent for a taschenbuch of *Hero*. The contract arrived, and was instantly buzzed back unsigned. These modest patrons of literature merely asked for 50% of all rights in all languages and in all dramatisations, TV, radio and film. Impudence. They included an option clause on same terms for *Casanova*, which incidentally has been made a play in Czech.

I may add that contracts for *Hero* exist in USA, England, Italy, France, Germany, Sweden, Norway, Denmark, Spain, Portugal, Argentina, Poland, Czechoslovakia, Slovenia and Hungary. At this moment it is being re-issued in Russia, Poland and Czechoslovakia.

The yanks refuse to reprint it, really because it is a furious plea for peace, ostensibly because it was published 'in the 1920s and lacks the realism and brutal detail now demanded of war books in America'. To which I urbanely answered that 20,000 copies in English had just been issued in USSR and a very large edition in Russian was planned. 'But of course the heroic defenders of Long Island and the Bronx are far better judges of war realism than the fat-arsed commuters of Leningrad and Stalingrad.'

My dear boy, we are surrounded with shits, and nobody except me does anything about it.

Hope you see Catha while in Paris (France). She is in a dreadful

flap about her Sciences Po. exams, and trying to persuade the vener-
able moron her dad to let her cut them and go on holiday instead. Pah.

I suppose you looked at TV. I had only a newspaper, but I thought
Viscount Mellors looked quite genteel in his gas-light duds. The Court
upholsterers and camera made her look really pretty. I wonder if she
was still that rara avis, a virgo intacta? Sir Richard Burton reports that
his lady friends told him the operation is exactly like having a tooth
pulled. My goodness, man, you ought to have had that in your quartet,
except for the improbability of any virgin over the age of five in Alex.
You will remember Rabelais.

Love to you both,
Richard

𝔰 *[Engances?, after 28 May 1960]*

Dear Richard

Just back from a scenario session in Paris at hideous expense—
luckily not mine but 20th Century-Fox.

Was hoping you and Catha might sneak down for the gypsies on
the 28th—kept an eye out. We are going to London for a fortnight,
again worked by the filmers on a lucrative bit of odd-jobbing. An ideal
way of resting for me, playing with a new form.

Then: an avalanche of children of all ages and shapes.

Are you well?

Love from us both
Larry
& C

[P.S.] *Time* calls me bronzed and chunky! Better than 'fat and pasty',
no?

> Both scenario sessions involved work on *Cleopatra* under the direction of
> Rouben Mamoulian. Although Durrell produced several hundred pages
> of script, apparently little or none of his work was used for the film, and
> his name does not appear in the credits. Direction of the film was even-
> tually taken over by Joseph L. Mankiewicz, who also wrote much of the
> final script.
>
> Large numbers of gypsies come every May to worship at the Church of
> the Two Marys at Saintes Maries de la Mer.

🙂 *Nîmes [before 9 July 1960]*

Ah Richard—thrice wicked man. We had decided to take this long week end off and booked a room at the Saintes where we go today Thursday. But why for godsake didn't you at least beat on the door on your way north and demand the ever-ready stirrup-cup? We were sure you would and were delighted at the thought! What a shame!

We did a gruelling 14 days in London working on a Hollywood movie-script at a good price and living in a posh hotel on smoked salmon. How nice it is to be back but . . . *of course* the bloody mason has run the well dry and now I have to carry water round Nîmes in tin cans. And the children when they come will have to wash in the rivers. Damn! I am now coming to the end of my literary chores and hope to have a month off. Ouf! I'm tired. Henry floated briefly through on his way to Italy.

No other news. Weather nasty and muggy but no damn rain. It simply will not rain and fill the well.

Every good thing from us both,
Larry

🙂 *Sury-en-Vaux, Cher, 9 July 1960*

Dear Larry,

We had intended to come over to see you both on the 5th, but Catha's friends had arranged to leave for Pamplona at 3 a.m. on the 6th; and I consequently had given up my room at the same date and left at 6 a.m. We were both tired with running around, and felt that it would be too much with each of us facing a run of 700 kilos. But it was a shame to miss you.

The Saintes are pretty well wrecked, with all this building and the rather odious types of city parvenus who have 'villas' just built and more paper-money than they know how to spend. Catha introduced me to a youth of 17, who averages 500,000 anciens francs per *month* selling some product I've forgotten. I shan't go back there. Catha gets away with it, because she is accepted as one of themselves by the natives, and spends her time out by the Vaccarés and so on.

Saw a splendid specimen of the Herrenvolk at the Brise. He marched up to the bar, vociferating: Wein, wein! They took a look at him, and offered him beer, which he rejected. At last after much shouting and waving he got a large tumbler filled to the brim with red wine. He then shouted: Cognac, Cognac! and eventually got a large verre de dégustation also filled to the brim. He drank off half the wine in gulps, then tossed down the brandy in one gulp, topped off with the rest of the wine, paid, and cleared out. Obviously he had a mission from God to teach the French civilised methods of drinking.

I have been musing over a possible parody, to be called Sex and Sex-ability by Jane Miller. But perhaps better not.

What a bind about the water, but it is always the trouble out on the causses, and indeed in other remote places. They tell the tale that pre-1940 Rebecca West bought land and built a house in a lovely situation some five miles from St Tropez, only to discover that there is no water at all there.

[. . .] Meanwhile, a London thing called *Today* offers me 100 guineas to do some preliminary debunking [of the David Lean film *Lawrence of Arabia*]. Perhaps I will. Curious how the F.O. and the Col. Of. hung on to their hero, but the anti-Curzonites were all fanatically pro-Arab, knowing nothing much at first hand about the mid-East. It is said that in his pro-Egyptian days Anthony Eden learned the Arabic of all the four-letter words. [. . .] Much of the pro-Arab policy was simply anti-French, as it was with TEL, who announces as his objective to get hold of Damascus and 'biff the French out of all hope of Syria'. [. . .]

The Midi struck me as noisy and expensive, compared with the tranquillity and comparative cheapness of this area.

Thanks to you, it worked out all right with Rowohlt, who sent a second 1000 DM to complete the DHL deal, and 1,250 on account of *Hero.* He was surprised and, I think, pleased, to have the taschenbuch script as soon as he asked for it. Malapropos, Mondadori has made a terrific effort to honour DHL by this Opera Omnia he is doing. The latest is 2 vols of DHL's poems, English with Italian translation en regard, far more complete than any English edition, competently edited, and produced in a style which no Anglo-Saxon publisher could rival.

Do you know one Derek Monsey? Golly (Gollancz to you) has sent me proofs of a novel, *The Hero,* which looks damn good.

Love to both,
Richard

♫ *Nimes [9 August 1960]*

Dear Richard

As you rightly surmised the children are down here in force which means every sort of pandemonium including jazz which they thoughtfully brought with them, and also jam on my typewriter. It is nice but . . . I'm losing weight. From cher maître to chair maigre. Congratulations on your excellent and very just review in the USA. I've passed it along to Cath at the Saintes. We hope to be seeing something of her, as we aim to bathe there frequently; in fact we are dickering with a doctor over a one-room flat to use as a camp site twice or thrice a week. Needless to say there is no thought of work; but having got through with this *Cleopatra* script I have secured our back door for this year and can draw breath. It was an interesting experience and I learned lots of stage wrinkles from Mamoulian in the process; of course the script is prime corn but as supercolossal what could be expected? I obediently put myself into the skin of Rafael Sabatini and thought up one extravagance after another. Great fun really, and not hard work writing for screen. Why not try some story-synopses . . . 800 words or so? You could get 10,000 dollars if you landed one. Don't do 'treatments', but just a synopsis. Ouf I'm tired though; need a month or so off when the children do go home. Then . . . I don't know; a comic novel? Much love to you; are you coming down this summer?

every good thing
Larry

♫ *Sury-en-Vaux, Cher, 10 August 1960*

Dear Larry,

Someone—a fan of yours—has just lent me the *Yale Review* for Summer 1960. Have you seen it? It has two highbrow articles on you, supposedly pro and con; though the praise seems to me as offensive as the blame. What ghastly parasites these 'critics' are—the poet's lice. I can lend *Yale* if you haven't had it. Makes me *sick*.

Thanks for sending on the *N.Y. Times* to Catha. This morning I have received an excellent article on Rattigan's *Ross* by Michael Harald, which leans heavily on my book, and once more demolishes the

Establishment myth. A pity it had to appear in Mosley's paper. I am offered 100 guineas to do a 3000-word article on the pseudo-Prince of Mecca for *Today*. But the editor is so ignorant he mixes up DHL with TEL, and I wonder if a rag like that is worth using. The moment my article appeared Diddle Fart would rush round with his two letters from Sir Water Closet on Downing St paper; Astor would ring up the boss of Odham's; and I should be betrayed by the free, liberal and enlightened British press as I was in 1955. Better hold off.

You say nothing about your water problem. Has it been solved? If not, what a bind for you all.

My young niece, who is a fan of yours, says you were on (obviously recorded) TV on the 7th—'What an attractive man he looks.' Sort of young Leonardo da Vinci, eh?

Have you read Fred Hoyle (astronomy prof at Cantab) on *Frontiers of Astronomy*? He links up sub-atomic physics, chemistry and long-range astronomy in a fascinating way—a little too matey in being 'popular' but with real knowledge. Some of his extrapolations—such as the continuous creation of matter from nothing—seem pretty hazardous, but he is a bright lad. The method of taking the temperature of the ocean 200 millions of years ago is ingenious—if reliable. They analyse the isotopes of carbon in fossil sea-shells, and infer that the average temperature was then $10\,°$ C. higher. If you haven't read the book it would give you ideas, I think, and perhaps compensate for the misery of too much jazz. [. . .]

How is that Claude? Is she able to keep her head above kinder and kitchen and get on with her writing?

Love to you both,
Richard

P.S. Please return the enclosed. Notice the genuine amazement with which this journalist finds I am read in USSR. It is percolating. Yesterday I gave a letter of introduction to a prominent Unescow who is to visit Moscow, so that he can meet *my* friends in the Union of Writers and Academy of Sciences. What next?

✿ *The Saintes [ca. 10–20 August 1960]*

Dear Richard:

Apropos *Ross,* while I was in London Mamoulian went to see it. He says that it makes very clear that TEL was forcibly buggered by the Turkish pacha, and Alec Guinness actually staggers across the stage holding his bottom and groaning—which deeply disgusted and shocked M. who is very pi indeed. He said he had never seen such a thing on the stage and was deeply outraged! This only to point out that the main point of your thesis appears to have been accepted and presumably the movie based on the play will have the same admission?

I need only add in passing that when De Mandeville fought his duel with Gool the British Council man it was because Gool said that Shakespear had been referring to him (De Mandeville) when he coined the phrase 'more honoured in the breech than the observance'. But you will have to wait for vol. 3 (*Sauve Qui Peut*) for further details.

Rain! Nothing but Rain!

Love
Larry

✿ *Sury-en-Vaux, Cher, 12 August 1960*

Dear Larry,

Yesterday I had for lunch Prof Moore of Southern Illinois. He didn't ask me to sound you, but he mentioned without asking me not to tell you, that the University Press think of publishing a collection of the many studies of your work which have appeared, including mine in 2 Ciddies. I suppose it's all crap really. An artist is an artist, and what the jackals yelp round the real lion is neither here nor there. I told Moore I saw no reason why you should object.

Moore has been recently to New Mexico, and has some Angie-Frieda-Brett stories. Everybody knew that Brett on her eyrie kept binoculars to see who visited Frieda down in the valley of El Prado. Moore mentioned this in his book [*The Intelligent Heart*], but she is offended, and refuses to see him. Also, she has made a will bequeathing her land to a doctor to build a hospital which must be called The San

Lorenzo Hospital. Angie has sold all the DHL MSS and pictures. He sold the pictures to a restaurant-keeper in Taos, a German baron who is called 'Frenchy' because he ain't American. This very astute Boche gave 4000 bucks for ten or a dozen, then showed them in his restaurant, and is selling them off at 4000 each. The artist himself never got a cent, and to my certain knowledge DHL and Frieda very nearly starved under the persecution of the military, the journalists and Jix. God, I feel sour and bitter against England. Shits.

I do hope your daughters will see something of Catha—she knows too little of English-speaking girls, though she is always quite lyrical about the beauty and charm of your Sapphie. [. . .]

What COLOSSAL crooks and imbeciles the yanks are. After those friendly talks between Ike and K, the pentagon wilfully continues the spy-plane, and thereby intentionally plays into the hands of Malinowski and the Russian army, who are furious because K. has cut them down by over a million men. Have they no sense those bloody Americans? Or are they so conceited that they think they can rule over a world blasted to eternal sterility by nuclear-fission bombs? It was an evil day when 'Western Economy' was based on the armaments 'industry'.

You are not nearly bitter enough. I am going to try to say, expanded, what is the truth set down above. And nuts to the F.O. [. . .]

Love to both, and Gott strafe England
Richard

[P.S.] Moore agrees with me that you are the only one who matters.

Harry T. Moore edited a volume of critical essays, *The World of Lawrence Durrell* (1962), for the Southern Illinois University Press.

Lawrence's paintings were purchased by Baron Hutton in Taos, who operated La Doña Luz restaurant, and later by Saki Karavas, proprietor of La Fonda Hotel.

Sir William Joynson-Hicks, known as Jix, as Home Secretary in 1928 and 1929 was responsible for confiscating copies of *Lady Chatterley's Lover* from Lawrence's agents and friends, and for the seizure of two copies of the *Pansies* manuscript in the mails. It was Sir William's successor, John R. Clynes, who was in office when thirteen of Lawrence's paintings were confiscated on 5 July 1929.

❡ Nîmes [ca. 12–16 August 1960]

Dear Richard;

Just dropped in to collect my mail after a hectic night of storm and drang at the Saintes; children soaked but exultant like the blasted nordics they are. Wet footmarks and a lot of insulting un-fan mail from hairy Christians who saw me on TV and objected to my notion that Jesus (possibly) had a sense of humour and is being read rather heavier than he meant . . . I have to laugh. No, my dear Richard don't send the *Yale Review*; it will appear in the course of nature. But a real pro and con on the quartet is rather handsome however withering, no? They are the Leavis gang of the USA—or have I got them wrong? Whatever . . . I don't know whether you understand (ahem ex press attaché talking) that the ratio of interest in anyone on the basis of press is purely one of inch-space. A wise Grub Street writer once said to me: 'What they write is unimportant provided they write at length; the bad is merely "controversial" and the "good" merely stimulating. The ideal press for a writer is a really mixed press, hovering between the downright vicious and the adulatory.' I thought he was joking until I saw it in the course of my work. When the fledgling governor of [. . .] came to me one day almost in tears with his press cuttings in his hand I was able to reassure him by saying: 'Sir, today you have made the headlines. That is the important thing. You will go from strength to strength after this latest blunder. Why, the *Daily Mail* is calling for your resignation. It will not be twenty-four hours before its rivals build you into a Strong Man of Strong Convictions affronting a lousy policy.' So it fell out and now the poor man is running [. . .] very badly to judge by the press. It is not sufficiently bad as yet to get him a portfolio of real importance in the CO back home. But that will come if he will only stick to his errors hard enough. Do you see what I mean?

I'm amused about the Russians . . . I expect that after the thaw the anti-régime people are delighted with your forthrightness! Now official policy is changing and we anti-coms are going to be pleaded with to be nicer.

Hoyle is good; the post-Einsteinian line is really poetical in its way; the new middle ages. More anon about this.

I enclose an accolade from Bouvier which delighted me; too much about treachery but a good wise and tender piece. They don't know what we have to contend with back home do they, though? Avanti. What are you writing, you lazy dog? We are off at dawn for three more days of Saintes; will try and contact Cath.

every good thing,
Larry

🕭 *Sury-en-Vaux, Cher, 16 August 1960*

My dear Larry,

My cool and unbiased opinion is that the *Yale* people on you are miserable shits who should be relegated to Satan's arse, as detailed by Dante towards the end of the *Inferno*. My dear boy, they are madly jealous because the one undoubted English-writing genius of the last decade is not American.

Yeah, I've heard Tom Eliot discourse on that square-inch theory, and I don't go for it. Of course, I agree that a genuine pro and con fight is by far the best for a writer. But my own experience is that when there is a conspiracy of enemies, backed by the Establishment and the newspaper owners, a continued campaign of abuse and calumny can and does do harm, especially when followed by a boycott. Luckily, lit'ry England is not so important as it thinks, nor lit'ry yankerie neither. Yesterday, I noted down the works of mine published this year and definitely engaged by contract for the future; and find I have just published or shall publish books (new, reprints, foreign translations) in Chicago, Carbondale Illinois, New York, London, Paris, Hamburg (thanks to you), Moscow, Warsaw, Prague, Milan, Sofia, and Tokyo. Mostly lesser breeds outside the glorious victorious subtopian state, but I begin to think that after all they have not altogether succeeded in obliterating me. The Russians have a programme sketched out until the winter of 1962—so why shouldn't I rally round the people who stand by me? Let England stew in its own Jews.

I came across a reference by Norman Douglas to homunculi—he says homunculi in bottles were still sold on the streets in Germany when he was a boy. Why? You would have been amused—a fan of yours called and was disappointed with *Clea,* particularly the homunculi—and my ingenious and mendacious defence would have made you roar with laughter.

My objection to Jesus and the other rhinos has always been that there isn't a laugh in the whole bloody bibble from Gen I to Rev last. I get to dislike Jesus more and more. He was such an ignorant and conceited fellow, imagining the world was to 'come to an end' for his honour and glory—whereas the good Hoyle gives us 5,000,000,000 years. He thinks birds live in nests, and grouses that he hasn't been 'appreciated'. He thinks plants don't toil, when everyone knows that the leaves and roots are incessantly at work, and any relaxation means death. His economics are those of a silly working man—if everyone sells all he has to give to the poor, where are the purchasers? The 'beatitudes' make me spit—blessed are the chumps etc, etc. Also, he was obviously a bugger—they all are, these saviours of humanity. The disciple on whose bosom Jesus did lean. Do you lean on the bosom of your disciple—I bet you'd get a stinker from Claude if you did. Tell me not of Jesus. Let us re-read Athenaeus and Aristophanes together, and merde to the Xtians and los yanquis e tutti quanti.

Now there is 'peace' in Cyprus, can't you sell your villa? Poor Dizzy, he didn't foresee this last capitulation.

Gott strafe England.

Love to you both and the niñas,
Richard

[P.S.] Don't take any scientists too seriously, they're all frauds.

🎵 *Nîmes [after 17 August 1960]*

Dear Richard;

I don't mind, if Moore wants to. What does it matter? It's very flattering that people might like to read around the bloody old quartet. Incidentally there have been some tremendous essays in French; *Critique* did a forty-page study of it which was cockle warming, and last week Bouvier also. I have a socking great shelf of stuff. But much more interesting than all this are some of the letters I'm getting from young writers who have been deblocked by the quartet. Deblocked from 'serialism'—the Charing Cross Road Proustian stuff. I think here I am having some effect. Young French writers moreover, who are sick of Butor and the atomic school of monochrome work . . . It is funny. I also now have two letters from young physicists telling me that in fact my notion of continuum has been fairly faithfully carried out. One presents me the quartet (the form of) in mathematical diagrams! You can imagine how I laughed. Of course while mathematically it is nonsense to invoke Einstein, philosophically I have unspooled some of his notions and suggested that fundamentally (more important than The Bomb) the questions raised bear directly on our notion of human personality—I think I'm teleologically watertight! Apart from that, what does it matter? Of course there are weak spots and lousy Rider Haggardish writing (some deliberately) and indeed all the faults in the world; but the faults are always inherent in the mere act of trying to create. You have to throw the paint about in quite a desperate way; the proportion of luck to conscious design is always difficult to estimate . . . As for the criticism . . . well, it doesn't matter either; it's nice to be praised and wounding to be cursed. But neither author nor critic can predict where the work will stand in ten years' time. (Stephen Phillips or Stendhal?) The work has its own destiny. And I don't ever forget the marvellous dictum of Wordsworth. 'Each work of art creates the public by which it is to be judged.'

Back off to the Saintes; what a lousy summer we've had—genre Kensington; yet the children think it's wonderful. They may be right. I know I'm over indulgent . . . but since the gods have given me three times what I asked for (a small living and the freedom to write) I feel I should be. I don't want to stir up contention; I want to excite understanding, to kindle. Sometimes this is best done by sitting on one's huge battery of complexes and private tensions. Sometimes the other way is better. It's all according . . .

every good thing;
Larry

[P.S.] Do you know Suttie's *Origins of Love and Hate*? Just been reissued in Penguins.

⚱ *Sury-en-Vaux, Cher, 20 August 1960*

Dear Larry,

You will doubtless have seen that the smut-hounds have already launched their prosecution of the Penguin unexpurgated *Lady C.,* although publication date is not until the 25th. Clearly, an information has been lodged either by a bookseller or someone connected with a periodical—who obviously have advance copies. The sudden prosecution is to surprise Penguin before they can get their guns into position and rally supporters, and also to prevent any copies of the book getting into the hands of the public. If Lane fights it will mean an Old Bailey trial for him, much as poor old Frere had to suffer over that silly bugger book he published (without having read) on the recommendation of one of the office sods.

What is the origin of this intense and prolonged persecution of DHL, when other writers get by unscathed? First, of course, being only a bloody working-man he had the incomparable impudence to possess genius instead of having attended Eton and Magdalen. Then he ran away with a prof's wife, instead of buggering camel-boys in the sands of Arabia Felix. Garnett (D.) whose pop, E. Garnett, was long a friend of DHL, says that would have been forgiven, but Ford Hueffer made an adverse report in 1915 on the loyalty of DHL and Frieda, either to the W.O. or the F.O.—I should think F.O., as Ford was hired by them to traduce his native land (Germany) at 50 quid a book. Ford is such a liar that I discounted the boast in his memoirs that he had been sent to report officially on the Lawrences, and that they were so anti-English he (Fordie) had to hide in a barn because he could not endure these insults to the King's uniform he was wearing. However, Harry Moore has proved that Ford was not commissioned until a fortnight after the date he gives for this interview. I suppose this can never be cleared up.

In this Penguin case my own view is that it was insanity to risk the publication in a bourgeois-philistine country such as England, where the Courts always take up the position that they know and care nothing about Art but do know Dirt intimately—obviously true. I am sure any piffling stipendiary magistrate will wave aside with lofty Imperial contempt the admirable decisions of Federal Judge Bryan and of the Supreme Court upholding him. Penguin don't realise that the majority in the US today are not descendants of puritans but of European immigrants, 30 million of them Germans, and a prodigious number of rhinos (man). In the West of America the paintings in the saloons would hardly be allowed in a Paris brothel, supposing brothels were still allowed in Paris. You know what the yank magazines for women are like. Until I read them I never realised how much American women enjoy the idea of other women being raped; with lurid illustrations. But Boston, Providence etc are just as puritan as ever, and I expect they manage to obstruct the local circulation of *Lady C.*

I am sending *Yale Review* by separate post. I suppose this creature Green is a specimen of the 'new Brit intellectual' Geoff Dutton told me he found at Leeds university. They study 'a field' so they can get an academic job, think as the BBC and gutter press tell them, and following the yank line denounce the decadence of such expatriates as ourselves, not to mention our obscure fore-runners, Gibbon, Byron, Shelley, Landor, Browning, etc. Why you are called 'British' with inverted commas escapes me, unless it is to stress your wickedness at having fled from the Hellfare State.

Did you see that in London a man was fined 2 quid for looking at the legs of women in the underground? I suppose if he had been caught leering at the bottoms of boy scouts they'd have given him 5 shillings from the poor box.

No, Larry, my main point against the bogus Prince of Mecca is not that he was so obviously an impudent sod, but that he was an impudent mythomaniac whose lies about himself and his alleged deeds were put into a film-lecture by a slick yank advertiser and taken up enthusiastically by HMG in 1919 because it distracted attention from the fearful slaughter on the Western front, the failure of the invincible British Armada, and similar uncomfortable truths. Only a propagandist could doubt his pederasty. What I want to see is the removal of his bust from St Paul's where it insults the tombs of Nelson and Wellington.

Do you really mean we are to have a third vol of good old Antrobus? That is the best news since Lumbumbum kicked Mr H's arse. It makes me very cross when people say they have 'to excuse' you for those admirable sketches—about the best F.O. skits ever written. I have now got the reply: Ah yes, that reminds me of 1912, when the London pundits said they had 'to excuse' DHL his poems because of his prose. That is a fact—you'll find it somewhere in his Letters. Personally, I wish the Antrobi and the Quatuor would go on and on like the *Arabian Nights.*

Did I send you my limerick on the Prince of Mecca and the Bey of Deraa?

> There was an old Bey of Deraa
> Who said to his sergeant: 'Ha-haa
> Just bring that bhoy
> Wid the gleam in his oi,
> I think I might—thankee—ta-taa.'

Ever
Richard

[P.S.] I re-open to say that when Moore next mentions the book of essays on you, I'll say I think you approve, and tell him to write to you. This would be widely reviewed, I think. Keep all your scripts, letters etc. American universities are beginning to bid for mine. Yours will be a nice mare's-nest-egg for the beautiful Sapphie and her sister. Claude will disdain such trash.

According to *The Trial of Lady Chatterley,* C. H. Rolph's account of *Regina* v. *Penguin Books Ltd.,* the initiative in the case was taken by the Director of Public Prosecutions under the new Obscene Publications Act, 1959. This for the first time required that a book should be 'taken as a whole' and allowed the defence of 'public good . . . in the interests of science, literature, art or learning'. Many distinguished witnesses testified, and in a historic decision the publisher was acquitted. Sir Allen Lane, founder and chairman of Penguin, was in court, although not physically in the dock.

The 'silly bugger book' (*The Image and the Search* by Walter Baxter), published by Heinemann (of which A. S. Frere was then chairman), was one of a number of novels made the subject of prosecutions during 1954 under the old Common Law about 'obscene libel'. After two juries had failed to agree on a verdict, the Heinemann firm was acquitted by order of the judge.

🎕 *[Engances, Summer 1960?]*

Dear R.

Just dropped into the mazet to answer mail and then beat it. Amusing this bunch—good piece by the Fascist man—I must say you seem to have got both wings on the run—le rouge et le noir!

> Much love.
> Will write from the Saintes.
> Larry

🎕 *Saintes Maries [after 20 August 1960]*

Dear Richard,

We are down here for a flat week so that the children can really get to grips with the sea. Confidentially Penguins have written me to ask whether, in the event of *Chatterley* taking a serious turn, I'd be prepared to testify to its qualities. You betcha! I've told them I'd take the first plane over to lend DHL any support I could. I also am being televised by the Canadians (USA hook-up) on the 30th of this month and I'll try and 'plant' something square in the middle of the interview. In the BBC film (the time when you defaulted) I managed to plant an attack on the 'unsportsmanlike' attitude to *Chatterley* and the hypocrisy of the DHL celebration going on while this book was banned! How much better we could have done in a cross talk (me interviewing you on the subject) which was what Jones wanted!

> Every good thing
> Larry

[P.S.] *Yale Review*!! I awfully liked the subdued note of discomforture and the 'grave doubts' about whether I'm a charlatan or not! However inch-space will win—provoking Answer to an Answer to a Tract!

🎕 *Sury-en-Vaux, Cher, 15 September 1960*

Dear Larry,

The enclosed came in a day or two ago from my Hollywood agent. In reply I said that I had intended to retire and to undertake nothing more than articles, introductions and such small deer; but that IF he could secure such terms I might be tempted; BUT that I don't feel I can undertake such a big job, demanding among other things a sense of popular response today, without the aid, advice and collaboration of a younger and more gifted author. The only person who fits the bill is Lawrence Durrell, and if he agrees and a reputable studio and publisher are found I am, as the stylists say, 'agreeable'.

This guy, Al [Manuel], is really [a] serious agent. I know that all sorts of mirific proposals and figures emerge from Beverly Hills, but Al got me several studio jobs at 750 bucks a week which kept us alive during the late finest hour of Sir Water Closet. We had bad luck over that *Casanova*. Al got me 10,000 bucks for a studio option, and the book sold 30,000. But at the crucial moment the producer fell sick, and was fired. His successor refused to touch any of his projects, and the other studios wouldn't take over. That Al was right was proved by the fact that someone else did a Casanova (hideously vulgar and inaccurate) which did well; and I wasn't so bad, for the Czechs dramatised my novel and the play ran for 60 or 70 performances.

Think about it. If it could be brought off it would earn a nice little sum—of course, I propose 50–50 between us—and a bit more security for the females for whom we are responsible. I think, if it is done, the book should appear first in USA, a fortnight before England, to prevent the malice of the Brits functioning—the yanks will be bad enough. If the book did only 30,000 in US it wouldn't be so ducking fusty.

Trouble is the good Al doesn't seem to realise that the Crusades numbered nine and extended from 1096 to 1291. If our Aucassin and Nicolette hero and heroine—the guy will have to fall for a bicot girl— are 20 when Urban II preaches the first crusade at Clermont, they will be about 215 when the shattered rearguard evacuates. Richard of Anjou is probably the only Crusader the yanks ever heard of, but our late dread Liege Lord failed to re-capture the Holy City, and the name of his beautiful Berengaria simply suggests a Cunard liner to those morons. Such is the cussedness of things.

If there is any flying in to be done, you can turn on the old Chancery good manners, and knock 'em in the old Kent road. You could stipulate that you (including me out) do the screen play, and I think Al could get you an additional 1000 bucks a week for 13 weeks.

Apropos—it strikes me as typical of the boches. They wouldn't come into the first crusade because they were quarrelling among themselves. When at last an army did start it began by making a pogrom of about 10,000 rhinos (man) along the Rhine valley. Pack of bastards they are. Of course, those ruffians of the 4th crusade sacked Constantinople and melted down all the bronze statues of antiquity to coin sous—blast them. Robert de Clari, whom you probably know, has an amusing altercation between the Doge of Venice and the Emperor Alexis:

'Non?' dist li dux, 'garchons maalvais! nous t'evons,' fist li dux, 'gete de le merde et en le merde to remeterons; et je te desfi et bien saches to que je te pourcacherii mal a men pooir de ches pas en avant!'

Such was the noble courtesy of the heyday of chivalry.

I am trying to tidy up here, expecting my friends (and landlords) from Paris (France) tomorrow, followed some time by Catha, who is cross about the rain and metro, but doesn't say when she arrives. God help us all, said Tiny Tim (me).

Yes, we shall probably be in or near Aix, and I must run down soon to see what this mazet is Cath has found. If it is on top of that hill above Aix (as she implies) it will be open to the mistral, and apparently lacks electricity and chauffage.

Well, Larry, let me have your views.

Love to all
Richard

[P.S.] Did you see the Catalogue of the DHL Exhibition in Nottingham (Eng)? I have just learned from a friend that its introduction said:

'Richard Aldington has written that "England owes Lawrence an apology". This exhibition may be regarded as a contribution to England's belated apology to one of her greatest sons.'

One up to the Notts and Jocks. Saeva indignatio sometimes gets home—eventually.

Nîmes [ca. 15 September–7 October 1960]

Dear Richard;

Ouf, the last brat is now airborne, and after twenty-four hours' clearing up we will at last be able to address ourselves to serious things. First, many thanks for your very generous offer about The Crusades but I won't be able to collab owing to the enormous amount of contracted work outstanding and the fact that already this blasted *Cleo* script which they have only just begun to turn in Egypt has delayed me by six months on *Acte* which had holes booked for it this spring by two European theatres, and on which I alas had to default. As far as Hollywood is concerned I feel I've purged my contempt, and have put aside quite a dollar cushion between school fees and the writer's reality. I am therefore free to stroke my art for a bit; if only the contract correspondence would quieten down . . . It will of course: then I'll complain I suppose. No pleasing writers. Meanwhile *Sappho* is shaping up for Edinburgh Paris and other places and this again will mean discussions etc and possible tailoring of scenes.

I should stick to one crusade and build it round some good tale like Aucassin (How funny: the other day I was reading it and thinking how Mamoulian would like it). But sell your short treatment first and then write it for the screen. Why a novel unless it's something near to your heart? But a direct screen treatment is easier, and they do most of the work while you spout notions. I should also see it on to the floor and gather up a steady thousand a week for a few months. Paddy Leigh Fermor told me in London that he is still living on his scenario of *Roots of Heaven*—three years later. I opted out of the floor work, or else I'd be sitting on a pyramid now chewing gum. They won't finish this ninety-day epic before late spring I judge from the present prevailing confusion.

But I think it's a heartening sign that you have been called back on such a big money proposal, a sign that the cloud has begun to lift in USA. Please follow it up however distasteful the work may be. (Sell them *The Cloister and the Hearth;* sure they have not heard of it.)

I don't know what has happened to the weather; one thunderspout after another, and all the roads washed to blazes. I gather Cath has got you two houses to choose from! We rented a workman's flat for the children's holiday by the sea and are wondering if they won't let us keep it on for next year. Modest price.

much love to you all
Larry

Poste Restante, Aix-en-Provence, B. du R., 25 October 1960

Dear Larry,

Anyone can infer that you've been in the F.O. from the way you date your letters. Is 'Tuesday' a date? Think of your miserable biographers.

You are quite right—the famous four must-get-heres can not possibly be filmed as you created them. And I rather or greatly resent books with so much beauty being butchered by H'wood for the vile sadistic proletariat who are temporarily top dogs, until the Russ moves in. Anyway, I hope you are getting a GIGANTIC fee, and that you are able to cheat any governments concerned out of their iniquitous tax-robberies. But beware of entering the USA. That may make you liable for tax even if you go for a few days only, and there is a fiscal gestapo to examine every foreigner before an exit-visa is granted, and to screw as much money out of him as possible. The bastards got 2000 bucks illegally out of me, but the lawyer I consulted merely shrugged and said: 'You are in the right but can you afford to fight the case over years to the Supreme Court?'

So much for America.

We are at the Hôtel de Sévigné which is run by the wife of a Félibre, who in the evening abuses the situation by making the guests listen to his poems read aloud. Still, it was owing to the Félibrige that we got the two last rooms in the place, which now has up the sign 'Complet'. There seems not to be a place in the town, although they are building dozens of those vile HLM (and destroying the whole 'atmosphere', to coin a useful word) but Catha may be able to get a flat which these hotel people will have available in November. I suppose I shall return to Sury soon.

Damn the Crusade. I am glad to have this excuse to get out of it. [. . .]

For the Toussaint, Catha (who at this moment is listening to some silly lecture at the Faculté) wants to go to her hideously uncomfortable Mas Dromar, so perhaps during those 6 days of unnecessary holiday we might meet either at the Saintes or at Arles.

By accident I ran into le Roi de Pologne on the Cours Mirabeau, accompanied by his Swiss—I know not how to qualify her. She is at least 50 and looks like a pi-jaw elementary school-marm. What a theme for you! Le Roi was super-abounding in political poppycock, such as that le Général is soon to be thrown out for the benefit of— hold your breath—le comte de Paris. Many of the plane-trees on the hill leading from Aix are plastered with a poster (doubtless put up by our old friend of Pologne) saying 'Le Roi. Pourquoi pas?' Or as I say: 'Le Con. Pourquoi non?'

I must say I find Miller most engaging—keeping youth and illusion to the extent of seeking Nerval (who was a bloody liar anyway) in the Mid-East, as doubtless he hunted Hearn in Nippon.

Love to both,
Richard

In his *Introduction to Mistral* Aldington states that 'In its widest sense "Félibrige" simply means the cult of Provence and Provençal speech.'

HLM tenements consisted of blocks of workers' flats.

Ŋ Sury-en-Vaux, Cher, 7 November 1960

Dear Larry,

Argumentative bastard to the contrary, I don't agree with Claude that England has changed much. It is still the same money-worshipping, snobby, half-bully, half-toady, bourgeois-philistine country it has been since the death of Charles I. Certainly it is now petit bourgeois instead of grand bourgeois, but that isn't much to boast about.

Lane won his case because the law has been changed, and the utter unfairness of the old law removed—that is a gain. For the rest, he won because he was able to spend 10,000 pounds on the case, which no lone writer (such as DHL in 1915 and 1928) could possibly have afforded. (The British are such canaille that while at any time during this century

10,000 pounds could easily be found for a jockey, a prize-fighter, a footballer, they would not subscribe 10,000 farthings or a fraction of them for a great writer in trouble.) That 10,000 quid went into the pockets of greedy cynical lawyers, who sell 'justice' and live by fleecing litigators, as the Brit government lives by robbing the widow and the orphan with 'death duties'. From the point of view of Scotland Yard it is equivalent to a fine, for Lane will never recover that sum even if he prints 500,000 paperbacks. Now we hear that many booksellers are not going to display the book (by request of Mr Tartuffe, Balham, Birmingham and everywhere else) and that it can't be sold in Scotland. The great point about *Lady C.* is that it is far too good for the sons of bitches.

Gott strafe England.

With which moral I drop my theorbo.

No, I don't—a letter in this morning from a Sth. African—a woman (now 64) whom I knew in London (Eng) 35 years ago, and haven't seen since. A woman's memory! Anyway she pleased me with this:

'I have what is probably Lawrence Durrell's first book of poetry. I have always been an intense admirer of him, and I have his *Black Book* which I value greatly. He sounds a most exciting person. Brother Gerald gave a very amusing portrait of L. when very young—I thought the mother of that family a very rare and understanding human being.'

Love to both,
Richard

P.S. My Sth African friend says: 'The Immorality Act has been a boomerang for the Sth. Af. govt. Apart from sailors, nearly all the charges are against farmhands and "respectable" farmers caught with native girls—practically every one has been an Afrikaaner pro-government man, and several have been parsons of the Dutch Reformed Church.' Why can't we share this with Roy?

Nîmes [before 14 November 1960]

Dear Richard;

Just a swiftie. Snow—and I'm out of wood, and olive too wet to cut so I must into town and fill up the car with chêne. Yes, I had a letter from Moore to which I have replied; he speaks of a book of two hundred pages but doesn't say how he is going to fill the space. I've sent him a checklist of muck which Claude keeps under the sofa; apart from your piece and about three others there isn't much from England except an awfully good general press, reviews etc. But it would be infra dig to print a merely good press. But there have been some goodish long studies (how posthumous can you feel?) in French, notably in *Preuves* (Dominique Arban) and *Critique*. There is also a huge German Italian Dutch and Scandinavian press which helps to light the fire coz I can't read it. I suppose something might be done that way. But am I quite ripe for this treatment I wonder? London is still trying to write me off as a latter-day Charles Morgan!

I'm writing to Rowohlt and will ask about DHL. (Claude says: 'Tell Richard I give in; after all he should know, he's English.' But she sounds unconvinced.)

I've just finished a new play . . . ouf! Now all that remains before Xmas is a *Holiday* mag article on Gascony. I'm waiting for that bastard Henry to come on down so we can do a swift five-day swerve together; after which I push him over the Spanish border and go back by inland roads (and some large meals) to my desk. Henry is stuck with Georges Simenon and Charlie Chaplin in Switzland, and is clearly being well fed because he is miles behind schedule and refuses to leave in spite of my abusive telegrams.

Yes, Temple's book [*D. H. Lawrence*] has had two v. important broadcasts consecrated to it; several local people have mentioned it. Alas we have no poste here; but Dominique is a wonderfully intelligent woman (she is the official translator of Dostoievski in French and wrote a book about him *Le Coupable* which is full of insight). She runs the internal literary side of RTF and is a honey as well as being a power for good and evil (I mean or). A woman you would treasure.

I've told Fanchette he should go ahead with our DHL letter; looks as if we will have to face the Scots and the bloody Irish over the issue. Tell me HOW did Burns get born there?

much love from us both
Larry

RTF: Radio-Télévision Française.

Sury, 14 November 1960

Dear Larry,

For lack of a new Durrell I have been re-reading the Divine Quartet (see Dante) and lo! this morning arrives your 'arrangement' of *Pope Joan*—a fascinating theme, considering she never existed. But I'm not going to start on the new book now, until I have completed this re-read. I must say that re-reading, without the spurious agitation of 'suspense', I am filled with admiration, more than ever. The people who crab you are insensitive, bloody fools. They want you 'to take a firm stand', to identify yourself with some vindictive and ephemeral party politics (as that detestable Orwell did) instead of reaching to the heart of life in words which will be as lively in 2200 as they are now. [. . .]

For heaven's sake don't sign that *Two Cities* letter about DHL without alterations. Look—how in hell do you and Fanchette know what Lorenzo's 'intentions' were in writing *Lady C.*? I talked with him (not about it for he very seldom mentioned his books and never work in progress) before, during and after, and I've no idea whether it was meant as a new gospel or a new chance to clean up a little dough since Joyce had re-started the cult of the four-letter word—remember? 'the Dead Sea, the old dead cunt of the world'—not bad. Or his intentions might have been mixed anywhere between the extremes. What he said to old Norman [Douglas] about wanting to put life into the young writers is a most obvious put-off, especially as about that time Norman was cashing in on British purity with that book of repulsive limericks—an insult to the female sect. And DHL's 'peculiar genius' is not above question—he was a great man, could be super-charming, was also in some ways a cad and a shit—ditto his writings. Last week going through the work of a woman poet, lately deceased, of that epoch, I found a most scathing denunciation of him—I hope no woman has ever written something as nasty as that about me. But we must judge people by their positive achievements, and there DHL scores.

Charles Morgan be damned. Why not Hugh Walpole?—the gerontophile—I must tell you Pino's story about him.

The chief change in England is that 50 years ago it was a great empire, and now it is America's cringing and whining jackal. It makes me laugh to think their master at the White House is an Irishman and a Catholic. They've been made to eat plenty of dirt since 1940, and I suspect there'll be plenty more in the next four years.

Cath sends me her required [reading] for the English course at Aix—Galsworthy, Forster, Orwell (2), Joyce, DHL, Mansfield, short selections from Byron, Sheets and Kelly. Plus Eliot (George, not the churchwarden). It might be the English (not American) part of the 'program' in a mid-West minor State university.

Love to both,
Richard

Pope Joan is Durrell's translation from modern Greek of the book of that title by Emmanuel Royidis.

❡ *Sury-en-Vaux, Cher, 21 November 1960*

Dear Larry,

[. . .] If you can blackmail your brother for a copy of his *Family* book I'd be very pleased. Catha read it in Switzer and loved it.

If you look up page 326 of *Portrait of a G.,* you'll see I put out various *hypotheses* about DHL's 'intentions', but only deny dogmatically Douglas's report. If you read the whole set of refs. you'll see I don't even exclude rivalling Joyce in 'words' and cleaning up a bit of dough.

My mind probably failing, but damned if I can see how anyone can NOW help Lawrence, who is a bowl of ashes mixed with a ton of concrete by one jealous woman to prevent another from pinching them. Only his work endures, and if people don't like that, what business is it of theirs what is said or done about 'Lawrence'? I should say that a defunct author whose book sells 200,000 copies in a day, with 300,000 to follow next week, needs nobody's help. Impossible to impose the book on priest-ridden Eire. Lane is in consultation with the Attorney-General of Northern Ireland, because there the book comes under the Act of 1857. In Scotland the book may not be sold, but the police can't stop Scots from buying a copy in England and bringing same in. The real joke is that Dame Edith is convinced that Connie is Lady Ida, and also *Lady C.* would 'destroy the faith of any young person of 18'. So, it seems, strong in her self-importance, she is nagging the Queen-Mum to get the case re-opened. As if the lawyers would listen! As far as I can see, the case can be 're-opened'—in the Court of Criminal Appeal. Under the 1907 Act, this is always an appeal against an Old Bailey or other Criminal Court conviction. I don't remember that the Crown has ever appealed against their conviction, but I suppose it could, though the customary 10 days have elapsed. Even then I think the appeal could only be on misdirection to the jury or some error in procedure. Nous verrons.

You don't say if Rowohlt has given any news about his DHL publications. What is he waiting for? Seghers is being rather unwise in not immediately announcing a pocketbook edition of Temple's work. I think I'll write and suggest it. Do you know Seghers? If so would you prompt on the same lines. [. . .]

Love to you both,
Richard

[P.S.] What an age of isms. My dear old friend Tom MacGreevy, for years Director of the Dublin National Gallery, has just issued a little book on Nicolas Poussin (about whom he knows a great deal) and stuffs it full of propaganda for nationalist Eire and Tridentine Catholicism. He makes a great fuss about the fact that quite half Poussin's pictures are religious. Well, so were most of Leonardo's, but look at his notebooks! Fragonard and Boucher painted religious pictures. In all cases I should say the subject represents the taste of patrons, not of artists.

R.

Lady Ida was Edith Sitwell's mother, daughter of the Earl of Londesborough; Lawrence had met her. Commentators have continually connected the Sitwells with *Lady Chatterley's Lover,* but the model for Constance Chatterley was probably another high-born lady Lawrence was undoubtedly in love with: Lady Cynthia Asquith, née Charteris.

§ *Sury, 24 November 1960*

Dear Larry,

Last night—after interruptions—I finished a careful re-reading of *Black Book.* Of course it is Joyce-ish, Lawrence-ish, Miller-ish, even

Eliotish—if he has anything he didn't crib from others—but at 24, why not? One has always predecessors. What gives me more confidence than ever in you is that I get more from second and third readings than from the first. It always seems a good omen of permanence. Most books are so soon exhausted.

Unfortunate misprint towards the end—Gregory 'sot' himself. I suppose we must be thankful the bastards didn't make you say 'Gregory shat himself'.

I note that Gregory quotes with approval Ezra's lament for the '14–18 war dead 'for an old bitch gone at the teeth'. We don't want his condescending croc's tears. If he had carried down in stretchers sick, wounded, and corpses, if he had lived and slept week in, week out, with wounds and death, stood by open graves as the young men were lowered in their blanket coffins, cursing bloody God and the blasted Government, then perhaps he might humbly—not with his conceit— take his place as mourner. He spent the war keeping out of it, like his mate Eliot; and in the name of five years of mute casualties I spit on that particular effusion of a draft-dodging yank. Selah. [. . .]

Match and *Time, Mountolive* in Italy, *Clea* in Germany—excellent. I hope it annoys ALL your enemies.

Your *Book* somehow wakened a long-lost memory of 1917, which Gregory could have used effectively. Back from the front after 7 months without seeing a woman; sent to Lichfield as officer cadet; discipline so strict the great hero TEL would have croaked in a week under it; cadets did all guards as if tommies, but woe unto the negligent. Just opposite barracks a large hospital for military syph 'patients', barbed wire entanglement (as in prisoner-of-war camps), day and night guards of cadets with fixed bayonets AND loaded rifles—'shoot at sight'. Close at hand barracks of WAACs, no barbed wire, but ditto guards. I clicked for 10 p.m. to midnight, just as the ladies were retiring, in summer, open windows. I don't think the coarsest tommies talked more blatantly and coarsely than those girls—who forgot the sentries could hear. It was as if they emptied piss-pots on our heads. And I madly in love with a girl [Dorothy Yorke] in London. I still wish it hadn't happened.

Conquering my aversion and dread of flu, I MAY go to Paris end of next week to see oculist, and get a dentist to restore lost false tooth. Then back here for a few days, and if roads not snowed up etc hope to

start for Aix on the 13th. This should give time to arrange flight to
Rome about the 20th. (Must find out if Rome plane goes from Marig-
nane or Nice.) Then back to Aix, and brood in spare room of Catha's
flat (which she entered yesterday) until snow seems ended. This place
is too difficult in real snow and frost. But IF these projects are carried
out, we shan't be at Camargue for the Saturnalia, and hence unable to
make use of your offer of Saintes Maries place. BUT it might be most
welcome in Jan–Feb. I'll reply to Claude.

The Russ sent me 250 pounds in 1959, and 750 in 1960. I'm not
counting on more than 250 in 1961, but they certainly owe me more.
They kept one or more of my books continuously in print since
1931—except for war decade—but started paying only in 1959. They
also pay Willie Maugham and Priestley—god knows why. Mr G.
Greene, the famous literary greengrocer, has to go to Moscow and
spend his royalties there. I think the literary Moscows know perfectly
well that I don't give a damn for political parties and rather hate the
proletariat—so do they, but they have to pretend otherwise. Did I tell
you I think I have persuaded them to re-issue DHL, who has been
'killed' there for 25 years? I sent them the carbon of my Rowohlt
script, telling them to make any use of it. Apropos, what IS that fellow
doing about DHL? Missing buses every hour on the hour. I wrote to
Seghers suggesting he should issue a paperback of our friend Temple's
book (I suppose you've seen it?) but he evades with all the cunning of a
. . . what? I can't think of anything sufficiently opprobrious.

I have just discovered that in N.Y. is a restaurant called Ying and
Yang. They'll have the Yoni & Lingam next.

Love to both, and all thanks,
Richard

✍ Nîmes [ca. 30 November 1960]

Dear Richard;

Just got back from a six-day tilt with the shades of D'Artagnan—a
sponsored tour of Gascony to gather dope for an article long promised
and long put off. Wow! We did some impassioned gastronomic research which had slain us both; black bread and Perrier for at least a
whole week. I see things through a hazy spectrum of goose liver and
pigeon; what eating country it is. And I think N 117 is perhaps the

loveliest drive in France—cutting north through the Aude valley from Perpignan to Pau. You start in Spain and end in . . . hospital. At least we nearly have. Yes, it was amusing to find ourselves keeping up with the Joneses, as they say, in *Match*. What rubbish it all is; the cabotin of the western world.

Of course we could make Maussane; I am just waiting for a firm date from the Marseilles television people to whom I've promised a few fond words about the state of main drainage in Nîmes. Tentatively they'll turn up the 7th. Apart from that, I have only a few odds and ends to tidy up before Xmas. We'll take off the 22nd I guess. Is the Saintes too long a leg for you to make? I feel it's important to just size up the flat, even if you don't want it; I believe you'll need to borrow a bed, as present camp beds are not too comfy for non-pygmies. And you may need a better heater than this silly one-bar job, in which case I could buy it off you for later use up here. Questions of comfort are so personal that it's impossible to legislate for anyone else's tastes; and we are rather used to roughing it. But I think you could keep warm, cook and have hot water to shower, which is something these days. [. . .] I think it would be worth looking at, so if you can ever make the Saintes for lunch one of these days flash me a telegram and I'll whistle down. Anyway the key can stay with the Butagaz man to be reclaimed when and if you need it. Incidentally just outside the Saintes there is a new eating place of absolutely top quality, Boumian. *Match* took us there for lunch—really superb food and a big fire. Mark a notch in your pistol . . . for future use when you have to dine a Hollywood magnate or someone else's girl friends.

Rome sounds crazy to me; at Xmas? I was stuck there once during December and didn't like it. Pity to visit such a heavenly town for the first time in mid winter; it's equally hell in August too I find. However . . .

Let us know how things firm up; it's turned damned cold here; must get some more oak.

love to you both
Larry

Durrell's 'The Gascon Touch' appeared in *Holiday* magazine, January 1963.

Butagaz: butane gas.

❡ *Sévigné, Aix, 8 December 1960*

Dear Larry,

Good lad! Looking forward so much to seeing you both and hearing all about god and suchlike.

This confirms rendezvous, 1200 hrs, approx, Saturday, 10th, Dec, at Oustaloun, Maussane. It is in the central place to your right as you face the wall fountain which says 'Défense de laver' and all the old ladies do their washing in it. But doubtless you know it. There is a fire in the grubbery.

We have booked Nice–Rome—50 mins by Caravelle—on the 17th, back on the 30th, alas, but C. has some sickening réveillon engagement.

Love to both,
Richard

[P.S.] Saw a very gastronomic English family here at the Royale—Dad, Mum, girl of 10, boy of 7.

Dad had ham and eggs
Mum had ham omelette
Children had cold ham, roll and butter
½-bottle of vin blanc—but none for the children.
Pah.

❡ *Hôtel Sévigné, Aix-en-Provence, 1 January 1961*

Dear Larry,

I hope you and Claude have now left the Zoo without an owl on your characters.

By the way, does your brother ever allow distinguished strangers to look over his menagerie? I ask, because a friend of mine is longing to see them—les bêtes. [. . .]

Le roi de Pologne is also unanimously elected roi des cons. He has made the most ghastly mess of that little piece on Rome [*A Tourist's Rome*]. He dumps it here in sheets, unsewn, with the airy message that doubtless Catha will sew them. (He was overpaid to do the whole job.)

About three quarters of the way through the little thing he suddenly changes to a larger type, and in 20 pages he contrives to produce more than 20 misprints and blunders. E.g. in correcting his ignorant author he turns the old church of San Stefano (the little round temple near the Tiber) into the impossible 'Sancti Stephani Rotondi'—an absurdity. What with all this and incompetent inking he has contrived to turn out a piece of work so slipshod and amateurish that a child would be ashamed of it.

To keep up the grouse—here comes Rowohlt, also correcting my ignorance. God knows what he has done to the text by way of improvement, but he has taken away my chaste I, II, III etc, chapter headings, and substituted Daily Shit captions. He produces Russell as 'Sir Bertrand Russell', labels Orioli 'Reggie Turner' and Reggie Turner 'Orioli'. Lady Cynthia [Asquith] is produced as a hard-faced woman of 70, instead of the most lovely girl she was when DHL knew her. Finally, a book with my name (fortunately inconspicuous) on it, is, without my consent, plugged up with crap about DHL from various bêtes noires of mine, including even Spender and Simone de Beauvoir. Hell.

What beats owt is that Heinemann received on the 9th Dec an important cable for me from *Moscow Literary Gazette,* delayed so long in sending it to my agent that it did not hit me until we got back from Rome (It'ly)—too late.

Rome was wonderful to me, though I think Catha was often bored, but she is not a Bildungsmensch. The traffic and the Americans and the go-getting are indeed hideous, but underneath and aside the real life goes on. And it is to me a terrific experience to renew contact with a place where art has really mattered. I went alone to Villa Borghese and mused much. Almost everything John Evelyn saw in 1644 is still there, with additions. Boney stole pieces from Camillo Borghese for his Louvre, and though Wellington sent his redcoats to restore the thefts I fear they were better soldiers than art critics, though Canova went to Paris to advise. The Pauline Bonaparte is charming, though the *Messaggero* cocked up a silly-season story while we were in Rome to the effect that she didn't sit for the statue—it was a pretty contadina. Pauline certainly posed to Canova for a completely nude statue, so there is no need to worry about the Venus Reclining one, about which the usual British matron cattishly asked Pauline if she had not felt 'very uncomfortable'—in the puritan sense—when posing for it? To which the Principessa most properly answered: 'No, the room was perfectly warm.'

This week-end I didn't take advantage of your very generous offer of the Stes Maries place. The weather is cold and wet, and Catha obviously wanted to shake me and whoop it up with her Camargue friends. Yesterday I found here a bottle of González Byass amontillado, and am peacefully sozzling in an otherwise unoccupied hotel. The place is closed until the 3rd, but as I am a Soci of the Félibres (the proprietor is, I think, a Majoural) I am allowed to have a lofty room with heat and water, on condition I make my bed.

Please give my love to your Claude who is so kind to me, and take plenty yourself.

Ever
Richard

[P.S.] I am reading Italian again like mad. How lucky it is that Pound and Eliot are only the Dante and Shakespeare of Rhode Island—outside, the competition would be distressing. Books in Rome all for pescicani of wealth. I had great difficulty in getting poor man's texts, and found only part of Lorenzo de' Medici's Poems, Raphael's works socalled (a poor thing, and the letter to Papa Leo about the ruins, suspect), and Alfieri's *Vita*. The best text of *Vita* is in that Library at Montpellier, owing to sexual vagaries of the relict of our (de jure) late sovereign lord, King Charles III of blessed memory—he was a Scotch bastard, got so drunk he was sick in his lovely wife's bed, Allah blacken his face. Can you read Alfieri's Plays? They seem to me almost as bad as Racine's, ma ché . . . We must all go to Rome, and be Knights of the Golden Spur.

Re Pound-Eliot—perhaps it would be better to say the 'Dante of Idaho' and the 'Shakespeare of Missouri', their respective home states.

Have you found the portrait of la Lucrezia in the Nîmes gallery? I *must* see it, and Catha can go worship Mithra. Her remark on a typical Mithra group in Rome was 'that wouldn't kill the bull'. But the point was to make him slowly bleed to death, sprinkling the neophyte under the drain. What a filthy religion. As bad as Xtianity.

50 minutes by Caravelle from Nice to Rome.

A Tourist's Rome is the separate publication of the introduction Aldington wrote for *Rome: A Book of Photographs* (1960).

Majoural: an official in the Félibres.

Pescicani: Italian for shark, war profiteer.

✑ Nîmes, Thursday [before 24 January 1961]

Dear Richard;

We both got back at last, but with such dreadful grippe that we were laid low for two days, and even now are hawking and spitting like costers. Both Paris and London were in the grip of grippe of a new nasty bronchial sort which we got . . . but the trip was fun and interesting; have a lot to tell you when we meet, but feel too frail to put it all into a letter today. I've sold my second play to Hamburg. It will open at the same time as *Sappho* goes on at Edinburgh, and I'm busy doing some alterations to it now so that the translator Schnorr can start on it pronto. Head spinning though. Keep going with good marc! Yes, my beloved and wicked Gerry's ZOO is a public one, in fact the Jersey Zoo; anyone can go. It's open to the public. He mostly isn't there, away on expeditions, but Ken Smith runs it like a clock. It's amazingly good for its size—lion tiger puma cheetah bears . . . all the works except an elephant. I tried to buy him one secretly in London and send it COD but there was so much paper work concerned with the transaction that I had to desist. I asked him to send you his crazy book about us, which he duly did. But I sent it to Cher, thinking you perhaps back there frowsting again. His collection of monkeys is really quite something and most of them, including a small gorilla, drop in for tea every day with the family . . . Scares me!

How long are you with us? We must meet and talk. I have to go to Marseilles about an affidavit (selling my house in Cyprus); I also am moving up legally on the business of marrying Claude sometime in the next three or four months. I hope to get the new version of the play into the post this week, do Marseilles at the week end and feel relatively free next week. I'll flash you a line; would so like to spend a night or two at the Saintes if I can. Failing that we might visit you or you us. Let us see how the landfall works. I'm afraid at the moment though we have no temperature we are both groggy with this beastly deep 'flu. But it will pass. I suppose you've seen what your Moscow friends have done to Pasternak's widow and daughter! When I read the Nobel citation I exclaimed to Claude: 'This means possible death or life imprisonment for Pasternak'; I knew a lot about him, admired his poetry (translated by the French) for many years; knew friends of his, and knew he was an uncompromising enemy of dialectical materialism (like yours truly); but as he had blood cancer they could afford to let him die normally. But they've got the family on a trumped up charge. I hope it makes you hang your head a little, you are so naive politically. This could NOT happen in the England and America you despise so much. But by the time you make your first sponsored visit to the marxist paradise you'll maybe lay a small wreath for me on the tomb of the Pasternak family!

> more anon and much love
> Larry

❦ *Sévigné, 24 January 1961*

Dear Larry,

I got a nice shock yesterday. Just before Catha was due back from Camargue, the hotel proprietor comes to my room—looking portentous—and says a young man, friend of C., wanted to speak to me. Suffering like yourself and Claude from the after effects of this bloody flu, I naturally saw everything en noir—obviously she had fallen off one of those wretched little screws . . . But no, the young man is writing a book on British frauds, and came to get extra dope about your F.O. hero, Tommy Lawrence. He also thought I could tell him about Aleister Crowley. I had to point out that among other weird manifestations of Brit intelligence is the fact that I am whispered about as an Aleister Crowley addict and pervert because I have an Australian friend called Alister Kershaw. They certainly have achieved the democratic idea—bats in every belfrey.

Well, Larry, I am pleased about your house and the new play, and still more that at last you seem to be disentangling the old matrimonial webs. However, I should have thought Claude had had enough of being married—it is a man-devised handicap nearly all to the interest of the male, who gets a free servant etc . . . That's enough of that.

Under separate cover I send you both, at last, copy of the notes on Rome (It'ly) which you lost and Geoffrey Montalk has typograpically [sic] murdered. All that remains is to ask Tom Eliot to write its obituary.

TLS has discovered a poet with the most exquisite name of 'P. Green'. I vow to Gad. Reminds me of the days when I used to make a weekly trip to said *TLS* to pick up cannon-fodder. One Tuesday I had to say to Bruce Richmond: 'Do you know what you printed about Edmund Gosse last week?' 'We had a review of his last book.' 'Yes, and you kicked off by saying he is the dean of French letters in England.' Do not let Claude see this—it will shock her.

I don't want to leave the Midi, but hotel and restaurants bonae sub regno Catherinae come expensive; so next week—roads permitting—I shall go and frowst in the Cher and hatch out plots against the Free World with my commo friends led by the king of Poland.

Did Ledigger [Rowohlt] send you a copy of my paperback on DHL? If not, I'll send one.

Your excellent brother sent me a Penguin of his *Family*, which is delighting me. I understand so well his keeping a jar of caterpillars always near. I used to keep them in my bedroom, and the housemaid always screamed and gave warning when she found one creeping up her . . . whatever it was.

Eternal love to both,
Richard

ℌ Mazet Michel etc [31 January 1961]

Dear Richard; Claude was struck down with cold and 'flu and so I brought her back here for a day in bed. She'll be up tomorrow I guess (Wednesday); now another trial. I have been convoked for Saturday to take my driving test at eleven fifty. How long it will last I don't know, but it might be wiser to have lunch here and tool down to the Saintes afterwards. Shall we then fix our date of Saturday for the eve? Shall I book a table for us? Cath will have given you such news as we have; she was a bit disgusted to find that we could do the Charleston (approx). Many thanks for the Roman book, despite the kingly typography it is very nice. I was interested in the pyramids—have you seen Hotson's dating of the Sonnets by a reference to such in them? A marvellous piece of detection and I think he's right.

Holiday complains that I've left Cyrano out of 'Gascony'; but didn't you tell me he was a fake gascon? I seem to remember.

I have done my Marseilles chore; you were wise about this week end. The Saintes was mighty cold and it takes two days to really warm the flat up.

much love
Larry

§ *Sury, 8 February 1961*

Dear Larry,

Herewith a brief note on Cyrano, which you can use to refute *Holiday*. The chief French authority on Cyrano is Frédéric Lachèvre, *Oeuvres libertines de Cyrano de Bergerac,* 2 vols. Champion, Paris, 1921. The only authority in English is Richard Aldington, Cyrano de Bergerac, *Voyages to the Moon and the Sun,* translated with Introduction and Notes, Routledge, London, Dutton, N.Y., 1922. [. . .]

It was great to see you both again, and to rouse no less than three night-owls with champagne—a notable event.

Excuse brief note—the bronchs are at it again. But the place is warm, and the greeting of the peasantry even warmer and more pleasing. Should I have made a good seigneur? I think not. Exaction of the droit de cuissage would have repelled me, so in consequence I should have become very unpopular.

The Russians have sent me a really magnificent fur bonnet in which I look a real shit.

Will write again.

All love to both,
Richard

The 'brief note' Aldington appended was a 600-word biographical sketch of Cyrano.

✥ *Sury, 17 February 1961*

Dear Larry,

[. . .] I think there is quite a bit to be said for English cooking, in
addition to kippers and Stilton. English game is more varied and most
of it home-grown, whereas the French 'chasseurs' spend half a million
sterling annually to import live hares, pheasants, and partridges from
Hungary, Czecho and Spain. If they have grouse, it is a rarity—and
have they blackcock, ptarmigan and capercailzie? I have never had a
pâté en croûte as good as a real Melton Mowbray or even a Lichfield
pork pie bought at Lichfield. To your applauded kippers I'd add
smoked haddock, smoked cod's roe and smoked tongue. I've never had
sirloin of beef here or in USA as good as those at Simpson's or any of
the old London taverns. There is much to be said for a kate and sidney,
and though I hear it no longer reigns as of old, the steak, kidney,
mushroom, lark and oyster pud at the Cheshire Cheese accounts for all
the indigestible quality of Willie Yeats's early poems.

I'll return le Bouffant soon.

Claude should be decked with a cordon bleu. I still think with
tender retrospection on that duck and navets—a chef d'oeuvre.

I did eventually get your letter about the 40 dollars, for which
many thanks. 40 dollars is nearly 200 NF, and I ought to be able to
live 10 days on that here.

You are kind to take so much trouble advising about the Laclos.
The trouble is that for years and years the 'press' and reviewers have
been telling it aloud that I am an 'inaccurate writer' (so unlike the accurate Mr TEL) and 'no critic' and 'no historian' [so] that the publishers—who are only half-educated business men—believe it. That is why
I was so cross with Rowohlt for plastering that little book with his silly
howlers, all of which I could have caught. Heaven knows what boners
have got into my text. You may have noted that Mrs Colin says
Doubleday 'may' want to 'make amendments' in the *Characters*. Now,
they are far too ignorant to be able to add one page, but in their mania-
cal way they will insist on 'cutting' a book which was carefully planned
to cover the subject without redundancy, and took years to get together. When I was at Princeton they showed me about 20 copies, re-
bound and worn, which were required reading; and one of the English
profs said the book saved him and his undergrads an immense amount

of poking about in other books. But Doubleday of course know or think they know the requirements of Mr and Mrs Nobody in the Bronx, and so the book is to be ruined for that abstraction—just as bloody Chattos ruined by cutting my *Remy de Gourmont.* If the state of affairs is such that one's work can only appear in mutilated form, better not let it appear at all. Especially on such barabbas-like terms.

To go on grouching. *All Men* is refused in London and N.Y. as being 'too long to be economically feasible' as a pocketbook. Hau kay, but how come the Russkis could print and get away with an edition of 225,000? Better business men? A more intelligent or receptive public? Did I tell you that Mikhail Urnov states officially that the new translation of *Hero* and the translation of Stories are completed? Instead of pulling about the order of the stories to please themselves—as any Western publisher would do without a by your leave—the State Fiction Pub Co wrote asking permission to put the last of the war stories first. It is certainly the best.

I got a typical Welfare State jeer at the Rome piece, which I sent to a 'friend' of 45 years' standing. The only comment is that I make a great display of my 'erudition' and 'make constant digs' at those who haven't got it. Wish we could hear Roy on this. I used to love his diatribes against Charlie Chaplin (a rhino, man) and his snivelling cult of the 'liddel guys'.

Everybody is a political or religious fanatic to-day, except us. Let us start a New Political Party, the object of which is to abolish income tax and reduce the cost of vintage champagne . . .

Do you see Cath? What is she up to? Is your weather as 'divahn' as ours here? The peasants are having kittens, saying the fruit and vines will bud and then be blasted by frosts.

Love to both,
Richard

Claude Durrell translated Marcel Rouff's *La Vie et passion de Dodin-Bouffant, gourmet* into English as *The Passionate Epicure* (1961).

◊ *Nîmes, 19 February 1961*

Dear Richard,

[. . .] We are off to London (England) to-night, to earn some dollars for a month or thereabouts. To re-Cleo the *Cleo* scenario. As usual, this is a last-minute rush invitation (nay, an imploring cry) so we have had no time to sort things out for the immediate future, but Larry is well up on the third play [*An Irish Faustus*] and there is nothing important in sight for some weeks, so why turn down the good lucre?

I hope Catha received the little parcel of cleansing-cream Jacquie (Larry's sister-in-law) sent her at the same time as she sent mine which has safely arrived. A great help in the Camargue where the water dries one's skin horribly. Give her my love and ask her if she wants anything from UK—our address will be Basil Street Hotel, Knightsbridge, London, but in any case c/o Curtis Brown or Fabers will always work if she forgets the hotel address.

Is there anything we can do for you there? If so, I hope you will tell us *sans façons*. It was so nice being able to spend that weekend with you at the Saintes, and I have preciously preserved the Aldington Tape for frequent re-listening.

Love,
Claude & Larry

⚓ Sury, 8 March 1961

Dear Larry,

This spring is too beautiful to waste in France. On Monday I drive south to fly to Venice (It'ly) for a few weeks. I 'gin to be a-weary of these frogs, anyway. Write here or c/o Cooks, Venice.

Very sorry about th' beautiful Liz [Taylor], but why have English doctors? Are there no Liberians available?

Heavens, dear lad, I have a terrific SOS from the King of Redonda, asking me to sponsor a selection of his poems. God help us all, said Tiny Tim. If I were Roy it would be different. 'Well, you see, man, we were both in the East African Deception Corps, and when it was stationed on Lake Victoria Nyanza, we used to get drunk together, so of course I had to praise his poems, but they weren't any good.'

Moore sounds cheerful about the little book on you. It won't do you any harm, believe me.

I am most excited about going to Venice—*there's no money in it.*

Love to both,
Richard

The novelist M. P. Shiel had bequeathed to John Gawsworth the title to Redonda, a tiny Caribbean island inhabited only by goats and sea birds. To gain assistance in claiming his 'kingdom' from the Crown, Gawsworth created many dukedoms for his friends, among them Aldington, Durrell, and Henry Miller.

✍ Mas Dromar, 27 March 1961

Dear old Larry,

In case you haven't heard it, here is another war-whoop from one of your faithful Sioux.

Do you think it's good enough to send on to Moore for his book? If so, best translate, as American kultur seldom includes a knowledge of French—a durdy people who like women and white wines.

Moore says he has got a good piece from a Frawg (cf. Ez Pound) at Yale.

I hope that book hits the yank press—such a nice sock at Messrs the Twaddling Eliots, Graham GreeneGroceres, and Evelyn Waughs.

> Mr Evelyn Waugh
> Is rather a baw;
> Mr Evelyn Wuff
> Writes plenty of guff;
> Mr Evelyn Wow
> Is a dreary old cow;
> Mr Evelyn Woff
> Was never a toff;
> But he ain't such a squitford
> As Mrs Nancy Mitford.

ever
Richard

Chère Madame,

Je me mets à vos pieds avec l'expression de mes hommages les plus respectueux,

R.A.

Yale professor Victor Brombert's article 'Lawrence Durrell and His French Reputation' appeared in *The World of Lawrence Durrell.*

❧ *Li Santo, 31 March 1961*

Dear Larry,

The local paper says you and Claude have committed matrimony. If so, all our loving felicitations. If not, why not? State reasons, and draw map.

Very glad about the dollars. What an advertisement the fair Liz has given the London climate in winter. What did you blokes make the girl do that she got double pneumonia? When I read that she was in the London Clinic I thought you might be returning at once to Engances, especially as Claude's letter indicated a certain nostalgie. Did I tell you that at first I got it into my muddled noddle that you were overseeing the filming of the *Quartet?*

There was a long article on L.D. in the Litt Supp of the *Gazette de Lausanne*—the only paper which has given (fairly recently) an adequate and documented article on the bogus Prince of Mecca. I sent it to Engances, so you may find it there when you return. [. . .]

Bryher wants to visit Gerald's zoo during a yachting tour she is making in or about July. Could you see that instructions are left with the curator for her to be well received? She says she has several times been bitten by monkeys, which seems to be the blue ribbon of zoophily. Also, Br. reports that Catherine Gide (daughter of Gide's adopted daughter) is crazy to work in the zoo. What is meant I don't quite know. Does G. need an assistant? Apropos, I have asked Bryher to send you two of her books when you get back to the Gard. They are really meant for young people, but the history is said to be very sound.

Love from us both,
Richard

[P.S.] Catha's comment on the reported marriage was: 'He doesn't know what a good wife he has got.'

⚓ *C/o Cooks, Venice, 7 May 1961*

Dear Larry,

We had the Queen's Majesty here yesterday, in a shabby replica of the Onassis yacht. Poor girl! What a life! Surrounded by shits at every step. I went out to Torcello on Friday, had the cathedral & Santa Fosca almost to myself, lunched (at a safe distance from los yanquis) at the Locanda Cipriani, where H.M. was taken. Never have I felt so keenly the advantages of obscurity, & the disadvantages of publicity. It was Flaubert, notre Maître, who wanted to be 'the little old gentleman who passes unobserved in the crowd'. Capisce?

Claude will call me horse, spit in my face, but by'r Lady, I find the Venetian menus a most welcome change from France's. I write in a small restaurant in the Campo di Santa Maria Lobenigo. Granzeola *with* the coral; then prosciutto al madera, & macedonia di frutte al mareschino. Delicious; & much too good for me, of course.

With Byron's apartment in the Palazzo Mocenigo, & a mere £5000 a year, two could jog along very nicely here. The Browning apartments in Ca' Rezzonico are closed, but he had only a mezzanine, reserved (in the great days) for impoverished clergy of the family. Ca' Rezzonico is now a superb museum of the Settecento & *much* better as an exhibit than the Ca' d'Oro.

I shall have to stagger back to France (Europe) in about 10 days, shall hide from Whitsun in Catha's mas (if she'll have me) & then frowst in Sury, & save centimes to return to civilisation in Italy.

Well, Larry, Gott strafe England. I don't care a fuck for old von Kluck and all his fucking army. *But,* if England doesn't get out of this obscene German-American-Germany war alliance . . . well, it'll get what's coming. It's done for, anyway.

Mà non ragiam' di lor . . . (Dante) How are you both? And the heirs? I think of you every day, & several times a day. May all be as you wish.

Et merde à la . . .

Love
Richard

[P.S.] On dit that Castro is now Cubu Roi. Good for him, & shit to USA.

❡ *[Venice], 17 May 1961*

[To Claude]

I leave here to-morrow with infinite regret, but after 5 weeks of aesthetic revelry, I can take in no more. 'And love itself have rest', signed: P.B. Shelley. I weave financial plots to bring Catha here in Sept—after the hordes depart. If only you & Larry could come too. There is now a plane from Nice (change at Milan) and I can be Cicerone thereafter.

Strange to think that (barring accidents) I shall be tomorrow in all the discomfort of Mas Dromar!

Love to both,
R

❡ *as from Sury, 23 May 1961*

Dear Larry,

No trade secrets . . . here is the agent's report received today. The poem reprinted in the ghastly woman's paper, was written when I was 20. I am glad for the quote—5 quid—but I wish they'd realise I did write some poems after I was 20.

By the same mail a letter from a retired yank prof, asking to quote (gratis) 68 lines of various poems in some treatise or other. He says he's too poor to pay anything, and writes from Riverside Drive, which is rather more expensive than Park Lane. Another cow asks (free) quotes from my memoirs—crap about Ezra. I think one should give permission—but I get peeved with yanks for always pleading poverty.

Very nice to see you both again, and also to make the acquaintance of the family. A charming lot God wot. I was very glad just to have had even a glimpse.

As C. and I drove home we noticed you and your sister *lolling* on the steps of that caravanserai. Antrobus thought disciplinary action should be taken—'looks so bad' he said 'what with all these natives and riff-raff'.

Love to both,
Richard

In 1961, once-fashionable Riverside Drive in New York City was in fact not nearly so expensive or exclusive as Park Lane, London.

❧ *The Saintes, Thursday [20 July 1961]*

Dear Richard—a swift line to thank you—we are fixing up the flat against the invasion, *tomorrow,* of the four children. We'd planned to start off up in Nîmes but the well went dry on us so we will reverse the process, staying here for ten days and then returning for a spell of garrigue with them. Then I have to go to Edinburgh to push out the boat with *Sappho;* quite exciting and frightening to hear it in English, at last, after ten years. They are spending a deal of money on the production and Margaret Rawlings is starring in it so it has every chance of being easy on the eye and possibly painless in the acting. The rest is up to the play. But it went so well in Germany that I dare to hope that people won't be asking for their money back at the guichets. For the rest we swim a lot and read a bit—but reflect hardly! On Saturday we are being visited by Denis de Rougemont, a writer I much admire. I think you would be quite *emballed* if not actually *degringled* by his *Love in the Western World*—philosophic work; yesterday quite at a hazard I wrote a poem, the first for about six years, and not as good as I'd wish. Often wondered why you don't [write] more. I remember an anthologist once grumbling that one had to go 'all the way back' to your *Collected Poems* to find something to 'represent you'. But perhaps you do write and don't publish? Haven't seen Catha whizzing about these last few days. We were all delighted at her success. The girl has turned some sort of corner and has come into the straight now—rather unpredictably to me—I mean I used to think that whatever qualities she had she would never turn out an 'intellectual'. Now I'm not sure. She's jumped into a new skin.

Won't you be coming down sometime soon a-visiting? Remember that our address here is No. 12. Au Grand Large.

Much love from us both
Larry

[P.S.] The King [John Gawsworth] is a good chap but not above getting eminent chaps to preface his poems (They are good—some, but some rather wishy washy I find) But I like him. He is a curiosity and inside a strangely modest man—despite all these literary 'trucs'.

Durrell's 'degringled' apparently derives from French *dégringoler,* 'to topple over'.

🔥 *Sury-en-Vaux, Cher, 24 July 1961*

Dear Larry,

Very cheered by your very nice letter . . . I was about to write to you again anyhow. I have just had a letter from one W. Neurath, managing Director of Thames & Hudson (ever heard of them) asking me to do a DHL for their Pictorial Biography series. They are sending a copy of Vyvyan Holland on Oscar (not yet arrived) to initiate me into this new departure. Obviously it must be much the same as Ro-Ro-Ro, though I hope its 'editors' make fewer boners. Ro would doubtless like me to sell them the English of the text they have, and pocket 50% for nothing. But there is another reason against this. The text for nos chers amis les boches was written before the trial, before the new edition of *Letters* (I have galleys here) and was slightly over-weighted with Frieda, vu the fact that she was a bochess. (Wish she weren't dead.) Anyway, (1) Do you think it ethical for me to undertake the Brit job if I make something as different as possible—can't alter the facts—utilising the new letters, and the different 'approach' now that DHL at last is vindicated, and (2) if 'yes' to that, ought I to let RO know at once? (If I do, they may try to shove in ahead of me.) Advise me, will you? Meanwhile, I'll mark time, and perhaps ask my agent to investigate terms.

A recent letter from Mikhail Urnov (who sounds a very nice guy) saying he is trying to place as much as possible of the RO book (he has English text) as a long article in one of their reviews. I very much want to get DHL started up again in USSR (Stalin banned him) and it would fit in nicely with the paperback of *Portrait of a G.* in USA.

Did I tell you that Spring Books want to use my *Decameron* for an illustrated? I think they can, although the book is in print (illustrated) with Folio Society, and in hardback and paperback with Elek; but not exclusively. No reason why a translation should not go the round. In USA my *Candide* was pirated (not being copyrighted) by practically every NY publisher. Out of 5500 dollars advances on the last two paperbacks in US, 50% has been boned by the publishers (with nothing in the contract to justify it, BUT they hinted that there would be no republication except on their terms) and so far I have not had one cent—they have placed the money 'to account' and so I get it sometime next year. Nize babies. I always object to Byron's 'Bar-Abbas was a publisher'—so unfair to Bar-Abbas.

I left my copy of *Sappho* at Dromar for Catha, but from memory I should say the only snag about the Edinbro' production is that it's too good for them. However, you'll get a better educated and less degraded audience there than in London. May it wow, and sweep out Murders in Cathedrals and Mr Fry e tutti quanti. You are right to take up poems again, but I am far too old. Sophocles wrote a trilogy at 80, and his sons were so scandalised they said he was nuts, and brought a legal action to get him bug-housed. But you still have maximum energy.

Apropos, your anthologist was hardly à la page about me. The first *Collected Poems* came out in 1923 when I was 30, and that is the volume these conscientious scholars invariably use, although there was an enlarged *Collected* in 1929, and another still further enlarged in 1934, while my later poems are only to be had in *Complete* Poems of 1948. It will show you how accurate reviewers are when I say that at least half the reviewers in England gave the title as *Collected* Poems (including Roy's!) and I don't think one had read the book.

Tomorrow my friend Alister is coming down by car. [. . .] Then on Wednesday Catha is coming, and bringing Jacques. I suppose I shall be told what is now planned. I don't think C. is an intellectual, although she wrote charming poems when she was 12, but I hope she goes in for this psychology racket. Bryher says that qualified females are well paid, but after Aix-Marseilles she may have to do a 'finishing year' in Paris.

Did I tell you Bryher was very pleased with her reception by Gerald? She and her buddy dined with them en famille. She must be back in Zürich now, and I am anxious to hear what she thinks of H.D. Br. said the daily report from the nurse was reassuring, and that before she left the specialist said H.D. may be better than she has been for years. However, at 74 no very spectacular recovery can be expected.

[. . .] I had a letter from the other king [Potocki de Montalk] (now in Dorset with one of his [. . .] daughters who was left a little property by T.F. Powys) and he tells me pompously that he prefers the Germans to the French. So what? Does he expect France to reel under the blow? What he and old Norman Doug never realised is that you can't high-hat the French as you still can the boches and the Ey-teys. La Révolution a passé par là.

Love to both,
Richard

'Ro-Ro-Ro' is Rowohlt, and for a time Aldington considered rewriting his English text of *D. H. Lawrence in Selbstzeugnissen und Bilddokumenten* for the Thames and Hudson series. The Lawrence biography was finally written by Harry T. Moore and Warren Roberts as *D. H. Lawrence and His World* (1965).

Harry T. Moore edited the two-volume *Collected Letters of D. H. Lawrence* (1962).

Catherine Aldington married Jacques Guillaume on 12 January 1963.

Saintes, Wednesday [26 July 1961]

Dear Richard—

Your letter explains why we have seen no sign of Cath the last ten days. She's whizzing about in her car. I'm glad Gerry did his stuff and showed Bryher around as he promised. I hope she's got scars to show—of her choice bien sur!

About Rowohlt, I don't think you need even discuss the matter with him as it is an English language project, and as your book will be essentially a re-make—an after-the-event essay. Nor will it affect Rowohlt's public in any way. Thames and Hudson, I have been told, are very rich and are planning to build up a sort of modern Batsford-type of fine art publishing house. They've done several finely produced books—among them Patrick Kinross's short guide to modern Greece. It sounds a good ploy to me and certainly nobody except you could handle the subject so effectively. I'm trying to urge Temple's book on Rowohlt.

The Saintes is very crowded but fortunately with ordinary trippers and not Bardots. Consequently prices are still low (for France) and the general ambience pleasingly scruffy.

We visited the mazet yesterday as a fact-finding committee would; we have, as you know, acquired the profile opposite with the other mazet. Now a chap has appeared who sounds as if he will fill the bill as a resident handiman and gardener (for the table): also a watch when we are away. The name is nice Alphonse Trintinac—strong Logère accent. Rather stupid but a partly-disabled specialist in polyculture. If he is all he promises we shall be lucky—plans to virtually live off our own land—is there anything quite so satisfying I wonder? We split the produce. Next year all capital expenditure will be through and the property firmed up. 22 acres so near to Nîmes . . . one couldn't lose on it if we sold out as we may one day and head for a Greek island.

Much love from us both.

Larry

Sury-en-Vaux, Cher, 29 July 1961

Dear Larry,

It is very kind of you to reply so promptly to my query about the Pict Biog of DHL. I'll go on those lines. Unhappily, my agent in London seems to have gone away leaving nobody on deck. She has not replied to my letter of a week ago mentioning Thames & Hudson, nor to an earlier letter from Spring Books who want to reprint the *Decameron* translation as an illustrated. The way people let one down! Anyway I shall write direct to Neurath, and begin the negotiations myself, leaving Mrs C. to bring up the topic of money—what is money, is it an 'erb?

I see from the yank contract that the US paperback of a *P. of a G., But . . .* is due 'between Sept '61 and March '62', so apparently they won't delay. There doesn't seem any time limit for the US paperback of *Decameron*, but they have paid for 125,000 copies; unluckily bloody Doubledays have snaffled half, although their contract gives them no such right. But I had to accept their ultimatum, for they could have queered the deal.

Good that you have a favourable opinion of Thames & Hudson. I'd never heard of them.

Catha is here, with Jacques, behaving like a little lady and gentleman. At the moment they are out in her car, taking one of the peasant women to do her week-end marketing. There are no estivants at Sury, but St Satur and Sancerre are lousy with them. She is already reading on psychology, and I think is sérieuse about the Diplôme. I think that Jacques getting fired and then failing to get money to set up a 'promenades' of his own was a shock to her, and she realises that she must qualify for a job or . . . Obviously at nearly 70 I can't last much longer, and I doubt there'll be much or anything in the way of posthumous royalties for her.

Cath tells me that the gent from Mauritius is inviting subs to his mag on the ground (among other things) that he re-launched 'the forgotten writer R.A.' [. . .] Tell him he's got to cut that out, will you. What next?

The H.D. news is not so good. I had a long letter from her friend Prof Pearson (of Yale) who saw her after Bryher left for her cruise. He says H.D. is better physically and is even able to walk downstairs and sit in the garden, but there seems little or no recovery of speech. Shit, eh? But of course this may recover, even if slowly. Arnold Gyde (late of H'manns) got a boche bullet through his napper in the BEF of 1914, was paralysed and speechless. Eventually, though he had to have a silver plate over the hole, he recovered completely, and is still alive. But then tissues of a youngster of 22 recover better than those of 75. [. . .]

'Some unsuspected isle in the far seas.' But as Byron's valet said: 'His lordship must be mad to leave Italy, where we had everything, to come here where there is nothing to eat but tough nannygoat and nothing to drink but turpentine.'

Are the children yet with you?

Love to both,
Richard

A split between author and publisher on paperbound reprint rights is usual. The 50% claimed by Doubleday is the standard commission in such a transaction.

Ϟ Saintes, Monday [after 29 July 1961]

Dear Richard—Tomorrow we return to the garrigue for a spell, and I'll check exactly what Fanchette did say, but to the best of my recollection it was not offensive. After listing all the people he had printed he added something like 'also work by Richard A. who has been unjustly neglected of late'. I didn't get a shock when I skimmed it. But I will check on it anyway. Myself I'm always glad to see your name crop up among les jeunes—for policy reasons. The helm is coming over steadily I feel and justice will be done after this period of tracas. As for your expectation of life—Claude always says when we swear at you and curse you for not going on writing: Claude always says—'He doesn't seem to realise that he has 20 years ahead of him—he's going to be so *bored* if he stops writing!' More anon.

Much love from us all.

Larry

🕉 *Sury-en-Vaux, Cher, 4 August 1961*

Dear Larry,

Have you heard from Sternberg and/or Moore about the balls-up over your bibliography? It was made by Larry Powell, an old friend of mine, and just as S.I.U.P. were going to press with the Durrell book, out comes an article showing Powell has blundered. Too late to make changes, so they scrapped it. A pity. But if it had got by, the pedants would have had a field day, and all attention would have been diverted from your merits to the other Larry's boners. I can't understand it. He is one of the few yanks who really care about books, and has built up a very fine library at Los Angeles. And of course having been Librarian for over 30 years he knows his stuff. I fear that, like so many yank experts, he takes on too much work, and handed this over to an assistant without properly verifying.

I am having agent and publisher troubles, but won't bother you. [. . .] Since it became such a swindle on authors, publishing is odious, and of course in my case I am at a disadvantage now because of the concerted opposition, which was merely the culmination of 40 years of denigration. Mention in a two-donkey shay production by left bank Parisites is of no importance. If I were worth it, there would be a real battle such as we fought for DHL; but obviously nobody thinks so, and therefore I bow out. Life, as Gogol said, Life. I wish the king of Poland were not such a feckless fool, and so perpetually a pauper. If he had done as I told him, I could have used his Mélissa Press to get out a few libellous squibs on the Establishment and perhaps one or two highbrow-aesthetic productions. He made a complete balls-up of the Rome piece, so I shan't bother to do the Venice.

Catha and Jacques came here, and are now with Alister in Paris. If it suits them they may spend the week-end here on their way back to the Saintes. But I daresay Alister will keep them in Paris, and they'll go straight back on Monday.

The news of H.D. is not good. She has made a remarkable physical recovery, but the speech centres seem badly damaged. And in the Swiss clinic they all speak German, which she hates. Bryher wants us to go to Zürich for Hilda's 75th birthday (Sept) to see her, if the quacks permit, probably for the last time. Then she must be flown to USA, where she can have proper attention, be near her daughter and friends, etc. All this is rather depressing.

Do you remember my telling you how a 'friend' in London circa 1930 stole a deed-box containing literary letters &c? Well, Texas University has just published a brochure on their TSEliot collection, and it contains 71 letters from TSE to me, eleven from Virginia Woolf, eight from Ezra, and one from Lady Ottoline [Morrell]. This was about a scheme of Ezra's, which he called Bel Esprit (!) designed to get TSE out of slavery to the Bank by getting enough annual guarantees of 10 pounds to raise 300 a year. I thought Eliot knew all about it, but he didn't. Somebody spilled the beans, and a Liverpool daily came out with a stinker, and somebody sent Tom four penny stamps as a contribution! You can guess how that distressed him. He came out of it very well, as a matter of fact, and these letters should illustrate the whole abortive manoeuvre—typical Ezra nonsense. As DHL used to say reflectively: 'In the days when we took Ezra seriously, Richard . . .' Some, but not all, of DHL's letters to me from the same box have turned up, and are in the new 2-vol *Letters*. [. . .]

Your old pal, Osbert, sinks deeper into the horrors of Parkinson's, and refuses all treatment. Edith, on the other hand, has fully recovered, and is still on her campaigns against Noise and DHL. Both will probably survive her.

Catha wants me to share with her the expense of a house for the winter at the Saintes. But what on earth should I do there, being nei-

ther a bull nor a gardian, with her absent most of the time at Aix and
Marseilles? Aix would be better, but she says it is too much trouble to
look for non-existent flats, which is true.

I won't ask if the children are happy, for I'm sure they are. But
how about the water? Is there no way of increasing the supply without
hideous expense?

Love to all,
Richard

Apparently Aldington had been misinformed. Alan G. Thomas and
Lawrence Clark Powell had collaborated on a Durrell bibliography published in *The Book Collector* in 1960. It was basically this bibliography
which Mr Thomas offered for *The World of Lawrence Durrell* and which
Moore and Sternberg rejected on the grounds that it had already appeared in print. Aldington was correct in assuming that Powell, one of
the most brilliantly capable of American librarians, would not be likely to
commit errors.

ℐ *[Nîmes, 16 August 1961]*

Richard me boyo—I'm just off to Edinburgh for the performance of
Sappho scheduled for the 21st—Be back early in September—shall I
bring you a deer-stalker?

Everyone sends love
Larry

[P.S.] It's heartbreaking about H.D. I'm sad for her & you as well.

On 9 August Aldington had reported on Hilda Doolittle's recent stroke:
'The specialist says her progress is excellent in all respects, except in the
most essential. She will probably not be able to write again or even read
Greek. So drowns a noble mind [. . .].'

ℐ *Saintes [end August 1961]*

My dear R.

Saw Cath and Jacques for lunch yesterday. Just got back exhausted
from Scotland. The play received a stinking press as I expected particularly from the *Pravda-Observer* chaps but . . . hold your breath, it

paid its way and completely paid off the festival subvention—an occur-
rence so rare that they even began to moot a West End run, which I
knew imposs. from the start! What a joke! It was well played and good
on the eye and the audience loved it. But . . . I knew it was romantic
and foresaw disaster critically. But what the hell! It went through after
ten years! And now for the second in Germany. I don't mind about
anything so long as the children are paid up! And they are for the
nonce. Cath gave me your news—you old grumpy. It will be wonderful to see something of you this autumn. Just reading Harry T.
Moore's DHL. I liked it—it's temperate and lucid and just. Hope he
does as well by us in the book to come. We shoot off the children next
Wednesday and return to the mazet for a brief spell of work—mountains of correspondence! Poor Claude. But all goes well generally
speaking.

So looking forward to seeing you again, both of us. Keep that pow-
der dry!

Love

Larry

*Hôtel de Sévigné, Rue des Bernadines, Aix-en-Provence, B. du R., 3
October 1961*

Dear Larry,

H.D. is dead.

On Tuesday 26th she received from USA a copy of her latest
book of poetry, seemed interested and pleased, and looked it over.
Next evening (Weds) her nurse went down to fetch her evening meal,
and on returning found Hilda unconscious. The House Physician gave
oxygen, but it was too late, she was dead. Yesterday afternoon—Monday 2nd—her body was cremated. The ashes are to be flown to USA
and placed beside the graves of her parents.

Bryher wired and wrote here, instead of to Dromar, so I didn't get
the news until yesterday morning.

Love to both,

Richard

In a letter to Harry T. Moore, Aldington noted the poignant coincidence
that H. D. was cremated on 2 October, the anniversary of their marriage
in 1913.

❧ *Nîmes, 4 October [1961]*

Dear Richard—

How sad about H.D. I know what you feel. And yet a poet's death is never wholly sad, in the sense of a life unlived—because the work is there, like the aftertaste of a wine of high vintage. And really we writers aren't human beings but bundles of témoignage, words scribbled on paper. Every good death should incite us. Every good sorrow should teach us to keep feeling, keep working! The only real way to love the world, I guess.

We shall talk about her when we do these absurd discs and things—thoughtfully; we may lead people not yet fifteen or sixteen to her work and they may find there an indispensable aliment.

All of which means she isn't dead. How could she be—any more than Roy? They've stepped behind a curtain for a cigarette in the wings.

Best love to you both from us both.
Larry

❧ *Hôtel de Sévigné, Aix-en-Provence, B. du R., 10 October 1961*

Dear Larry,

Nutting has been answered, so my letter was superfluous, as well as feeble. Weintraub, an American scholar who is completing a study [on] TEL and GBS (how much did GBS re-write 7 Pills?) writes me:

'. . . Nutting's insinuation that you concocted the letter to Mrs G.B.S. alleged to be in the British Museum (but which he couldn't locate) was so annoying that I wrote an indignant letter to the editor announcing that I had just re-read the letter and was sure that Nutting's statement was typical of the quality of his research in the rest of his book. But the *STimes* didn't print mine (so they wrote me) because another letter actually quoted the "missing" letter. [. . .] But at least your statement is now actually confirmed by the quotation, which has received the *STimes*'s wide circulation.'

But will make no difference to the official 'hero' cult. Those letters in the B.M. are first-class evidence because they are the *only* TEL letters which haven't been 'edited' and touched up by the Lawrence Bureau.

I loved Antrobus and the barber—will return, but want to re-read. Idle thought of an idle fellow—could you do a farcical study round the idea of one of the Dip Corps gradually showing signs of going Bolshie and deserting to the enemy? Not our Dips, of course, but some Ruritanian mission. The Dips gradually hear about it, Polk-Mowbray wants to poison the feller to avoid an Occidental scandal, when happily it turns out that the guy is nuts and is certified, singing the Red Flag as he is strait-waistcoated and taken off to the bug-house. Perhaps too risky?

Catha came over to see me, and we lunched at Vauvenargues. Very pleasant. Jacques and his family at last have got that 'promenade' and start taking cows round on those little screws of ponies next week. Hope they succeed in making some dough. More fools in heaven and earth, Horatio.

Apropos cows—when is the Durrell Miscellany coming? I must stir up Illinois.

The *Times* obituary of H.D. headed it 'Miss Hilda Doolittle' and mentioned in an aside 'in 1913 she married Aldington', with the additional information that we translated from Greek and Latin together, 'bringing out a volume entitled *Images, Old and New*'. Funny, ever since 1915 I had thought it was a book of my own poems, but the *Times* must know. [. . .]

Love to both,
Richard

Stanley Weintraub's study, *Private Shaw and Public Shaw*, was published in 1963.

✿ Hôtel de Sévigné, Aix, 7 December 1961

Dear Larry,

I was glad to have a signal from you at last, though very sorry to learn that you are both ill. I can the more sympathise since for the last fortnight I've been battling with bronchitis and what the Scotch call 'a sair hoast'. The rain and now this mistral don't help.

With this a cutting from the *Times* in which you are named among a host of victims of Dame Edith, Jack Murry, E. Waugh, old uncle Tom Cobley and all. I trust Dame Edith isn't selling your love letters to her. She by the way is said to be writing a book to obliterate DHL. After trying to high-hat him for half a century she finds the collier's kid cock of the literary walk, and the coal-owner's bairns in the discard. Osbert, by the way, has had pins stuck in his noddle by the quacks, and is on the road to recovery from Parkinson's. It could have been done years ago if he hadn't been such a mule. The cutting, by the way, is from Sotheby's ad., and it is amazing to read of the stuff now being auctioned in England. The whole ex-upper class must be broke.

Glad to know that the play went over so nicely, and hope it keeps the pot-au-feu a-boiling. The yank book on you is postponed until Jan—perhaps as well since there is then more chance for discussion of a non-creative book. S. Illinois hasn't much prestige, but the book may help a bit. The DHL illustrated and our tape are out. Neurath took one sniff at my Rowohlt DHL, and you couldn't see his arse for dust. Possibly his sturdy British pride was outraged by some of the things I said about the cowardly bullying and high-hatting stupidity of the DHL persecution in his lifetime, and the Pecksniffian pretence of 'admiration' when in spite of them he became a world seller. *Lady C.* has now passed the three million in Penguin alone, not to mention the yank piracies and translations. There is a (bad) French version in a pocketbook with an intro by Malraux, which shows that he knows a lot about erotic books and has precious little knowledge of DHL or appreciation of his unique powers. Rowohlt editors from time to time consult me on their reprints, and I urge the merits of the travel books and pieces, but whether the editors pay any attention I know not. They are certainly in no hurry to reprint the *Hero*. They may be right and the book may have outlived its public, though the recent English paperback has now reached 25,000, making at least 130,000 (there were 75,000 Penguins) to date. But people have supped so full of horrors and threats that they have become apathetic to them, and can no longer respond to the book's saeva indignatio. The lament for a butchered generation is taken to be 'personal resentment', as some British academic cunt recently stated in print. Well, if I hadn't been there I couldn't have suffered for others as well as for myself.

Shakers is a chance for you. We've had MILLIONS of books by

academics and Dame Edith—about time a poet had his say. The great difficulty is to determine what is Shakers and what isn't, both in the canon and the apocrypha. My own view is that he was quite venal and the head of a syndicate like Dumas père. One may imagine such a scene as this:

Shakers discovered solus, scribbling. Enter an actor.

Actor: I say, Bill.

Shakers: Shut up and go away. Can't you see I'm still slaving to keep you bastards your jobs?

Actor: I know, I know. But I want you to add a bit for me in that Macbeth scene.

Shakers: Whaffor?

Actor: Well, er, it's like this. There's a cute little piece always comes to that show, and I've got me eye on her. Now if you'll give me a few extra lines in that scene—you know, one of your twiddley bits— people'll notice and she'll notice . . .

Shakers: Balls to you. What the hell . . .

Actor: Yeah, but lissen, Bill. It won't take you two jiffs, and I'll cough up a rose noble.

Shakers: (At last interested) Make it two?

Actor: (Reluctantly) All right—she's worth it.

Shakers: (Scrawls and then reads lines beginning To-morrow and to-morrow and tomorrow etc.) Will that do?

Actor: It's a bit corny, I must say, but it may give me a chance to produce my voice and do a bit of business. Here's the dough.

Shakers: O.K. and now fuck off.

Work upon that now, as your and his friend Dekker says some-where.

> Love to both,
> Richard

❦ *Nîmes [ca. 7–11 December 1961]*

Dear Richard;

Delighted to hear you are still in the parages and most amused by enclosures! I'm sending you a photostat of some letters with Sir Osbert

which should chuckle you. I fell foul of him by accident; the letters repose in California. [. . .] By the way, a book which will interest you *Le
Matin des magiciens* (NRF) gives a popular and readable account of
what the hell is happening in contemporary thought—how magic, poetry, maths, physics, alchemy, psychology etc are coming bang up
against a totally new notion of a formula applicable to every field . . .
It's much what we've all known; but this is the first pop account which
is at all readable and well done. Also has excellent things on Nazi Black
Magic; do have a look if you can find it in Aix. I really think it would
amuse you. By two chaps, Bergier and Pauwels.

Yes, you are right about Shaks; the only things one can really be
sure were all him are the two appalling verse-treats, *Venus and Adonis*
and *Lucrece;* and of course the Sonnets . . . I may be mad to see an actual situation there described, but really there is no other sonnet-
sequence of the period (I've read them all) quite like it; it's absolutely
non show off and non Petrarch and depicts I think a real situation . . .
How the hell can we know? But Sh's attitude to a dark skin, to black
beauty, echoes here and there in the plays; myself I think he was half
Jewish like Montaigne. But of course all this is romancing. Only Madame Blavatsky could tell us for certain. But I don't think he thought
of himself as a writer at all, and his reputation with his contemporaries
was nearer, say, to René Clair's than Valéry . . . Well, we shall see. I
still haven't got the contract, and until I do I don't try to cross Niagara
in a barrel, a Durrell.

More anon,

much love and some sneezes from us both.
Larry

⑨ *Sévigné, Aix-en-Provence, 12 December 1961*

Dear Larry,

Catha thinks you and Claude always (like the other nobs) go to England for Xmas . . .

If not would you consider a Xmas dinner (evening) with us at the
cabane? We would provide turkey etc and try to give these poor frogs

a decent meal for once in their lives. Will you ring up here as soon as possible, since it will need planning. Number: Aix 16 - 63.

Love to both,
Richard

꧁ *Nîmes, 12 December 1961*

Dear Richard,

I always love you, but especially now when you're sharing my own recovery from the bronchs—you can have half of my self-pity—there!

Larry says I'm mad, and it's too late to plan anything for Christmas, but he's used to me and said go ahead when I suggested that you just might not have planned anything special, and so DEAR MISTER ALDINGTON? WOULD YOU CONSIDER SPEND-ING CHRISTMAS WITH US? No draughty children's bedrooms— a nice warm room at the Hôtel du Midi (on us) with a good hot bath, and all your waking hours Xmas Eve & day with us? I *can* do a decent Christmas dinner, and it would be so very nice if you could say yes. And if you can't, and have other plans, will understand of course. But if you hesitate, remember it would please us so much. Perhaps Catha and Jacques might like to come and have lunch here the next day, or some-thing like that . . . A eux de decider. We haven't seen you for a very long time, and Christmas [. . .] seems to be a splendid chance.

By then, too, we should no longer be coughing and spitting and sufficiently recovered to enjoy the Festive Season.

On vous embrasse tous les deux, espérant que vous direz Oui!

Claude

꧁ *Nîmes, 28 December [1961]*

My dear Richard:

Question I meant to ask you but which slipped my mind in the course of all the Christmas chat was this: do you know offhand what the insignia, shield or rebus of the Tarquin family was? It might have some bearing on the little psychoanalytic game I'm playing with Will

S: or trying to, I should say. Will send you a carbon in a day or two for you to blast out of the water with a well aimed charge of dynamite.

'Twas splendid to see you in good heart and unworried, and a delight to hear that your fortunes are steadily mending. Fortune the jade! But we both had the impression that you looked ten years younger and far more happy & relaxed than at any time since we first met. I hope the drunken cowbabies at the cabane enjoyed themselves in their own fashion. One of these days I shall be coming through Aix and hope I shall be able to nobble you for a drink. I've got awfully stale and need a week end away from the machine to recharge the batteries.

> Much love from us both
>
> Larry

Durrell's 'Shakespeare and Love' essay was eventually printed in Pierre Singer's translation as 'L'Amour, clef du mystère?' in *Shakespeare*, Collection Génies et Réalités, 1962 (not published until 1965).

ƒ Sévigné, Aix, 4 [January] 1962

My dear Larry,

Yesterday I sent off some pedantries about Tarquin. I thought you might have wanted a sentence or two about the origin of the Lucretia legend and what little (very little) is now known about the historical Tarchu. But I see it is all irrelevant to your purpose.

When I got back here to the hotel I found your carbon, and read it at once. My first impression is that you have chosen the wrong form, and wasted on historical criticism what 'God meant' for art. You have sketched out the rough plan of a 'reconstruction' Renaissance novel which might be the wow of the century. Why waste on miserable pedants what is 'meant' for mankind? Of course, you have Oscar in the way, but you can walk round him without getting out of your chair. And there is the novelist's difficulty that you would have two 'Wills'. Of course the creative impulse moves in its own way, and your Balaam's ass may refuse to trot that path. But do consider it. I think you may have here a great opportunity. Consult the Muse.

From the point of view of 'historical criticism' I fear you may be an easy target for the academic batteries if you publish in this form.

Tell Claude (upon whom be Prayer and Peace) that in her passion for Shelley she has typed Adonis throughout as Adonais. But you'll have noted this.

The real Othello was [. . .] a Venetian general, Cristoforo Moro, who murdered his wife, fled, and was murdered by bravi hired by his wife's family. A squalid tale, which Cintio, and then Shakers much improved. By sheer chance I have Cintio with me, and he begins: 'Fu già in Venezia un Moro molto valoroso . . .' So already by his time (1504–1573) the surname Moro had been melodramaed into 'un Moro'. But that might mean merely 'dark-haired', like the Elizabethan 'black' (remember Lodovico il Moro) or at most a bicot like Bourguiba and the FLN (may Allah blacken their faces). I wonder how much of *Andronicus* (if any) is Shakers? Years since I read it, but it sounded like some ranting imitator of Marlowe. Conceivably Shakers might have written such lines as:

> He dies upon my scimitar's sharp point
> Who touches this my first-born son and heir.

(There's 'heir' again!) Isn't it now turfed out of the canon?

Yesterday I searched this highly cultured university town for an English text of Shakers. In vain. They had heard of the bloke, and had one or two Gide versions and an English *Merchant* 'for the use of schools'. But otherwise nicht, nullus, niente.

I thought it was to Nutting's credit that he resigned over Suez— hard to give up a career at that point [. . .]. If that coup had succeeded we should be much further from the universal anarchy the idiot yanks and doctrinaires and commies are spreading. But acting as tout to a film produced by Sam Spiegel! Out, haro. Dr Weintraub (of Penna) who is the only person beside myself to have laboured the whole bloody mass of evidence without bias, says Nutting's book is poor and unscholarly. I read only one *Sunday Times* extract, but that was enough to give away N.'s incompetence. History and biography demand standards different from those of F.O. propaganda and Parliamentary oratory. But you are quite right. My cue is to keep quiet, and let the wrangle go on. If the yanks do, as seems possible, paperback my TEL, the battle is won. Hardly any of them read the original book. They just allowed the London establishment to review and to suppress it.

> Love to both as always,
> Richard

In discussing Durrell's proposed Renaissance novel, Aldington had earlier mentioned Oscar Wilde's *Portrait of Mr. W. H.*

Nîmes [after 4 January 1962]

Dear Richard;

Many thanks for your letter; yes, it is awfully wobbly, I know only too well: a mere newspaper article in its present state, and I'd never dream of releasing it in English or German in its present state. Actually I'm just waiting for a book or two before expanding it in a number of directions into a forty or fifty pager; but I couldn't in fifteen pages, and for a pop market start throwing Spenser Sidney Dyer Barnfield and company at them; and it was either starting a hare or tamely paraphrasing Sidney Lee and ending up with the old nothing-can-be-said ploy—which is after all the reel truth of the matter. I shall take it all apart and add things like the Hobbinol bit from Spenser and some Barnfield and various other bits, including some from Shakes himself. I think the central case isn't so bad; tho of course it's a bit ludicrous a mixture of astrology and Freud. But what else can one do? I'm sure he wasn't a bugger but heir-haunted, and even those nice bits in *Richard* about the infant actors which make buggers slaver are just envisioning his own little heir at Stratford; probably had plans to get him into the company when he was fifteen. Instead of which the boy dies on him. But with an artist who is always using other people's stuff to work on it's awfully hard to know anything for certain; and most particularly with this wicked chameleon. However they brought it on themselves. I'd never have written a word about Sh. unless they'd provoked me. I'm wrestling with *Faustus* . . . O dear, more difficulties with magic! But *Acte*'s success has suggested that I wasn't so foolish to go back to the *Spanish Tragedy* and make it my starting point . . . But of course serious people everywhere would be agin such a neo-neo-neo-attitude. [. . .]

> much love from us both
> Larry

Nîmes [ca. 8–12 January 1962]

Dear Richard;

[. . .] I'm planning a bit of a Bold Belloc next week to cool the heated mind; one more article for *Figaro* and I'm off. Would you be there Wednesday *next* week? I'd love to pop in on you. I wonder if I mightn't lodge the night in your little hostelry? Would they have a room? Then next morn I could make tracks. I want to feel the wind in my grey curls for a few days, and feel careless like a daft undergrad. I haven't had a real bit of mooching time off alone for years now; and this play is getting me worried as it has to be delivered end Feb for production next season. I think a changement of a few scaramouche days might prowl up my fancy and cocker my typewriter. Tandis que Claude has a big translation on hand here and would be quite safe and happy for a short while. Will you ask your chap? I'll roll in for lunch I imagine; only place I know for rendezvous is Café Leyden on the Mirabeau.

Why don't you make a case for Marlowe writing the sonnets? And blow me down. It's just possible.

> much love
> Larry

[P.S.] Never thought of a historical novel; it must be very difficult to avoid the Avaunt kind of tushery?

Claude Durrell was at work translating Marc Peyre's *Captive of Zour*.

Sévigné, Aix, 13 January 1962

Dear Larry,

Do you have to pay Italian income tax on your Italian royalties? I have a communication from Mondadori showing that they deducted as tax nearly 12% on my last account. After my name on the form they put 'Inghilterráx', and of course I am a British subject, but fiscally domiciled in France. Isn't there an exemption arrangement between France and Italy? Instruct my ignorance. The tax officials in the Cher are ignorant of all these international arrangements, and suspicious because they have to deal mainly with peasants and petty commerçants who always cheat.

This taxing royalties is an American device, introduced by them whenever they take over a country. It is the same in Japan where I am taxed 20% on royalties. Of course they do it themselves—'taxation without representation is tyranny'. The American Congress has always been an enemy to authors, so we should be their enemies, and lose no chance of a smack at the bastards. Even our copyright there is not for life and 50 years, but two periods of 28 years. And until recently there was no American copyright in foreign books not set up and published in USA within six weeks of original publication. Thus my version of *Candide* has been pirated by several yank publishers [. . .] who made a fearful outcry against my protests and coughed up inadequate sums most reluctantly; Shits.

Yet I believe the insufferable Gladstone started it all by taxing visiting American authors during the War of Secession. Silly thing to do. [. . .]

To my dismay Catha has scratched up a prof of English here, who told her I am 'a successor of Milton'! I've been called a lot [of] things, but never that before. Catch me acting as sec to old Noll or any other filthy Roundhead. Prick-eared curs. This French cow eagerly asked if I'd give a lecture, to which Catha sagely answered: 'Mon père est un sauvage.'

Love to both,
Richard

♂ *Sévigné, 6 February 1962*

Dear Larry,

I'm sorry I had a tin ear on the phone. I am going deaf, hate the phone, and the French phone service is about where the yanks were in 1900.

Will you repeat any instructions by letter?

Your copy of THE book [*The World of Lawrence Durrell*] was sent by air. I trust you are not displeased? Sternberg asked me to suggest some free personal copies. I gave him Haley, Snow, Jeffares (Leeds) and Geoff Dutton. So don't overlap. I asked for them to be sent at my request.

I don't think Haley can review in the *Times* because it is a yank book and purely literary. Therefore, the prey of the *TLS,* where you have such warm-hearted friends. Old Snow meets everybody, likes any acknowledgement on the literary rather than scientific side, and might help. The reason for Jeffares is that he runs that series of monographs on recent authors, and might be moved to commission one of you. Dutton is now chief literary adviser to the new Australian Penguins, and joint editor of two lit'ry periodicals. And don't shoot the pianist.

I must get back to Sury—too expensive here. Then I feel I may be in Catha's way. As she spends much of her spare time here with me, she doesn't make friends with students of her own age. Similarly, I won't go to the Saintes, as I rather spoil the fun for them.

Tell Claude that *Times* X-wd. 9,901 is a corker. She'll get it out, but I couldn't. X-words are a great resource for busy publishers. Thus, Frere used to drive a full 1000 yards to his office about ten, in a company-owned Rolls, look through his already opened letters, tell other people to answer them, and then settle to the serious business of the *Times* X-word. He would then lunch on expense account, play cards at the Garrick with Duckworth and other intellectuals, return to sign his letters, and receive a few obsequious authors at a levee to tell them business was so bad they couldn't have any money. He generally dined one of them at the Savoy—expense account. It's a damn shame he didn't get his peerage.

Love to both,
Richard

🎜 *Nimes [ca. 6–13 February 1962]*

Dear Richard;

It was less your earhole I think and [more] my exuberance at having such a lovely large book all—ALL about me. What pleasanter intoxication than to lie back on the sofa, select a chocolate with a soft centre, and then open a book devoted to praising your own damn swordsmanship? Nothing. I know nothing so nice. When I got to the end I said plaintively: 'Why aren't there more books like this? Really good books on worthwhile subjects.' But joking aside it is admirably conceived and executed; it's extremely varied as far as approach goes. The contributors are all very different and all have a separate approach to the books. There is a maths man who diagrams the whole thing out with tangents and cosines; and there is another who has unrolled and examined all the gnostic references; another has bracketed the Tarot references. All in all, even if it were not about me, I think it would be interesting. It's certainly a marvellous service to me and I can't thank you enough for leading the dance. I'll organise some copies for chaps. You know, I hope Snow won't be piqued because Gerald [Sykes] has left in his crack about me not being 'unco British'. It is mild enough I suppose but usually people should be careful of direct quoting; think Gerald might have left it out. Sometimes one says something ironically or in a context, and it comes out at an unjust angle. Like poor [. . .]; everything I told him as a joke got printed like gospel, and what I said seriously was bypassed or mangled. However. The book is serious without being professorial; the one silly piece is not the fault of the poor man Green. The book was issued so fast and all so different that Mr Green found himself arse upwards—a wayward British position, examining my philosophy through my story for 14-year-old boys, and accusing me of being a poor copy of Buchan. It's really a scream.

The first volume of the Miller-Durrell correspondence has come in typescript; it's rather funny in bits. Of course I was insufferable at twenty-five and I guess it's good to [be] made to rub my own nose in it. Wondered if it might amuse you to read? I notice your name crops up all over the place.

Much love from us both.

If you leave, do let us know when.

Larry

Durrell is mistaken about the Martin Green article; it had earlier been printed in the *Yale Review* of 1960, and thus the author had had sufficient time to revise his stand.

Durrell's one juvenile is *White Eagles Over Serbia* (1957).

Lawrence Durrell/Henry Miller: A Private Correspondence appeared in 1963.

❧ *Sévigné, 13 February 1962*

My dear Larry,

Auspicious omen—your checklist and letter about the book on that feller Durrell arrived at the same time as the new (and vast) DHL *Letters.* I am much relieved that you aren't displeased by the Illinois book, and most devoutly hope it'll be of some use to you. But what? As a matter of fact you don't need it, and we are cashing in on you. I never heard of Mr Green, but then I have never heard of anybody who really matters—only the old strumperumpers. (Place me that word!) Buchan be damned. He was guilty of the sin of sending Lowell Thomas to Akaba and its romantic security—the Western front flinging its heavies and shrapnel about without so much as a thought for the valuable lives of yank journalists.

Your checklist must bring back your youth, as DHL's letters bring mine—I can see his blasted genius waiting to trap me long before I ever saw him. I find him 'musing' on flowers in a garden in 1908 just about the time I was 'musing' over the butterflies on a large lavender plant.

I am pleased with Moore's introduction. He makes the right points and quotes, which I can praise since they all occur first in my *Portrait.* And he isn't shamefully modest. A fearful chore, well done, largely by his wife I think, but no matter. You ought to have the book—but 84 bloody shillings—bit of a dental extraction even for an overpaid genius. Perhaps Heinemann will send you one. Ought I to thank them as well as Moore? Perhaps I ought, though we are scarce cater-cousins [. . .].

I don't think old Snow has anything against you. In his last letter (9th Feb) he says: 'Do give my warm regards to Laurence (*sic*) Durrell if you should see him. He is, of course, a very different writer from me, but I have great respect for him, and envy his gifts. Tell him that I go round American colleges explaining that his name is *not* accented on the last syllable.'

Not unfriendly? The 'very different writer' is plain even to my dim intelligence. Note the touch of the ex-Cambridge don in 'American *colleges*'—not universities.

Probably I shall start back for Sury on the 27th, unless some new deluge of snow and ice arrives. I struggle with my indolence which doesn't want to order in coal with instructions how to get garage open, or to write the Guénauds begging for sarments and the furnace to be lighted, or to get my car serviced and 'revised', or to pack, or to make that boring route 7 journey in a blizzard of trucks and road-hogs.

The *Figaro* says Willie Maugham is selling his pictures and devoting the proceeds with the rest of his fortune to founding incomes for poor writers. The Brit press has not mentioned it—they wouldn't. I resisted my impulse to write gratters to WSM, first because the *Fig* might be a canard, and then I didn't want to seem to be putting in my claim—though who better deserves a slice?

Your *Cefalû*, evidently sold out, has again appeared in the Aix shops—in the vitrine of the Provençal almost next to some new catchpenny French book on the bogus prince of Mecca.

No more violence in Paris, thank goodness. But we still have to get over to-day's funeral. *L'Humanité* headlines, banner, call for two days of fight for LIBERTÉ—communist 'liberty'. No Paris papers but I got the Nice Morning, which apparently didn't have a strike.

Yes, I would like to see the Durrell-Miller (note the inversion) script. I feel rather like old Wyndham (remember?) who, if one happened to mention meeting a common friend, always enquired with hostile suspicion: 'What'd he say about me?'

Goak—the Italians are about to boost Ponza for tourists, and an article 'selling' same advises all morons to buy *All Men* 'which is placed for the most part in Ponza'. Per Bacco. True, some people say Ponza used to be Aeaea, but I have never even been there, and know nothing about it save what I read reverently in old Norman's sketch. Apropos, why doesn't some demented publisher re-issue that marvellous book of Ramage on south Italy, with Norman's most cogent and amusing essay as introduction? Why, because they are a pack of ignorant pimps and spivs. That's why.

Love to both,
Richard

[P.S.] Bryher is sending me some of the books I gave Hilda, and among them is Ruskin's *Praeterita,* which I've re-read. I perceive again what Norman meant when he wrote: 'Ruskin isn't a man, he's an emetic.' A little sweeping and unjust perhaps.

> The funeral for the eight demonstrators killed on 7 February in fighting between left-wing anti-fascists and government security forces drew several hundred thousand mourners.

> Aldington is referring to Craufurd Tait Ramage's *The Nooks and By-Ways of Italy.*

ᛃ Nîmes [ca. 13–18 February 1962]

Dear Richard; It's good that things are shaping as they are; the wheel is coming round, as I always said it would. This year and next you will see quite a large cuddle up all round. By God, though, we are getting the most devastatingly wicked mistral, knocking down trees and whatnot all round. Yes, the events in France are bad as always (sorry my *a* has stuck). Will try and disengage it. AAAAAAAAAAAaaaaaaaaaaaaaaaaaaaaaaa aaaaaaa no go. But actually the OAS which is such a bore here can only be helping negotiations the other end? It is of course touch and go, but with the French as politically as silly [. . .] as the Gyppos there is nothing to be done; let them overlay each other in the Metro in an excess of zeal. At least the general knows what works with Arabs, and I hope with his own countrymen. Balzac is easy meat to take or not as you feel, but I remember a note from your agent which you showed me in Aix which mentioned *Le Rouge et le noir*; well now, thanks to your early tuition I have only read *De l'Amour* in French; but now I've just read the Rouge and the Chartreuse in French and I realise how deficient the present Moncrieff versions are. They are faithful to meaning, yes, but they haven't got the quirky idiosyncratic feel of the original. The French of Stendhal isn't very good (excuse me); it has a Dauphinois ring. But the poetic usage he adopts is so very weird that it keeps you on the qui vive with every sentence; you have, so to speak, a smile or a frown ready because you don't know whether in the final add up the thing is going to be comic irony or a serious truth of some sort. You can't take chances with him; he loves the upside down, elliptical, odd man out way of writing. It's a very special ironic flavour that one degages from him. It hasn't yet been done. But it's damn near to the Aldington irony, though of course different context and different moeurs; but I should say that you were born to interpret him in an equivalent quirky english. Could quote you a number of splendid double-takes, introduced at vital moments of the action when the author has no right to intrude, and which make fun of everything, chiefly the author, which are quite genial. Yes, very much your author I think. Ponder him. He is a target well worth your deadly bow and arrow.

I've nearly finished *Faustus*; another peroration and the bloody Devil can rise and eat them all. It may be better than I fear. I'm sick of this aaaaaaaaaaaaaaaaaA AAA aaaaaaaaa a a no go. It's full of derision. More by hand.

Larry.

So long as the corpses have no bullet holes it's okay; it's the price of curiosity. You remember the stricture by someone on the Athenians? The Modern French, to the life. Bam Bam Bam . . . Another Pompier bites the dust. The new issue of *Olympia* has been suspended for pornography and I am in it . . . another procès-verbal. O dear, twelve years of close confinement with nothing but Fénélon to read. Yes, the Moore compilation is really very good. I'm delighted, particularly because you lead in. The letters are terrible, but will make you laugh a great deal. I was 25 and v. serious indeed. Miller's long swing away from traditional forms impressed me much as DHL's wild activeness [?] must have knocked you off your plate. I'm hoping to finish the new play tomorrow and then to have ten days rock building before the next game—a scenario to end all scenarios called La Machine à Plaisir—no, not the autobiography of a washing machine. Your french must be better than that!

Why not come over for a glass? The director of the Midi told me yesterday they were missing you: 'ce cher M. Aldington'. He is a fan of ours by the way.

You don't think *Seraphita* and *Louis Lambert* should be done in U.K.? They never have been. Are they the worse for being applied Swedenborg? Am I the worse for being post-Einstein . . . Answer!

Now the pen has run out as well.
Blast! It's the mistral!

Love

Larry

Durrell's 'Pursewarden's Incorrigibilia' and 'Frankie and Johnny' appeared in this issue of *Olympia* (No. I, 1962).

'La Machine à Plaisir' was Durrell's working title for the novel sequence *Tunc* (1968) and *Nunquam* (1970), published in one volume as *The Revolt of Aphrodite* (1974).

⚓ *Sévigné, 18 February 1962*

Dear Larry,

[. . .] Moore's notice of Eliz I is interesting. I wonder if Jennings is right, and that she was a virgin? Hope not, poor girl. Ben, who knew no more about it than we do, says she had 'a membrana' (whatever he meant) but 'tried many men for her delight'. So unlike our own dear David Windsor. The tale is that everyone thought it was high time he ceased to be a puceau, so the arrangement was made for him to spend the night with a chorus-girl. But he was so nervous that he made no approaches but just sat on and on and on, until in exasperation she said: 'Now, do you want to come to bed, or do you want to go back to your little grey home in the West?' Ben trovato.

Those silly *Sat Rev* people in N.Y. want only 700 words on the new DHL *Letters*—a bad sign. All this whooping up of *Lady C.* has done harm to his real reputation. It deserves at least 2000. Heinemann's format is rotten—print often greyish, paper too thick, so each tome weighs about 5 pounds, and the monument becomes a couple of tombstones. Also for 84/- they give only a case-binding. [. . .]

Rowohlt have sold 30,000 more copies of my *DHL* to Ex Libris AG, Zürich, whatever that may be. Of course they are going to bone half my royalties. Hope the Hamburg floods got him.

I wish Dorothy would write to tell me how Ezra is. I suppose you didn't see the item saying he'd had a heart attack. By'r Lady, it is just 50 withered years (Francis Thompson) since I first knew him. In those days as amusing a cuss as ever slipped on a banana skin.

The Folio Laclos is much better designed and printed than Heine-mann's scurvy DHL and only 27/-, stitch-bound. But the illustrations are feeble as hell.

DHL was a good pal. He was very jel because *Point Counter Point* was a best-seller and badly jolted by reading the prologue to the *Hero* in typescript. Listen to this, written to Aldous:

'. . . if you can only palpitate to murder, suicide, rape, in their vari-ous degrees—and you plainly state that it is so (*sic!*)—*caro*, however are we going to live through the days? . . . And if murder, suicide, rape is what you thrill to, and nothing else, then it's your destiny . . . R.A. is exactly the same inside, murder, suicide, rape—with a desire to *be* raped very strong—same thing really—just like you—only he doesn't face it, and gilds his perverseness.'

Of course I've murdered and suicided pretty often, but I could never get any damned woman to rape me. Just my luck.

Love to both,
Richard

Rowohlt: see note on page 185.

Lawrence's letter to Huxley of 28(?) October 1928 is printed in *The Collected Letters of D. H. Lawrence.*

𝕊 *Sury-en-Vaux, Cher, 15 March 1962*

Dear Larry,

Why have you and Claude gone into hibernation (or purdah) now that April is round the corner? It grieved me much to miss your party, but before I heard about it I had already fixed time of arrival here, and then champagne at midnight is not a good preparation for a long drive by an octogenarian. [. . .]

In confidence to you and Claude the enclosed copy of a letter from the sec. of USSR Writers' Union. After consultation with Bryher and my solicitor-brother I have rather grudgingly accepted for us both. Catha can visit schools for feeble-minded children, and I shall at least have the pleasure of annoying some people in G.B. We shake hands with murder some time in second half of June, but I have to find out when Catha will be free. As it is for three weeks I shall try to get to Samarcand, and find out what Flecker was talking about.

I have just turned down another TV invite. A letter came from Joan Rodker (presumably a scion of old Wyndham's Ratner) asking me to take part in some show about the soldier-writers of the two fracas. The other names given were all chair-borne warriors of the knife-and-fork brigade, BBC war embusqués who wept for the soldier at a guinea a tear. Blasted cheek to ask me to bolster those bastards. I thought of my last two passages across the Somme battlefields— tramping up through the infinite litter of the defeated German army and the chaos of graves, with Cambrai and other towns burning; and the return by slow cold train after the Armistice through that tragical desolation of death. You can't make a show of such memories. [. . .]

Very peaceful and pleasant here, which makes me feel very cheerful and urbane. Not a sound. And a Little Owl comes to feed in the grass, and then perches on the quince tree, looking, I confess more foolish than wise. Glaucopis.

Love to you both,
Richard

This is the text of Alexei Surkov's 9 February 1962 letter to Aldington:
  You probably know that your books are widely read, published and loved in the Soviet Union.
  We appreciate you as a distinguished writer humanist who has devoted all his life to the cause of peace and human happiness. That is why we would be honoured if you would accept our invitation to you and your daughter to visit the Soviet Union and spend here 3 weeks as guests of our Union (The Union of Writers of the USSR). Your numerous Russian readers would welcome your presence here in July, and you will spend your 70th birthday among us.
  And of course all the expenses during your and your daughter's stay in the Soviet Union, as well as the flight from Paris to Moscow and back, will be covered by the Writers' Union.
  We do hope you will accept our invitation and will let us know as soon as possible about your decision.

'Shake hands with murder' was used around the time of World War I to denote any agreement or friendly contact with Germany, and many of Aldington's generation felt the same about a liaison with Khrushchev's Russia.

Lewis satirised John Rodker as Ratner in *The Apes of God*.

✍ *Nîmes, Monday; no, Tuesday [after 15 March 1962]*

Dear Richard;

Silence was due to a few days bronchitis—essentially psycho pso-matic I know: brought about by the need to correct the *Quartet* quickly for a one-vol edition this autumn; heavens the slips and skids and barely negotiated virages . . . O dear; I keep wanting to sit down and re-do it all over, but there isn't time. Meanwhile in the case of Claude the silence is entirely due to the DHL letters which I ordered secretly for her as a birthday present, with the result that she gives me cold meals now and has hardly stirred from the fireside this forty-eight hours. (And still on vol I) When will she get normal again? It's not fair.

I'm delighted about the Russian trip, but particularly the timing, as you cannot do yourself any harm now and may do us all some good; also it will make a terrific change in landscape to plough northward through the huge tundra-like wastes to the town where these misbe-gotten sods continue to misbeget; and if you get down south you will find the people livelier and happier and quite fun I'm sure after what I heard from people like Fitzroy Maclean. Try the Black Sea end (where commissars go to get away from it all). Bring me back a Samovar and a collected Rozanov. On second thoughts better not mention him, nor Babel.

Don't know who is there en poste at the moment, but what a pity Patrick Reilly has left for Washington; you would have loved him and he would have been of the greatest use. I haven't got a dip list so I can't check.

Take them a breath of fresh air; and you'll find that all the fish foods and vodka etc laid on by the ministry are tops to eat. It's some-thing everyone ought to do once. But it's going to be cold, so take warm undies, Cath too.

Will you be passing through Germany? Why not stop and see dear Ledig? I think you [would] like him, and Robert Schnorr. Altogether it's very good to feel you will be doing a short sharp trek before the summer breaks on us here. Don't stay away too long.

We've had bloody neither norish sort of weather which persists;

but the potager is now in commission and soon will come our own eggs and salads in abundance.

much love; more soon; I must boil myself
an egge it seems thanks to DHL.

Larry

⑨ *Nimes, 26 March [1962]*

Dear Richard;

Your letter was a scream; true to your old form! No, but the Russian journey is excellent, just what you need—I don't mean Russia, but a change, a long journey. And sponsored as it is it will be comfy as they can make it; and what a blow to our national heritage to have them firing guns for your birthday instead of us. Serves us bloody right. Makes me chuckle with pleasure though—touch of malice in this; I can hear them in the Charing Cross Road! Excellent. Excellent. By the way as a foreign sponsored guest H.M. Mission need not cross your path, and won't feel hurt if you ignore them; it's possible that from tact they won't intrude an attaché on you, so as not looking like poaching; or to make your hosts feel suspicious etc. They may not, in fact, *know;* but I surmise they will be told and that likely they'll send the press officer (think of me and don't bite him) to stand at the back of the reception committee at the airport and murmur Welcome, depositing a card with phone number 'just in case', and saying that H.E. would be delighted to receive you if you have time but will quite understand etc etc. If on the other hand *you* feel it appropriate to make your number the procedure is simple and need not involve you in any trouble. Just ask your host, translator, to take you to the Embassy and ask them for 'The Book'; you will be conducted to the front hall of the residence where it lies on a table. Sign therein (and for Cath too if you wish) and beat it. Nothing else; you can turn down any invites which they may feel compelled to launch at a man of your eminence by pleading a crowded agenda. And this, by God, will be too true and well they will know it! In fact when you are handed your itinerary be a wise man and insist on having every other day off to loaf. They tend to pack about thirty visits a day into things, and you get corns or have breakdowns. My tours of

England were a great success with Marxists because I insisted on a one-day loaf between full days of visiting; mind you, I laid on translators etc, and let them understand that they could see anything they wished that didn't need special permission and organisation. This went very well; but for their part they crammed, and many a hot and footsore Brit stumbled to my door with blazing feet with a plea for a hassock. You have been warned!

I don't think you need feel undue concern about C.P. Snow; he is very well padded and protected by very powerful concerns like the *Sunday Times* etc. After all they elected him the British mandarin and they will defend him tooth and nail, you'll see. I don't know any details, only the bare fact, from a letter. I think Leavis is lobbying frankly; he hasn't been news (controversial) for many a long year and thinks a dust up will blazon him forth again. If you add to the chorus you are only helping him . . . and may get him an important cultural appointment in UNESCO or something. Wouldn't that be worse? Wary does it.

love
Larry

🦋 *Sury-en-Vaux, Cher, 20 May 1962*.

Dear Larry,

[. . .] Do you ever see the *TLS*? Harry T. Moore writes 'I suppose you saw *TLS* on the Lawrence *Letters*—first really nasty review, and a monument of nastiness. Obviously the Leavis crew who have taken quite a beating since the Snow business.' I know nothing about this *TLS* review—enlighten my ignorance.

You will doubtless spit in my face and call me horse for saying so, but I think that it was A Good Thing to send a personal copy of the Durrell Book to Haley and not to the editor of the Tempus-Fuckit. He sounds to me as pleased as a waggonload of monkeys by the little compliment, and I doubt not that he is even now telling the bishops at the Athenaeum about your tendencies.

Have you seen a yank (Philadelphia Uni) book on Sydney Schiff by one Prof Theophilus Boll? Eminemment cocasse. This sent me to old Wyndham's *Apes* (Chez Lionel Klein Esq) which is certainly a vituperation of Dantesque virulence, and far in excess of poor old Sydney's demerits. I fear the greatest demerit in Wyndham's eyes (as in all the other Apes) is that Schiff had a large private income. Wyndham's libellous portrait of Edwin Muir as 'Keith, the Unknown Idiot' is uproarious, but as your smug mate TSE would say 'the emotion is in excess of the situation'—but Muir deserved a kick in the arse for trying to patronise DHL. Apropos 'emotion in excess of the situation'— well, if my uncle had murdered my father to get hold of my mother and kingdom I'd feel goddam emotional and fail to achieve the ataraxia, the 'ristocratic phlegm of the highbrow saint from Saint Louis.

Love to you both,
Richard

𝄢 *Nîmes, Monday [before 13 June 1962]*

Dear Richard;

Sorry we've been off the air for a week or so; partly due to all the fuss over Claude's father's death which cost her a week of hell in Paris and the subsequent slump of morale; but she's back at the crease now and hard at it as the big Gyppo translation has arrived at long last. For my part I have been closeted with the rep. of the third programme, pouring out my little heart on to tapes for a series of programmes they are doing. 'Explain in four words what it took you four books to try to explain'; I thank god for my barren years of experience with all these tricky media. It would be awful otherwise; the man had just come from 'doing' Robert Graves whom he found brilliant until the machine was switched on, when poor Graves began to twitch and gibber. Took him ages to forget the tape recording his thoughts. Is it a matter of generations? Yet you took to the tape like a duck after the first playback and would make a v. good broadcaster and you are the same generation as R.G. The interviewer was D.G. Bridson, writer, old admirer of your work, friend of Pound and TSE, and ex *Criterion* critic. Ring a bell?

I'm still coiled up in this foul play which I wish I didn't never start—it's getting so complicated with witches and vampires etc. Henry turned up in Majorca for the Formentor Prize committee and fell a victim to their verbosity—he calls it getting 'flu; he's in Paris and I've just had a word from him, en route for Berlin where he's got a play coming up soon. We've both been invited to edinburgh for a congress this august and are planning to set them by the ears if we can by taking Alf Perlès in his beastliest mood. Soon you'll be heading north for the steppes, no? Cath looks forward to it, quite rightly; everything is worth seeing at first hand I feel and any journey will brisk you up and make a contrast to the lonely Sury life. Avanti. By the way, other day comes a letter from Toby Mannering addressed to Scobie care of me; typically unstamped (150 francs) it was written in the old vein; he is now Budgie's agent in the Midlands for earth closets. Letter came from a nursing home in Leamington Spa (traction?); with the next post comes another letter equally unstamped from Budgie, posted in Paddington Station. He says ('Dear Old Friend') that he has invented a new type of closet even more arcane, and is sending me a sample. Every time I get a chit from the PTT now I bristle for fear this joker will actually send me an Elsan with astrology round the brim . . .

much love from us both
Larry D.

Alfred Perlès, Miller, and Durrell referred to themselves as 'The Three Musketeers' after their 1937 meeting in Paris. Perlès has written novels, plus a book each on Miller and Durrell.

§ *Sury, 13 June 1962*

Dear Larry,

I was barely 15 hours en Camargue, as I've explained to Claude— just a rush for her mother to see Cath.

Oblomov is not dead. After a cable from Moskva to say 21st June is all right, I have to-day a note from the 'Counsilor' (so he spells it) of the Paris Embassy to say there is *no* flight on the 21st so we must go 22nd. The Consulate need Two days for visas! Why? Since they are asking us to go? But I suspect that it is a rule (as it was with France in 1946) that even a Consul-General can't give a visa without cabling name and particulars to the Foreign Office in USSR.

Oblomov is also right here in Sancerre, in the person of the local tailor, who has made my clothes too small though urged to give me space. I think there is just time for them to be made tolerable. As what hits the eye first is important, I have determined not to go dressed as a bohemian but as a pseudo-gent, with would-be impeccable black jacket and small-check trousers, and another of dark blue with grey. A nylon shirt and silk tie should, added to this tenue, dispel any illusions of proletarian sympathies, though I think it mightn't be polite to wear an armlet with a swastika.

You an OBE! What damn cheek of the bastards. You should have been pretty stiff about refusal. When they gave a cow like Dick Church & Spender! *Man!* a CBE!! That was offered in malice. Buggers, shits.

I'm in a quandary about Gawsworth, having received the same request from Gardiner. The fact is, Larry, I don't know what to say, so I haven't said anything. If Gawsworth were not such an unwashed bum and pub-crawler I might have been able to get him a pension from Bryher. But at the moment I am working for the widow of Carl Fallas (who has worked all her life and is now virtually starving) and I feel Gawsworth must be passed up.

Do you want a set of Russian stamps unused? I'll bring some anyway. And of course I'll send cards, but they'll be devilish laconic. I'll keep comment until out of that particular propaganda area.

I had a letter from Geoff Dutton. His mother has died, and he is (rightly) thinking of throwing up the University and going to live at Anlaby, which of course is a mansion with famous gardens. If Geoff can afford it he would be a bloody fool to go on stewing in that pot of pundits and pedants which any university is. He was jubilant at receiving the copy of the Durrell book I ordered for him. He is going to Brisbane to give what are known as Commonwealth ('A common wealth sounds like a common whore,' signed: J. Dryden) Literary Fund lectures, including one on you; and he said the book would be most useful to him as he could be the first in Ozland to make use of the material. As a matter of fact it's all muck, and one of your Scobie jests is worth more than the whole volume. But the world is redundant with fools who must be answered according to their folly.

This Russ trip is a blind, and like Mr Weller Sr on another occasion, I don't take no pride on it, Sammy. I shall be thankful when it is all over, and I can re-frowst in peace here.

> Love to both,
> Richard

Readers unfamiliar with the British honours system should appreciate that the O.B.E. (Order of the British Empire) is a decoration more widely distributed and considerably lower in status than the C.B.E. (Commander of the British Empire).

Fallas, novelist and travel writer, was a friend of Aldington before both entered military service together in June 1916; he predeceased Aldington by three months.

ℒ Moscow, 4 July 1962

We had 5 interesting days in Leningrad, but tiring. Yesterday here I had to meet an audience of readers in a public hall—most friendly & enthusiastic. I have signed copies of my books everywhere, scores of them. We return to Paris on the 10th & I'll write from Sury. By the way, at the do yesterday I met Ivy Litvinov & her daughter.

> Love to both
> Richard

Ivy Litvinov, who had been a friend of D. H. Lawrence, was the widow of the Russian statesman Maxim Litvinov. Mrs Litvinov, daughter of the scholar Sir Walter Low and novelist Agnes Herbert, died in 1977 at Hove, in England.

ℒ Sury-en-Vaux, Cher, 14 July 1962

Dear Larry

I enclose a little Muscovite souvenir for Claude and also some stamps. There is supposed to be a clear run of the present issues from one kopek to 50; and to these I have added a few others used and unused. Observe that the 150th anniversary of Dickens's birth is commemorated in the USSR but not in England.

We were treated most hospitably, & lodged in first-class hotels in Moscow and Leningrad. I had a suite consisting of entry, large sitting room, bedroom, and bathroom. I had to have the sitting-room on account of the numbers of interviewers and readers. The interviews as translated to me were scrupulously exact and the numerous photographs excellent—some day you may look them over. I knew I was read there, but didn't know how widely, and I certainly didn't know that I am revered and loved. I was inundated with flowers and letters of good wishes—one elderly woman came a 12-hrs rail journey just to see me for ten minutes. No matter where I went the mention of my name by the interpreter brought instant attention and smiles and even hand-clapping. I was given many birthday gifts, including a samovar, choice Russian teas, and a huge souvenir cup, amber cuff-links, and at least 30 illustrated books—most of the latter are being sent on by post. The finest I brought with me—an illustrated book on the eikons, published in East Berlin. Among the stamps you will find a monk painting, and the dates 1360–1960. This represents Andrei Rublëv, the most famous of the eikon-painters.

I can't speak too highly of the kindness with which we were received. As to 'depressing'—I found them the most cheerful and warm-hearted people I've ever met. Such a pity they have to be communists. I met Tolstoy's grandson at Yasnaya Polyana (the old Tolstoy estate which is now a national monument and museum) and also Gorki's widow plus numbers of their writers. I have two publishers there—one of whom sent a bound testimonial to my merits to the birthday feast, while the other was present and announced he was commissioning a translation of *Women Must Work*. I also met Ivy Litvinov at the Moscow Library of Foreign Books, which was started some 30 years back by the present directrice and already has 3 million books including practically all mine which were on display. In Leningrad Public Library I saw Voltaire's library (bought by Catherine the Great) and was allowed to handle some of them and to read his amusing comments. Thus a translation of Shakers is inscribed 'Le barbare Shakespeare traduit par le charlatan Le Tourneur.'

Catha behaved excellently and was most popular with old and young alike.

Well that's enough of that. In spite of every kind consideration for my age I did get tired, and shall be glad to rest here. Do let me have your news.

The comma on my tripewriter is bitched—and it will take ages to mend in this holiday season. I also enclose a night photo of the new Moscow University.

Love to both
Richard

ℐ Nîmes, Monday [after 14 July 1962]

Dear Richard—sorry not to have replied sooner. The children invaded end of last week! Usual chaos. But we were both delighted by your account of the Russian visit and by the fact that they took you seriously on your own merits and [did] not try to twist your arm into a hammer and sickle. Bravo! Perhaps there is some truth in 'the thaw' after all and if the people seem relaxed it almost certainly means that the power of the secret police has been curbed; the Yugoslavs turned from zombies into cheerful crazy Balkanics in about a week, after the same thing happened! But all in all I am *so* glad you accepted and they dealt with you so warmly and honourably; of course the British nose was put slightly out of joint, and the significant change of tone (more in sorrow than in anger) was most amusing. I've been invited (Henry too) to a writer's congress at the Edinburgh Festival (August 15); all found and all free, and no work involved. We'll have some fun, coming up against Sartre and Russell in open debate! Claude will stay with the kids. Ah! the postman is on the hill. I must get this off today. More soon, my dear R. Claude is writing too.

Love
Larry

ℐ Sury, 19 July 1962

Dear Larry,

Nice to see your moniker again, but do let me have news of Claude and yourself when you have time.

Your letter crossed one from me, containing some little souvenirs. I was presented with a samovar as one of innumerable birthday gifts, but couldn't bring you one because of space on the plane. As it was we had about 30 lbs of excess baggage. One of the gifts I most value is a folio of coloured reproductions of the Eikons, which were hardly known even in Russia until the suppression of the monasteries—remarkable things. The book has been the life-work of a learned Hun, and is published in East Berlin in this magnificent edition de luxe which for some reason is not allowed to be sold anywhere in the West, so I daresay there aren't many copies in the Cher. This was really a great compliment. The book was shown me by one of their best-known contemporary novelists, Konstantin Fedin, who boasted that he had received it as a present from the Writers on his 70th birthday. Evidently my interpreter noticed my yearning over it and must have reported it, for lo! at the birthday banquet it was duly presented to me by the head of the Writers Union, Alexei Surkov, who whispered me that he'd had the devil's own job to get hold of a copy. The other most valued gift is a cheap toy dog brought to Catha (in the belief that she was still a child) by a poor woman who came a 12-hrs rail journey just to see us and talk for ten minutes. But most of the visitors were young couples who shyly announced their intention to live up to the love affair in *All Men*—uphill work, I should say.

Thanks indeed for sending me the rather half-hearted apologia from the *S. Times*—which I had seen. I incline to think that they do these things better in USSR, as witness the enclosed 'address' which was presented to me handsomely bound in blue leather with my name and age on a silver plaque, read in Russian and English amid great applause, and spontaneously signed by many of the authors present. Then my other publisher, Grigori Vladekin, got up and made a similar extravagant eulogy, winding up by saying that he had just commissioned a translation of *Women Must Work*. The day before we left a short extract from it (the novel) appeared with a laudatory article in the *Literary Gazette*. I was so beset for interviews I begged for exemption, and thereafter I was kept free. I must add that the reporters were courteous, avoided politics almost entirely, and (as translated to me) were strictly accurate. The photographs were innumerable and excellent—I have some here, and Catha has others.

The *S. Times* piece was due solely to the persistence of a reader of mine who happens to be the English chief of the Italian Tourist Bureau in London. He took the trouble to ring up and inform of my birthday and the Russ visit the *Times, TLS, Telegraph, Guardian, Observer, S. Times*—with the result of this small tiddler. As a matter of fact they could have used the birthday affair as news. *Tass* asked me for a special short interview for their foreign illustrated service, and I know the thing was on the Moscow radio because it was heard by a friend in Paris. The news was killed on purpose. I am not in the least mollified, and can afford to feel more contemptuous than ever of their bugger heroes and of them.

Catha will give you her version when you see her.

Love to you both,
Richard

❦ *Sury, 26 July 1962*

Dear Larry,

I got to-day from the Red Fiends in Muscovy a whole set of amusing snapshots of the birthday feast. I reluctantly pass one on to you and Claude, mainly because it is such a good shot of Catha. The bloke to her right is Alexei Surkov, head of the Moscow Writers Union, a poet (!) and a member of the Supreme Soviet. Their top writers are all in that affair, just as we automatically go to the Lords.

A letter from Gawsworth. He wants me to contribute to that muck about him, and I just can't. Would you allow me to write a briefest piece saying I am prevented from writing about J.G. as I had hoped, but that I associate myself wholly with the admirable remarks of L. Durrell? If you agree tentatively, I'll send you a sentence or two for you to approve or disapprove, and if the former to send on. Further, J.G. brings out a sculptor, Hugh Oloff de Wet (grand old English name!) who wants or says he wants to do heads of you and me. Clearly, this is a device of J.G.'s to tickle my vanity. I am going to suggest that it is unnecessary for the cutter to come to France. You are soon going to Edinburgh, and I feel sure you will consent *to sit for us both.* Who says the wisdom of Salaudmon died with him?

What a pack of fools.

Love to both
Richard

Twenty-four hours after writing this letter Richard Aldington died of a heart attack at the Maison Sallé.

INDEX

This index covers not only significant names and titles specifically mentioned, but also indirect references. A few subject listings have been included. Items discussed in a paragraph which continues onto the following page are indexed only to the first page. Endnotes are not indexed unless special considerations so warrant.

11